Smoke and Mirrors

THE SUSPICIOUS DEATHS
OF THE BIOWEAPONEERS

SMOKE
AND MIRRORS
THE SUSPICIOUS DEATHS
OF THE BIOWEAPONEERS

C R HARRIS

LENNOX BOOKS

GLASGOW, SCOTLAND

Lennox Books Limited
272 Bath Street
Glasgow
G2 4JR

Dedication

To Paul for the thousand and one reasons that made this book possible, and to the team who worked on this book: readers, reviewers, editors, graphic artists, and not forgetting booksellers for whom every author has deep appreciation and gratitude. The input, care and encouragement have been invaluable – thank you all. There are too many to mention by name but too few to forget each individual's contribution.

CHAPTER ONE

Paris – Autumn 2004

For three whole days, Chloe had listened to Charles's theories, his paranoia, even his obsession for an investigation into the deaths of the biological weapons scientists. There was no reasoning with him—as far as he was concerned, there were no accidents and no reasonable explanations.

Chloe Moreau walked from the Métro to the main office of *La France*, a leading daily center-left newspaper. Early morning Paris mist formed droplets on her tan trench coat; she had tied the belt, and would have put up her collar against the weather, had she noticed it. The colors of autumn were vibrant and the promised Swarovski moments of winter had yet to arrive. The traffic noise was muffled, and the only clear sound was the click of her boot heels on the pavement.

William S. Burroughs reputedly said, "Sometimes paranoia is just having all the facts." Chloe's mind was frantically sorting out fact from coincidence, trying to decide what she would tell her editor and whether to commit to this lengthy project on so much conjecture. In her heart she knew she would, with or without the blessing of her editor; she wanted to know the truth. Turning off the main road, she took a shortcut to the office's underground parking garage, reserved for senior staff. It would save time, as she wouldn't have to clear security at the main entrance.

Chloe became aware her footsteps had developed a soft echo. Either she had a stalker, or an innocent pedestrian was following her. She could hear her self-defense coach telling her, Don't rationalize away your fears, don't be a victim; plan against an attack. She regretted there were no Tasers, mace, or rape alarms in her bag. But it was Paris, a quiet tree-lined boulevard off the Périphérique, an area not known for muggers at the peak of morning commuting.

She pulled the cover off her umbrella. Now it could open at the touch of a button, it would serve as a truncheon, and although it was light-weight, she hoped it would be enough. She pulled her messenger bag in front of her to act as body armor against a low-level knife attack, opened it and stuffed the cover in a pocket, then took out her apartment keys and placed them between her first and second fingers to act as a weapon. She thought about what else she could use from her bag to surprise her attacker. Drawing a clown nose with her coral lipstick would be a surprise, but not a defensive strategy. She put the lipstick back.

Chloe extended her stride, and for a couple of steps, the echo was out of sync. Then her follower's footsteps changed, a leaf crunched underfoot a few meters behind her, and they were in step again. This made her feel less paranoid and more threatened. *Where is everybody?* Had she missed a bomb alert while she was on the Métro? She looked up at the surrounding offices, unable to tell in the mirrored glass if anyone inside could see her. It was an unlikely time of day for staff to be looking out of the window; they would be staring at computer screens, catching up on emails, performing the usual routines of starting the workday. No one would notice her from the windows, and they couldn't offer help even if they did.

She could hear her own breathing, fast, deep, her body working itself into flight or fight mode in an adrenaline rush. If she made the hundred yards to the parking garage and got through the security gate, she would be safe. Without the appropriate security key and pin code, her potential attacker could not follow her. She wanted to look around, maybe stare down her opponent. Instead, she quickened her pace. She could hear the rustle of her stalker's clothes, perhaps from a waterproof commando jacket. He or she must be closing in. Chloe considered making a dash for the entrance. Six months ago, when she had been in peak condition after completing a marathon in three hours, she might have tried, but not now, not in these boots. She might manage an elegant jog but it wouldn't be enough to escape. She cursed the vanity and impracticality of the boots.

The moment of reprieve came from a cruising taxi. The Taxi Parisien sign glowed yellow in the mist as it turned into the street, on its way to the busy boulevard where, no doubt, it expected to find more potential passengers. She moved quickly to the curbside and hailed the taxi, waving her arm frantically. She expected it to cruise past her, they usually did, but she had put more effort into the wave than usual, not caring if she looked ridiculous. When the taxi stopped, she bundled in, computer bag over her shoulder, messenger bag slung across her front, shopping bag of papers, keys in one hand, and red compact umbrella in the other; she landed on the seat in a complete muddle and struggled to close the door. She exhaled, she was unaware she had been holding her breath. For one brief moment she wondered if this was part of the plan, perhaps she was supposed to get into the taxi. Let's face it: taxis never seem to stop when you really need them.

"Where to?" He turned, he had the look of a taxi driver, and he asked the right question, an abductor presumably wouldn't need directions.

"I would like to get back to here. Do you think you could drive around the block? I think that person over there is following me." Chloe rummaged in her computer bag for her camera; she wanted a picture of her stalker.

The taxi driver shrugged, locked the doors, put the meter on, and drove slowly up the street. Her stalker knelt on one knee as if tying his shoelaces. Dressed all in black; combat pants, soft boots that did not need retying, a zipped jacket, and baseball cap, not the commercial kind, but the sort that made your head look square. He didn't look like a mugger. He looked more like...

Chloe took her photo. She thought it would be subtle, unnoticed in the gloom and mist, but she hadn't allowed for the automatic flash feature. The only benefit was the man on the pavement was startled and looked up, so she took another photo. At least she could identify him. He looked familiar.

By the time they had circled the block and returned to the underground garage, there was no sign of the man in black. Safe in the confines of the taxi, she couldn't decide if she was disappointed or reassured. She concluded she was overthinking it, paid the taxi driver, gave him a large tip, muttered things about being paranoid, and was encouraged by him telling her, "Better safe than sorry." She walked down the slope to the pedestrian entrance, used her personal security key, entered the pin number on the keypad, pushed the cold metal gate open, and was relieved by the closing clunk of the heavy bars and grills once again settling in their five-point lock; the noise reverberated through the garage. She leaned back against the gate, and felt the outline of the bars through her raincoat, solid and reassuring. She exhaled long and slow, made her shoulders relax, and felt slightly foolish. She smiled. She wasn't sure if she had overreacted or taken a wise precaution. Her few days with Charles had given her the start of a cold, and a mild dose of paranoia.

She made her way to the elevator, through puddles of fluorescent light and pools of gray shadow, past concrete pillars streaked with car paint and rubber bumper marks, a testament to the need for parking and the impossible number of spaces promised by the property developers, none of whom, it seemed, actually drove.

A vehicle stopped at the garage entrance and she heard the noise of the metal shutter rolling up. She paid it no attention and assumed a colleague had arrived for work. Instead, she focused on the numbers above the elevator as they slowly counted down its descent to the basement. The elevator stopped at the ground floor. Silently and impatiently, she implored the car to come down to the basement for her, rather than going up with its new passengers. She pressed the button three times in quick succession in the hope the elevator would note her urgency. She wanted coffee and companionship—in that order.

Chloe never found out whether the elevator came down or went up. The recently arrived car stopped alongside her with a tire squeal, and a passenger got out. As she turned to look, she felt a blow to her neck. Her hand closed over her umbrella, an instinctive reaction; the umbrella opened. Her attacker's response was a single expletive, "Ben zona!" Everything went black. She knew she was falling but could do nothing to stop it; her landing on the concrete was hard, but she felt no pain. She was unable to move. Urgent voices whispered instructions to get her computer bag, the shopping bag, her phone, and a computer storage key. Her last thoughts related to the computer storage key they were looking for; Charles's final intimate act and ultimate demonstration of his paranoia had been to conceal it in her bra, nestled under her breast, next to the underwire.

She became aware someone was bending over her, patting her hands and calling her name.

"She's speaking English—I think. Is she English?"

"Not really. I suppose in one way yes, the other no, English father and French mother. She is bilingual but I don't think of her as being anything other than French."

What, she wondered, *is Jean Pierre doing here?* Then everything went black again.

She awoke, or more accurately, the catchy "Chihuahua" from DJ Bo-Bo booming its repetitive lyrics and Latino beat at full volume in her ears blasted her consciousness into a response. Her first act was to take out the iPod earplugs. There was a strong taste of ammonia cloying at the back of her throat.

"There you are," said Jean Pierre. "Don't play nice soothing music from the patient's own iPod; you need to hit them with something they can't wait to get out of their ears." He turned from the doctor to Chloe and cradled her shoulders as she sat up. "I think you fainted and you've given your head a bit of a knock on the garage floor. In fact, you've made rather a mess. I'm not sure if the janitor's job description includes washing your blood off the garage floor. You okay?" He gave her a stare and she realized he was telling her to play it down.

Chloe pulled down the oxygen mask from her face. Shook her head to try to clear the muzziness, and said, "I think I'm okay." She gathered up the iPod. "Yours?" Jean Pierre nodded.

"Did you faint or something?" Jean Pierre took the iPod and put it in his jacket pocket; he sounded unconcerned, as if fainting was something women frequently did for no reason. "The medic tried smelling salts but you wouldn't respond."

"Something," replied Chloe and decided not to say more. The doctor leaned over to check her pulse and respiration. He took the oxygen mask away, and shone a light into her eyes.

"How do you feel?"

"Absolutely fine. I probably should eat breakfast more often, so sorry to inconvenience you," said Chloe brightly, going along with Jean Pierre's suggestion that she had fainted, and hoping her lies would be undetected. She rubbed the new red wheals on her wrists. Her head throbbed. She couldn't believe the medic had overlooked the blow to her neck. But, she wanted to get upstairs, sit down in the office, and collect herself. A computer bag placed between the elevator doors prevented them closing. Jean Pierre wouldn't want to waste more time than necessary getting back to his desk.

"I think you should probably come with us to the hospital and be under observation for a few hours at least," said the doctor.

"That's all right. Now she's up and awake, I can keep an eye on her." Jean Pierre sounded determined.

She could see the SMUR (Mobile and Emergency Resuscitation Service) sign on the ambulance, Jean Pierre had been sufficiently concerned to call the equivalent of an intensive care unit with a doctor for her, but now Jean Pierre, for reasons best known to himself, was encouraging her to dismiss the medics.

"Thank you, but I'm fine. Really." Chloe hoped Jean Pierre was right, she felt awful and wanted to go to sleep.

"Take it easy for a couple of days. Any further symptoms, go visit your physician. That was a nasty blow to your head. You have a mild concussion," said the doctor.

Chloe nodded and immediately regretted the instinctive action. She felt the back of her skull and found the swelling and wound dressing. It was evidence of the damage from her head crashing into the concrete. She smiled at the doctor to encourage him to leave. He shook his head as he packed his medical bag, clearly unhappy at her decision, then patted her shoulder, picked up his equipment, and went to the ambulance, leaving the bloodstained blanket he had placed under her head on the floor. It was a disposable world.

She looked around and could only see her messenger bag, which lay on the floor next to her, unzipped. Her umbrella was open and rolled around on the floor, reacting to the air movement from the departing ambulance. She pressed the button to collapse the umbrella, looked inside her bag for the slipcover, once the umbrella was secured she checked her purse and credit cards, they were untouched.

"Let's go up," said Chloe, picking up her things and the discarded blanket.

Jean Pierre helped her to her feet and they made their way to the elevator and rode in silence to the fifth floor. He settled her at her desk before going to get coffee.

He returned with a latte and a supportive smile. "So what was that about? And how are you feeling—really?"

She cupped her hands around the mug, more for comfort than heat, and drank. The warm foamy liquid soothed her throat. "What time is it? How long was I out? Who called the ambulance? They took my computer, my camera, my key ring with the computer storage key on it, my phone, and all Charles's papers I had in a shopping bag. I feel as if someone has had a bottlebrush up my nose, encased my limbs in lead, and emptied a duvet inside my head. Apart from that, I'm fine."

"Oh good! Lots of questions. That's all right then! No damage to brain functions, but you sound like you're on speed. It's probably an adrenaline reaction. So now, will you give this investigation up? I told you not to mess with the Mossad a week ago."

"How do you know it was the Israeli Intelligence Service?" Chloe thought about what had happened in one week. It was extraordinary, only one week. It seemed a lot longer.

"I don't, but you didn't faint. They shot you with a tranquilizer gun on the side of your neck inside a secured garage, so not your average mugger. I found you. I was on my way to an interview. I don't know how long you were out. It's nine o'clock now, so maybe you can work it out. I called the ambulance because you were having difficulty breathing, probably a reaction to the drug. Your wrists were bound tight with cable ties—thank heavens for a Swiss army knife." Jean Pierre paused between comments to check her reactions and make sure she was listening.

"Why SMUR?" asked Chloe.

"I didn't think the paramedics would be any good for diagnosing what was wrong with you. I thought you were dying from the injection, in which case your best bet was to have SMUR with the resuscitation facilities and the expertise of the doctor in the ambulance. I felt it was the safer bet. But you were getting over the effects by the time they arrived. I probably came across you at the worst time."

"Thanks. But why did you feel I shouldn't go to the hospital?"

"Do you know how much paperwork there would be for Anne Marie if you were hospitalized from the newspaper premises? She'd kill you—and she wouldn't make any mistakes or halfhearted attempts either."

Chloe could imagine the anger of their editor and it wasn't a pleasant thought.

"You should give this investigation up. Really, it's not a suitable case for—"

"Don't you dare say a woman."

Jean Pierre shrugged. "I was going to say a journalist working alone. Leaving a Post-it note on my computer is not keeping me in the loop. Our esteemed leader was not pleased you took off for a week and I didn't know what you were doing or why. I thought it would be better to call an ambulance than prepare a eulogy. How the doctor missed the mark on your neck, I don't know. Perhaps he thought it was a love bite." Jean Pierre lifted her shoulder length hair away from her neck and looked at the wound. "It could look like a love bite; anyway, will you give this investigation up?"

"Hell, no! As I was walking into the office I had my doubts, I thought Charles was paranoid. But this only confirms his suspicions. I may have a bad headache, but I'm not going to be bullied. And Anne Marie knew where I was at the beginning of the week, and I took a few days' holiday at the end."

"You were with Charles."

"There's no need to sound like a jealous husband about it; yes, Charles brought me the files from the States and we were working."

"Great! So what will you do now you've lost all the evidence?"

"I haven't, Charles has the real papers, there was only recycling in the shopping bag and the storage key is..." She paused, lifted up her sweater, revealing a white half-balcony lace bra, and pulled out the key.

"Great storage facility! Anytime you need anything filed or retrieved, do let me assist." His smile faded quickly. "You know you can't transfer those files on to anything other than a laptop which you can never connect to either the paper's network or the internet. I suggest you transfer these to a new computer which you then leave in Anne Marie's safe. If they'll mug you for the information, they'll certainly try to access our computer system to find the files. I'll warn the IT department there'll be more hackers than usual."

She pulled a face, reacting to Jean Pierre's flirtation and despairing of more paranoia. Jean Pierre took this as a sign she was feeling better.

"Let's go look at the CCTV recordings from the garage. See if we can tell if it was the Mossad. If you're feeling up to it?"

They walked slowly across to the elevator, Jean Pierre put a protective arm around her, frightened she might faint, and they went down to the ground floor. The security office was compact, banks of TV screens lined one wall, showing staff coming and going through public areas, and the guard set up one screen to re-run the garage footage they were interested in. They watched the car arrive. You couldn't see much, most of what was happening to Chloe took place on the floor, shielded from view by the car.

"How did they get through security?" asked Chloe.

The security guard moved to the recording of the car entering the garage. "They appear to have a key and the code."

"Were you carrying a bag with 'Target' on it?" Jean Pierre had taken over the controls and was replaying the recording at the point where she was waiting at the elevator just before the car arrived.

Chloe laughed. "Yes, it was Charles's little joke."

The ubiquitous American discount store had a red bull's-eye on its shopping bags, he had referred to as Tar Zjay, thinking it funny to make it sound French and chic. Whether it was the effect of the cocktail of drugs in her system, or a reaction to her fears, she felt tired and tearful. It had been an extraordinary week. It had been one of the most frustrating weeks of her career. Normally journalists get questions answered, she had spent the week accumulating more questions and doubting if she could get any, let alone all, of the answers.

CHAPTER TWO

Paris – A Week Earlier

If it hadn't been for the Israeli deaths in the explosion at Kirkuk a week earlier, the photo might have remained forgotten in Chloe's desk drawer. It turned out to be an awful, slow day at the office, and it started badly.

It was not the first time her husband had not returned home for the night. She had gone to bed wondering if it was all her fault. She had put his note, which she thought had said he would be back on Saturday afternoon, in the pocket of her jeans. When he hadn't arrived home late Saturday night, she had gone to check the note only to find it a mushy mess in the freshly washed jeans' pocket. She assumed it must have said Sunday and went to bed disappointed, but when he didn't return on Sunday evening, she was concerned. She imagined accidents, muggings, affairs, and general indifference. If there was a genuine reason for his absence, why didn't he phone? It was a symptom of the problems their marriage faced, not the cause.

She arrived at the office with a bad case of the Monday morning blues; she was frustrated with her job and her personal situation didn't help.

The new office décor was a study in porridge but in spite of designer attempts at bland, it was full of color. Journalists were hoarders. It was the color of the paper, the doodles, the shape of the torn-out copy that helped your memory retain the information. No one trusted computers for the important stuff.

Now in the hexagonal interlinked micro-spaces, referred to as the pigpens, in her untidy, paper strewn, book-laden cubbyhole, she would settle down, phone a few contacts for a final quote or opinion, and finish a piece she didn't find satisfying. Jean Pierre, who covered French national security issues, worked at the next desk.

She briefly considered tidying her desk to pass the time, but the effect would be short-lived, and afterward she would never be sure if she couldn't find something or if she had thrown away a now vital piece of information in a fit of enthusiasm. She opted to do her expenses instead, and as usual, found items on her credit card statement she no longer had receipts for and receipts at the bottom of her handbag for expenses she no longer remembered incurring, and annoyingly found a receipt she couldn't find last month when she did her expenses.

Journalists were milling around the office, more trips to the water cooler, frequent caffeine intakes, and longer lunches than usual. Toward the end of the day, Chloe gathered with others at the bank of TV screens, scrutinizing the scrolling items of breaking news, just in case a lead could provide compelling copy. They were also afraid carefully researched pieces might break on a competitor's TV channel before their presses even started to run.

Today's news comprised announcements of economic data and the sad but inevitable losses in post-war Iraq. A press agency newsflash trailed across the screen, "Bomb blast in Kirkuk, five Israelis killed." Yet the item never made it to the bulletins. Instead it ran as, "In Iraq another bomb exploded, this time in Kirkuk, five killed." Editorial control had removed the presence of the Israelis altogether.

Chloe had a nagging concern. *Why edit the Israelis out of the story?* After searching through piles of cuttings and notebooks on her desk, she eventually found a manila envelope in her desk drawer. The Iraqi post-mark was two months old.

She took the photograph out of the envelope and ran her fingers along the edge of the card; someone had taken the trouble to mount the picture on a chamfered-edge art board, as if the quality of presentation would give substance to its credibility. It was a rather grainy picture, reminiscent of the number of fake pictures in circulation at the end of the Iraq war. The words Mossad Metsada were written in pencil under the image, together with a grid reference. Google Earth identified this as southwest of Kirkuk, Iraq. It was a barren space with a couple of trees she could clearly cross-reference with the photograph.

Jean Pierre had returned to his desk where he sat, looking relaxed, almost smug. His chair was tilted back, one polished black loafer placed on the edge of his desk secured his recline, as he contemplated his computer screen. The mouse under his right hand occasionally clicked as he navigated around emails and webpages.

He was tall, good looking, and aging in the way men do, and women envy, and he knew it. About six-foot-two, naturally slim build—he ate without censure, hazel eyes, dark, short curly hair with a few strands of gray at his temples. Maybe it was a lack of confidence, but he tried too hard to make a favorable impression and the result was unappealing, like an enthusiastic spaniel, cute, but after a while, tiresome.

He routinely flirted with Chloe, without any serious intent, she didn't believe she was his type; she was just target practice. She had re-married six months ago, which was turning out to be a mistake, and he was getting over a divorce. However, it would be a lie to say she didn't appreciate his attention; it gave her confidence a much-needed boost.

"And how is my petite blonde today?" He emphasized the word "my."

She didn't think five-foot-five meant she was little, and the blonde was more about the highlights applied to the typical northern European brunette—not rich enough to be interesting, not pale enough to be mousy. The proprietorial use of the possessive pronoun she overlooked, because he was her essential guide to internal politics in the newsroom, which he believed meant he held a special position in her life. He could wish or maybe she hoped he would continue to wish, she wasn't sure.

When the photograph arrived, she had taken the view checking out this story wouldn't pay off, either because national security issues would block publication, or you couldn't get any facts to support it. She didn't feel any differently about it now. It was too vague to be anything but a tease.

Chloe thought it unlikely anyone could find the Mossad in Iraq. They were like ghosts; they came and went without a trace. But the news that a bomb had killed five Israelis in Kirkuk, alongside the photo's implication that the Mossad was active in Iraq needed further investigation.

She ignored his greeting, because there would be a lengthy amount of banter to follow if she indulged him, and she got down to business.

"Who are or what is the Metsada?"

"Mossad," he replied without looking up. "Israeli Special Operations Division which conducts highly sensitive assassinations, paramilitary, and psychological warfare projects. In other words, don't mess with them. Why?"

"I was sent a photograph."

"Yes, I know, you've had it in your drawer for two months. You managed to suppress your usual curiosity. Why the sudden interest? I assumed you had wisely decided to leave it alone."

His knowledge of her desk drawer contents didn't entirely surprise her. They opened all mail in a secure room to protect employees against explosive devices and pathogens. It was a precaution mainly against cranks; serious attempts would probably be successful. The process bred rumors. Little remained confidential.

"Your first instinct was better," Jean Pierre continued, "you should leave this alone. It's either a fake or an anti-Israeli campaign. I doubt you'll get any budget to investigate. Anyway, what can you see on the photograph? A group of guys burying rugs shrouded in white sheets, ready for excavation when life settles down again. Perhaps they're going to make an insurance claim."

"I don't think so! Surely the implication is the Mossad is involved in mass burials." Not only did he know she had the photograph, but he had taken the trouble to examine it closely. She wondered if he would have stolen the story from her. He was competitive and it troubled her she didn't know the answer. Journalists were a cutthroat breed; each one thought they had the divine right of exposing the truth, and were unique in the qualities they brought to a particular story. Clearly putting the photograph under a box of winged female products was no deterrent.

"Maybe, maybe not—who knows?" He chuckled.

Jean Pierre was right, but Chloe was bored, frustrated with "establishing trust with the readers," "gaining a readership," and other such similar phrases from her editor. She was desperate to get involved in a good story. She had arrived at *La France* a couple of years ago, recently widowed and expecting scope to continue her former role at *The Washington Post* as an investigative journalist.

At first, the editor felt she didn't understand France's privacy laws and developed other excuses to keep her involved in European Union stories. Recently Chloe had discovered no one liked covering these stories and the editor usually left new reporters to cover the EU until they resigned, or came to her with such a fabulous story she was compelled to let them investigate. Chloe hoped this story might be her opportunity to escape the monotony of the EU, and a cursory look into known activities of the Mossad in Iraq had to be worth a few calls and emails. She got out a fresh spiral-bound notebook, a new pencil and started to make a list of contacts and questions. She was looking for two sources for every piece of information, reliable sources, preferably prime sources, people who knew firsthand what was happening. When she had completed the list, she picked up her phone.

"Hi, Chloe, it's good to hear from you. Interesting questions, but I can't give you answers. I can confirm Israeli Security Services have been operating with the Kurds in Iraq since 1968." The Washington CIA press officer, Marlene, was a friend as well as a work contact and usually helpful.

"So do the Mossad have an office in Kirkuk?" She had to ask the question but didn't think Marlene would answer it; even if the CIA knew, the press officer wouldn't know, or wouldn't tell, it didn't make any difference.

"I couldn't say, but the six men killed in the Kirkuk bomb blast were Israeli."

Chloe made a note, the death count had risen. "How many were injured?" Perhaps she could interview a survivor, if they hadn't already been spirited back to Israel.

"I'm sorry, I can only repeat information from Israeli intelligence, this is as up to date as we have, you might get more with a direct approach."

Chloe doubted that. It was a useful confirmation, but nothing new, and not as much as she had hoped for. "Thanks, Marlene. Have a good day."

"You too, Chloe. You should drop in for lunch next time you're in town, although I don't suppose you want to swap Paris for Washington. In fact, how do you ever get back to the office from lunch, with all those opportunities to shop? I should visit you. We miss your challenging intellect here." Marlene laughed. "There's just an excess of testosterone over common sense in the press room these days."

Chloe couldn't remember the last time she had been shopping in a "let's have fun" sort of way. She had bought a pair of boots on impulse a week ago, they were on sale, and feminine in an impractical way. It was a spur of the moment thing, not a planned "shop." If Marlene came over they wouldn't be socializing, it was against CIA policy to get close to the press. Marlene always kept things professional, an occasional sandwich lunch with members of the press was as much as Marlene allowed herself and Chloe respected her more for it.

"I'll keep that in mind. Let me know if you want to come over. I hope to see you soon." Chloe paused. "There wasn't anything else you could add to this line of inquiry, was there?" Another pause. "Was there any other information that might be relevant?" Chloe waited and let the silence work. So far, Marlene had given her standard responses, straight off the briefing sheet. The most useful information would come from intelligence Marlene had, but would have to think about. If she waited with an expectant silence, she might get more. Silence was the best interview tool any journalist could master.

"You could email Jonah Evans at Fort Detrick. They might have answers for you." This was a typical Marlene response, saying nothing, but merely suggesting a follow-up inquiry implied there might be an interesting story. A chill ran through Chloe. Someone had just walked over her grave.

Chloe hung up. She was pleased with the lead, and feeling nostalgic about her time in America. She wondered, not for the first time, if it had been a mistake to come back to France. But with this story, it now felt worthwhile.

Why did the Mossad need an office in Kirkuk? It wasn't difficult to join up the dots. If the troops couldn't find weapons of mass destruction, it didn't mean Iraq didn't have the capability to produce them, just that they didn't have any stockpiled. Rumor had it that the stockpiles had been sent over the border to Syria. The issue was all about the knowledge, the people involved, who knew what to do and where to find the materials to commence manufacture.

Chloe emailed Jonah Evans at the National Interagency Confederation for Biological Research, at Fort Detrick, Maryland.

His response was simple and direct: the Mossad had been getting detailed information from UNSCOM, the United Nations Special Commission, about scientists working on potential Atomic, Bacteriological, and Chemical activity. The list contained the names of three hundred Iraqi scientists, all working on ABC weapons.

ABC weapons. Chloe shook her head in disbelief; only the military could select an acronym more suited to preschool and innocence than weapons of mass destruction.

It was not enough for an international investigative journalist. It summed up her day, nearly interesting but not quite there.

She was preparing to leave when Charles Forbury, a former colleague at *The Washington Post*, returned her call. His office colleagues referred to him as a stiff-assed Brit with a first-class mind and a Pooh-Bear body; an Oxford graduate with first-class honors in PPE from Brasenose College. He embodied the best and the worst of a posh education: self-confident, competitive, polite, sexist, full of charm, and an uncanny ability to fit in anywhere. They had been friends, as well as colleagues, expats spending American holidays together. Smoke-filled backyards on Independence Day, copying the best barbecue traditions; turkey and Stove Top stuffing at Thanksgiving; it was imitation American culture, like Disney reproducing Europe, in essence correct but not quite right. They were happy days.

"There was an Iraqi establishment at Mosul known as Group Four looking into long range missile development," said Charles. "It appears the Mossad are killing all the scientists on the UNSCOM list, possibly including those at Mosul. And the only thing I know about Mossad at Kirkuk is their bomb-making factory exploded last week."

Chloe was busy taking notes of these three unrelated facts that together seemed significant and wondering why the Israelis had a bomb-making factory in Iraq when he continued.

"Look, Chloe, if unexplained deaths of scientists involved in biological warfare is of interest, there are seven or eight in America, three in England, a dozen or more in Russia, four in France, and several in Germany, about forty in total; they'd all be interesting. Anything's better than going to Iraq on a wild goose chase. Even if you find the bodies you'd have a hard time linking it to the Mossad."

"Sources?"

"Oh, it's all sound stuff. I just ran out of budget for an investigation. It's also not politically acceptable as a topic here—you know, you're either for us or... you know the rest. Look, I can send you a synopsis and if you can get approval, I'll bring the files over next week. I could do with a break. How about four days by a Normandy beach?"

"Charles, you're delusional. It's autumn. It'll be cold..."

"I know, I like cold—it'll be wonderful. Cozy open fires, thick coats, woolly mittens..."

"Oh stop; you're beginning to sound like Julie Andrews." She hung up.

One news flash plus one photograph, fake or not, had aroused journalistic curiosity, and an unrelated inquiry. No matter how dramatic the subject, unless the readership of the paper was interested, it was unlikely to get a budget.

Charles emailed his synopsis. It was brilliant, detailed, and provided her with a compelling argument for further investigation. The facts would have to be overwhelming to spark a debate about the dangers of so many countries having biological and chemical weapons programs, usually in the guise of "defense projects." She felt sufficiently confident to make an appointment with her editor for the next morning.

The final blow in her day came when Monique canceled their squash match. Chloe swore gently as she put down the phone; she wanted a game to release her tensions before she went home. Any conversation with her husband would need to be calm and quiet. All day, gnawing away in the back of her mind, she had worried about Walid. *What if something has happened to him?* The fact this was the sixth time in four months he had disappeared without letting her know his plans left her worried and annoyed. It was at best rude, and left her uncertain as to whether to contact the police again and look hysterical—which is what he had called her reaction to the first time he disappeared for two days. What concerned her most was she didn't feel jealous anymore. She was questioning in her mind if she loved him, or just the thought of him. She couldn't tell. She needed to see him. The fact she was away so much didn't help matters. But he knew she would be away two or three nights a week when he married her.

She phoned home again, but there was no reply. He often chose not to pick up the phone in the apartment, so it didn't mean anything. She tried his cell phone again, but it was switched off, which was usually the case. He didn't switch it on unless he wanted to make a call, and never listened to messages.

"You're having a bad day." Jean Pierre returned his chair to the upright position, the metallic clunk of the mechanism protesting at the stresses beyond its design limitations. In two years, he had broken four chairs, but it didn't stop him tilting them back. He was sufficiently skilled at his job for it not to be an issue.

"Sort of."

"Would you like a squash opponent? I'm sorry. I couldn't help overhearing your conversation." Chloe looked at Jean Pierre. It seemed a serious offer, it seemed genuine concern, but all the same she waited for the banter and the jokes to start when he continued.

"I could do with the exercise, and you could do with the stress relief. I'm divorced. I know the signs. You've tried to call Walid at the office, you've left endless messages; in return, you've suffered from the unanswered telephone calls, the ignored texts, and you've even used the office phone to check if your cell phone was working. And if I'm not mistaken, at one point you even sank as low as asking his department secretary for his whereabouts."

Chloe shrugged. He was observant; he was a journalist, paid to read people and situations. She didn't want to discuss it. She accepted his offer graciously.

They were both members at the Aquaboulevard club and he gave her a lift around the Périphérique and parked with ease. She noted this fact with envy, she would have spent an age looking for a space, one seemed to just open up for him. He didn't seem surprised by the ease of parking and she had the uncanny feeling it was always like this for him.

They changed and went to the court where he unceremoniously began to thrash her. This had been a really bad idea, she was an adequate player and usually did well in the women's league at the club. After twenty minutes, he stopped and said, "You feeling better?"

"No. More stressed." She was sweaty and panting. "It would be really nice to actually hit the ball."

Jean Pierre laughed. He came over and started to coach her. After ten minutes, she had mastered a return to the tricky corner shot he kept playing. They started to keep score again and this time she managed a few points and felt considerably better by the end of the game.

Jean Pierre made his farewell at the court. He clearly had a date and was in a rush. She was grateful for the game. After a shower, she felt she could face anything, including the difficult conversation with her husband, assuming he was at home.

CHAPTER THREE

Paris to the Cotswolds

The next morning, Jean Pierre approached as she sat waiting outside the editor's office. She knew he had been watching her work, intrigued, jealous of her contacts and her ability to work in both English and French with equal proficiency. Chloe concentrated on her papers and hoped he would go away.

She wasn't looking for confrontation and didn't want to be wound up by his banter. Her head was buzzing as she rehearsed the words to persuade her editor of the merits of the case. Her strategy was to go for an initial budget to disprove the theory. If her contact said it was a load of nonsense, so be it—it was interesting but just a series of coincidences. If, however, the scientist didn't dismiss the idea out of hand, then there was the potential for a global investigation.

"Was everything okay at home last night?" asked Jean Pierre.

Chloe was surprised, she hadn't expected his concern; he seemed too much of a flirt, too self-interested for real compassion.

"Yes. Apparently, he was in Frankfurt with some students. One of them had an asthma attack and was hospitalized overnight. Walid felt he should stay with the student." She hoped she sounded more relaxed about the situation than she felt. If this excuse had been true, why hadn't the department secretary known he was taking students to Frankfurt, wouldn't he have had to clear it with someone first? She had told him she might be away the following night, nothing was fixed yet, and he had just shrugged. If he cared, he didn't show it. He had said he was tired and gone to bed early. He had been asleep when she left this morning. Nothing had changed.

"Good." Jean Pierre shrugged. He clearly didn't buy the excuse either. "Apart from that how's it going?"

"I don't know yet. I'm waiting for Anne Marie." She hoped he would take this as a cue to go away.

"Ah—the sweat, the anxiety, the..." He smiled broadly, enjoying her discomfort.

"Piss off!"

"Chloe—language!" He went back to his desk laughing, leaving behind the pleasant citrus and earthy aroma of Eau Sauvage.

Chloe found herself distracted by the aftershave; it had been a favorite of her late husband, Michael Moreau. It was at times like these she missed his encouragement and faith in her ability.

Anne Marie beckoned her over. The glinting chrome, brushed steel, and black leather office had no personal touches. A phone, a single flat screen computer monitor, with keyboard and mouse were the only items on the desk. The editor of the most prestigious newspaper in France believed in the "clean desk, tidy mind" theory of work. Of course, this was easy to achieve in an office six meters square with all round full height storage. A new glass wall to the side of the office had an integrated electronic blind and at the flick of a button on her desk, the glass would change from clear to opaque. It was like the third eyelid of a reptile and staff referred to it as the eye of the dragon, and the office itself as the dragon's lair.

Anne Marie looked up with a slight smile of encouragement. Encapsulated in her glass domain, she controlled the budget for the investigative reporters and the future of this project. Today, her hair was a rich chestnut, to Chloe's mind it was the most aging of colors, but over the weeks, it would mellow to soft ginger with gray roots. At some point in between it would achieve a soft auburn shade that knocked ten years off her age, and set off her translucent porcelain skin to best advantage.

Anne Marie had arrived at the post of editor-in-chief quite late in her career, but had achieved significant success. Over her ten-year reign, you could count the number of apologies printed by the paper on one hand. The circulation of the paper had increased by a third, quite an achievement when newsprint was in a steep decline as the public moved toward bite size headlines delivered by multimedia handheld devices.

She was tough and demanding, but wanted her reporters to succeed. Chloe realized Anne Marie must have been waiting a long time for her to make this appointment and show her true colors as an investigative journalist.

"Right, Chloe, what've you got?" Anne Marie didn't look up and didn't ask her to sit, and so Chloe stood, clutching her papers in front of her with damp hands, feeling about ten years of age standing in front of her teacher, asking for a favor.

"I think we are in the middle of a sequence of murders or unexplained deaths—of infection microbiologists and DNA biological warfare scientists."

Anne Marie looked up, her eyebrows raised over her half-moon glasses; pale blue eyes alert; at least she was showing some interest.

"DNA?"

"Since the completion of the DNA sequencing of the human genome in June 2000, these scientists are now better able to complete the work started in the Soviet Union. They can target biological weapons based on the genetic code of a particular race or nationality."

"Any common threads? Did these scientists all work together?" Anne Marie removed her glasses and leaned forward.

"Yes and no." It was a weak answer, and Anne Marie regularly burned up journalists leaving only charred remains. Chloe had won two Pulitzer prizes for investigative journalism while working for *The Washington Post*, so she should have had some sense of professional self-esteem. But her recent marriage to Walid showed a lack of judgment, and events of the last year rolled around in her head clouding all sane thoughts.

"Which is it? Did they work together?" Anne Marie picked up her glasses, took out a chamois leather from her drawer, and proceeded to polish them.

Chloe answered, trying to sound confident and authoritative.

"No. But there is a common thread. Some worked in the same country. They all met at conferences, and because of their specialties, I would say yes."

"Presumably your case is going to be against a secret service. And how easy is it going to be to prove anything, not against one agency, but several global intelligence services?"

"I think—"

Anne Marie's phone rang; she picked up the receiver and listened. "One minute," she said to the caller and covered the mouthpiece.

"Okay, I'll cut you some space, but only limited. Keep me informed on progress. Don't waste time. You can work on this, but I expect you to carry your share of the normal, non-sexy, non-prize-winning investigations—understood? So what's the next step?"

"Ken Antipov..."

"Sounds Russian."

"He was, but now he's British, probably the top man in this field, a senior scientist at Porton Down."

"Does he give interviews?"

"He's governed by the UK Official Secrets Act, but he does give information on background and will check a correspondent's copy and comment on any inaccuracies. I would expect he—"

"And you want to interview. Where?"

"He's in the UK at present." Chloe looked at her notes. Anne Marie let out a sigh. "He'll be attending a conference shortly, which—"

"Yes—go!"

The interview was over; Anne Marie hadn't looked at notes, or asked about primary sources. The timely interruption of a phone call had saved Chloe. Editors didn't usually let reporters have a travel budget without a realistic prospect of a result, all expenses were scrutinized in order to keep costs down. In the past, newspapers would have collaborated on an item of international interest, but either the multimedia news channels or just pride of ownership meant these large investigations seldom got off the ground.

Chloe returned to her desk, secured four days holiday from her subeditor, an appointment with Ken Antipov at his home in Oxfordshire for the next morning, and sent an email to Charles:

Charles, I'll pick you up at CDG airport – email flight times.

Regards, Chloe

She looked around for Jean Pierre to share her good news, but he had already left the office so she stuck a Post-it note on his computer screen stating "out of office for a week," left a contact number, and departed before Anne Marie could change her mind. With an overnight bag packed and discreetly hidden under her desk, she was ready to go, rejoicing in her preparedness and optimism. Things were looking up.

Chloe left the office and walked briskly to the Métro station. The Gare du Nord was busy as she boarded the Eurostar to London. After a sleepless night spent wondering why she was getting involved in this particular story and trying to control her expectations, just as she was about to fall asleep disquieting thoughts about her husband filled her head. She'd been married for just six months now, and as a newlywed, she hadn't expected to be considering if there was any future with this man. She was incredulous at his thoughtlessness. The money spent on a bed in a small London hotel was wasted. It was a relief when morning came. She went to the station and took a train to Oxford.

She rented a blue VW Golf from the car-rental office near the station, and she drove the seventeen miles through mixed farmland framed by bedraggled hawthorn hedges, dotted with red haws, to the village post office in Wychmoor Wood. It was a new modern unit, the loss of charm was apparent in the regimented parking spaces for essential rural transport.

Usually English village post offices were wonderful, you just needed a reason to stand in line and you would know everything. Not so here, it was quiet. The tiny shop had every square inch jam-packed; cluttered shelves filled with a mix of bread, cakes, greeting cards, brown paper, string, various envelopes, and every type of stationery schoolkids and small local businesses might need.

The postmistress was preserved behind a glass screen, a focus on security in a changing world where even small rural post offices were a target for the unlawful. Her directions to Antipov's house were explicit; she was experienced in directing delivery drivers in a quaint village where they used house names, not numbers. Not much anonymity for a leading biological weapons scientist, the real test would be the security at his home.

The village didn't have the classic appeal typical of the Cotswolds, there were some individual stone cottages along the main road, some thatched, some tiled, which lent character to the scene. However, these were interspersed with a variety of architectural styles ranging from the modern, mainly glass, A-frame Huf Haus, to a sixties, mottled orange-brick two-story with large windows.

Chloe had been twelve years old when she left this village. Her mother had packed up their possessions and they had returned to her native France, just after the inquest concluded her father's death at the British Chemical Defense Establishment at Porton Down was an accident. Chloe didn't believe it was an accident, he wasn't stupid and it would have been a particularly stupid accident. It seemed Chloe had followed a pattern of grieving widows in returning to France. Now memories of her father were so hazy she wasn't sure if she remembered the event, or the picture of the event.

She thought her dad, James Robert Culshaw, would approve of her investigation into the recent deaths of other microbiologists who had died in suspicious circumstances.

Chloe had just parked outside Antipov's house when her BlackBerry announced the arrival of a text message from Anne Marie. It was succinct and gave no background information.

Chloe, cum bk, no i/view poss with antipov – he's canceled.

Named as spy by bbc this morning. anne marie

She was checking the news on the BBC website when the local police turned up. One unarmed police officer got out of the car and took up his post by the front drive. She swore under her breath and wished she had ignored the text message and knocked on the door. Soon the world's media would be on Antipov's doorstep and he would need protection from the press or other factions. Anne Marie was right. A Russian spymaster had exposed an unnamed Moscow agent in a recent book. The BBC had revealed the spy known as "Rosa" was Kolenka Antipov.

Chloe needed a plan B. First, before the police organized themselves, she would check out the security at Antipov's home.

It was a beautiful Cotswold stone farmhouse. Small golden lichens niched into crevices in the mortar and weather had mottled the stone roof tiles. The farmhouse had long ago been divorced from its land, and the remaining plot was about two acres. Chloe walked along the lane at the side of the house, to several other new houses. She could see through Antipov's net curtains, the two small ground floor windows had concertina grills inside to protect the house from intruders. There was a small front yard, and an eight-foot wall enclosed the garden. At the end of the garden, there was a paddock with a post and rail fence and two bay hunters in the field. She wondered if the horses belonged to Antipov or if he rented out the field. What disturbed her was, although there had been changes—a different house name, a recent development of houses where the back garden had once been—and there were new security measures—fresh mortar indicated where the height of the walls had increased—she realized this had been her first home.

It seemed an extraordinary coincidence. She got out her phone and emailed instructions to a research assistant at the newspaper's office in Paris, to check who owned the property on the website of the Land Registry for England.

While she was waiting for the response, she went across the road to the Spotted Pig pub. The pub did coffee in the mornings before opening up the bar for lunchtime drinkers, so she ordered a coffee and the landlady was quite happy to engage in a conversation. Chloe engineered a discussion about the police arriving; did she know who owned the house? By the time her latte was ready, she knew Ken was an active member of the pub quiz team, and was essential to beating the pub at the other end of the village in an annual match where the victors gained bragging rights for the remainder of the year. The woman spoke warmly about Ken. She was oblivious to the television news running behind her, declaring him one of the worst spies in modern history. Chloe felt she knew Ken Antipov when she left. How he seemed to fit into this little Cotswold village, and was loved and respected.

She waited for her email in the parking lot. It didn't take long to find the holding company owning the property provided their services to the Ministry of Defense and they had acquired the property from the estate of James Robert Culshaw twenty-five years ago.

CHAPTER FOUR

Paris

Walid Merbarkia awoke in a cold sweat, screams reverberating inside his skull. He put his arm across to get reassurance from his wife, but she wasn't there. He sat up and looked for his cigarettes on the bedside table, but there weren't any.

"Merde!" He padded into the bathroom for a pee, the cold terra-cotta tiles drilled sharp needles of pain into his bones. He put his right foot onto the toilet seat and massaged the stumps where two toes were missing, but still hurt more than the rest.

He had a quick shower and a hasty shave, resulting in a small cut, which he dressed with toilet paper. He went into the kitchen and poured a coffee, bitterly regretting his decision to give up cigarettes. In his imagination, he could see the red and white packet of Ryms, feel the cellophane, soft and slippery, smell the sweetness of the filters, as he took his first nicotine fix of the day. A new packet was the dawn of his day. Instead, he made toast and checked the time.

He was supposed to be meeting Ahmed first thing this morning. He looked at the hook on the back of the door, Allah be praised, she had left him the car keys. He should, traffic willing, make it on time. He had a vague recollection she was hoping to go to England to interview someone, but wasn't certain she would go.

He arrived at the café on the Champs Elysée fifteen minutes late. He would now be rushing everywhere for the rest of the day. Ahmed Talbi was an important source of income for Walid; but if the Sorbonne dismissed him from his position as a lecturer, his wifely alibi would come under scrutiny by immigration, and his home life would generally become more complicated. Much of his kudos as an academic specialist would also be lost.

Moving into teaching in France, from being a curator in a museum in Algiers, had seemed a significant change, but he was happy at the Sorbonne, he felt safe and enjoyed his colleagues and the students. He still missed Algiers, the waterfront, old fishermen clustered around the tables in the cafés, the laughter over a game of dominos, and the smell of cigarettes. Everything reminded him about his need for a smoke. It was the stress; he should never have got married again, it complicated everything.

Ahmed owned an Islamic art gallery just off the Rue de Rivoli. It was close enough for those enthused from their experience in the Louvre to walk to the gallery and purchase priceless artifacts for their private collections. Walid and Ahmed always met at the café to do business. Ahmed Talbi liked his clients to think he personally acquired the items, direct from source. It was all part of the charade; he knew how to sell to exceedingly wealthy clients.

Walid sat down on the aluminum chair, the chill penetrated through his pants, leaving goose flesh across his thighs and a mild cramp in his calves. The table, covered in a blue gingham cloth, was set back from the gaze of passing pedestrians, under the wall-hung awning. Shafts of sunlight twinkled through the holes in the worn navy canopy, giving the impression of a night sky.

It was an unseasonably warm morning; the café was on the sunny side of the avenue, but soon it would be too cold to sit outside. Golden brown leaves, mixed with dull red and burnt orange, the debris of autumn swirled in the wind and rested on the pavement. A pot of coffee was already on the table.

He greeted Ahmed in Arabic.

"You're late," said Ahmed who continued the conversation in French, preferring to be inconspicuous. He poured the coffee, and offered him a cigarette. Walid recognized the blue packet of Gitanes, not Ryms, but good all the same.

"A thousand apologies, traffic was awful," he lied. "I'm lecturing this morning, but you said it was urgent and it couldn't wait 'til later." He took a cigarette, reached into his pocket for the gold plated brique lighter that still lived there and cupped his hand to shelter the flame as he lit it. Walid inhaled the smoke deep into his lungs, and enjoyed the moment before exhaling slowly.

Ahmed, a small man, had enormous amounts of nervous energy, tiny movements of his body, eyes checking constantly, hands clenching, opening, touching: his ear, his face, even the act of smoking was completed as if the nicotine police were waiting to pounce on him. At first Walid thought Ahmed was on drugs, or in the early stages of Parkinson's, but now he recognized it was a state of hyperactivity; Walid didn't know what drove or motivated the other man, but once you got used to his ways, he was pleasant enough and certainly paid well.

"I thought you would think this worth finding time for." Ahmed handed him a twenty-five-by-twenty-centimeter color photo. He was reluctant to hand it over, while at the same time eager for an opinion. Walid studied the image carefully. It was a test. His reputation as an expert depended on him getting the answer right. From the flat overhead picture, it was difficult to tell if he was looking at a bowl or plate.

"An Iranian luster bowl?" Walid paused for a moment to study and enjoy the intricate pattern.

"Yes." Ahmed looked pleased.

"At a guess, I would think Kashan, early thirteenth century?"

"Spot on." Ahmed leaned back in his chair, now confident in his choice of expert.

"Looks okay," said Walid, handing him back the picture.

"You sure?" Ahmed anxiously studied Walid's face for any sign of hesitation.

Walid looked at the Sotheby's catalogue on the table. It was a test where Ahmed already had an answer. "I can't be sure unless you have the bowl with you." Why did Ahmed need his opinion? The experts at Sotheby's were happy with the provenance, or the catalogue would have the key words "in the style of" or similar get-out clauses.

"It's lot 426 in Sotheby's sale next Tuesday. Can you check it out and if you're sure it's genuine, make the purchase—usual commission." Ahmed put the photograph into a soft leather briefcase and shut the clasp.

"What's the estimate? I would have thought somewhere in the region of forty-five to sixty thousand euros. Do you have a bid ceiling?"

"Right again, but no ceiling. The client's just been into the gallery and I needed to know you would be available at such short notice."

"Yes, next Tuesday will be fine. It's admin week, so no classes." *It's going to be a busy week*, thought Walid.

Ahmed got up, shook Walid's hand, and left. Walid hastily swallowed the remains of the coffee, stubbed out the cigarette, and made a dash for the car; he tore the parking ticket off the windshield and placed it in the glove box with the others. He rummaged about in there, looking for some anti-heartburn tablets to reduce his chest pain, but couldn't find any. He'd have to wait until he got to the university. Eager students who had paid considerable sums of money for the Sorbonne were now waiting for him and would enjoy his passion for Islamic art.

CHAPTER FIVE

London

Louise Chappel watched as the ultrasound picture appeared. There was no mistake; it wasn't a figment of her sister's overactive imagination. Her sister actually was about nine weeks pregnant. That meant it was Robin's baby. The nurse looked up, smiled, and made no comment. She'd probably seen it a thousand times before.

Laura wriggled and rustled on the disposable covering as the nurse slid the sensor across her abdomen. "It tickles."

Louise and the nurse exchanged glances. The child was about to have a baby. The picture on the computer screen updated, and the baby was moving. Suddenly it was real to Louise, she felt protective of both her young sister and this unborn child. She hadn't expected to feel quite so strongly about it.

Robin was a submariner, which meant he was conveniently away for about six months, he didn't want to be precise about the date of his return, and so Louise had agreed, under protest, to be the birthing partner, at least until Robin got back and the couple could make plans.

Plans were big in the Chappel household. Her mother had drilled into them *the* life plan. Good education, driver's license, good degree from a "proper" university—not one of these modern places—in a subject that would make them employable, a good job with prospects, followed by a relationship which would lead to marriage, homeownership, and finally a family, and this would provide their parents with the payback and gratitude together with the grandchildren they deserved.

Laura maintained it wasn't her fault. The doctor should have made it clear: the pills she was taking weren't *the* pill, and they were only a mini dose to help control her periods. Louise was sure the doctor had been clear, but Laura had only heard what she wanted to hear —she was "on the pill" and could have sex now.

Louise was firmly on the correct trajectory, although finding a life partner was proving difficult, she had embarked on buying her apartment. Existence seemed to be a choice between work and personal life.

What hurt was Laura was now the darling of their parents' eyes. Laura, who had moved from driver's license to parenthood, skipping all the required steps in between, seemed to have landed on her feet, after about ten days of passion on her back.

Louise's phoned chimed.

"You promised you'd take today off," accused Laura.

"That"—the nurse pointed to the phone—"shouldn't be on in here."

Louise shrugged an apology and left the consulting room to move outside to check the message. She knew what it would say; they would need her at work.

Louise made her way back to the consulting room and told her sister she would have to leave. She had been there for most of the appointment; there was little she could add now. Laura protested loudly, the nurse rolled her eyes in despair at the fuss, and Louise left.

She hurried to the office, and thought about what might await her as she made her way through the security system into the headquarters of British Intelligence (MI5), at Thames House. Entering through the pods had long since lost its enchantment. At first she thought it was much like entering the elevator on the starship *Enterprise*, there was a whoosh noise as the pods revolved. In the past, Louise—a confirmed *Star Trek* fan—would have muttered, "Bridge," but not today. Having to come into the office for some urgent security event, when off duty, was wearing thin. Today was supposed to be a day off in lieu of working the weekend.

Graeme Scott, her manager, was waiting at her desk. "Into the briefing room—now!"

"What's the flap?" Louise threw her coat over her desk. She switched on her computer and logged in, an essential requirement for health and safety, and to log the hours she spent in the office.

"Art Expert is on the move again."

"Art Expert" was the codename for a forty-one-year-old Algerian living in Paris who worked at the Sorbonne and advised on Islamic artworks. Periodically he would come to London and attend an auction. Sometimes he just delivered pieces to London galleries from a gallery in Paris. Rarely, he purchased a piece and took it back to Paris. He had become a regular disturbance to peaceful weekends and days off.

"Can't we get better information from the French to avoid all these sudden panics?" said Louise, as she gathered a notebook and pen from the top drawer of her desk.

Graeme shook his head. "I can't work out whether he talks to French intelligence, or maybe he's a French agent. Maybe he's both, maybe he's a terrorist, or maybe he's just innocent. He may be implicated in money laundering for Al Qaeda, and sometimes I think the French can't work out the options either."

"I thought he was an academic." Louise tried not to sound breathless as she followed him into the briefing room, her slight five-foot-six lithe frame needed to run to keep up with the long legs of her six-foot-five boss.

"Perhaps that's just a cover," said Graeme, grinning. He also found the fascination with an Art Expert somewhat lackluster when there were many more high priority targets to focus on.

The briefing had little detail other than Art Expert was en route to London, would be arriving at Waterloo station within the hour, and should have twenty-four hour surveillance. The meeting ended and Graeme turned to her.

"So what do you think?"

"Doesn't his wife know what's going on? I thought she was supposed to be a leading investigative journalist. Seems odd she married him at all, I don't see the attraction. Can't we ask her what he gets up to?"

"Good question."

"Anyway, I think we should find Art Expert a job in London," said Louise picking up her notebook.

"It's not a bad idea—can you start to think about something suitable, and you better include something for his wife too."

"Okay." Louise felt pleased. Finally, Graeme seemed to be prepared to trust her with an assignment. She could only hope it was genuine and she wasn't being patronized.

CHAPTER SIX

Chechnya

The Chechen Obshina were usually reliable, but today they were two hours late. Lying in the undergrowth on the damp ground, the Algerian wanted to relieve himself and a cigarette would have been welcome. He eased onto one hip, if he moved he would leave a heat signature on the ground. Ten more minutes, he looked at his watch, just ten more minutes and he would leave. He was too old for cloak-and-dagger events, he should have sent someone else. But he needed to be sure that Aden would supply him, and for that, he had to see him in person. From his elevated position, stationed a hundred meters up the hill from the road, in a sparse wood, mainly shrubs, he could see halfway around the bend in the road. Perhaps they weren't coming.

He was about to stand up when a battered, rusty white van and small trailer came around the corner of the narrow dirt track. He watched. Was it them? The van drew to a stop, six men alighted and quickly detached and dragged the trailer back along the road toward the corner. One man dug a small hole in the gravel road; two men carefully placed an improvised explosive device in the prepared space and covered it lightly. They then hid the trailer in the bushes.

He recognized Yuri, directing his men to take up places in the woods. The sound of an approaching vehicle pierced the still air of evening.

Now he understood why he was wearing a ghillie suit with a thermal imaging block, and had been instructed to remain concealed until Yuri called him by satellite phone. A ghillie suit might prevent his discovery from a heat-seeking camera on the ground, but it wouldn't stop the Russians finding him with the more sophisticated infrared camera from a helicopter.

Aden had been insistent; on no account was he to make himself known to the group, even if they appeared to be leaving without him. He must camouflage himself and hide in the undergrowth. Yuri had a little *zachistka*, a clean-up operation, to take care of.

He recognized trouble; Russian Spetsnaz troops, probably eight of them in an armed personnel carrier. Yuri set off a smoke canister. There was no breeze and the smoke hung in the air. It was subtle; it could have been an early evening mist to the uninformed; but it was sufficient. It distracted the driver of the armored vehicle from noticing the recently disturbed road.

The device went off and the vehicle lurched to a halt. Yuri shouldered his AK-47 in favor of a small pistol, and four seasoned arms dealers ran with him to scavenge the wreckage for useful items. Two shots rang out; there would be no injured Russian soldiers to tell the tale of what happened.

The driver of the van remained behind the wheel. At the back of the white van, Merbarkia recognized Mikhail, who was ready to provide backup from the machine gun bolted to the center floor. He remained at his post until the unit began to return, and then jumped out of the van, his Kalashnikov rifle dangling from the strap, and lit a cigarette.

Lying in the undergrowth, Merbarkia felt sure that Yuri would now phone him, it would not be safe to remain here long. The Russians would send a helicopter to find the troops. The speed of the assault had probably precluded any radio message summoning help; it had been a slick and well-rehearsed operation.

His attention moved from Yuri and the group to Mikhail, pacing back and forth behind the van. Alarmed, the Algerian noticed a small thermal camera in the palm of Mikhail's hand. The camera itself didn't cause alarm, but the sly way Mikhail used it did. As Mikhail brought his hand up to smoke, he was looking through the eyepiece.

What was he looking for? Who was he looking for? Russians? The thought of Russians being in the wood was alarming. It would suggest that the attack had been expected. It was the surreptitious way Mikhail glanced into the eyepiece; it wasn't an effective search technique. He puffed at his cigarette; it could hardly be called smoking. The cigarette was a cover to enable him to put the camera within eyesight.

He watched from the damp earth. What was wrong with the picture? Why was he concealing his action? That was it. Yuri would know he was hiding, camouflaged; the instructions were clear, if they were to complete the rendezvous, Yuri must phone him.

Mikhail seemed to turn toward his position and lifted his rifle, ready to fire. The Algerian slowly, imperceptibly pushed his chin even further into the leaves and earth to reduce the target area. He was so hot sweat was pouring down his face, stinging his eyes. He was sure he must show up on any thermal imaging. Was Mikhail supposed to be looking for him? He could only hope that the suit would shield his body heat from the camera. New cameras were so sensitive it made it increasingly hard to hide. He regretted he was unarmed.

The group walked back dragging the trailer filled with their spoils, their nervous laughter and joy of survival filled the woods. Yuri carried a Russian helmet, a strange trophy.

Couldn't they see what was happening? If he moved to a safer position, he was sure Mikhail would fire. But it was Yuri who drew his pistol and fired a single shot.

Mikhail was on his knees, clutching his leg, with blood pouring out of the wound. The red stain covered the green fatigues and puddled over the dusty road. The thermal camera lay abandoned. Although he couldn't hear what was being said, he knew the signs, Mikhail was begging Yuri for his life.

Yuri said nothing but kept walking toward Mikhail, leaving the rest of the group to bring the trailer. As he drew close, he took careful aim, delivered the executioner's bullet. He went up to the body and placed the Russian helmet on Mikhail's head. The message was simple and clear, Mikhail had been working for the Spetsnaz. The shot and the silence that followed conveyed the shock of betrayal.

The rest of the group, now silent, but well disciplined, continued their task and hitched the trailer onto the back of the van. Yuri picked up the camera, a useful asset, then reached inside his tunic and took out a satellite phone.

"Algerian? You ready?" Yuri asked. He answered the phone but made no reply, anyone listening would not get a voiceprint to be able to check his identity. "Let's go!" said Yuri.

Yuri motioned for the others to get inside the van. He took a final glance at Mikhail, and a look of regret crossed his face.

The Algerian rose like a leviathan from the sea of leaves. The ghillie suit added to the prehistoric appearance. As his urine met the cold earth, it gave off a steam cloud in the chill of the autumn evening. Relieved, he then strode down the hill, each step jarring his aching frame, and got in the van.

Dealing with the Chechen Obshina was always risky. He concluded they were mad but the Chechen separatists sold reliable equipment.

When the van stopped, they all got out and the Algerian was surprised by the extent of the surrounding destruction. The Russians must have attacked the village again, since his last visit. The dingy suburb had disintegrated into a shantytown. Rusty corrugated iron was the only building material, and the shacks had no windows, just a single air vent.

"I'm sorry about the business with Mikhail, we weren't sure." Yuri nodded his respects.

The Algerian digested this information for a moment. Yuri had knowingly endangered his life. Yuri would keep. He would deal with him after the delivery of his goods.

"Is Aden about?" It was essential to conduct his business and leave before the Russians found him. His visit to Chechnya had hardly been a low key, unobtrusive event. If Mikhail was looking for him, then the Russians knew he was here.

Aden exited the nearest shack. A seasoned Chechen campaigner, he looked much older than his forty years. He beckoned his friend over.

The interior of the shack was simple; it took a moment for the Algerian's eyes to adjust to the gloom. In one corner, there were four chairs and a plain wooden table with an oil lamp, which lit the room; it was functional.

The Algerian outlined his plans. Aden was disappointed the target was London, not New York or some other major American city. But he took delight in the audacity of the plan and explained how they had improved on the briefcase bomb design.

"We have placed thin beryllium reflectors on either side of the plutonium to increase the effect and reduce the amount of plutonium, and it now weighs eleven kilograms. It will give about a ten ton explosion; it will be effective over four hundred meters and we would expect a hundred percent fatality within three hundred meters. We build these to order, the material is at its best for about a hundred days."

"Detonators?"

"We'll supply and ship those separately, we are using polonium-210, they ship in packets that look like sugar packs you'd find in a café, and we'll send a specialist to fit. Then you'll need to deploy within a couple of weeks."

As soon as business was done, the Algerian slipped away. Unable to trust Yuri for transport he walked for several miles before phoning a friend who would spirit him out of the country into Georgia where he would appear to be a foreign business executive, before flying home.

CHAPTER SEVEN

London to Paris

Chloe left the Cotswold village of Wychmoor Wood, took trains, tubes, and eventually got on the Eurostar back to Paris. It was full of soccer fans, a sea of blue and white. Chelsea was about to play Paris Saint-Germain in the UEFA cup, at the Parc des Princes. Clearly the fans were going to have a good time, their mildly inebriated enthusiasm was contagious but distracting. They weren't making trouble, just in an expectant mood.

To the tune of "Yellow Submarine," they were singing, "We are going on a European tour, European tour, European tour."

When they got bored with that chant, they moved onto "Lord of the Dance," with the words, "Chelsea, wherever we may be, We are the famous CFC, And we don't give a f***, Whoever you maybe, 'Coz we are the famous CFC."

Her head was pounding, partly from lack of sleep and partly from her brain being in a loop. Why would the Ministry of Defense buy her father's house after he died? It didn't make any sense and the only person who could have shed light on it was her mother, so only a psychic could give her those answers now. She made her way to the first class section of the train and paid for the upgrade, which she couldn't reclaim, and regretted the lack of a decent expense account.

The train journey provided thinking time. She needed to make a decision about Walid. Chloe had met him at an art gallery event. Jean Pierre had suggested they go, not as a couple, of course. As companions, on the clear understanding if either should meet someone the other would be okay about it. True to form, Jean Pierre had met a slightly drunk, giggly blonde, showing a lot of cleavage enhanced by silicone implants under a cowl-neck on a red, pencil-slim dress. The couple had left the gallery arm in arm twenty minutes later.

At first, Chloe had wished she had not gone to the event at all, and although she was managing to circulate the exhibit, she felt out of place without an escort. When Walid had approached her, it had been a relief. He was Algerian, spoke French with an accent, a warm and thoughtful man. They were good company for each other and shared interests in classical music and art. The next night he had invited her to a small intimate café for dinner and afterward they had walked along the Left Bank of the Seine, enjoying the lights and talking about tourists in the city. He had suggested a concert the next night, and she had suggested a charity reception for sick children at the Louvre the night after that, and soon they were spending part of every day together. She had found his company easy and enjoyable. But there was nothing more. He might hold her hand as they walked along, or put his arm around her shoulders to guide her, but there was no suggestion of anything other than friendship. He had never resented her frequent absences to Brussels or Luxembourg. He had seemed too good to be true. But she had begun to wonder if he was married, she didn't think he was gay, and it seemed impertinent to ask. What she knew was she was fond of him, and was the happiest she'd been in two years.

A few weeks later, he had proposed and the relationship had found the physical intimacy she thought had been lacking. She had concluded his old-fashioned values had prized a chaste courtship. She had expected things to carry on that way for several months, a commitment with an eventual marriage, but they married quickly to save the anxiety and uncertainty of a visa renewal and perhaps this had focused his attentiveness and passion. She didn't remember actually agreeing to the wedding date. It was all a blur. If he had married her for a visa, then it was probably time to admit her mistake and get a divorce. She got off the train and made her way across Paris.

She took the train from the RER station to Sceaux, a pleasant community six miles south of the center of Paris. She walked past the shops and through the black wrought-iron gates to the apartment block. The apartment Walid had chosen had few redeeming features, constructed in the sixties, the rooms at the front looked directly onto the street and the rooms at the back looked onto a wall, being a half level belowground. It would have made a great bomb shelter. It was life in a bat cave; he wouldn't have the shutters open on the street side, and opened only those of the rooms in use on the garden side. Perhaps he was mentally ill or moderately paranoid.

She had assumed they would live in the city, in the elegant apartment she had inherited from her grandmother. It was the first compromise of many, and at the time, it seemed reasonable to let him choose their first joint home. She had agreed she would rent out the apartment in the 8th arrondissement near the Parc Monceau. She missed the convenience of the location, unused to commuting to work. She mourned the loss of the spacious rooms with their wood panels, and silk brocade drapes in jewel colors, the balcony overlooking the boulevard where she could listen to the rumble of cars over the cobbles, amplified on wet days. But she couldn't bear to rent it to strangers, it was full of memories of her grandmother and her childhood. She would visit occasionally to check all was well, but if Walid didn't start contributing to household expenses on their apartment in Sceaux soon, she would have to rent it out. While the future of her marriage seemed uncertain it seemed stupid to let go of the apartment she might need herself.

Chloe opened the door, and made her way through the gloom to their bedroom, opened up the shutters so she could see to unpack her overnight bag, and re-pack for a few days by the coast with Charles. She closed the shutters and tried to make contact with Walid. His cell phone was off. His voice mailbox at the university was full. Some things didn't change. She left him a note on the kitchen table and set off for the airport to pick up Charles.

Chloe wondered just how confidential these papers were if he felt the need to deliver them in person. Perhaps he just wanted a break. She met him at the terminal meeting point and they embraced French style, he pushed her back to look at her.

"I can see France agrees with you, you look terrific."

"Let's face it, I would be hard pressed to look much worse than the last time you saw me —I can't believe it was two years ago."

She drove to St Vaast, to the Hôtel de France where she had booked two rooms. They didn't talk much in the car. Charles was travel weary and dozing. Arriving at the hotel, they made their way through the rose arch, a few pink blooms remained, resolutely holding on to the end of summer, and they crossed the courtyard. Red Dutch canopies over the windows added color to a gray day. The Virginia creeper on the white-washed walls was vibrant in crimson and blood-red leaves. They would begin to fall with the first hard frost.

Inside was welcoming; raspberry Toile du Jouy paper covered the reception walls, idyllic rural scenes of a bygone era. She had picked the hotel because it held personal memories for her. Many celebrations with her mother, including her mother's last birthday lunch. Neither of them had known it would be the last at the time. The food was excellent. It was always warm and cozy. For a long time after her mother's death, the thought of the hotel was too painful, but now it brought treasured memories and wistful smiles at the familiar.

Reception gave them adjoining rooms, Chloe felt there was an implication in their proximity, but Charles was too tired to notice. He decided on a nap, leaving strict instructions to wake him for dinner.

Her heart lifted when she entered her room—so pretty, so feminine. Small floral paper went up the walls and across the ceiling, sympathetic curtains hung at the window, not overmatched but a sophisticated harmony.

Charles was awake when she knocked on his door. They made their way through the narrow corridor to the dining room.

"I'm ravenous, I could eat a horse," he said.

"I don't think My Little Pony is on the menu tonight but I could be wrong. You should be careful what you wish for, this is France and horse might be served."

They went downstairs and were seated by a window overlooking the courtyard, the nights were closing in. Chloe wasn't ready for autumn to end.

Dinner was a candlelit, romantic affair, a log fire blazed away in the corner, and she wasn't sure how Charles would take the ambience, so she overcompensated by being too animated. After dinner she left Charles to linger over coffee and liquors with the locals in the bar, communicating with Gallic shrugs and dubious Franglais. Chloe made her way back to her room; they had agreed to meet for a late breakfast and to start work with a walk along the jetty.

Chloe slept well. The following day she enjoyed dressing in jeans and a sweater, it made a welcome change from formal businesswear. She met Charles in the restaurant, the smell of ash lingered from the previous night's log fire; the ambience had changed in daylight.

The croissants were hot and flaky and the coffee rich, Charles savored the aroma and made the usual remarks about Americans not being able to make coffee.

"Yeah, and they can't make croissants worth a damn either," Chloe responded. Charles laughed.

They collected warm coats and set out for the marina. It was a brisk and chilly walk. The wind was piercing enough to blow any jet lag or sleepiness away. Yachts were bobbing and straining at the mooring ropes securing them to the pier. The shrouds beat against the aluminum masts intermittently with the wind, as the gusts peaked, the noise became a deafening crescendo, which faded away to a few irregular beats.

"Do you remember the SARS outbreak in China?" said Charles. "That seemed to be the start of it all. A scientist working in America had traced the virus back to a lab in China—"

"You mean it was a biological weapons accident?"

"Not exactly, but the scientist had an outbreak of guilty awareness. There but for the Grace of God go I. Before you could say 'whistle-blower' he was dead."

"How do you know that's what he was planning, if he was dead before he blew the whistle?"

"He told his wife that's what he was going to do and they agreed they could both accept the consequences. They assumed he would be imprisoned under an act of treason at best, and at worst, killed as a traitor. But it was worse because he lost his life and didn't improve the world situation."

"Yes, but you've just said she's telling the tale now—so what's the problem?"

"You may have noticed I didn't give you the scientist's name and that's because his wife won't go on record because 'the authorities' "—he made air quotes with his hands—"have threatened her entire family. Nasty, gruesome, and grisly deaths and just to prove a point, one of her husband's colleagues was stabbed several times, placed in the trunk of a car, and set alight."

"Merde."

"If you want out, now would be a good time to say so and we can have fun on a yacht." He grinned.

"No. I'm just a bit surprised that's all."

"How's your mother?"

"She died, quite suddenly, about eighteen months ago—why do you ask?" Chloe was surprised at this sudden interest in her personal life.

"I'm sorry. I know she was one of the reasons you came back to France and I owe you an apology."

"It's not necessary. I know you thought you were right. But it was bad enough to have to make the decision to turn off the life support machine without everyone telling me either I was right or I was wrong. I was neither. He was my husband. I did what had to be done. It didn't make it right or wrong."

"I know that now. I'm very sorry, I shouldn't have said anything, I suppose I just came to realize there was no hope of Mike recovering more slowly than you did. I hoped that when you asked for help on this investigation it meant you had forgiven me."

"There's nothing to forgive. It was impossible to stay in the States afterward though, everyone in the office seemed polarized by your hostility toward me, and they either agreed with my decision or questioned it. Some of those people didn't even know me but they had an opinion. The comments, the sympathetic looks, I knew I would never move on with my life if I stayed."

"I'm sorry, you deserved better. I didn't realize it had become so bad. I really regret saying anything and I'm devastated to hear I made things so much worse, but I was angry."

"I know, it's grief; we were all angry, it seemed such a waste."

"Anyway, I thought I should make sure you don't have anyone close who could be compromised by this investigation."

"I remarried."

"What? When were you going to tell me about that?"

Chloe looked out at sea. What was she supposed to tell him about Walid? *I'm married, but I made a mistake.* Charles wasn't her type so it wouldn't have made any difference. When she had worked with him, it had been an abrasive experience. He was a dominant character, and she was obstinate, the result was explosive.

"He's a lecturer at the Sorbonne. He's kind and easy company. We enjoy going to galleries, music concerts, and..." Chloe smiled, pulled what she hoped was a face that dared him to ask any further questions.

"I'm glad." It was all Charles left unsaid that mattered, and she read the disappointment in his face, which surprised her.

"Where were we?"

"Exposing SARS as a Chinese biological accident."

"There seem to be links here. Either these scientists were about to expose issues, were reaching retirement and contemplating life as an author, or were about to engage in some other worrying breach of security, which resulted in their deaths."

The exposé went on for about an hour before Chloe declared it was time for coffee. She was cold and needed time to think. This project was a lot more interesting than she had originally thought, but there was one worrying fact. Charles had all this evidence but still didn't have enough facts to publish, not one person would go on the record, but collectively it had to amount to a planned retirement strategy for biological weapons scientists.

They made their way to a patisserie and ordered coffee and cake. She watched as he emptied two packets of sugar into his coffee, stirring methodically in a figure-eight motion. After Charles finished a douceur au chocolat, with Neanderthal noises of approval, he finally returned to the matter at hand.

"So what do you think?"

"I'm not sure, I have this theory placed somewhere between the *Titanic* was sunk as an insurance fraud, and the Americans never landed on the moon."

"I don't think that's fair."

"No, you're right; it's far less cohesive than either of those two conspiracies. This is a global, disparate issue. It lacks anyone, in over forty cases, prepared to give a statement. You haven't published, in spite of comprehensive research. Why on earth do you think I will do better?"

A man in a dripping wet raincoat walked into the shop, ordered a coffee, and sat at the next table. They exchanged nods, neither party wanting to engage in conversation.

With his back to the newcomer, Charles put a finger to his lips. He clearly didn't want to discuss this within earshot of anyone.

"So tell me about the new man in your life. Does he have a name? Come on, time for girl talk, and tell me all."

"When did you ever know me to engage in girl talk?"

"It's an expression. Come on. Tell."

"His name is Walid Merbarkia. He's six-foot-one, good looking, has a Mediterranean complexion so always looks like he has a great tan, dark hair—no gray—well none so far, soft gentle brown eyes. He's Algerian, a lecturer in medieval Islamic art and Arabic at the Sorbonne. Is that enough?"

"Algerian? Not nearly enough, how did you meet, how long did you know him before you got married, where are you living? Tell all." He stressed the word "all" and that was the last thing she wanted to do.

"We met in an art gallery, six weeks, apartment in Sceaux—a suburb south of Paris. Now we're done." Chloe got up, the rain was only beginning to ease but she wanted to walk and think of questions. She felt he was railroading her into this investigation and it didn't seem a promising enough project.

"Only six weeks?"

That was Charles the reporter, throw a bunch of disparate facts at him and he would pick out the follow-up question.

"Walid's visa..."

"You got married in haste to save him filling in a bunch of forms?"

"It seemed silly not to get married early and save the anxiety of waiting for a visa renewal. It would be more straightforward and guaranteed we would be together."

"You don't think by any chance he saw you coming, do you?"

"Charles, I resent the implication that Walid took advantage of me. The subject is closed."

They walked in silence. Chloe was fuming, because he was right. She didn't like to admit that she didn't remember her wedding day at all. There were pictures of her outside the Mairie with Walid, looking happy. She was wearing a blue sequined dress, and couldn't imagine what she had been thinking, it was an old, full-length evening gown, it was too big for her, she'd lost weight since she came to France and it looked tawdry and ridiculous on a sunny afternoon. She had the Livret de Famille, her marriage certificate, the official document. She remembered getting all the papers together and going for a medical and waiting for the blood tests, she remembered going to the lawyer to get the Certificat de Coutume, but there was no evidence of the Certificat du Notaire, the prenuptial agreement, and she knew she wouldn't have married him without one. None of her friends or family had been invited. It disturbed her that she didn't remember the day. Perhaps it was a reaction to the stress of the moment.

The first two months after they got married were great, but overnight, something changed. Chloe had asked about it. Walid swore nothing had changed, but it had. It was something to do with the extra work he had taken on appraising artifacts for a gallery, whether it left him short of time or under pressure, she didn't know, but he had changed and she didn't like it. They came across a wooden bench overlooking the marina and sat.

"Okay, Charles, if you were going to continue with this assignment where would you expect to get the hard evidence?"

"I think you must be able to find evidence in Iraq, because of the numbers involved, but that will be dangerous. I think you will find answers in Miami, because two witnesses weren't called at the inquest and it would be interesting to hear their stories now and compare against the statements they gave at the time."

"Okay. You said in the synopsis, the link was biological weapons scientists who specialized in DNA microbiology. Why do you think DNA is the link?"

"I have had plenty of time to think about that, and just consider a weapon you could deploy without any damage to property, no contamination to water supplies, no loss of energy resources, and no expensive rebuilding and reparation. It would also be a cheaper form of warfare compared to conventional weapons. The war in Iraq is costing about 1.8 billion US dollars a week—armaments, troops, supplies. Imagine just sending in one missile and ending the war."

"I'm not sure an ethnic weapon can distinguish between Taliban and Afghan, they have the same ethnicity. What's the point of going to war, if it's not to encourage financial transactions and boost the economy, I'm not sure this will catch on." Chloe shivered in the cold wind, reached into her trench coat pocket, found her gloves, and put them on. "Anyway, that doesn't explain the demise of these bio-med scientists."

"The link they also share is they were about to go public, publish a book which might have been damaging, or blow the whistle. One couple working for a highly regarded research project in the States discovered money flowing from their organization, going out the back door for black ops. They went to visit her sister to tell her she should leave town before the press landed on her doorstep, something unpleasant was about to break which would concern them."

"So surely the sister is a witness..."

"To what? They didn't tell her what was going to happen. Sure enough the press were on her doorstep for a comment, the couple were killed before the end of the day."

"How?"

"Car accident."

"Michael was killed in a car accident, are you saying it was a suspicious event?"

"No... but..."

"So you do believe in coincidence?"

"Good point"—Charles sounded defensive, which she hadn't intended—"but you can't accept all these events as just coincidence, there are too many events and there is a pattern."

There was no doubting Charles's sincerity or the strength of his feelings on the matter.

"Come on, let's walk, I'm getting cold." They got up and, turning their backs to the wind, they made their way back to the hotel.

"Why are you so sure?" she asked.

"Because I have met with some of the individuals involved." He looked into her eyes to emphasize the veracity of his claim.

"Did you remember investigating the Marconi incident?"

"Yes, they lost thirty employees in the 1980s, most either murdered or they died in unsatisfactorily explained circumstances."

"The statisticians said at the time, the odds of it being a natural phenomenon were 14,000,000 to 1, or something similar."

"And your point is?"

"No one could prove anything. When we looked at it twenty years later, we still couldn't prove anything with our investigation. If secret intelligence services were concerned the Marconi employees would leak elements of the Star Wars Project, or were killing them in an attempt to get information, there was no way of proving it."

"So you're going to give up?"

"Hell no, Charles, why would I give up? My father was a biological weapons scientist. I've always wondered about his death. But at the end of the day, people have accidents, they die and other people are left to ponder the universe and wonder why."

The remaining days flew past; they pored over his notes, the documents, his clippings file, drew link diagrams to see if they could find other common themes to the deaths, and devised a plan. Chloe showed him her Mossad photo; a few phone calls later they had established several correspondents in the States had received these photos, but the map reference points were all different. Maybe, using all the map reference points, Chloe would be able to find three hundred missing Iraqi scientists. She would need to establish what was happening in the rest of the world first. Iraq was a separate issue, although related.

Chloe dropped Charles off at the airport. She had planned to go in and have a coffee with him, but changed her mind. She hadn't heard from Walid. He hadn't answered his cell phone or responded to her daily messages.

Charles gave her a Target shopping bag they had taken on all their walks, although he only showed her papers in his bedroom. As they said goodbye, he made a great fuss of putting a computer storage key on her key ring and drawing her in close.

"Come on, give me a hug," he said.

She moved closer to him, unsure about sharing her personal space with him. It was strange how she didn't feel comfortable with American hugs anymore. Perhaps her English DNA liked distance and formality. With his hand firmly against the small of her back she thought he was going to kiss her, she tried to draw back but he held her hard against him. She was shocked to find his hand cupping her breast, placing something underneath it, against the hard wire of her bra.

"It's a computer storage key, the real one," he said, while making sure her top was readjusted. "There's only recycling in the shopping bag, and nothing important on the storage key on your key ring. But the computer key in your bra—that's the real item. I'll get the real papers to you tomorrow." Charles spoke into her hair, in a clinch that would look amorous to anyone watching, but to Chloe it was clinical and chilling. She was glad when he let her go. Charles's paranoia was beginning to get to her.

CHAPTER EIGHT

Sceaux, Paris

Chloe went back to her shuttered apartment, and got an immense feeling of freedom in opening everything up, front and back, letting light and air into the colorless home. It might be cold, but it seemed to help.

She took the computer storage key out of her bra and put it in her pillowcase, she thought it would have been equally safe in her briefcase, but deferred to Charles's paranoia.

Walid had left her a note scrawled at the bottom of the note she had left him. *Terrific, so now we're pen pals.*

Anne Marie phoned. "Ken Antipov has just been found dead at his home. Can you run a piece?"

"My piece isn't about deaths—there are over forty of those, it's those deaths that are suspicious."

"I want a piece on my desk tomorrow afternoon." She hung up.

Chloe felt annoyed; Anne Marie was downgrading the project to a pseudo investigation. She started working on the piece but didn't feel this was the right time to go to print. She'd finish it tomorrow. She made a couple of phone calls and initial information suggested suicide, nothing suspicious. Given he had been exposed as a spy she could believe it had been suicide.

The milk in the fridge was off, which suggested Walid hadn't been back to the apartment since she'd left for Normandy and she was about to walk to the shops in Sceaux to get some food when the phone rang.

"Why are all the shutters open?" It was Walid, he sounded tense.

"I'm spring cleaning." Perhaps humor might defuse the situation.

"Close the shutters."

So nothing much had changed. She opened the front door and kissed him. Perhaps they could find some of the original love and if not love, at least a sense of respect and care for each other.

"It's good to see you," he said. He kissed her, drew her close, and kissed her again with feeling. She was surprised. Perhaps he realized she'd had enough.

"Shall we go out for dinner?"

He said they should go into the city and have dinner on a Bateau-Mouche. She thought it was a facile idea, and it would be busy on a Sunday night, but it seemed to please him and she wasn't about to have an argument about where they had dinner.

Chloe hadn't had a dinner date on a Bateau-Mouche since she was a teenager, and the atmosphere was guaranteed to have you believing you were in love with whoever accompanied you to dinner. If Quasimodo himself had been sitting opposite, she would have been enchanted. He insisted on a private table at the front of the boat. She could only hope he planned to pay, at three hundred and fifty euros it wasn't a cheap evening. Walid was charming. Some issues, like communication, the shutters, and his failure to contribute to the household expenses, seemed inappropriate.

Chloe didn't want to discuss her unsuccessful trip to the Cotswolds, or her time with Charles. Walid didn't want to discuss the fake art piece in London and didn't offer an explanation as to where he spent the remainder of the week. Instead, they behaved as if they were on a first date; they talked about the beauty of Paris, the Pont Neuf, and the illuminations. She asked him if he wanted to join her in Florida for a few days, they could fly out on the Wednesday, she would need to work on the Friday and then they could spend the weekend relaxing before returning on the overnight flight on the Sunday. Perhaps Walid would benefit from a break. Hopefully, if Anne Marie agreed, she would be leaving for the States the day after tomorrow. He seemed to think it was a good idea. Maybe it was a start, it reminded her why they had married, and how easy his company was.

If she had expected more, she was disappointed, he slept on the sofa saying he had a bad back and didn't want to disturb her with his tossing and turning. She had pointed out if he had a bad back maybe she should take the sofa, and the arguments had started again. In the end, she gave in and took the bed. When she got up he had already left, but no note this time, she didn't know where he was. She could only hope a trip to Florida would provide a fresh start, but she wasn't optimistic. It was like being married to two people, the man she married, lovable, loving, and caring; then there was the inconsiderate, insensitive man who ignored her.

She took the train to work and walked from the Métro to the office. She had placed the computer key back in her bra. Part of her thought she was becoming paranoid, but it amused her. She had the Target shopping bag with Charles's recycling, her computer bag, a messenger bag slung across her tan trench coat; it was misty and she was thinking she should probably have taken the car.

CHAPTER NINE

Paris

Jean Pierre escorted Chloe back to their pigpen, sat her down, checked she didn't still feel faint, and went to fetch her coffee. Chloe was beginning to think about going home. No one would blame her if she took the rest of the day off. Her head was pounding, and she would have liked the opportunity to bathe her head and remove the rather conspicuous white wound dressing. She wanted a chance to think calmly and quietly about what had happened.

She'd been a target while researching the Mafia, but being the focus of multiple secret intelligence services was sinister. The man in the car wasn't wearing black combat gear so there were two events and perhaps they weren't linked.

Jean Pierre canceled his appointment and sat with her. "I suppose the most urgent question is: what are you going to tell Anne Marie?"

"Anne Marie? What's there to tell? I was mugged."

"Not exactly, you were mugged in the staff parking garage, an ambulance had to be called, and in case security was asleep, we went and reviewed the footage alerting them to the issue. Anne Marie will already know, so what are you going to tell her?"

Chloe caught sight of a reflection on her computer screen; Anne Marie was standing behind her.

"I shall have one more coffee, and I shall go and tell her as much as she wants to hear. It's a two-minute event. I was mugged, robbed, ambushed, bushwhacked, attacked, I don't know, whatever you want to call it. Someone was sufficiently organized to be able to drive a car through the newspaper's security system and take my computer, my camera, my phone, and a bag of recycling. Probably the key issue here is the breach of security to the building, and that has little to do with me, except that now I need a new computer."

"Is that all?" said Anne Marie.

Jean Pierre's chair crashed to the floor as he stood up. He righted the chair, and motioned to Anne Marie to take his seat. "If you could give us a minute," she said.

Jean Pierre left.

"I wonder how much you would have told me if you hadn't seen me standing there."

Chloe shrugged, she didn't know the answer to that question and couldn't think clearly.

"Are you sure this is the right topic for you? I understand you want to move to some real news, not the continuing cycle of EU, but I wouldn't want to feel you were taking this to avoid the EU stories. There will be other stories, perhaps with more chance of a successful outcome. I want to know if you want this investigation. I think we know it will be dangerous."

"Yes, I want this story. I think knowing the truth about how someone died is important. To say nothing of exposing the intelligence services if they are systematically killing public servants."

"You don't think your feelings about your father might be clouding your judgment?"

Chloe was surprised Anne Marie knew about her father. "I don't know. Possibly."

"That's an honest answer. All right, you can go ahead but on the clear understanding you must keep Jean Pierre informed at all times. He's not your boss, you're not working for him, no matter what he thinks, but I want to be able to pick up a phone and talk to you twenty-four hours a day. Is that clear? If working with Jean Pierre is an issue, I'll assign someone else."

"Crystal clear. JP is fine." Chloe liked Anne Marie's direct approach. Anne Marie's cell phone rang. She listened.

"So bring it up. No. Now. Immediately," Anne Marie said and turned to Chloe. "So what's next?"

"Dr Biryukov in Miami." Chloe wasn't convinced, but Charles was sure she would get enough from a trip to Florida to justify the rest of the investigation. "There are two witnesses who saw the attack—"

"Keep me informed of actual progress. After the Miami trip we will have a full review to see if this investigation can go anywhere."

"Right."

A security guard came across to the pigpen and waited. Anne Marie held out her hand.

"That's my camera," said Chloe.

"Yes, would you like to tell me what it was doing in a taxi?"

"I took a taxi to escape my follower, but I took a picture of him. It must have slipped out of my bag. I thought the muggers had taken it."

Anne Marie shook her head; she didn't want to know the details. She switched on the camera and looked at the images. She pursed her lips. "That could be useful." Anne Marie had recognized the stalker.

Anne Marie got up, handed her the camera, and said, "I think it's time you went home, just file your piece on Antipov and go. You better collect a new computer on your way out; if you phone ahead they'll load all your backup files onto it for you."

Chloe nodded, and regretted the action. "Could you put this in your safe?" asked Chloe, handing Anne Marie Charles's storage key.

Anne Marie took the key and put it in her pocket, she seemed to know instinctively what was on the key, or was suffering from a distinct lack of curiosity.

Chloe wished she had the courage to ask Anne Marie if she recognized the man in the picture. But if Anne Marie had wanted to say who it was, she would have told Chloe. Maybe Jean Pierre would know.

Jean Pierre returned, took one look at the photo, and said, "So what do you think of that?"

Chloe didn't like to admit she could barely see the picture, everything was blurred; she would need to put the image onto her computer to have any idea of who it was.

"You do recognize him, don't you? I mean you must have recognized him when you took the picture."

Chloe assumed her vision would clear soon. It was getting better so she had discounted a detached retina or anything else that might make her change her mind and visit the hospital or an ophthalmic optician. She hadn't really seen the stalker when he was on the pavement, she was too busy looking at the little window on her camera to get her picture.

"You don't, you have no idea."

"It's not that I don't recognize him, I can't see him."

"Really? Are you okay?"

"I expect I will be, but humor me, who is it?"

"Patrick Dubois. I hope you see there is a need for us to at least keep each other informed of what actions we're taking."

Chloe could only nod. So her first day on this investigation and she had engaged the interest of two secret intelligence services. That must be some sort of record.

"Anne Marie says you're to go home after you've filed your piece. Do you want me to call a cab for you? It's on the paper's account."

Chloe shrugged, she felt worse now than earlier, she just wanted to go home and try to sleep it off. Charles had been right to be cautious and send the files by courier. In the meantime, she would collect her new laptop on the way out and she could file her piece from home.

CHAPTER TEN

Extract from La France

Leading Biological Weapons Scientist Found Dead
By Senior Correspondent Chloe Moreau

Kolenka Antipov was found dead in his Cotswold home in the village of Wychmoor Wood yesterday. Antipov defected from Russia to the UK in 1978 and after an extensive debriefing, led by James Culshaw, went on to become a leading scientist at Porton Down, the UK defense facility. Antipov was privy to NATO secrets, working on pan-European defense strategy and researching protection against biological weapons coded to an individual DNA.

The BBC alleged Antipov was the spy code-named "Rosa," working for Russia since his defection. Another Russian scientist felt the use of a female code name for a male spy was unusual and, knowing Antipov as a close friend, dismissed the allegations entirely.

When the BBC made its announcement, one of two things should have happened, either Antipov should have been arrested or had some protective custody. The establishment's response was to send one, unarmed, local police officer to his house, which was an old farmhouse with low security, set in the middle of idyllic countryside with undulating fields stretching out to the horizon.

Antipov was a popular figure in the village, where most seemed unaware of his job. One villager told me, "He said he worked for the Ministry of Defense, it was assumed he probably worked as a translator or something at GCHQ in Cheltenham." He was a leading member of the quiz team at his local pub, the Spotted Pig, played tennis socially, and was a keen gardener.

Several villagers in his local pub were quick to dismiss allegations against him as inconceivable and are shocked he might have taken his own life. Antipov, aged fifty-eight, was found in his garden shed next to a gasoline-powered lawnmower, and initial reports suggest he died of carbon monoxide poisoning.

Dated 21 September 2004

CHAPTER ELEVEN

Paris

Walid arrived at the usual café before Ahmed. The Champs-Elysees was so full of tourists it was easy to blend in. It made him feel secure. Here, he knew where the nearest Métro station was, how to order coffee, and the general location of the main attractions.

He ordered a double espresso and a pot of coffee for Ahmed. Ahmed had been quite clear only to buy the piece if it was genuine. If he had a client that wanted the piece for decorative purposes, he should have made the fact clear. Ahmed had been angry on the phone.

He glanced at his watch. Ahmed was late. He opened his wallet to pay for the coffee. He paused for a moment and looked at the picture of his children, twin boys. Hardly children, he thought, they would start their military service next week. After his wife died, he had applied to the Sorbonne; he hadn't thought for one moment he would get the job, but had seen it as a new beginning and accepted. He had asked a neighbor to look after his boys for a couple of weeks until he had found somewhere for them to live in Paris. It had been a shock when the boys told him they weren't coming. He found out later their uncle had been visiting them, and now they were angry young men with jihad on their minds. He had remonstrated, pleaded, and eventually realized if he continued opposing them he would lose them forever. Walid would be glad when they joined the army.

The people at the next table left. Walid was alone outside the café where they could smoke and the waiter would soon light the patio lamps to keep customers warm.

Walid noticed Ahmed standing on the opposite sidewalk waiting. Walid waved and Ahmed crossed the road in haste, carrying two aluminum briefcases.

Walid rose and offered an outstretched hand. Ahmed put the cases down and embraced him. Instead of the usual small talk Ahmed launched forth.

"You did the right thing. I missed a sale. The client's furious but pleased. So..."

"If your client wanted a decorative piece you should have said." Walid poured a cup of coffee for Ahmed. He watched as Ahmed tore open two sugars simultaneously and agitated the coffee with his spoon. Waves of coffee sloshed around the cup and just managed, by the smallest margin, not to produce a tidal wave in the saucer.

"No, you did the right thing—but now the client wants you to go to Iraq to pick up genuine pieces. How do you feel about that?"

"I think we could make it work. I have a couple of weeks I can take as professorial research leave. Can I assume you'll take care of the requisite import licenses? And deal with the shippers? Getting any artifacts out of Iraq won't be easy."

"Of course. Here are the first two pieces." Ahmed handed two black and white Polaroid photos to Walid. Walid was distracted for a moment as Ahmed got out his cigarettes.

"I can't tell anything from these." He handed the photographs back.

"I know, but that doesn't matter, because you will be able to see what is available for yourself, and if you get offered anything else, well, I need good pieces. You can phone me for further instructions. I'll send a letter of introduction to two specialist suppliers in Baghdad. I think it would be appropriate to send a gift." Ahmed reached down and placed a small aluminum briefcase on the table, he opened it to show Walid the blue box set in foam rubber. Ahmed indicated to Walid to take the box out of the case and open it.

Walid picked up the cut glass vase with care. The crystal danced with rainbows as the sun caught the cut facets. He could tell the quality of the piece by the weight and the sharpness of the cuts. There was no mistaking the value of the item.

"Arts of fire," said Walid admiring the piece. He watched as Ahmed lit a cigarette, and turned the packet toward Walid. Gratefully, he took one and lit it.

"I would like you to take this one as a carry-on; I have a similar but smaller item you can put in your checked luggage. You will have some problems with airport security. The lead in the glass affects the scanners, but all you have to do is open up the package for them. If my client likes them, I shall be sending him containers of the glass, he thinks there is a market and we can trade."

"Okay." Walid put the glass back in the case, and put it down carefully beside his chair. He couldn't see why there would be a trade for ornate glass in a war torn country, but Ahmed could sell ice to Eskimos.

He handed Walid another aluminum briefcase. "Go on—open it. It's a present."

Walid put his cigarette down, took the case carefully in his hands, and placed it on the corner of the table next to its twin. He flipped the locks and opened the lid. Nestled in the gray foam was a large stainless-steel canister, a digital display showing the humidity, a temperature gauge, and a slim plain cardboard box. Inside the box was one of the most beautifully illustrated pages of the Qur'an Walid had ever seen.

After a few minutes of examining and admiring the art he said, "I have heard about these briefcases that control the humidity and temperature for artifacts, but I have never seen one. It's amazing. But I'm sorry," he said, closing the case and handing it back. "It's beautiful, but I never trade in pages from the Qur'an."

Ahmed checked the case was closed securely and then locked it. "Trade? This is a gift."

"I'm sorry, my answer's the same." Walid felt embarrassed. It was an extremely generous gift. "Well, um. I'm going to lose my job, shortly, if I keep turning up late. I have a department meeting to attend."

Ahmed shifted about uneasily, reached inside his jacket pocket, and gave him a large envelope.

"All the details are in here for the trip." Ahmed held out his hand, the meeting was over. Walid got up and shook his hand, deal done. The embarrassment would pass. He picked up the briefcase with the glass vase.

Walid hailed a taxi, and just made it to his lecture on time. He wished he didn't have scruples. He would have been able to sell the illustration for a magnificent sum. The only question in his mind was why Ahmed would want to offer him this gift. Was it a test? He rubbed his chest; these meetings with Ahmed were giving him indigestion.

*

Ahmed watched him leave in the taxi, poured himself another coffee, and watched to see if anyone was interested in Walid's departure. He couldn't detect any unusual movements, or any surveillance.

Ahmed wondered if he was right to trust Walid. He didn't know anything about him. He came recommended, and the fact Walid Merbarkia was a man of principles might work to his advantage. He double-checked the closures on the briefcase were secure and walked off to the Métro.

Considering the large number of lead crystal vases transported in the mix of artifacts constantly going to and from Iraq, it should confuse customs and security staff at the airports.

CHAPTER TWELVE

MI5, London

Louise studied the surveillance material; she knew what she was looking for. Had Art Expert been contacted or tipped off to prevent him making a bid? She still couldn't find any contact, direct or indirect. No one liked behavior outside the norm and she needed to find a reason as to why he had deviated.

Graeme told her to attend the briefing meeting with James T and she wasn't looking forward to it. Why would Art Expert take the trouble to come all the way to London to look at pieces at Sotheby's and not make a bid? Art Expert had been in London for thirty-six hours. The surveillance team hadn't seen him make any contacts. It was all odd; yet so far, she had only drawn a blank.

She picked up the computer and made her way to the briefing room. She must remember to get the cameras out of Sotheby's. She would get instructions from Graeme after the briefing.

Louise kept her briefing short; Art Expert came into London by Eurostar, they watched, and there appeared nothing to report. He had managed to lose surveillance after the sale, and she couldn't confirm where he had gone next. She was glad it was only Graeme and James T at the briefing. James T was section head and Graeme's boss. He came to a decision quickly but she was never convinced he was a details man.

"Louise, could you show us the salesroom footage?" said James T.

Louise booted up the computer, put the disk in, and projected the images onto the big screen.

"Pause!" James T barked out his command.

Louise paused the frame and looked to see what Art Expert was doing.

"There you are, back row, third in on the left." James T pointed at a seemingly innocuous individual.

"Well, well, that answers one or two questions," said Graeme.

Louise looked on, very perplexed. *What can they see?*

"This is Patrick Dubois of Direction de la Surveillance de Territoire, or DST."

Louise felt under scrutiny, his penetrating glance checking to see if she knew about the French secret service. "I think you'll find that is the face of Patrick—check the image against the database. Naughty, naughty, so they are following Art Expert without consulting with us."

"Surely they know we would have full surveillance on Art Expert. They notified us he was coming, so why would they do that? Surely they know we would be watching. Perhaps the question should be, is there anyone else in the room Patrick could be watching?"

"Good question, Louise. I think we should call Patrick in and ask him." James T smiled. "It's always good to be able to call the French to account; they're so goddamn superior."

"I'll get on it," said Graeme. "There still remains the question as to why nothing happened—unless Art Expert was spooked by Patrick's presence. Do you think he would have spotted him? Louise spent a long time looking at this surveillance data but she didn't pick him up."

Louise could feel herself blushing.

"Louise, could you go back through the data and see if you can spot if Art Expert notices Patrick." James T gave her an encouraging smile.

"Certainly."

"I don't hold out much hope, Patrick is good. We only spotted him because we know him, and we were looking for spooks in the salesroom." Graeme looked at Louise; his doubt in her ability showed in his face.

"Ask the chaps in digital analysis to do a check on all the faces in the salesroom."

"But there must be over a hundred people there." Louise knew how much work this would mean.

"They better get started quickly. We need the results as soon as possible on this one—I don't like Art Expert coming over and not buying anything. I like even less Patrick was there without telling us. I don't believe he has suddenly become enamored of Islamic art, and if he has I would have to wonder where the money came from for such a hobby." He nodded to Louise, his cue for her to leave, and she picked up all the files and disks and left.

*

James T leaned across the table and picked up the next file. Graeme was still considering Art Expert and Patrick; it was all odd, and he didn't like oddities. They were usually trouble.

James T looked up at Graeme. "Are you still thinking about Art Expert?"

"Yes, my instinct says this is big trouble, my worry is we haven't got to the bottom of what exactly his role is, if he has any. I think I'll make some more inquiries in Algeria. Someone must have some background on him. Why has he taken up refuge in France? Has he any family? Are any family members involved in extreme activities? The usual stuff. There's nothing here to trigger this level of investigation, but it would be worthwhile, and as Louise said, we are always reacting to his visits with no notice. She suggested we get him a job in the UK which would make consistent surveillance easier."

"Good idea. A colleague from my old college in Oxford has an Islamic art foundation that might have a suitable opening, and Art Expert's wife used to live in Oxfordshire so it might work quite well. We could set up a three-year art research grant and ensure it goes Art Expert's way. I'll check it out. I think Louise is a bright girl, you need to work on her confidence."

"I don't like trainees to be too bright and confident, it makes them careless, and we lose them."

"We're losing far too many graduate trainees after three years' training, which is about where Louise is, isn't she? We're not losing them because of mistakes. We're losing them because of overwork. The exit interviews had 'not being appreciated' as the top reason for leaving."

"Right."

"Well, it costs a lot of money to get them to this stage and we can't afford to lose them. I know it's hard right now, until we get more staff in, and the number we have off with stress and depression isn't helping. But let's face it, Louise has stuck at it and her hours last month were excessive."

"Were they?"

"You should know how many hours she does, Graeme. When did she last have a vacation?"

"I don't know."

"Well you should. Try to make sure she gets three weeks off and soon. It'll be a lot easier than having her signed off sick. The current doctor's notes are for a minimum of six weeks."

"All right I'll look into it."

"Did you read the security note from the FSB today?"

"Do you think they're headed here?"

"Let's face it, first target of choice would be the United States, but these briefcase bombs are coming from Chechnya or Georgia to Iraq for onward movement to Europe; I would suspect the target list would be London first, with Frankfurt, Paris, or Madrid as second choice."

"You're taking this seriously then?"

"Absolutely!"

"Why? On what evidence?"

"I phoned the Lubyanka, and the FSB had an agent with the Chechen mafia. It would appear the Chechens have a scientist who is cloning the technology of the briefcase bombs, and they have found a buyer, an Algerian, apparently, or maybe called the Algerian, they weren't sure. These weapons cost upward of $30 million each. Finding that amount of money is a challenge for most terrorist organizations. This man wanted several."

"Are you serious? I thought the Russians had denied Lebel's claims—sour grapes or muckraking by the former chief of national security because Yeltsin sacked him?"

"You had to look at the denial rather carefully, what they denied was the weapons program's two-man suitcase bomb of about one kiloton. But the KGB had about a hundred briefcase bombs made for their own use; they made no comment on those. The briefcase measures about twenty-four inches by sixteen and eight deep."

"That's no bigger than one of those aluminum briefcases you'd use for a video camera or similar."

"Right, inside there are three aluminum canisters containing plutonium or uranium—the design isn't fussy, it isn't a sophisticated device, it's a dirty bomb using a trigger of polonium-210 and beryllium-9 which has a life span of 138 days. A specialist would be required to renew the trigger device. That's the good news; the bad news is these triggers are packaged in foil packs about the size of a packet of sugar you'd find in a café."

"And you think they're coming here?" Graeme was giving James T his full attention, Art Expert was no longer his number one priority.

"I'm just saying we need to keep our eye on the ball—there are big issues out there. We're looking for two things: the perpetrator and a briefcase, or if the briefcase is already here, an item about the size of a sugar packet which should be fairly easy to shield from present security scanning—unless we're lucky and the packet ruptures, in which case we'll have a nuclear trail to follow."

"Okay, I hear your point. Is our Art Expert anything to do with this? After all he's Algerian."

"I don't know, it might explain why the French are so keen on close surveillance. I'll make some more inquiries. Don't forget what I said about Louise."

CHAPTER THIRTEEN

Paris to Atlanta

Chloe got home and booked two tickets to Tampa via Atlanta. She had decided not to tell Walid anything about the events in the office parking garage, and was still trying to think of how to explain the wheals on her wrists. She had put ice on them, a calming face cream, but nothing had reduced their angry, swollen appearance. Perhaps Walid's present mood would continue and he wouldn't notice.

She need not have worried. When Walid arrived home, he was sick. He managed to pack a suitcase in between trips to vomit in the bathroom.

Getting to the flight had been uneventful, but on board, and encouraged by Chloe to keep hydrated by drinking water; it appeared she had put his system into constant turmoil. The flight attendant was sufficiently concerned to make inquiries about any doctors on the flight, but there were none.

The lines for immigration were long, and it had taken Walid twenty-five minutes to arrive at the desk for Non-US Citizens. Her passage through US Citizens and Resident Aliens was much faster. Chloe wasn't of interest to immigration as she still had a green card, but they took Walid into a glass booth to question him. The interview took fifteen minutes and Chloe was concerned, it made her think about the things he had said over dinner and on the flight.

One thing in particular bothered her. He had told her he didn't want her going to London again, he said it was dangerous. She didn't understand why he felt safer in Paris and he hadn't explained why he felt her life could be in danger. It made Chloe think about the incident in the parking garage. She had assumed it was to do with the investigation, but there was now another possibility linked to Walid. She suddenly remembered what her attacker had said; it was "Bat zona." A Hebrew, vulgar phrase, meaning she was the daughter of a whore, and she didn't think her mother would have liked being called a whore. Walid didn't have any links with Israel, so the attack was everything to do with the investigation and nothing to do with his former Algerian connections.

Her stalker was Patrick Dubois, a member of the French secret service, and he hadn't attacked her. Had he been there to protect her? Or warn her? Did he want Charles's files but had missed the opportunity to talk to her about it because she had panicked by his proximity and taken off in a taxi? Her head still hurt. It was impossible to know, so she would continue as planned and not tell Walid about the incident under any circumstances. Being caught between two national intelligence services was not appealing, though the fact they showed so much interest was encouraging. The story obviously had some substance.

Walid's interview with the Transportation Security Administration concluded with an apology, and the explanation that Walid Merbarkia was a common name and it was just confusion, but the answers he'd supplied should make things easier for future trips.

They picked up their bags from the carousel and rechecked them for the Tampa flight. Then it was off through security again, to enter the terminal for internal flights. Having deposited everything in trays on the scanner, she cleared the security hoop without any beeps. She returned to the scanner conveyor belt to reassemble luggage, laptop in case, bag in front pocket of carry-on, shoes on feet; she picked up Walid's jacket and looked around but he was nowhere to be seen.

Chloe was reluctant to go back through security and repeat the performance. She wasn't sure she it would be allowed and Walid couldn't have gone far. She had his shoes, wallet, phone, belt, and jacket, which had his passport in the top pocket. Had a security officer picked him up? Perhaps immigration had changed their minds about allowing him entry. Perhaps he had been abducted by those pesky "Resident Aliens."

It seemed an eternity but it was only a couple of minutes before Walid reappeared. He looked awful. Chloe would have to get him to a doctor before the next flight. At the medical center she listened to the doctor's explanation, he wouldn't prescribe anything without tests, and he didn't want to make anything worse. It was probably just a virus and Walid would get better in twenty-four hours. However, to help Walid get through the next flight and on the assumption he was a fit man and able to fight off any normal infection, he suggested Gatorade.

"Gatorade? The sports drink?"

"When you are constantly sick you disturb the electrolytes in the system, any isotonic drink will rebalance the system and that may be enough to stop the vomiting."

"Any particular flavor?"

"My suggestion would be Ice—it's the most neutral flavor."

The little newsstand had Gatorade and Walid drank the whole bottle, which Chloe thought unwise, but he was desperate for a solution and so decided to go for it. They sat at the departure gate to see what effect the drink would have. After half an hour, they were optimistic and when they boarded the next flight, they were confident Walid was on the mend.

The rest of the journey was uneventful; Chloe picked up a rental car at the airport and drove them to Siesta Key on the Gulf Coast. Some friends had let her use their beachside apartment. They showered and fell into bed exhausted. They agreed to sleep until they woke, oblivious to any ideas of jet lag adjustment, just an end to the exhaustion would do.

In the morning, Walid seemed okay so they went for a walk before breakfast. The tourist guide proclaimed this beach one of the most beautiful in the world and it was easy to see why. The white quartz sand was soft, warm, and dry, like powdered sugar, kept immaculately clean by tractors clearing the trash and levelling flat any irregularities left by children's play and tides. The smell of the tractor diesel jarred in the soft ocean breeze, as did her phone ringing.

Walid walked on, leaving her to answer her phone.

"Chloe Moreau."

"Where the hell are you?"

"Well, good morning, Jean Pierre, and how are you?"

"Biryukov's work colleagues have canceled. They said they have nothing to say to you."

"Okay."

"You don't sound bothered."

"I'm not really, it was just on the off chance; as you can see from the list, it's a pretty busy schedule anyway."

"I can hear the sea, where are you?"

"On a beach in central Florida, I'm off to Miami this afternoon."

"Are you being followed?"

Chloe looked around. She watched as brown pelicans practiced formation flying routines. Wings beat in unison, then, one by one, they swooped down low over the ocean and dived in sequence. The pelicans came up from their dives facing a different direction from the point of entry, a performance dive routine with sub-water half twist. The beach was getting busier with keep-fit fanatics, clad in T-shirts, shorts, and baseball caps, Sony Walkmans for the over sixties, iPods for the young. All participants marched with arms swinging and with a single objective, to deprive the grim reaper of an early reward.

"No, I can't see anyone dressed in black combat gear. It's too hot."

"Don't be facetious. It'll cost you your life."

"You sound like Charles, a bit of trouble and you resort to paranoia."

"Yes, it's a healthy regard for danger, it means we like living." He hung up.

She didn't share his views about the danger, she wasn't wearing enough clothes to have any papers or computers concealed on her, and after her attack, surely no one would expect her to bring any files to America.

She ran to catch up with Walid. Running along the sand reminded her of vacations as a child in Wales, always running to catch up with her dad. They were the best childhood memories: sailing a small Heron dingy when the wind and waves allowed, and occasionally going into Abersoch where they would sail on a Seagull with one of his friends. They would fish for mackerel with a line and spinner, stopping only when the bucket was full. These were memories of which she was sure, there were no photos, only the smell of the salt breeze and the feel of clothes stiff from sea spray. It made her smile; these were the closest memories she had of her father. Her mother would sit patiently on the beach, in wind, sun, or underneath an umbrella, always engrossed in her book, and always with a picnic basket waiting for their return. Chloe wanted to know what had happened the day he died, she couldn't believe he'd had the accident they described.

CHAPTER FOURTEEN

Florida

Chloe was loath to do any work. Her relationship with Walid seemed to be back on track. Or maybe she just hoped it was going to return to the loving relationship they'd had when they got married. She kept asking herself why she was so keen for it to work. She had inherited Protestant values from her father, which stated that anything worthwhile required work, and Catholic values from her mother, which led her to believe that divorce would be a sin. She didn't really subscribe fully to either viewpoint, it was probably more a case of refusing to accept she had made such a stupid mistake, and sold herself for a marriage certificate to facilitate a work visa. Some would call it stubborn, she preferred determined and resolute.

They had even discussed communication and about letting her know where he was and when he would return. It had seemed a positive discussion and she was optimistic things would improve. It was only a start, but if they couldn't communicate with each other, the rest of the problems were incidental.

She left Walid enjoying the sunshine and reading on the beach in Siesta Key, having agreed where to have dinner the following night, and then she drove down the interstate to Naples and across the Everglades Expressway, known as Alligator Alley. She didn't see any alligators, only an armadillo bumbling along quite fast and always ready to curl into a ball, his body armor instantly available against an attack. The Everglades Expressway was almost devoid of traffic and she was sure no one had followed her.

Chloe checked into the hotel and thought about the next day's appointments. She was keen to find out if there was any truth to Charles's theory. This death was an unusual case, where two witnesses, under the influence of a noxious substance and viewed as unreliable, were certain Dr Biryukov was killed. The police investigation had concluded two passers-by had asked him the time and while consulting his watch, Biryukov had suffered a fatal heart attack. The two men had performed CPR on the pavement until the medics arrived. The witnesses said these two men had injected the scientist with something in his neck; he had fallen to the ground where they had done something else to kill him.

Chloe rubbed her neck, the memories and injuries too fresh not to give an empathetic twinge for Biryukov. The similarity of the blow to the neck followed by further interventions worried her. Could this murder, if that was what it was, have been carried out by the same people who stole Charles's bag? She blamed Charles's influence for making her paranoid and jumping to illogical conclusions. If the Biryukov's own physician was confident it was a heart attack, she should start by assuming anything else was Charles's cooked up theory.

The next morning Chloe went to the local paper and spent an hour skimming through the archives for the weeks before and after the scientist's death. She hadn't expected to find anything, but it was her sense of curiosity for the unusual that sometimes gave a reward. The only news item of interest, which made her laugh, was a police car, stolen the day prior to the death of the scientist, and returned two days later. It had been washed and impeccably cleaned. She introduced herself to the reporter who had covered the police car item; the young reporter was delighted she had found his item of interest but didn't have anything else to add to the piece. She left the newspaper and went to police headquarters.

The investigating officer was Detective Bob Anderson. A uniformed sergeant escorted her into his office. Bob looked up, but didn't get up. He reached across into his in-tray and slapped a manila file down on the desk. Chloe got the feeling he wasn't pleased to see her. His dark hair had been buzz-cut within a quarter inch of his scalp. His eyebrows plucked to avoid a uni-brow. They certainly emphasized his displeasure in a frown that had four deep furrows across his forehead. His face was evenly tanned, except for the white crows' feet, which wouldn't have shown, had he been smiling.

"I'm busy and fed up with answering questions about this dead case. It was a heart attack. Was there anything else?"

"I just need to clarify a few things."

"Why are you wasting my time?"

Chloe thought carefully for a moment. "A biological weapons scientist in China was murdered by the authorities, together with his wife—"

"And what's that got to do with—"

This time, Chloe interrupted, "It was the first death, but not the last, there have been a series of deaths of biological weapons scientists, and Dr Biryukov falls within a pattern. You are probably right, there is nothing sinister about having a heart attack, but as it is part of a pattern, I would like to ask a few questions so I can rule this as a coincidence."

"So"—Bob Anderson got up, came around to her side of the desk, and sat on the corner—"what do you want to know?"

"Tell me about the witnesses, they seem to be the only point of dissent in the account of a heart attack."

Bob intimated the police knew them, he couldn't recall the event in full but he thought it was aggressive panhandling. "You shouldn't meet with them alone, not a pretty woman like you. It wouldn't be safe."

He leaned forward, looking down the front of her shirt. Chloe didn't move or acknowledge his interest. He was like a dog begging for scraps at the table. If you didn't react, the thrill of the chase was missing and usually someone in Bob Anderson's position would just go away. It was exactly as she expected, without any response from her, he went back and sat down at his desk, like a dog returning to his basket. Chloe asked for copies of their statements, read them, and told Bob she didn't think meeting them could add anything. She didn't tell him she already had an appointment to see them later on, and the fact he had suppressed their statements from the coroner's report was the most compelling reason to talk to them. His patronizing views about her safety made her even more determined to see these witnesses without a police escort.

The medical examiner had been satisfied there was sufficient evidence, together with prior medical history, to conclude he had died of a heart attack. With four hundred and forty-five violent deaths in Miami Dade County in 2002, you could see why the police would be happy this was not another violent death from homicide, suicide, or a firearms incident. The murder rate was five times higher per head of population in the United States than in either France or the United Kingdom.

"One final question, I understand you, um, how shall I put it, lost a police car the day before this incident. Was this a related event? Would you like to comment about that? Why do you think it was returned a couple of days later?"

Bob Anderson picked up the manila file and thumbed through the pages, beads of sweat had broken out on his forehead, and Chloe hadn't noticed any change in the effectiveness of the air conditioning. This was why you traveled over four thousand miles to Miami, you couldn't see this reaction on a phone call.

"Kids joyriding. Well done, I see you've done your homework. An interesting coincidence, but not related to this case. Well, that seems to be all." He stood up.

The stress he exhibited told Chloe two things: either the police car had been used in the incident, which was sinister, or it was unrelated and merely the police department's embarrassment at the loss of the vehicle and its subsequent return. Chloe had never heard of kids, joyriding or otherwise, voluntarily cleaning a car.

Chloe got up and shook his hand. His palm was sweaty, but he didn't seem to notice. She smiled sweetly, thanked him for his time.

"One final point, was an autopsy carried out?"

"Not necessary, he had just seen his doctor. It wasn't an unexpected death."

Chloe wondered if it was worth talking to the funeral home to see if the mortician had noticed a mark on Biryukov's neck, if the mark on her neck was anything to go by, it would be very noticeable—but then of course her medic had missed it. The mark on her neck had been concealed by shoulder length hair. Biryukov was nearly bald, and the mortician would have had plenty of time to take note of the mark and report it.

Chloe's next appointment was to meet Biryukov's family in South Beach. She had telephoned the house and by good fortune, the son, Jeb, had agreed to meet. She doubted the wife, Lorraine, would have agreed to it, and had expected the meeting to be canceled, or a no-show. She hoped the daughter, Missy, wouldn't come. It was too painful to think what Missy would be feeling at the sudden death of her father.

Chloe parked the car and made her way up the short path to the entrance of the art deco hotel, styled curves framed the doorway, painted in ice cream colors. The entrance hall was cool, potted palms and aspidistras wafted in the breeze of the overhead fans, large blades looked like woven palm fronds, but were probably plastic. She wished she had remembered a jacket; her arms became goose fleshed in the air conditioning.

She looked around the bar and was surprised to find Lorraine, Jeb, and Missy already seated at a coffee table in a window alcove overlooking the sea. The chairs placed two by two formed a square, dark wood chairs with broad flat arms, split cane sides, and overstuffed cushions in a vibrant tropical print overlaid with quilted toucans.

Chloe looked at her watch. She was fifteen minutes early, and wondered how long they had been waiting. Missy lounged across the chair, playing with her phone, with the bored indifference of a teenager required by parental authority to attend a meeting that was clearly of no interest to her. Her cropped blue jeans were fringed, and a white tank top completed her outfit. Her long limbs were a study in tan without shadow.

Jeb sat in a composed manner, a hand placed over each khaki clad knee. A pale blue button-down, short-sleeve shirt was tucked into the chinos. The shiny black leather belt matched the wingtip shoes. It was American formal-meeting wear. In comparison to his sister, he was pale and looked more studious than sporty.

Lorraine looked at her watch and looked like she was regretting the meeting already. She was dressed in a short straight blue skirt, bare tanned legs, classic low-heeled shoes, white top, and three-quarter-sleeved linen jacket in white with large blue flowers—maybe a stylized form of hibiscus. Her shoulder-length, color-enhanced, chestnut hair had recently been in hot rollers, no curls lasted long in eighty percent humidity. Having checked the time, she folded her arms across her chest.

Chloe took in this family scene; she doubted they had dressed to meet her. She would have expected blue jeans, or shorts and a T-shirt. This meeting was a distraction on their way to the main event of their day.

Chloe approached the table. "I'm sorry to keep you waiting." She introduced herself and handed business cards to Lorraine and Jeb, Missy ignored her arrival.

"That's all right, we're early," said Lorraine.

"We're always early," said Missy without looking up.

"It doesn't do to keep folks waiting." Lorraine sounded tense.

"No danger of that..." replied Missy.

"Can I get anyone a drink?" said Chloe too quickly, but not wanting to start the meeting with Lorraine and Missy at each other's throats.

"We can't stay long," said Lorraine, and put the business card down on the coffee table.

"I'd like a Coke," said Missy.

Jeb rolled his eyes. "I'd like a beer," he said, resigned to the fact that now drinks were being ordered and they wouldn't get out of the meeting quickly.

"Root beer," said his mother, not letting him indulge in underage drinking.

"Okay, a Coke."

"I'm going to have a coffee, would you join me?" asked Chloe.

Lorraine nodded. Chloe got the attention of the waiter and placed the order. The good thing about ordering drinks in a hotel, particularly hot drinks, is they seldom arrived quickly, which left your interviewees with nothing better to do than chat.

"Firstly, I'd like to say how sorry I am for your loss."

"Why, did you know my father? In fact do any of you journalists know what it's like to lose a husband and father?" Missy sounded angry, but she didn't look up from her phone. Chloe understood the anger, she had been angry for years—but the circumstances had been a little different. At present Missy believed her father to have died from a heart attack.

"I think I have some personal understanding, I was widowed two years ago and my father died in an accident at Porton Down when I was twelve years old."

There was an uncomfortable silence.

"I'm fifteen."

Chloe didn't reply.

"Porton Down? So your father was…?" Lorraine asked.

"Yes. My father was a scientist."

"I'm sorry. We didn't mean to be rude," said Lorraine. "Missy, well none of us meant to be rude, we are just rather sick of journalists asking questions. I guess you'd understand that, but Jeb said you didn't want to talk about my husband."

"Let's start again." Jeb stood up, the imprint of his hands had formed damp patches on the knees of his chinos. He offered a hot, but dry, handshake and introduced himself and his family.

Chloe smiled. "There is a reason journalists can be hated, but they also do a good job of exposing the truth and keeping those in power at the highest levels honest—or we try to. I wanted to ask you about Ken Antipov. I understood he was a colleague of your father's, both here and possibly in Russia before they both defected."

"Yes, they were close friends. But they only worked together briefly, maybe six weeks on a project at Fort Detrick after their defection. There were five scientists in total, all recent defectors from Russia. He said they had been involved in compiling a list or something; he said it was a strange project group. They had all worked on projects together in Russia before they defected. Normally they just met up at conferences. Ken is flying over today. We are on our way to the airport to meet him."

Chloe was shocked they hadn't heard. If she told them now the interview might be over, but she couldn't withhold the information, dishonesty would be the end of their cooperation.

"I'm sorry." She paused. "I thought you would have heard."

Chloe waited, hoping the silence and the crestfallen face would prepare them for what she was about to say.

Lorraine looked shocked and looked at both her offspring. She reached for her purse and took out a packet of tissues. It was a precautionary measure. Missy had returned to interacting with her phone, and Jeb hadn't drawn a conclusion from the body language.

Lorraine looked down and gathered her thoughts. "Missy? Is Kirsten still planning on going to see that movie you were so excited about?"

"Yes." Missy didn't waver in her attention to the small screen.

"Call her and say your plans have changed and can her mother drop by and pick you up from here."

Missy looked up brightly, stood, and announced she would need to go outside to get a signal for her phone so she could make the call. Her flip-flops slapped against the terrazzo floor, fading away as she reached the revolving door.

"Go make sure she just gets in the car and doesn't get distracted, will you?"

Jeb got up with the resigned air of the babysitter and followed his sister. A group of tourists laughed loudly in the corner. Chloe waited for Lorraine to take the initiative.

When he was out of earshot, Lorraine asked, "What happened?"

"Ken Antipov died a few days ago."

"When?"

"Sunday."

"That was the same day he spoke to me and arranged for me to pick him up at the airport." Lorraine had taken out a tissue from the packet and was twisting it into a knot in her hands.

Chloe made a mental note, Antipov was making travel plans on the day of his suicide. It was strange behavior for someone planning to end his life. It was also odd that while he was under some suspicion of being a spy that he could make travel plans. Clearly the Ministry of Defense weren't treating him as a spy. She wondered if the ministry was planning to make an announcement to clear his name, they most certainly hadn't taken any steps to either arrest him, or protect him.

"Was it an accident?"

"I'm not sure what the conclusion will be, but on the face of it, he committed suicide."

"Ken? Never."

"The police found a suicide note on his computer, and they believe he went into his shed, started the lawnmower, and apparently died from carbon monoxide poisoning. As I said, that's the initial view, it will take forensic evidence to confirm what happened."

"I don't believe it. They must have got to him."

"Why do you say that?"

"I don't believe Ken would take his life, and certainly not on the day he spoke to me. We were laughing and making plans. He was looking forward to telling me all about his cousin's trip from Moscow with all the family news. If he had planned to commit suicide he would have sent me an email with all the family news, he wouldn't have been making travel arrangements, and he would have let me know why he was ending it. I couldn't have stopped him with the whole Atlantic Ocean between us."

"Did he talk about the BBC revelation that he was a spy?"

"Not really, it was old news; he had been under suspicion before. All the defectors are watched closely and there is an underlying concern amongst some people that the scientists might have loyalty elsewhere. It wasn't true, he had chosen to live in Britain and was loyal to British values. He was hoping the Ministry of Defense would make a statement which would have quieted down the media, but they said they didn't think that ill informed remarks by a reporter more anxious to make a name for himself than report the truth needed to be dignified with any statement which would only lead to another round of media reports."

"So, what do you think happened to Ken?"

"Putin's hit squad. He has given the KGB, FSB, or whatever you want to call them, permission to terminate anyone who was part of the Soviet Union and now works against Russia."

"Would that have included your husband?"

"I can't talk about that. My husband had a heart condition; he'd had a minor attack a month before the fatal attack. He was taking tablets and we both knew he was probably living on borrowed time. Now you tell me all five are dead, it does seem odd. I suppose you're going to ask about the witnesses and what they said they saw?"

"I understand they were potheads, and not reliable, I don't think you should worry about anything. If there is something, I'll let you know before I publish, but as you say, with all five gone, it is odd. Can I ask you if your husband knew or worked with any of these scientists?" Chloe got out the list of forty scientists and handed it to Lorraine. She didn't hope for too much, Lorraine was clearly distracted.

The waiter arrived and placed the coasters and cold drinks down on the table, he set out the cups, the creamer, sugar, and a carafe of coffee. The waiter gave the bill to Chloe who placed the dollar bills together with a suitable tip on his tray and he left. Chloe poured out one cup of coffee. Lorraine added sugar and cream to the cup.

Jeb returned. "I said I'd pick them up after the movie and take them out for dessert."

"Thank you, dear." Lorraine continued to study the list as she mindlessly stirred her coffee.

Jeb unscrewed the bottle of Coke with a hiss, and as he emptied the drink into the glass, the ice chinked and cracked.

"Sorry," said Lorraine, handing the list back, "I don't recognize anyone else. Should I? Are they alive or dead?"

"That sounds ominous..." Jeb clearly wanted to catch up.

"Not really," said Chloe. He might consider himself head of the family, but eighteen years of age and on his way to college didn't qualify him to get involved. "It was just on the off chance. I didn't know. I didn't know Antipov had been such a close friend. The names are a mix of those alive and those who have met with unexplained deaths recently."

"What are you saying? The deaths weren't accidents?"

"I don't know. I'm just investigating."

Chloe wanted to leave. She didn't want to have Lorraine questioning the death of her husband because it wouldn't bring her any peace. She was better off thinking he had died of natural causes—at least for now. On face value, it looked as if a busy police force had been sloppy in accepting a natural death too quickly. But she had no evidence of anything untoward or a cover-up.

"Are you saying Ken is dead?" Jeb asked.

"Yes, I'm afraid so, on Sunday."

"He can't have died on Sunday. He sent me an email, I'd been asking him which courses he thought would be most useful to take at college, and he forwarded the flight confirmation email. What happened? Was it a car accident?"

Chloe considered her response, she was looking for evidence, she needed to focus on that, rather than on how this damaged family was going to cope with another death. "I don't suppose you could let me have those emails, could you? It might help the coroner decide on his state of mind, and maybe show the order of events that day." The police in England should have accessed Antipov's computer by now and they should already have this information and be asking the same questions.

"I don't understand, are you suggesting they think it was suicide?"

"On the face of it, that does seem the explanation the police currently favor."

"Never. I'll use the hotel's computer." Jeb was up, he took Chloe's business card off the coffee table, and strode across the hotel lobby, he spoke briefly with reception and entered a door marked Business Services. Soon Chloe's BlackBerry alerted her to incoming email. She opened the emails from Jeb, looked at the time the flights were reserved, about half an hour before he was supposed to have gone into the shed—it didn't seem plausible. The email from Ken was chatty, full of news and enthusiasm for their meeting. Clearly, this was not what you would have expected from a man contemplating suicide. Finally, she had some evidence to cast some light on one death—there was a long way to go.

Jeb came back, "Got 'em?"

"Yes, thank you," said Chloe. "They'll be useful." She forwarded them to Jean Pierre, he would make sure they were archived safely.

"Do they look like the actions and thoughts of someone who was about to commit suicide?" Jeb couldn't conceal his anger; he leaned over her, checking she could see the emails on her BlackBerry.

"As I said, I'll make sure the coroner gets them." Chloe tried to remain impartial and composed, but she shared his anger.

Chloe felt tearful, the grief for Michael was as raw as the day of his accident. She never knew what triggered these sudden attacks of grief; she kept thinking each one would be the last. They were now spaced further apart but they still came. With all this news of death and the obvious grief of the whole family, it wasn't surprising she was feeling sensitive.

Chloe got up to leave. Lorraine was still shocked. Chloe could tell she was wondering if anything could have happened to her husband, or whether it was natural causes and Chloe couldn't tell her, not yet. Either way, it wouldn't bring him back.

They say you can only start grieving when the criminals have been brought to justice, the body has been found, or the truth has been uncovered. Chloe wasn't sure it was true; sometimes you just had to be strong and accept your loved one was gone. Rebuilding starts from that point.

CHAPTER FIFTEEN

Miami

Chloe stood opposite the main entrance to Memorial Hospital and looked at her watch, she was a couple of minutes late, she hadn't been sure if she was being followed and so had circled around the hospital a couple of times before ducking into the parking garage. After the cold air conditioning, she was enjoying the late afternoon sunshine. Maybe Bob Anderson had been right, these witnesses were Latinos, out of work, unreliable, no hopers, potheads, addicts. But she couldn't agree Latinos were unreliable. You couldn't denigrate nearly a quarter of Florida's, and sixty-five percent of Miami Dade County's, population as being unreliable by their ethnicity.

There were two neat, clean-shaven, young men waiting on the opposite corner of the street. They looked like students. Below the knee, stone-colored chino shorts, one wore a white polo shirt and one a turquoise Miami Dolphins T-shirt. Chloe crossed the road, got out her notebook to check the names.

"Diego Velazquez and Emilio Rodriguez?"

The taller of the two said, "I'm Emilio, he's Diego."

Chloe introduced herself and gave them each a business card. The white T-shirt of Emilio had the emblem of Miami University School of

Medicine. Her assumption they were students was right, hardly the out-of-work dropouts the police had described.

"Thank you for agreeing to meet me here. I read your statements at police headquarters, but I wanted to check out a few things. First of all, are we standing where you were waiting that night?"

The two Hispanic American students took her around the back of the hospital to a staff entrance and they stood next to a Dumpster. They would certainly have been out of sight of the entrance to the building.

"And that night, were you high on skunk or coke or…"

"What? No! Of course not. We were drunk, that's all. Good old Jack Daniel's and beer."

"I'm sorry. I was led to believe…"

"Yes, the police are going around calling us potheads—we know. It's not true. It's caused us all sorts of problems on campus. We have been interviewed for a range of things because of their efforts to discredit us. I think the worst accusation was we were drug dealers. We both took blood and urine tests to prove we were clean."

"I'm sorry, I can only go on the information I have been given. I tell you what, why don't you both relive the events that happened that night for me. The conversation you were having at the time, everything."

She got out a pencil and waited. The first attempt to tell her what happened involved the two young men repeating what they had said in their statements. She waited. They knew she expected more.

"On the basis of what you have just said, I wouldn't have bothered including your statements for the coroner either. Let's try something. I want you both to close your eyes and visualize what happened that night. What were you talking about? What could you smell? What were you touching? Don't tell me what you saw, just what your senses were experiencing."

The men shuffled from one foot to another, embarrassed by this request. It had been three months since they had made their reports and she wondered if it was all too late. Maybe they wouldn't remember.

She prompted them. "What could you smell?"

"The Dumpster smelled of rotten vegetables." Emilio surprised himself with this observation. Diego carried on, it was dirty, greasy on the edge; Emilio got the slime on his jeans where he had leaned up against the Dumpster in an attempt to steady himself. They both had a bottle of beer in their right hands. As they stood next to it, Chloe noticed the Dumpster didn't smell rotten; it was clean and smelled of disinfectant.

"What were you talking about?"

There was a long silence. They didn't look like they would be planning a bank robbery.

"You have to understand we were drunk."

"Yes."

"And this was pure fantasy."

"And..."

"Emilio had just found texts on his girlfriend's phone, sex texts. She's a nurse at this hospital and we were waiting to confront her. We were planning stupid things against her. Pure fantasy, but it made us feel better."

Chloe understood why they were in the shadows and drunk. Now there was enough detail in their accounts for it to be credible. "Did you finish the beer after the doctor came out?"

There was a pause. Emilio said, "No. I put my beer down on a ledge on the wall behind the Dumpster, to get out my phone to call for an ambulance and the police." He looked for the niche to show her. "It's still here!"

He brought out the bottle and shook the contents. "It's still half full."

Chloe thought for one horrified moment he was going to drink the beer, but she said nothing and was relieved when he put the bottle down.

"So what did you see that made you think these men weren't helping the doctor?"

"He was struggling and shouting out 'No, no.' Then they injected something into his neck and then after he had fallen to the pavement they sprayed something on his neck, and waited."

"I thought they squirted something in his mouth," said Diego.

"What did you do next?" asked Chloe, not fazed by the variation in their accounts of the night's events.

"We waited for the police and ambulance to turn up," said Diego.

"Just waited? You didn't want to go and help the man?"

"No, we were frightened. We didn't want to be seen." His tone gave her the sense they were genuinely afraid and she believed him. He looked ashamed, but for Chloe there was no shame in being safe.

"You did the right thing. So you stood there watching, but you didn't pick up your beer again. Why was that?"

"The police and ambulance arrived nearly immediately, almost before I had called them, perhaps someone in the hospital called ahead of me. The other thing was because I started to take pictures with my phone." Emilio was stunned at this information, in the heat of the moment and the police involvement, and with alcohol impaired memory, he had forgotten. Chloe was elated. There might be some real evidence.

Emilio got out his phone. Diego was trying to take the phone from him. "Let's see!"

Suddenly they both realized they had proof, they were not imagining things, it wasn't a drunken stupor, there was evidence. Emilio tugged the phone back.

"They're not there," said Emilio.

"It was Sabrina's phone," they said together.

"Wrong phone?" asked Chloe.

"The reason I had seen the sex texts on Sabrina's phone was that I had swapped phones by mistake. So that night I had her phone. When I broke up with her we swapped back phones."

"Let's go and see your ex-girlfriend."

"If she's on the day shift, she should be walking down those steps, in"—he consulted his watch—"about five minutes."

"Perhaps you could wait with me," said Chloe. "I think she would want to know it would be all right for her to give me the pictures. What's her full name?"

"Sabrina Flores," said Emilio. The tone of his voice led Chloe to believe he was still in love with her.

Five minutes later a nurse, still in scrubs, came down the stairs with an energy that showed she was pleased to finish her shift. Chloe went forward and introduced herself, and told her about the pictures on the phone. Sabrina hesitated and blushed when she saw Emilio and then agreed to take Chloe back to her apartment.

"I don't use that phone anymore. For a start it stinks of rotten vegetables." It was all that Sabrina left unsaid, and the sadness; she too still had feelings for Emilio.

They walked to her apartment. It was an open plan studio, in soft sand and aqua colors. They went to the living room area and Sabrina took a plastic bag with a phone out of a drawer in the dresser and gave it to Chloe.

"I don't know if the battery is dead, but I got a new telephone number with my new phone. I was sick of the nameless sex texts, I never knew who sent them and then there were the angry calls from Emilio. It just seemed easier to have a fresh start."

Chloe smiled. "May I?" The last thing Chloe wanted was for her to delete the photos. She was right about the phone smelling. Chloe pulled a face and Sabrina laughed, it broke the tension. The battery was fine, and Chloe got a brief glimpse of the photos, they looked blurry, but on a big screen and with image enhancing software who knew what she might find.

"Would you mind if I emailed these photos to my phone?"

"No, not at all, do you think they will help?"

"I think so, and they will go to prove your ex-boyfriend was telling the truth about that night's events."

The girlfriend seemed genuinely pleased and Chloe hoped they would get back together. Chloe began to believe she would find evidence to prove Charles's theory. She checked her phone; she had received the photos. Her initial excitement subsided. Apart from a good picture showing the police car license plate they might be too indistinct to be useful, she couldn't tell. The next step was for her to get them printed out in a large format, even blurred photos might tell her something. She forwarded them to Jean Pierre for analysis.

The photos were all time stamped, she checked the time on the phone was accurate and handed the phone back. Now she would have an accurate timeline of the events that night.

It had been a good day's work, and she was feeling elated as she walked to her car. She was looking forward to spending a weekend on the beach with Walid. It was going to be wonderful. She called the apartment from the privacy of her car. There was no reply. She called the management office for the apartment block.

"Hi, this is Chloe Moreau, could I leave a message for my husband, Walid Merbarkia, he's staying in apartment eleven? He's probably on the beach."

"Hi, Chloe. No need to leave a message, he left for Paris after his meeting this morning, he said to tell you he had to get back urgently. He left the keys here in the office for you and he'll see you next week."

Chloe was gutted. What meeting? Who had he been meeting? She had been looking forward to the weekend, the two days, the warm sunshine he said he craved, the time together, all gone in an instant. She regretted the additional expense of booking flexible tickets, but she might have wanted to stay on a couple of days if she found out anything exceptional. He would have had no problems turning up at the airport and asking for a seat on the next available flight. She couldn't think of anything that could have required him to get back to Paris before Monday. She also realized she couldn't go back to the beach apartment that night; the drive would take about three and a half hours, and she wouldn't get to Siesta Key before the office closed at five. She decided to drive partway and stay in a hotel when she was too tired to drive anymore, she would get the key when the office opened in the morning. She would get on the road before the numbness of his betrayal penetrated. She realized the manager was still talking to her.

"I hope you enjoyed your stay, I hope you can come back and spend longer with us next time. Just leave the keys to the apartment in the drop box on your way out."

"Right, thank you." She hung up.

Chloe was shocked, if she had been in any doubt about the state of her marriage, she was quite sure of the next step now and would contact a lawyer and start divorce proceedings as soon as she got back to France. She would start to move her possessions into her apartment in the center of Paris. She was saddened, after the time on the beach, she had hoped they could get the relationship on track, but now she knew it was impossible. They had only had one real conversation, about communication, and he could have called her, her phone had been on all day. He hadn't called. He hadn't even left a message in person.

The drive back to Sarasota went slowly. Apart from watching traffic weaving between the lanes, she had too much thinking time. Tomorrow was the third anniversary of her husband's death from a senseless accident and it still hurt.

A truck driver had run a red light and plowed into the side of Michael's car. It hadn't killed him outright; the nightmare had continued until they told her there was no hope and she had given permission to switch off the machines. Even at that point you heard of people waking up to the astonishment of the doctors, and so she had waited, hoping he would take possession of his body and will it to function again, but that hadn't happened.

The police hadn't caught the truck driver—who had abandoned his vehicle and fled—and no amount of effort had traced the truck owner, or the origin of the load. They had assumed the driver was an illegal immigrant. It didn't matter, it wouldn't have brought Michael back and she didn't believe his death needed a culprit prosecuted for her to have closure. Friends were not so forgiving, and the daily inquiry regarding police progress in the matter had ground her down. She had felt there was no space for her to recover so she had packed up the house, sold or shipped the contents to France, and taken up residence in the Paris apartment left to her by her grandmother the previous year.

It had seemed like a good idea at the time, a new beginning. She would be able to spend weekends with her mother. After ten years of married life spent in America, she had wanted or maybe needed to spend some time with her mother, also a widow after an accident. Six months later her mother had been walking back from the bakers when she collapsed and died. There had been no warning of any ill health.

Feeling tired, she checked into a hotel just outside Venice. It was too late to ring Jean Pierre, that would have to wait until morning.

She woke up when her phone rang, the merry tune of Scott Joplin made her smile, it would be Walid.

"Hi, I knew you would call. Where are you? Are you okay?" said Chloe.

"Wake up, sleepyhead."

"Morning, Jean Pierre. Sorry, I thought you were Walid, and at this time of day I didn't bother checking."

"I take it the trip to Florida hasn't been wasted."

"I'm not sure, I thought we had an agreement, but he left the apartment and didn't even leave a note, he just left a message with the manager."

"Wake up! One, that's too much information—unless you wanted to tell me about Walid which I think if you were awake you wouldn't—and two, I was talking about the emails and pictures."

Now her eyes were wide open, she had slept badly and still felt dopey. "Sorry, you woke me up."

"It's six o'clock for you, I have been waiting to call, sorry if it's still too early but I don't care—those pictures are great and the emails are fantastic. The situation with Antipov has moved on and the coroner opened the case and adjourned it after hearing all the police evidence pointed to suicide. You'd think they'd have got into Antipov's computer, or at least asked his ISP to give them the relevant emails, and the financials would have shown the flight booking. None of that was mentioned in court."

"They held the inquest quickly, didn't they?"

"Yes. There's going to be a public inquiry into the role of the BBC and the MOD into his death."

"MOD?"

"Yes, people are asking, after your piece on Antipov's death, why the Ministry of Defense didn't provide him with a safe refuge, or protection, or the police didn't arrest him. Anne Marie is pleased with you."

"Wow—that's a first."

"Now these pictures, they are a bit grainy and blurred, but they are cleaning up well. I think we should be able to get a clear picture of what was happening, and how fast it all happened. Interesting. When will you be in the office?"

"I fly out tonight. I'll probably come into the office tomorrow morning. I know, how sad am I and on a Sunday too, but I want to do some more analysis on the other cases."

"Okay, do you want me to pick you up at the airport?"

"That would be fantastic. I'll email you my itinerary."

"Okay." Jean Pierre rang off before she could thank him.

Chloe was close to tears; the small act of offering to pick her up at the airport, and on a Sunday, was unexpected and left her making a comparison between the generosity of a colleague and the thoughtless actions of her husband.

CHAPTER SIXTEEN

Mosul, Iraq

Waiting patiently, making mental notes, the Algerian watched. How many American soldiers were there in a patrol? What type of weaponry? How frequently did they patrol? The Algerian smoked his water pipe and looked around at the other customers in the teahouse. There was a relaxed atmosphere, some of the fear during the more active elements of the war in Iraq had gone, and Mosul was a calmer place.

Satisfied he had enough information he crossed the street into the complex alleyways of the bazaar. He moved slowly from stall to stall, examining the offerings, feeling the quality of the rugs, praising artisans for their wares, sampling food, and periodically checking to see if anyone followed him. He wasn't sure. There was one man who seemed to be busy in the market, going from stall to stall, looking, touching, conversing, much as he was, and yet he never stopped to buy anything, and there he was again, weaving in and out of the stalls.

The Algerian made a sharp right and quickly doubled back on himself, coming out behind the man he thought might be tailing him. Now he would be able to observe his reaction.

There was no reaction. The man didn't talk to himself, mutter into a coat lapel, or make any phone calls. He was either good at his job, or he wasn't following him. There was nothing to suggest any concern—the

Algerian reasoned he was being too cautious. Having decided all was clear, he made his way to an Islamic decorative art stall and asked for Dawud.

He couldn't afford to wait long. If this was a trap, he should leave now. He forced himself to wait without looking at his watch.

"I'm Dawud."

He turned and looked at Dawud. It was so dark he was unable to tell if he resembled the photograph he'd seen in Chechnya.

"You have something?"

"Come with me." Dawud led him through the bazaar to the bridge. He followed. The Algerian felt exposed and conspicuous on the bridge. He looked down at the murky Tigris.

"Is this the best place to meet?"

"Would you prefer we meet in the Church of the Al-Tahira?"

"What's wrong with the ..." he paused, "the Mosque of Jonah?"

After the exchange of the code phrases, he knew this was his contact. They approached a man who was waiting for them at the far end of the bridge.

"This is your chemist—Zahid bin Kalil," said Dawud.

"Dawud says you can provide me with weapons. Is that true?" The Algerian looked around nervously as he spoke.

"I can at the moment but the American troops will find the lab soon." Zahid spat on the ground, showing his contempt for the Americans. "It's only a matter of time. The Israelis came and either took the scientists or murdered them all."

"All? And you?"

"I was lucky. My mother was ill so I wasn't at work or my home. Either they forgot about me or they'll come and get me soon."

"Were you successful?"

"Yes."

"I want to see the results."

"When?"

"Now." The Algerian was suspicious. This man was too lucky. Perhaps he was a plant.

"How do I know this isn't a way of uncovering my lab?"

"You don't. You have to trust the people who gave me your name." There was sufficient menace and arrogance in the voice for him to consent.

"Dawud doesn't need to know where the lab is."

The Algerian nodded. Dawud left.

They walked for about ten minutes until they arrived at the outskirts of the city, and went inside a small industrial unit. It was dark inside. From the window-light above the door, the Algerian could make out the contents. It was filled with all sorts of scrap metal, old plows, ten gallon drums, a roll of rusty razor wire, a couple of spent tank shells, and a roll of copper piping. The chemist did not attempt to put on any lights and picked his way carefully through the items.

"This way."

At the back, the chemist moved a panel of corrugated iron to reveal a trapdoor in the floor that he opened. Merbarkia followed Zahid down the stairs. As he descended, the chemist began removing items of clothing, his jacket, belt, then unbuttoned his shirt.

"Take off everything except your underwear," said Zahid. "I'm afraid we don't have much protective equipment so I'll give you two injections—one against anthrax which I have in the lab, and the second is an antidote for the waterborne plague. I don't know or want to know where you got the culture from but it's very effective."

"I'll take my chances." There was little trust between them.

The chemist shrugged and continued to dress in a white T-shirt, white cotton drawstring pants, and a large surgical gown. He turned his back to the Algerian.

"If you could do up the ties? You need to ensure the ties bring the two sides together so they overlap."

"Right."

The chemist assisted Merbarkia to put on protective clothing. He put on black Wellington boots and handed over a pair.

"The equipment is the best we can get, it's inadequate. I should be working in a negative pressure environment. The respirator masks, however, are genuine and effective."

Finally, they put on two thin pairs of surgical gloves.

They entered the lab through a simple makeshift barrier system of two sheets of plastic stuck to the roof of the unit with duct tape. It wasn't an air lock and was unlikely to provide any real protection.

The protective clothing was low tech, but the lab was not short of equipment.

"I'm impressed—where did the equipment come from?"

"The centrifuge was payment for a delivery of sarin gas. The steel dryer came from manufacture of a foot and mouth virus. I'll get some better protective clothing after I deliver a typhus virus suitable for use in a crop duster plane."

The Algerian was impressed. "I have my part of the bargain." He handed over a sheaf of papers stapled together; the chemist sat down and started to read the formulae. He got to the end and nodded.

"It would have been useful to have these details before I started work, but you won't be disappointed in my results."

Zahid walked across to a row of red plastic petri dishes where a culture was growing. "Once the victims catch this plague, it's contagious. So you only need one victim, preferably a sociable character. I can show you the results on this computer. It's not dramatic—but it is effective."

Zahid and the Algerian watched video clips on a laptop placed on one of the wooden lab benches. The Algerian recognized the victim as one of the hostages taken about a year ago. He was surprised at the choice of death for a hostage but if you needed a victim to test out a virus, this was as good a test subject as any other.

The video clips were time and date stamped and showed the death by virus taking place over several days. The subject was given a glass of water and no indication there was anything amiss. For the first couple of days you couldn't see any ill effects, the man began to flex his arms and legs as if they were stiff, finally he had a nosebleed, and shortly after that, he collapsed and death came within the hour. There was no writhing around in agony; it reminded Merbarkia of collecting butterflies, you put the carbon tetrachloride on a cotton ball in the glass jar and the butterfly would flutter briefly before resting and slowly going to sleep. It was more peaceful than he had expected. He wasn't sure if he was disappointed or not, but he thought it would make a powerful weapon. You would be sick long before you knew it, and in the most contagious phase pass the disease on. Some of the symptoms could derive from a workout in the gym, being arthritic, or any number of psychosomatic disorders. It would cause large numbers of people to present for medical attention with entirely unrelated ailments. It could cause panic and overload the hospitals. It would be a superb weapon for his purpose.

"Where did you get it from?"

"The bioweaponeers rush to any outbreak of a suitable virus, Ebola, bird flu, cholera, to collect samples. Different strains react differently, and they take them back to the lab to see if they can weaponize them."

"Weaponize?"

"To weaponize is to control the timing of the effects and the potency."

"How long will the substance be stable for? Does it have to be kept at any specific temperature which will make it hard to transport?"

"It needs to be kept cold, but not frozen. It's a live culture. It should last about three weeks." The chemist could see the Algerian's approval, so he continued. "One last point, I'd like to move to Europe."

"What?"

"I have shown you what I can do for you. Now I have two choices, I can try to move my equipment across the border into Syria—not an easy task, the equipment is heavy and I work alone. Or I can wait for the death squad to get me. Now I have a third choice, you could set me up in Europe with a lab and I will provide all the weapons you could want."

The Algerian nodded his agreement. Chemists were useful. He could use him right now, and later he would be an asset. If he became a liability, well, all wars had casualties.

CHAPTER SEVENTEEN

MI5, London

Louise looked up as Graeme traversed the office. He looked determined, but at least he wasn't angry. Louise was worried that the large pile of fat manila files he carried were on the way to her desk. She was overloaded with work already and most of it had deadlines.

She had to join her sister for a prenatal class immediately after work and she couldn't work late again. Laura was dropping hints about moving into Louise's flat. Laura, unsurprisingly, had fallen out with their mother who was taking a strict approach to all aspects of her pregnancy, including going to bed early and continuing at school for some final exams. So now Laura wanted to move out. Louise knew Laura would need vetting by MI5 if she was to move in with her, and she wasn't optimistic of the outcome. It wasn't that Laura was indiscreet; she just spoke first and thought about it afterward. Presumably, the submariner would return to base soon and take Laura out of the path of a head-on collision with their mother.

"How's the job offer for Art Expert coming along?"

"It's ready. I'm just waiting on your word."

"Anything for his wife?"

"Nearly, just tying up the loose ends. I'm not sure she will take it though. She's a journalist at heart, and I can't see her eager to teach students, even for a short duration."

"Well, now is probably as good a time as any to make an offer. The Americans have just picked up Art Expert in Iraq."

Louise smiled at Graeme's pronouncing Iraq as "I-Rack," which he did when discussing any American involvement. He felt the Americans were not playing with the other boys and girls on the team, and put this down to the fact they were in a different field of operation.

"How have the French taken the news?"

"To say they are angry is an understatement. According to Patrick, they were cultivating him as an asset, which is why Patrick was at Sotheby's. He was using the trip to contact him and make a request for help. Art Expert is a strong character; in fact, he's quite alarming really. The GIA held his first wife hostage and he let her die rather than comply with their request for help."

Graeme keeping her in the loop flattered Louise. "So what was his response to Patrick's contact?"

"Interestingly, Patrick also lost him after the sale. Maybe we were all too relaxed about this character. I find it very odd that he managed to ditch two sets of surveillance. We have no idea where he went. Was he skilled in losing his tail? Or was it just a coincidence our team and Patrick both lost him? Patrick is very pissed off."

"And the GIA?"

"Yes, the Armed Islamic Group. Algerian extremists, ruthless, make Al Qaeda look like pussycats."

"What were the grounds for the Algerian's pickup?"

"Oh, they are convinced he's a cell leader. Say they have DNA evidence to prove he was assembling bombs in Afghanistan, have pictures of him at a training camp, and so on."

"Are we going to get the opportunity to cross-check the information?"

"Not so far, which you can imagine is driving the French to the boiling point. However, I have some details via the back door and you need to check them now. It doesn't give you much time, but Patrick Dubois is coming in for a case conference at eleven and I need to speak with some certainty about the evidence. Understandably, the French want Art Expert back immediately, before the Americans start to interrogate him. He is due to be on a plane this afternoon for Egypt and after that he's hardly likely to want to be a French asset, or anybody else's for that matter."

"Does his wife know?"

"I wouldn't think so, why?"

"I would have thought a French national and American Pulitzer Prize–winning journalist won't be best pleased to find her husband has 'disappeared,' and she might make things quite hot for the Americans through the press if she were to find out. The French have no love for the Americans' involvement in Iraq."

"Um, not a bad idea, we'll keep it in reserve. It might be better for us if she focused on getting her husband back, rather than her current investigation into the deaths of the biological weapons scientists. I don't like where that investigation is going. I wonder if Patrick is aware of how much progress Chloe Moreau has made. Can you consider ways of slowing down her investigation? The last thing we need now is an investigative journalist pointing at the security services and saying we have been covering up state-sponsored murder."

"Well…if you have the file?" Louise gasped as Graeme deposited all the fat manila files on her desk. "And you want this done by eleven?"

"Get Fiona to help."

"That's highly unlikely; she's working on a panic too. Data analysis is completely overrun today."

"Do your best. Focus on the pictures and the dates where we have Art Expert doing something here. Finally, there should be some DNA, which you could send to the lab for the additional test. Not the normal test, but the sensitive one that can throw up differences when there is a close match, just in case Art Expert has a cousin, brother, or twin we don't know about."

"Right. The sensitive test probably won't be ready today."

"Do your best." Graeme shrugged. What was he supposed to do? Everyone wanted everything immediately. In the end, the system got so congested you had to say everything was urgent or it fell so far back in the queue it never saw the light of day.

Louise opened the file, it was in a complete mess, Graeme had been working on it, and so the papers were all out of order. He had probably intended to do the work but something else had come up. That was what happened; Graeme got a problem and passed the work along. The problem was there was no one to help her; she was the end of the line. She picked up the reference pictures of Art Expert she had made from the Sotheby's footage. They were excellent shots designed specifically to work with photo recognition software.

She picked out the Afghanistan training camp pictures. They were grainy, but on face value, she would guess it was Art Expert, she analyzed the dates and times to reduce the work before taking the file to the lab.

She smiled. "I'm afraid I need this by ten-thirty?"

"What? Line jumping again?" Trevor looked up and grinned, he liked Louise.

Louise smiled. Rumor had it Trevor was desperate to find a new place to live. It dawned on her this would be an easy solution to the Laura problem. He seemed harmless enough, would pass MI5 scrutiny easily, and she would be able to relax at home without having to keep up the pretense of being a civil servant working in IT. Friends now asked her technical questions about their computers and there had been some awkward moments.

"Are you still looking for somewhere to stay?"

"Are you offering?"

"Possibly."

"That's rather a large bribe, isn't it?"

"I didn't mean it as a bribe, but if it works…" She smiled sweetly. She didn't play the coquette well, she didn't practice enough.

Trevor laughed. "I think we might make quite good roommates. Do you rent?"

"No, I took the plunge, I bought."

"Even better, could I put up pictures?"

"As long as there aren't too many; I don't want the walls looking like Swiss cheese when you leave."

"Can we have a drink later and discuss the details? You don't need to ask anyone else, I definitely want a room and I'm sure we can agree on the rent and so on. And I could move in tonight! Now when did you need this work done?"

"Quarter to eleven at a pinch. Presentation is at eleven, and it is rather time critical. If you get me the work done, I'm sure I can find clean linen for the guest bedroom tonight—I didn't realize you were desperate."

"I'm sleeping on a friend's living room floor, he has a large smelly Labrador and two small children who think it fun to sit on me when I'm asleep—God knows when they sleep, but they get up at about half past five in the morning. I am so desperate to move I cannot—"

"Okay, you've made your point, I'll bring an agreement when I come back and we'll see how far you've progressed."

"We can only do our best." Trevor grinned again. The thought of living with Louise had made his day.

Louise left, feeling guilty; it was obvious Trevor liked her and she knew he would do anything to gain her approval. If he wasn't such a geek he would probably flirt with her. But it would prevent her sister asking to move in, and if there was nowhere else to live, well Laura would just have to find a way to get along with their mother.

She took the DNA across to the lab, it would be at least eight hours before they would give her any true results. The quick and dirty results (presumably the ones the Americans had already used) could be done in a couple of hours, but not the detailed results she needed. She settled back down at her desk and began to compose a timeline on the American file, and correlate the information she had on Art Expert. She wondered idly how Graeme had got hold of the files and smiled, she could see him springing a honey trap with some CIA agent, she reprimanded herself for such thoughts, got a pen, pulled up a new file, and decided to call it "Janus." Art Expert was either straight or facing in two directions and she would decide which based on the evidence.

CHAPTER EIGHTEEN

Paris

The eye of the dragon opened long enough for Anne Marie to beckon Chloe to enter the den. Chloe picked up the computer bag, took a large breath, and prepared to do battle. She had heard Anne Marie didn't think the investigation would get anywhere and it was time to move on.

Anne Marie pointed at the conference table. "Spread yourself."

Chloe contemplated for the briefest moment climbing on the table, lying spread-eagled, and making snow angels, but didn't think Anne Marie would appreciate it. It was a damp sort of day and Anne Marie's hair was pulled back into an unruly ponytail, which made her look wild. So she pulled out an IBM ThinkPad, booted it up, and opened a couple of files and an Excel spreadsheet which had helped her to decide which of the forty suspicious deaths Charles had identified were most likely to provide the evidence she needed in order to publish. She also got out a pile of index cards, color-coded to provide the same analysis. She kept everything neat, the photographs and current evidence she kept in the briefcase, and had no intention of spreading out, thus allowing Anne Marie to pick up files in a random pattern. She sat and was relieved when Anne Marie sat opposite; she had a habit of wandering around at these meetings, picking up files and papers when the reporter failed to deliver the information fast enough, or if she got bored.

"Let's start with Antipov and we'll see what the next steps are. Firstly, I want to congratulate you on the Antipov piece. It raised quite a stir." Anne Marie sounded pleased, but there was no expression on her face to match, she looked stern, inquisitive, and tired.

"It's created a smoke screen. The inquest opened and adjourned. Now that there is going to be a public inquiry, the inquest won't need to reopen. The truth won't come out. The public inquiry will use set terms of reference, which will look at the events leading up to the death, not the death itself. It won't have access to forensic evidence or blood tests, because they won't be relevant. The real issues will be buried underneath a mound of irrelevant details, like an interview with the Downing Street cat. It will take a thousand pages to conclude there were minor faults in the way the BBC acted, but that they acted in good faith, and although in hindsight, the MOD could have done more, at the time they did what seemed appropriate. Apart from the remarks the cat makes, I could write it now, but it will take months to hold the hearings and to write the report by which time the media will have moved on, family and friends will want to leave things alone, and no one will push for the inquest to reopen to answer the real question. Did Antipov take his own life?

"The emails don't point to suicide so the question has to be who murdered him and why?" Chloe was surprised Anne Marie knew about the emails, and assumed Jean Pierre had given her the good news.

"I suppose it depends on whether he was 'Rosa' the spy. Either he was the spy and the Brits didn't know, which seems unlikely, or they would have arrested him after getting the evidence (if not the source) from the BBC. If he was Rosa then maybe he was a double agent, in which case why wasn't he given protection? Or the final option, he was a spy and the Brits knew and didn't offer him protection, knowing the Russians would either spirit him away or dispose of the problem and prevent any embarrassment. The Brits hate to be embarrassed," said Chloe.

"There is a further possibility, which you are overlooking; the issues relating to Rosa and spying are a smoke screen. To fall within the pattern of bioweapons scientists being killed he might have been viewed as about to blow the whistle on something. He might have been killed because you made an appointment to see him." Anne Marie paused allowing her comments to have full impact.

Chloe froze, thought about it, absorbed it, and remembered how she made the appointment. Her initial request was to meet Antipov in Porton Down, or in London at the MOD offices, which he declined. Antipov had phoned her and arranged to meet at his house in Wychmoor Wood. Why not meet in his office? What was he going to tell her? Something about her father's accident?

"That's a possibility," said Chloe calmly.

"You shouldn't feel responsible."

"I don't." Chloe wondered why Anne Marie was trying to make her feel guilty. *Is she trying to make me back down from the inquiry? Had someone got to her?* Even editors pulled away from inquiries if there was enough pressure.

"There's not much here that looks like suicide, and I never trust a suicide note written on a computer, it's too impersonal, and suicide is a personal act."

Anne Marie was making the point that Antipov fell within her inquiry of unexplained deaths of scientists and it was persuasive.

"What do you want to do next?" said Anne Marie.

"I don't think I want to interview scientists at Porton Down to see if anyone knew what he might have been going to say, so I think I will let the inquiry run its course. At some point, I would like to see if anyone in the pub saw anything. The Spotted Pig is right opposite his house, they would have ringside seats. It's a quiet village, strangers would stand out."

"I think Antipov is a candidate for your suspicious deaths' file. I will make inquiries at the BBC as to how they found out about Antipov being 'Rosa.' You have to say the timing, coming immediately after you made your appointment and just before you would have met, is suspicious. He certainly would fit if you follow the pattern of whistle blowers. Now tell me about Miami."

"Biryukov's family are happy to accept the official verdict of a heart attack, he'd already had one mild attack, and so it wasn't totally unexpected, although the sudden nature of his death has left them all in shock. Two things stand out: the theft of the police car immediately prior to the incident, and the witness reports of what they saw and the police attempts to discredit them."

"Yes, but without proof, you're just left with unreliable witnesses. I believe the police said they were potheads and panhandlers."

Chloe was surprised Anne Marie knew this much, Jean Pierre could have briefed her, but she thought it unlikely. "The witnesses were medical students who have had to prove through blood tests they haven't taken drugs in order to be able to continue their studies. Secondly the rumor they have any police record is libelous."

"Have you checked police files for their previous records, or are you taking the words of students?"

"Yes, but these are medical students who would have had to declare any prior convictions before starting their courses to become doctors. The whole point of discrediting the witnesses falls apart if they have any evidence to support what they said. They may have been drunk but that doesn't make them potheads, panhandlers, or unreliable."

"What evidence? There isn't any. And with Charles Forbury gone..."

"Charles?"

"Yes, sorry, I thought you knew. Charles was killed in the air accident in Sudan yesterday, there were no survivors. I know what you're thinking but it wasn't related. It was a mechanical failure on the plane. Just one of those things." Anne Marie turned away. Chloe had her doubts about it just being a mechanical failure, but Sudan Airways didn't have a good track record in air safety. Another carrier and Chloe might have shared her fears.

It was a sad fact that two journalists die in accidents and murders every week on average. They die in every part of the world, mainly from bombings and shootings, air accidents were a close third. Finding out the truth was a risky business; it took you to dangerous parts of the world, to war zones, areas of general anarchy and countries with differing safety standards.

Chloe thought about being with Charles in Normandy. Suddenly the regret in his face made sense; he didn't want her to be compromised in any way. This investigation was too important to him. If he had given his life, well she would be more determined to prove without any shadow of doubt that these scientists were being murdered, state sponsored cynical murder.

It explained why Anne Marie was pulling away from completing the investigation; she thought that Charles's death was connected. Chloe paused, and drawing all her inner strength together to avoid tears, she put her head up. She would grieve later. Charles had cared deeply about this investigation, and she would honor his death by following through. She was now more determined to get to the truth and wasn't going to be put off.

"The photographs from Emilio's phone are brilliant. We have been able to read the license plate of the police car, and the reporter at the Miami newspaper has asked for the license plate of the stolen police car so we can match it up. So far, Detective Bob Anderson has been slow in responding. I have a request with *Crime Stoppers*, a local Miami television show, where the producer remembers covering the theft. They are looking through the footage to find the license plate number. She's sure the police gave the details to the program. It's one of those pieces that sticks in the mind, the police aren't supposed to have their cars stolen."

Anne Marie pursed her lips. She wasn't pleased. There was the briefest of frowns then acceptance. "Good investigative work, so what happened that night?"

Chloe had the sequence of events from the witness statements, backed up by the photographs, and police evidence. The doctor descended the steps of the hospital staff entrance where two passers-by had asked him the time. The two men had injected something into the doctor's neck, and he had fallen to the floor. The two men had leaned over him, and put a syringe into Biryukov's mouth, or sprayed his neck, the accounts varied. The police car arrived two minutes after Emilio had phoned the emergency services, which was surprisingly fast, but not impossible. The ambulance arrived immediately after that, perhaps not surprising for a hospital site. The two passers-by were taken away in the back of the police car, leaving the paramedics to take the doctor to the hospital emergency room where he was pronounced dead on arrival.

It had been a well-executed murder with prior planning, stealing the police car, and then spiriting away the assailants. The photographs, however, would prove the use of the stolen police car. This death fell into the category of a cover-up.

The methodology suggested secret intelligence involvement, but so far she couldn't name the security service involved. It had all the hallmarks of Mossad, a well-disciplined team, with a good plan, well executed. But it would have been more logical for it to be the FSB, the Russians seemed intent on silencing their former employees.

Chloe continued, "We do have the faces of the two perpetrators and one profile, but matching these pictures against known secret intelligence agents won't be easy. They don't post pictures online."

Anne Marie agreed, albeit reluctantly, to delay publishing the findings on Biryukov. "It feels like a Mossad operation. It shows planning, teamwork, and they have covered every possibility. I don't think this was the Russians, they don't usually work in teams."

Chloe wanted a series of articles to show one scientist after another had been murdered, each death covered up by the police, which suggested some secret service involvement.

The interview in the dragon's den was never a comfortable experience.

"So what's the next step?" asked Anne Marie. Chloe wanted to go to Scotland. There was the presumed suicide of a scientist there and Chloe thought this case fit the pattern.

"All right, go, but take Jean Pierre with you, I don't like where your investigations are leading, and I think you might be in danger. But first, I want you to go visit Patrick Dubois at the DST."

"Why?"

"Because he's looking for you, and you have a compromising photograph showing him following you. It would be interesting to hear his explanation. If you get Patrick on the back foot, he's unpredictable. He might tell you something."

Chloe got out of the dragon's den and went to the women's restroom, entered a cubicle and vented her grief. She cried 'til there were no more tears. She cried for Charles, she cried for Michael, she cried for her father and the sense of loss she had shared with her mother, and lastly she cried just because she was so tired. This investigation had been absorbing her night and day, and even when she was asleep, she dreamed she was being chased. Afterward, she drew breath, went to a basin, splashed her face with cold water, put eye drops into her eyes to clear the redness, put concealer on her nose, and a fresh layer of lipstick to brighten the picture. She pulled herself together and went out to her appointment.

Chloe was anxious about meeting Patrick Dubois at the DST. She had the photo of him in her bag. The problem with asking a spook for information was you were never sure if they could be trusted. If they went on the record, which was hardly ever—even as an "unnamed source"—you were still not sure if they were using the paper for their own purposes.

Over the years that Chloe had dealt with him, she had derived a strategy of part flirt, part intellectual equal in discussing world affairs with Patrick. She liked to think this had him a little off balance, but in reality, she had as much chance of knocking him off balance as a mouse an elephant.

She went up the two sets of steps to the black imposing façade of the Ministère de L'Intérieur in the rue Nélaton near the Tour Eiffel. She met Patrick in the reception area of the Direction de la Surveillance du Territoire (DST) offices, he took her through security, and across to the elevator bank. She started to talk but he held his finger to his lips, he wanted everything on tape.

"Spooks!" she muttered.

Patrick smiled back, and his eyes danced with amusement. Chloe hadn't had many dealings with Patrick, apart from her investigation into the 1992 assassination of the Palestinian Atef Bseiso, which the Mossad had conducted on the street in Paris. It was retribution for the hostage taking and eventual killing of the Israeli athletes at the Munich Olympics. She had learned a great deal about how the Mossad operated from that inquiry. French intelligence had wanted to draw a line under the event, and hadn't welcomed her inquiries.

Patrick took her to an interview room, pointed out the camera was active; he was protecting himself against any entrapment by a journalist.

"I wanted to ask you about a global situation regarding the number of bioweapons or biomedical scientists who seem, over the last couple years, to be meeting rather unusual ends." Chloe sat across the table from Patrick.

"Anyone in particular you wanted to talk about?"

"How about Ken Antipov? He seems to be the most recent and high profile suspicious death."

"Ah, well you would have to ask the Brits about that one. I did like your piece though, I thought it highlighted the issues well."

As usual with Patrick, Chloe was never quite sure if he was lying or perhaps concealing but it left you feeling he always knew far more than he said. These were everyday skills for a spook. She felt lulled into a false sense of security.

"All right, let's talk generalities." She told him about the evidence she had on the Biryukov case, and two further American scientists, the two British scientists, and the Russian scientists.

"Okay. I get the picture, you're following up the conspiracy that implies scientists who, for reasons best known to a mystery assassin team, seem to be meeting rather unusual deaths disproportionate to the statistical probability for the group."

Patrick had a way of cutting down a huge amount of effort to a single dismissive statement. Chloe felt as if she had accused a righteous individual of a crime based on absolutely no evidence. She didn't think Patrick was a righteous individual; she thought he was ruthless and manipulative.

"And is it your contention that the security services are involved?"

"Should it be?" She leaned forward to add emphasis to the question.

"Chloe, you shouldn't come here on a fishing trip—that's not why we meet with journalists and you know it."

"So why did you agree to see me without qualifying the interview?" Chloe leaned back in her chair. She was surprised. She had scored. Patrick had an ulterior motive for seeing her. But disappointingly, he hadn't the slightest interest in her story.

"Chloe, you are always a delight—but unfortunately married." Patrick looked at her; his brown eyes turned up in the corners when he was amused. He managed this with the barest of smiles at his lips. It was as if he was laughing at his own joke. He was handsome in a classic way, dark brown tight curly hair, unruly when long, high cheekbones, a northern European skin that was usually slightly tanned, adding to his good looks. He could be charming when he wanted to get his own way and yet he could blend in and you could pass him in the street without noticing him.

"What about Walid?" Chloe understood immediately, he wanted to discuss Walid.

"Let's come straight to the point: we have an active interest in your husband. Where is he right now?" No more games, he was serious.

"He's collecting some artworks in Iraq for a dealer in Paris, who is paying him both expenses and commission. It's all aboveboard, he pays tax on the income and he knows his stuff. He wouldn't accept something that had been looted from a museum or anything like that."

Walid still hadn't been in touch. When she had returned from America, there had been a simple note on the kitchen table saying that he was on a buying trip in Iraq, he said he would be perfectly safe, and would back in a few days, a week at most. There were no phone calls, letters, texts, emails, or any communication at all. She had gone to a lawyer and started divorce proceedings that morning before going into work; it hadn't been a hard decision, she felt relieved and had stopped agonizing over it.

"It's a bit more serious than paying tax or illegal art dealing; our interest is in a stream of money for Al Qaeda operations in Europe," said Patrick.

Chloe paused; it was her turn to wonder if Patrick was fishing for information or whether he was informing her of serious accusations against Walid.

"Patrick, Walid wouldn't have anything to do with that. He absolutely abhors fundamentalism, his first wife was killed because he refused to get involved with the GIA—you've got the wrong man."

"Chloe, just how much has Walid told you about his life in Algeria?"

"Not much but I trust him." Chloe wasn't sure this was true anymore. He couldn't be trusted to keep in touch.

"No doubts at all?"

"None."

Patrick's penetrating look made her blush, something she hadn't done in a long time. He knew she had doubts.

"He's a man, isn't he? Every wife has some doubts. He's away a lot. Is he faithful? You know the sort of thing."

"Chloe—we both know the doubts concerning both of us are not whether he is faithful to your marital bed. You worry about his activity in the Muslim underworld and so do we. We are just not sure if he knows the money from some of the deals he does for this art dealer in Paris are going to Al Qaeda cells. We know this—it's not speculation. What we don't know is Walid's involvement."

"I don't know what to say. I am sure he doesn't know and if he did he would stop immediately."

"When did you last hear from him?"

"A few days ago, why?"

"Really?"

"It was last Thursday or Friday." *Did his message on Friday count as hearing from him?* She wasn't sure.

"Would he work for us? Would he give us information on Al Qaeda networks?"

"I shouldn't think he has any information and even if he did the answer would be the same. No."

"To quote George Bush you're either for us or against us—which is Walid?"

"That's a ridiculous statement."

"Maybe, but I'm asking the question all the same."

"Yes, but you're asking the wrong person. Walid left Algeria to get out from all that stuff and lead a normal life. What you're offering is a return to fear, looking over your shoulder, always concerned about your loved ones, anxious if they're late, would you volunteer for that?"

Patrick smiled. It was a stupid question. He worked in the intelligence community and he probably spent a lot of life looking over his shoulder.

"Well, Chloe, you wanted some information about missing scientists. I can tell you approximately three hundred Iraqi scientists have disappeared since the end of hostilities in Iraq. You could say changing the status in Iraq, from being at war to having an army of occupation, has not been good news for the scientists. Off the record and for your background information only, I would expect the trail to lead to the Mossad. If you find any trail at all. One thing you have to admire about the Mossad, they have the most efficient wet team in the world. And in Iraq, hiding three hundred bodies isn't difficult; dig up any mass grave, check how the bodies were killed. Mutilate your corpses to fit, age the corpses a little, and add a few to each mass grave. It's not as if we have good dental or other medical records to do a match on all the bodies being found."

"Three hundred? Why?" Chloe opened her notebook.

"Same reason the Mossad ever completes the circle. They are concerned for the safety of Israeli citizens. It wasn't long ago Iraq landed a Scud missile in Israel. What if the shell had carried a biological weapon? If Iraq no longer had the capability to make biological weapons, the world would be a safer place. Yet what's the point of destroying facilities, you need to destroy the knowledge."

"Yes, but..." Chloe thought about showing Patrick her photograph from Iraq but decided to keep it in reserve. He seemed to be happy to give her leads without needing to trade information.

"Yes, but no one else would be disappointed if they disappeared. The Americans don't want them to join some insurgents and give them more effective weapons than the car bomb. We wouldn't want them to join some Al Qaeda cell and share their information about biological weapons. So it is convenient for everyone to let the Israelis have the list of names and turn a blind eye."

"Where did the list of names come from?"

"UNSCOM—off the record of course."

"Of course! How? I can't believe they just handed them over."

"How many UNSCOM scientists have died recently?"

"I don't know."

"Get the answer to that question and find out what happened to their computers."

"Yes, but surely the team didn't keep a database of facts and personnel on their personal computers."

"Perhaps not. Was there anything else?"

"What about the scientists in Britain and America?"

"No comment."

"Patrick!"

"There's nothing to say. As far as I can determine some of these scientists died naturally, some died in suspicious but inconclusive circumstances, and some were murdered—not unusual in today's world. Some misguided animal rights activists could have killed them. Many of them would be conducting testing on animals. Not many people want to be human guinea pigs for plague. I don't know I'm speculating."

"That's it—that's all?" Chloe had hoped for more.

"We have looked at some of the same information as you, and if they were professional hits, you would expect the evidence to be inconclusive. These are discreet killings, if that's what they are. I have to say you are unlikely ever to get your story, maybe the Iraqi scientists are the way forward."

"So leave the other deaths alone?"

"Yes—definitely! Bright girl."

Patronizing git, she thought. "Is that a warning?" Was this her cue to be worried? Should she show him the photograph of him crouching down on the pavement, pretending to tie his shoelaces? She decided she would leave that for another day. He must know she had the photograph, yet hadn't asked about it. They were both suffering from a seeming lack of curiosity about the incident.

"I didn't say that, but it might be wise to listen to advice on this one. If you get close to exposing what is supposed to be secret, they will not hesitate to stop you. Be sensible over this."

"'Stop me'—a euphemistic term for..."

Patrick leaned forward and put his hand over hers to emphasize his warning.

"Yes, Walid's life is at risk if he shares the information I have given you about the money going to active cells. What you tell him is up to you, but confrontation and indignation with the art gallery owner will get him, and probably you, killed. We can protect you—you're a French national—but Walid... It's your decision."

"You mean you win both ways. Either he works for you and three cheers for Patrick, he has a new asset. Alternatively, if either Walid or I tell the gallery owner, who, by your reckoning is Al Qaeda, then they kill Walid. Three cheers for Patrick, a channel of funds comes to a temporary halt. Nice one, Patrick."

"Lunch?"

"Lunch?" Chloe leaned back in the chair and laughed.

"Chloe, let's be friends, I don't want you to think I like the choices. But, Walid is the link here; if he tumbles to this information by himself and he comments on it, they'll kill him. If the Americans find the trail of money, he won't see the light of day for a long time—if ever. I am being a friend here—can't you see that?"

Patrick had a wonderful way of making everything sound so reasonable. If he had suggested she lie down in front of an oncoming train she was sure she would have thought it was a perfectly good idea.

Chloe agreed to have lunch with him; he was someone you wanted to have on your side. They went down to the restaurant opposite the office and had a simple lunch. The discussion was neutral, weather, politics, and the normal conversation you would expect over lunch with a work colleague. But Patrick was no ordinary individual and she was left wondering why he'd wanted to have lunch with her when he ordered coffee for them both and suddenly blurted out, "Why have you filed for divorce from Walid?"

Chloe was surprised and shocked by the question, she had thought her actions were private. She had only visited the lawyers this morning. "I don't think that's any of your business."

"Nothing about Walid is private. Look, I wanted to have this conversation without any official record. What I want to tell you is classified, but I think you can help us. What do you know about him?"

Chloe was not going to be drawn into that conversation.

"Let me tell you what we know about Walid and his brother, Qasim. When Walid was born his mother was very ill after the birth, she continued to live for another couple of weeks and she gave birth to another boy, so technically twins although they don't share the same birthday. The mother then died and Walid's grief stricken father agreed to let the mother's sister have the second child, as looking after one child was going to be difficult, two would be impossible, and the sister couldn't have children of her own. Walid's father remarried."

"Don't tell me the wicked stepmother story—oh please, tell me you're going to be more original than that." Chloe was beginning to feel manipulated by this whole "let me tell you a story" routine, and the problem with Patrick was she didn't believe him, he was a professional liar.

"No, actually Walid had a very happy childhood, did well in school, went to college, and had a solid career, married, had twin sons."

Chloe was shocked by the news of the twins, she knew about Walid's first wife, but she was surprised he had never mentioned his sons before. It explained where his money went.

"Life was not so pleasant for Qasim, his adoptive parents were not kind, and the father was a violent man, angry with the French, the Algerian government, and most things in life. He was killed in 1994 in the civil war, fighting for the GIA. Qasim joined the GIA after that, and then went on to Al Qaeda."

"What's this got to do with Walid?"

"Walid's father decided it was best for Qasim that he would believe his foster parents were in fact his real parents, and it would have been difficult to explain just how alike Qasim and Walid looked if they weren't twins, so there was no contact. We don't know if they are identical because there are no photographs of them together and we don't even know if we have any pictures of Qasim, on each occasion the photograph could have been Walid. We don't know how they met, whether it was through family, or coincidence.

"The GIA took Walid's wife hostage to get Walid to take part in an action, I don't know what was involved only that Walid preferred to watch his wife die rather than comply."

"GIA?"

"Armed Islamic militants fighting for an Islamic state in Algeria."

"So what had this got to do with Walid now?"

"You can't bring logic into any discussion relating to Qasim, he is a flawed individual who will use anybody and anything to achieve his objectives. He has the opposite disposition to Walid, who I think you would describe as warm, gentle, and cultured. Qasim is taciturn and self-centered, with a ruthless desire to achieve great things as an Al Qaeda leader."

"So your question about Walid and the money laundering is, in fact, a question about whether he has changed sides? Where are his sons?"

"In Algeria, the plan was that they would join Walid a week or so after he left for Paris; he was stunned when he found out that they had been meeting with their uncle for months, and were planning to join the fighting in Afghanistan. He seems to have deterred them from going to Afghanistan until they finished school, but it's strained the relationship. He visits them from time to time. If you are planning on divorcing this man, just make sure you know which man you are divorcing."

Chloe went cold. If they looked that similar, which man had she married?

"Patrick, how can I thank you for filling me in. It's been a great help." It was a clever story, she decided. Divorcees usually complained about the changes in the man they married. What better tale to tell. She would love to know the truth from the fiction. If Walid had sons, why hadn't he told her? If he had been going back to Algeria to visit them, it would explain the absences. It would also explain why he was short of money. Three cheers for Patrick, who might be French but seemed blessed with the gift of Irish storytelling.

CHAPTER NINETEEN

Paris

Chloe told Anne Marie she didn't get much from Patrick, and would be using the photograph in the future. When she got back to the apartment, it had been searched, thoroughly and carefully. She routinely used a series of low-tech methods to check if Walid had returned, there was talcum powder under the front mat, which now showed large footprints, and she had left all the contents of her drawers in a meticulous order. Now bottles were facing the wrong way, and scarves left precisely lined up were in disarray. She had been expecting a visit from the security services, in a way she was surprised it had taken so long. It was another encouraging sign. At first, she couldn't identify if anything had been taken, but she wasn't sure about Walid's possessions, maybe something was missing.

The next day the original materials arrived from Charles via FedEx. He had enclosed a handwritten note with the files, which she put in her bag. It seemed odd receiving them after he had died, a handout from beyond the grave. She gave copies to Anne Marie to keep in the safe. But all the new evidence, the photographs, emails, and so on she kept on her own laptop that she left hidden behind a panel in her city apartment. It was unlikely the security services would find it unless they took all the oak paneling off the walls and she doubted they would do that. She liked and trusted the concierge. He didn't know about the secret compartment in the paneling. She didn't think he would let anyone go up to her apartment for any reason at all, he knew she was an investigative journalist and her privacy was essential. She had alerted him to bogus TV technicians, essential gas leak repairs, telephone engineers, and the usual entry methods of the security services and he had agreed if he couldn't phone her first they didn't get entry.

She had decided that going to Iraq would be the next step. That would need Anne Marie's agreement. She would be a fool to go without the paper's contacts and security arrangements in place.

The first delay was her inability to find her hepatitis A injection certificate, without which the newspaper wouldn't let her go to Iraq. The appointment was made and the injection re-given, but she was left wondering if the searchers of her apartment in Sceaux had taken the certificate, it was very odd that it would disappear. The next delay was in getting a visa:

> *Journalists and public media personnel after submitting applications for Visa either through Iraq's missions abroad, stating the name of which Iraqi mission they want to receive their Visa, or through the office of their respective newspaper, news agency, or satellite TV in Baghdad with a letter directed to the Press Department at the Ministry of Foreign Affairs (MFA) indicating the name of the Iraqi mission abroad through which they want to receive their Visas, or through the journalists' Embassy in Baghdad with a note to the Press Department/MFA requesting the Visa and indicating the name of the Iraqi Embassy from which the journalist would like to receive his/her Entry Visa.*

Anne Marie had tried all avenues and was still waiting. Chloe had wondered if she should go as a British subject, rather than a French national working for a French newspaper. It would have been a lot simpler as the nations forming the coalition forces got visas in a straightforward way. But having started down the French route with the paper she was in the system, if you could call the chaos a system.

For three weeks, she waited for the officials to provide her travel documents, she phoned, begged, emailed, photocopied documents, re-photocopied documents lost by the embassy, provided replacement forms, and was beginning to think someone didn't want her to get a vi-sa—everyone had some problems, but her catalogue of problems seemed to sum up the total experience of every French journalist going to Iraq.

In the meantime she conducted desk research into a suspicious death in Frankfurt but didn't come to any conclusions, and had found someone on the air crash investigation team in Russia to send over the documents relating to an accidental missile strike on a passenger plane which killed several scientists.

She had also asked for the investigation team in the Sudan to send over the report into the crash of the plane that had been carrying Charles. It was worth a look, but Anne Marie seemed convinced it was business as usual for that airline.

She was surprised she still hadn't heard anything from Walid. She didn't know any details about his trip, other than he would be in Bagh-dad briefly and expected to be back in about a week. When he didn't return when his leave ended at the Sorbonne, and she hadn't had any communication from him, she became worried. She decided to talk to art dealers in Paris who stocked Islamic items to see if she could find the gallery that had sent him to Iraq.

At the end of day one, trailing around in the rain, she was getting desperate. No one would give her any information on the phone; the university department was unhelpful and disappointed in his failing to inform them of his absence. Phoning art dealers had drawn a blank. Over the phone, she couldn't tell if the denials were genuine. It was the merest chance she opened the glove compartment in the car to see if she had left an umbrella in there, when a pile of unpaid parking tickets fell out. She was both horrified and delighted. They were all from the same area of Paris and she guessed Walid got these tickets when he visited the art dealer. This narrowed down the search and she found herself inside a shop managed by Ahmed Talbi, not far from the Louvre. It was an up-market shop, with items priced in tens of thousands of euros.

An anxious, jittery little man appeared out of the back room. He introduced himself. He didn't offer to shake her hand and she felt her presence as a woman left him deeply disquieted.

"I wanted to know if you had heard from Walid Merbarkia?" Chloe asked, having decided the best way to find out the truth was to appear as if she knew Walid worked for the shop. That way she could tell if the denials were genuine.

"You better come this way," he said, leading her to the back of the shop. He offered her a seat at a table and they both sat. "Walid Merbarkia?"

"Yes, he's collecting for you in Iraq."

"And may I ask, who's asking?"

She flashed her press card. Ahmed looked alarmed.

"No publicity. Nothing to say. Not even off the record." He jumped up, signaling her departure.

"Yes." Chloe smiled to alleviate his fear and stayed seated. "I am just investigating the disappearance of individuals from France working in Iraq. There have been a number of journalists kidnapped, and more recently just killed. Engineers helping to rebuild Iraq have been taken hostage and I understand Walid Merbarkia is missing. I thought you might be able to tell me more about his whereabouts, and what he was doing in Iraq."

"I'm afraid I can tell you little, my clients rely on discretion. I couldn't possibly let my work or my name be attached to any information I might have."

"No. This would be strictly background. You have my word."

"He had some appointments in Baghdad. I can't give you more details."

Chloe didn't think this was true for an instant, but he had no reason to trust her.

"What other visits do you think he might make?"

"I believe he wanted to visit the Sulaymaniya Museum, but he wasn't sure whether he would have time to arrange a visit to the north on this trip. Travel in Iraq, you understand, is still difficult and dangerous."

"Let me leave my card." Chloe got up and the little man looked relieved. "Please call me if you think of anything else that might be helpful. Perhaps you could call if you remember any of the addresses of your contacts."

At last, Chloe had found out for whom Walid was working. If Patrick had been more forthcoming she might have got this much information over lunch. He felt all searching for Walid should be left to official channels, but as he pointed out, Walid was not a French national, and so Patrick wasn't interested.

CHAPTER TWENTY

Iraq

As Ahmed had predicted, airport security had stopped Walid and asked him to open his case so they could look at the glass vase.

"It's the lead in the crystal," explained the official. "It means we can't see through the vase and determine the contents of the case."

On reflection, the gift seemed out of place. Why would you send someone who was interested in individual artistry a quantity produced item? This vase was clearly a collector's item made by artisans but not a designer piece.

Walid need not have worried; Ahmed's contact received the vase with enthusiasm. The vendor had a small warehouse full of interesting items, and Walid made several purchases.

Walid had one final appointment, which was outside of the safe "Green Zone," to meet an art dealer on Ahmed's most important sellers list. A van drew alongside him on the pavement, the door opened, and four individuals surrounded him, put a coat over his head, and bundled him into the van, which made a hasty departure. The voices inside the van were American. On the pavement, no one paid much attention to this melodrama in Baghdad. The residents were used to this insanity.

At first, he expected a simple interview, similar to the Atlanta airport, but soon it became apparent the Americans were sure he had been to a training camp in Afghanistan, was an Al Qaeda cell leader, and had been involved in some terrorist activities.

There was no way of convincing them of the truth, no way of proving his innocence and no way he would confess. It was strangely ironic. If the French had picked him up with similar evidence he probably would have just quietly disappeared—permanently—and if the GIA had picked him up with similar evidence he would have been beheaded with maximum publicity. What would the Americans do?

"Are you a member of Al Qaeda? Are you a member of the GIA? Do you support Osama bin Laden? When were you in Afghanistan? Who else was at the training camp? What is your terrorist mission?"

The questions were endless, unimaginative, and always translated. No one checked if he could understand or speak English. To hear the question once was boring, but to hear it repeated in Arabic hour after hour was exhausting. He began to play games in his mind. *Is the translation accurate? Could they have chosen better words for the translation?* He said nothing. If you said anything, he knew the interrogators would play with your words. His protection was to say nothing. After twelve hours of aggressive non-stop questioning, it was suggested he might like to have a shower, at which point his clothes went for forensic tests, and the humiliating blue overalls were supplied with ill-fitting underwear, no shoes or socks. The shower reminded him of scenes from *Schindler's List*. The powerful image of the prisoners disrobing had stayed in his mind.

When they moved him from his cell to the interview room, they applied wrist manacles, chains linked to leg irons, and a black hood with goggles over. It was a psychological war they were playing and he felt little fear or interest. They were showing him they had total control of his actions, movements, and senses. It was supposed to intimidate him but it was as if it was happening to somebody else and he was an objective observer.

He no longer cared whether he lived or died, he felt responsible for his wife's death. Nothing they did mattered.

He was shackled to others, unseen, unknown, and all silent. The human shuffle train stopped, the guards unlocked a door, took off the goggles and hood. He made his way with tiny baby steps into the gloomy room. They pushed him into the chair so forcefully it overturned. He landed heavily on the floor and saw the large tank.

He heard the shouted order, although his hearing was disturbed by the blaring white noise. Two soldiers set him upright and they manacled his wrists and strapped his ankles to the chair. A soldier waited on each side. There was a pause. Bright lights surrounded him. The instigator of the order was in the darkness. He saw the cigarette glow red and fade. He wished he could smoke. He could smell the cigarette, but couldn't distinguish the brand. He thought about his morning routine, opening the new packet, the first inhale and he could almost taste it. He waited for the interrogation to start again. There were no questions. At a given sign, they tipped the chair back.

At first, he did not struggle. He would welcome death. As the icy cold water hit the back of his head, he gasped. The degree of coldness surprised him. The water came over his eyes and flowed up into his nose. He wasn't under long. They would know he had no air. He'd experienced this before, but this time it was easy. He only had his life to give, no one else could be made to suffer.

Next, he thought they would ask him questions. No questions. The freezing rivulets of water cascaded from his hair down his neck, causing an involuntary shiver. He took one breath and immediately, they tipped him back again. This time he was ready for the icy water and involuntarily retained his last breath. He might be ready to die, but his body would still fight to survive. The blackness seemed to welcome him. A dull pain took over his chest as if a heavy weight had been applied. A light shone brightly into the water. He was floating toward the light. It was so peaceful. He saw his wife, not the image he so often saw, the one that pervaded his waking hours and nightmares where she was begging him to help her. Now her arms were outstretched to greet him. Her eyes filled with love. She looked happy. He couldn't hear her. She was pleased to see him. It meant everything. She absolved him of any guilt.

He came around with a mask on his face.

"No!" he shouted, but he heard nothing. His body had ceased to function. Paralyzed? Drugged? He closed his eyes and held on to the images of his wife. He never wanted to forget. She had forgiven him. Nothing else mattered.

His blue coverall had been undone, and a soldier was sticking electrodes onto his chest.

Unusual to start electric shock torture with so much water around, he thought. He looked at what might have been an officer with two large defibrillators standing over him. There was a large cart full of electronic equipment beside him, as he lay on the hard concrete floor.

The electrodes were now firmly in place.

The officer waited. *Timing in these matters is everything*, thought Walid. It was the anticipation that caused as much damage as the eventual pain. He couldn't work out what was going on. *Why would they put me on the floor for electric shock torture? Why electrodes on my chest? Is it more effective? Is this how the Americans do it?* He waited. Memories he thought buried in Algeria, resurfaced. The agony, the arching of his back 'til he thought his spine would break; loss of control, his urine, warm, trickling down his legs, and finally soiling himself. That had been the worst. Strange, he should remember the humiliation as much as the pain.

"All right let's take a print."

Whirring into life a small strip of paper cascaded over the machine. The officer, dressed in blue medical scrubs, tore the printout off, and looked at it.

"Okay, let's get a gurney in here and take this man to the hospital. You can unhook him for now, but I want him reconnected and monitored around the clock. Any change—call me."

Hospital? Walid thought this was all part of the game. Let's pretend this is all going to stop now. He was supposed to relax and in an unguarded moment, it would all start again.

"Hospital?" The unseen voice had a gravelly quality to it. The man remained in the darkness.

"That's right, I am placing this prisoner in sick bay."

"No; the information this man has is needed urgently."

This was a new tactic, two officers fighting over a corpse in waiting. It appealed to Walid. He wasn't quite sure where the situation was going, but he was beginning to think maybe he'd had a heart attack. He certainly had a severe pain in his chest, but that could have been the effect of some shock treatment.

The doctor in the blue scrubs leaned against the cart. "Let me explain the situation to you. Let's pretend this prisoner is a car. Your car's engine has just stalled, but it didn't restart for you. So, you called in the garage to jump-start the engine. The engine may be running, but it most likely will stall again unless we fix the underlying problem. It could be the fan belt, it could be the alternator, or maybe the car needs a new battery."

"Don't patronize me." The gravelly voice was displeased.

"Major—you need to understand when anybody has a massive heart attack and the heart stops beating, we can sometimes bring the patient back. But there's no guarantee we can bring him back next time for you, unless we sort out why your prisoner died. If you want information, it's better to keep him alive."

"Keeping him alive is your job—so you better do it." Gravelly voice lit another cigarette.

"That's an end to interviewing for today." Walid thought it looked like the scrubs man was winning the power play.

"What?"

"If you are going to hold me responsible. He's what—a fifty-something-year-old who's just had a major heart attack. He's been tortured before, and a lot more brutally than any measures you have at your disposal. There's a limit to how often you can torture someone. The effect is cumulative, you know."

"He's younger than that. Tortured before?"

"Look at all these little scars—burn marks if I'm not mistaken. Could be acne, but unlikely. It would be most prevalent on his back if it was a skin condition. Look at the loss of two toes. Look at the deformity of the remaining toenails. It could have been a severe nail infection. It's more likely pliers took out his toenails."

"GIA," mumbled Walid through the mask. No one listened or heard him.

"Get this man into a hospital gown. Remove the ironware."

"No. He knows about an imminent attack in London, it's important and critical."

There, you see, thought Walid, *a simple question and I could have told them I know nothing.*

"If this man's had encounters with the GIA, he won't survive more of the same treatment. It's time to do something different."

"All right, he's off to Kandahar the day after tomorrow. Psych Ops can sort him."

"I thought he was off to Bagram?"

"He was, but there's no point in sending him to Bagram if his heart's going to give out."

"I'll want to examine him tomorrow to confirm he's fit to travel. You may want to hold off on your travel arrangements until I give confirmation. There may be complications."

Walid took all this information in. So, he'd had a heart attack. He wasn't surprised. He'd had intermittent chest pains for a couple of months now. They had begun when he started working with Ahmed.

CHAPTER TWENTY-ONE

MI5, London

Louise put her handbag in her desk drawer, turned her workstation on, and was about to fetch a coffee when Graeme came over.

"Join me in the briefing room. Bring all the materials you have on Art Expert and his wife."

Louise still felt anxiety at these meetings; whether James T attended or not, she still managed to feel inadequate. Graeme had booked the room, and arranged for catering to deliver coffee. It was Graeme's way of showing approval for her work. Louise knew it was a manipulative attempt to engage her, but she was pleased and flattered by the attention of her boss. She was good at her job, and knew James T had issued an edict and there would be hell to pay over the next manager to get a letter of resignation from a recently qualified intelligence officer.

Louise arrived in the meeting room with armfuls of manila files. Everything was on the computer, but it was the ability to correlate miscellaneous bits of information that seemed easier on paper, rather than in the standard searchable computer format.

"You shouldn't be carrying such a heavy load in your condition, here, let me help you." He took the files and put them on the table. His remark surprised her.

"It's okay, I can manage." What did he mean, in her condition? Anyway, the offer was a bit late, she'd already carried them in. Normally she could be drowning under a sea of files and he would not notice.

"This is your opportunity to tell me all about Art Expert and his wife—how are things going? What's new? And what are our options?"

Louise was taken aback. Normally these meeting went at the speed of a gazelle in flight, and she barely had time to draw breath. She sat down. Sometimes she felt Graeme lived life so fast he refused to take in the details of the situation and she was frightened he relied on her judgment too much.

"Art Expert is still in Afghanistan. The Americans aren't sharing much, but it would appear they aren't making much progress. Our analysis of the photographs doesn't conclude the pictures the Americans believe to be Art Expert are actually him—close but not a match. A job offer was issued to Art Expert for a research fellowship for a fixed contract of three years, and his wife has accepted on his behalf. This decision was made easier for her when the Sorbonne dismissed Art Expert for unauthorized absence..."

"Nice touch."

"On a separate note I have Art Expert's wife considering a twelve month guest lecturer spot at the school of investigative journalism."

"Really?" Graeme's criticism was unguarded. "He gets a prestigious foundation and she gets school?"

"I made it appealing, a paid three day week but only half-day lecturing."

"Do you think it will be enough?"

"I don't know, the problem may be if she divorces Art Expert. Patrick took her out to lunch and told her a tale designed to make her more sympathetic to her husband. It might give us a few days, maybe even weeks, but if she isn't interested in staying with him then I doubt she'll take the job. The additional complication that we aren't sure about is the relationship she has with a work colleague."

"Romantically speaking?"

"There's not much I think we can do about that. I mean she drew up the divorce papers immediately after her return from Miami, when Merbarkia first went out to Iraq. It appears the Sorbonne wasn't the only one fed up with his unannounced absences."

"Your suggestions?"

"Firstly, I think we should get Art Expert released as soon as possible. The advantages being his marriage won't fall apart, not immediately anyway. I think no matter what the situation is, she will be sympathetic for a while and not likely to pursue a divorce until he's over the trauma. He will be over here where we can monitor the situation, and perhaps create an asset. We need more quality inside information; he is the only potential source I am working on at present."

"Agreed."

"Secondly, I think we should see if we could get his wife's paper to give her a twelve month sabbatical. After being 'kidnapped' in Iraq it would appear to be appropriate to give her some time to recover."

"Mmm—kidnapped? What are you suggesting?"

"We need to buy some time. His wife, Chloe, identified the art gallery her husband has been working for and Patrick is concerned the gallery owner will do a runner, just as they are getting to the end of a complex communication network and getting him tied into some senior Al Qaeda figures."

"And who is going to kidnap her?"

"Well, she is due to do some investigation in Iraq. Patrick did everything he could to delay the visa, but it's come through and she flies out next Wednesday."

"What is she investigating in Iraq?"

"Patrick Dubois persuaded her that the Israelis have killed off about three hundred Iraqi bio-med scientists."

"Fact?"

"Probably more than three hundred, but I don't think we want to have this factually confirmed, and she is an excellent journalist."

"You don't think it's a bit extreme?"

"You mean my underhanded kidnapping and kind treatment is less ethical than an upfront extreme rendition and torture solution?"

"No. Not at all, I think it's an admirable solution. I'm just not sure she will be viewed as a sufficient threat to warrant such a drastic solution being sanctioned, and it could be viewed as a French problem."

"Not if she gets to the bottom of the Antipov incident. She seems to have uncovered all the facts in Miami." Louise paused; she thought it was a creative solution. The stakes were high, but there was a nagging doubt about it all. It just didn't sit right with her, but she knew Graeme would find the solution appealing. "I think you need to look at the whole picture here. The benefits are that we can contain the bio-med story, not only the Israeli involvement, but also she is close on some of the other American bio-med scientists and she is turning her attention to our scientists—including Ken Antipov. It will put an end to her muddying the DST waters in Paris over Art Expert and more importantly, the delicate balance of information flow in Iraq. It will also deliver us Art Expert, an important potential asset."

"And you have a detailed plan for the kidnapping?"

"New radical Islamic groups are appearing all the time, we just need to create our own version and think of some suitable demands. The release of all women held under extreme rendition, for example."

"And how do you propose to fool Al Jazeera into complicity?"

"I thought we would keep it simple and just send an email with pictures. Our kidnapped journalist holding a newspaper up, so you can see the date, hooded men with crossed guns behind—a bit like a coat of arms."

"Louise, I admire your ingenuity."

"I think when Art Expert's wife gets back from Iraq—perhaps a month would be sufficient for us to broker some deal with the Americans over Art Expert—we could lean on the psychiatrists for her to accept a sabbatical. Put that idea to the paper on the grounds of medical compassion."

"I like your style: simple and measured. Keep this to yourself for now. Who else knows about this idea?"

"No one."

The catering staff arrived with a tray, and Louise was rather flattered he had ordered coffee for them and was treating her with respect. She didn't know why he was being so nice, it made her wonder who had been getting at him.

"Good let's keep it that way. Kidnapping a journalist under the guise of Islamic fundamentalism is likely to cause a whistle blowing incident. Secrecy from everyone is essential. From now on you are not authorized to discuss this with anyone other than myself, and don't discuss it with James T, he may need deniability. That includes the psychologist helpline and any other mumbo jumbo nuts currently employed for your well-being. Is that understood?"

"Crystal clear."

"Oh, I'm supposed to ask you how you are feeling. Do you need some time off? A proper vacation, say three weeks, let me know when, but not of course before we've finished this job."

With that he left the room, Louise sat there in some shock—a holiday? Usual time off? Did he think she was pregnant? L. Chappel, of course it all made sense now, some routine security checks had found telephone calls from the hospital maternity services advising her of appointment times, and so they assumed she was pregnant. They would look idiotic when Laura had her baby, and she was still slim and trim. Laura's submariner had been in touch and would be back for the birth. Anyway, the usual caveat about taking vacation time was there, "not before we've finished this job."

CHAPTER TWENTY-TWO

Baghdad Airport, Iraq

Anne Marie had been surprisingly supportive of Chloe's request to go to Iraq. It would be an expensive trip. She would need the newspaper's security arrangements with known fixers, drivers, and translators and couldn't consider the trip without those safeguards. Neither of them could have predicted how long it would take to get the visa.

Chloe's flight to Iraq was uneventful, unlike the transition through the airport, with security checks everywhere. Finally, Chloe was clear and went to meet her driver and translator, both engaged for her by the paper. The journey they were about to embark on was dangerous. They were going to cross Route Irish, the most dangerous six-mile transit from any airport in the world. Route Irish was a shooting range, if the American troops didn't get you, well there were suicide bombers, and failing that, nervous private security guards. Chloe put her body armor on, ensured the wind would not displace her voluminous black head-scarf, and made her way to the exit.

The newspaper had booked her into the al Hamra hotel in Baghdad. It was the new hub for international journalists. Other major hotels had been bombed or taken over by the Americans.

She had no idea where Patrick came from, but he gripped her elbow tightly.

"Hello, Chloe, had a good flight?"

"What do you want, Patrick?"

"I'm taking you to Mosul, I'm going to pay off your driver and translator and have them start work at the end of the week."

"Patrick, I gave my word to Anne Marie I would not go chasing down Walid."

"Yes, but she knew you didn't mean it."

"You think we can find something out?" Chloe wanted to believe him.

"Not we—no, we can't get any further, but I believe you could."

Chloe watched as Patrick paid off the driver and translator, and with a hefty tip, judging by their reaction. He turned, picked up her carry-on, and propelled her back into the airport.

"Where are we going?"

"Transport."

"Full of small talk, aren't you?"

"Right now I'm more interested in getting you out of sight. You were expected here today."

"Of course I was expected, you've just paid off the driver and translator."

"Don't ask me how I know, but this little diversion may well save your life. Was your husband completely innocent?"

"I have asked myself that question over and over again and have to conclude he was innocent, and what's more, he didn't support or comply with those urging him to action, nor was he prepared to give in to any form of coercion."

"Come on! We can consider that later. Let's go! You can call me Patrick but my role and my papers state I am Patrick Dufrene, your translator, and it is important we stick to that script. Okay?"

"Why?"

"I don't think the Americans would take too kindly to my using their transport system for my own ends."

"American transport?"

"We don't get a lot of choice; we have to go with what's available, and this is more like a war zone when it comes to transport."

They made their way through the airport and on to Landing Zone Washington, a field of concrete where two Black Hawk helicopters were waiting. Eleven soldiers, with duffel bags, M-16s, and helmets, all wearing body armor, climbed on board, followed by Chloe and Patrick. There were four canvas sling seats in each row and Patrick sat next to the soldiers leaving her the aisle seat.

The whine of the engines was mind numbing and she wondered about the possibility of getting her earplugs out of the carry-on on Patrick's lap. He had put his own small backpack under the seat. Chloe decided to wait until they were airborne and see if the noise abated any.

Chloe reckoned it would take about three hours to get to Mosul, and was surprised when they landed a few minutes later, but it was to refuel. They disembarked and waited behind a concrete barrier. Chloe got her bag off Patrick and took out her earplugs, though she didn't think anything would block out the noise, it vibrated into your body, like a jackhammer through concrete.

They landed an hour later. They couldn't have arrived at Mosul yet. Patrick urged her forward and they disembarked.

"Welcome to Forward Operation Base Balad."

"Is this near Mosul?"

"Not exactly. But we aren't flying scheduled air, or even cheap bucket shop. Think of it as hitchhiking, you just have to go where the ride takes you. It's okay as long as it will help you connect to the next ride."

They wandered off toward the operations office, a temporary unit under a camouflage net. The female administrator gave her a surprised look. *The novelty of a woman traveling,* she supposed.

Chloe left the conversation to Patrick and was dismayed to find the next flight would be in the morning. Bone weary, and head throbbing from the helicopter, it didn't matter, just as long as Patrick could negotiate somewhere safe and quiet to sleep.

Patrick beckoned her to follow him, and they made their way across a muddy path to another terrapin building. He checked the number on the key fob, unlocked the door, and they entered a tiny room with two bunk beds.

"Top or bottom?"

"Um..."

"Okay—so top it is for you."

"I don't suppose you found anything so civilized as a shower?"

"For you? My dear." He gestured for her to follow him.

Chloe showered, changed into clean underwear, put the khaki trousers and jacket back on and left the body armor and the rest of her gear packed on the floor, ready for a hasty exit should it be needed. It was wonderful to take off the body armor, she had never had to wear it for such a long period and her breasts were sore. *Are all war correspondents flat chested? Or is there a trick to these things?*

She clambered onto the top bunk and fell asleep immediately. It seemed no time at all before Patrick was shaking her.

"Wake up, it's time to go."

They waited in the office for the transfer bus and everyone piled in, the soldiers from the night before looking bright and cheery, sipping coffee. *What is it about Americans? They always manage to turn up to flights holding Styrofoam cups of coffee with neat sippy lids. Don't they ever learn to drink from cups without lids?* She thought Patrick had been lacking in initiative not to forage for some coffee or food.

It was cold in the helicopter, but the heat from the bodies crammed together soon took effect and she was grateful she had the aisle seat.

They landed at Tikrit, exchanged the current caffeine loaded soldiers for some freshly laundered ones and set off again; arriving two hours later at Forward Operating Base Diamondback on the south side of Mosul.

Patrick sent a signal from some electronic wizardry and a local turned up in his battered truck. Patrick and the driver exchanged quiet words in Arabic, and Chloe wished she knew what they were talking about.

"We'll get something to eat here and you could shower too, if you like."

"Food would be good, but I'd like to get on and get back. Anne Marie will be worried sick I have disappeared." She was beginning to think this trip would be a waste of time. It all seemed surreal; the nervous soldiers with their body odor, the military helicopters, Patrick pretending to be a translator. She didn't see how she could do anything Patrick and his colleagues in the DST or DGSE hadn't already.

"Do we get an opportunity to talk?" Chloe knew it was important she didn't say anything to blow his cover, but she was curious as to what her role was and why.

"Shortly."

They left the house by truck, which had all the advantages of being a local vehicle, and less noticeable. Chloe was acutely aware personal safety was a key issue. She was wearing khaki trousers with a light sweater and the flak jacket under a black full-length winter coat and black headscarf. Patrick, who had thought of everything, had provided the new coat. He was determined they would not stand out and it was clear he was tense and watchful of all going on around them.

The driver dropped them off in the square opposite the bazaar. Chloe followed Patrick across to a teahouse. She kept her eyes lowered and talked in a low voice with Patrick. How could she judge his honesty? Her instincts relied on eye contact.

They took their seats at a table and ordered tea.

"We managed to track Walid as far as a visit to a stall in the bazaar after his trip to the museum. There was no point in further interviewing museum staff; they have nothing to offer. However, this stall in the ba-

zaar has information, but they are afraid. I'm hoping your visit will enable us to get more information."

"But if everything I say has to be translated by you, how is this going
to work?"

"Someone in that market stall will be able to hold a conversation
with you."

"Let's go."

"Be patient, everything moves slowly here, and it pays to take time to
check."

When Patrick was satisfied, he got up and she followed him into the
bazaar, always keeping a couple of paces behind him. Normally Chloe
would have enjoyed the experience of buying local food, haggling in the
process, but they didn't stop as they made their way to the stall. The bazaar wasn't busy, but there were enough people walking purposefully
through the aisles for Chloe to have to move out of the way of oncoming men. Patrick stood in the walkway past the stall, looking at rugs,
while she looked at the artifacts. Certainly, this stall would have attracted Walid. She was unable to tell if the tiles were old or copies but Walid
would have known.

A man approached her and she debated the etiquette of talking to
him, but had to establish some communication.

"I'm sorry, I'm French, and I don't speak any Arabic. Do you speak
any French or English?"

"Wait." He went into the back of the stall.

"Can I help you?"

She looked up and could have done a double take; it was like looking
at Omar Sharif in his Dr Zhivago era.

"I am looking for my husband."

"I am sorry, I don't know any French nationals." He turned away.

"No, wait—he's Algerian, and missing. He came to visit the museum.
He would be interested in buying Islamic artifacts. He might have come
to your stall to buy pots and tiles."

The man turned back toward her, reacting to the desperation in her voice. She reached into her coat pocket, and he drew back.

"It's all right; I'm looking for a photograph."

She handed him a picture of Walid looking happy, taken on the beach at Siesta Key. The shock and fear on the stallholder's face surprised her.

"And this man is married to you?"

"Yes." There was no point going into explanations, she wasn't going to lie about a conversion to Islam, she was just looking for information.

"I wish Allah the merciful may help you find him."

"When was he here?"

"I have not seen this man."

"I think you recognized him. You were shocked because he is my husband—but I think you do know him." There was a pause and although she should have lowered her eyes, she returned his gaze, hoping to convey her need to find Walid.

"He was here, but he left in peace."

"Where did he go?"

"Chechnya, Afghanistan, Pakistan? I do not know, a man like that does not tell anyone his plans."

"No, this man would have been open about his plans. He was supposed to go back to Baghdad. Did he mention going back to Baghdad?"

"I will ask anyone else that saw him what he said. Meet me here, tomorrow morning at eight."

Chloe left and followed Patrick through the bazaar, stopping at various stalls to purchase food and coffee.

"Well?" he eventually asked.

"Confusing; but I need to go back tomorrow morning at eight."

"We'll be on our way back to Baghdad tomorrow at that time."

"But he might have more information."

"He recognized the picture of Walid; I think we have all the information we need. He was here."

Chloe wanted to argue but the driver arrived to take them back to the suburbs where Patrick made a tasty lamb dish with the ingredients he bought in the bazaar. Chloe was impressed. The man who lived in the house also seemed appreciative of Patrick's culinary skills. They retired early, Chloe's body clock didn't know if it was dawn or dusk, but she was ready for bed.

She slept restlessly, dreaming about Walid and the man in the bazaar. *The phrase "a man like that," what did he mean? Why did he think of Walid in those terms? It sounded menacing, but he recognized the photograph. How had Patrick known he had recognized the photograph?* Walid drifted in and out of her dreams, she was chasing him through the alleyways of the bazaar, catching glimpses of him, but he was always gone when she got there.

Chloe woke up feeling tired, got dressed quickly, re-packed her bag, and they left in the truck, making their way to FOB Diamondback.

"There's a transporter going direct to Baghdad in an hour."

Chloe wanted to talk to Patrick. Why hadn't they gone back to the bazaar? Bloody spooks, they jumped at their own shadow.

The C-130 was certainly a more civilized and quicker way to travel in Iraq and they landed in Baghdad an hour later.

"Why couldn't we have done that going out?"

"Because this is Iraq, there are no internal flights, there are no schedules, and no passenger lists. We did okay."

She supposed he was right but she wanted to talk to him and knowing Patrick, he would just disappear when they got back.

They ran the gauntlet of the six-mile terror strip from the airport to Baghdad in a small armored personnel carrier with some American soldiers, who seemed to be expecting them. They deposited Chloe and Patrick outside the hotel. The hotel was ten stories high, creamy concrete and glass. It was a place where security was taken seriously, gray concrete walls had been built in front of the hotel to lessen the effects of a car bomb. Three hotel security guards inspected them and their paperwork carefully. Satisfied, they allowed them through and Chloe checked in. It felt relaxed after the tensions of the last couple of days traveling and Chloe was impatient to get to her room.

Chloe didn't comment when Patrick came upstairs to examine her hotel room. She felt confident she wouldn't attract any more or less attention than any other journalist. Her room was on the sixth floor and when they arrived, he pushed past her and entered first, took out a piece of kit that looked like a cell phone, and proceeded to walk around the room. It wasn't a large room and it didn't take long. Chloe watched him in silence. He beckoned her to go to the bathroom, where he put on the bathtub and basin taps and flushed the toilet.

"Thanks for checking the plumbing."

"Okay, Chloe, your room is bugged. As I said to you before, you appear to be expected and that is a dangerous position to be in."

"So what did you learn about Walid?" Chloe waited while Patrick decided what to say.

He eventually replied, "If he was in the bazaar recently, who are the Americans holding?"

"The Americans? Did you tell them he was engaged in money laundering?" Patrick usually made sense, but she didn't understand his question about the Americans.

"No. But they did make the link and they have a habit of picking up anyone they want to question and sort of borrowing them.""You mean kidnapping." Chloe was furious. If the Americans were holding Walid, what was the point of the trip to Mosul?

"No, because that would imply demands. No, the Americans have a term for this, they call it 'extreme rendition.' Usually they say nothing at all about the person, they just disappear and at some later point reappear—well, with any luck."

"So where is Walid?"

"That's the point, I am not sure if it is Walid, or whether Walid was in Mosul. But the Americans are holding someone who looks a lot like Walid in Afghanistan."

"So get him back."

"He isn't a French citizen."

"So..."

"So that makes it complicated." Patrick looked away, embarrassed by the situation. "What are you investigating?"

"Missing Iraqi scientists. Just as you suggested."

"I didn't say come here—I thought you could do some desk research. You won't find them. They probably did a runner to Syria or maybe they were all killed by Israeli hit squads in the confusion and aftermath of the war."

"Is that for the record?"

"Don't be ridiculous. How many people know why you are here?"

"Several, at the paper."

"Who exactly?"

"Anne Marie, Jean Pierre, my sub editor, the fixer, translator, and driver here...I think that's about it."

"Umm. Obviously it's not a popular assignment. I suggest you go home, I'll see if I can find anything on the record. But go home. Shower, change, and I'll get you transport back to the airport now."

"The problem with spooks is they believe all this cloak and dagger stuff."

"Do you realize how easy it would be to kidnap you?"

"Well, with my driver and translator alongside me I don't feel too vulnerable—oh no, wait, you dispensed with their services until tomorrow."

"Chloe."

"Don't Chloe me—just what has this jaunt to Mosul achieved?"

"Actually, a great deal. But please just shower, change, and get packed up, ready to leave and we can discuss this some more."

"There is no discussion. I came here to do a job. It's a job I intend to finish."

Patrick looked around as if assessing the situation.

"Last call for a simple, safe trip home?"

"Goodbye, Patrick."

She watched Patrick leave the room, and had an overwhelming desire to go after him and go home. But instead, she turned off the taps and went to unpack the few possessions she had in her bag.

CHAPTER TWENTY-THREE

Baghdad, Iraq

The next morning she awoke with a feeling of foreboding. Was it going to be like some of the other investigations into disappearing scientists, a lot of suspicion and little substantiated facts? What if the driver and translator didn't turn up? What would she do? You couldn't just get a taxi.

Reception phoned at eight prompt to say there were two visitors in the lobby. Great, they were here and on time. Her fixer had done a great job in sorting out three interviews with the new ministers in the Iraqi Governing Council. These cabinet ministers had only been in place since the beginning of September, and the first interview was with the Minister for Higher Education and she planned to ask him about the brain drain of academics into Syria. However, the supplementary questions would be into the disappearance of government scientists. She had an interview with a leading scientist at the university, again to ask about disappearing scientists, and finally, a visit to a baby formula factory, which was reputed to have made chemical weapons in the past. It was going to be a busy day.

Chloe went into the lobby where Halim, the translator, met her and took her to the car where Faruk, the driver, waited. With over one hundred and thirty-five journalists killed in Iraq, every interview was set up with care and you could only hope your security was sufficient. She could have engaged a security company and had an armed guard, but that drew attention to your presence and she preferred to be low key and unobtrusive. Some reporters used a two-car system, traveling in the first car with a second car with security following and able to make a getaway with the reporter if necessary.

As they arrived in the square, they were running a little early, and Faruk drew to a halt so that a small truck could pull out of an entryway. Several men around the rear of the truck were guiding it back. Although they had stopped a suitable distance from the maneuver, the security detail came toward them, handguns drawn. It was a familiar scene; security companies were nervous and carried out their duties with dangerous zeal. Although uneasy, Faruk and Halim were not concerned at this stage. However, as they approached the car, they didn't lower their guns; Halim and Faruk raised their hands and got out of the car slowly so as not to cause alarm.

Chloe knew this was no security detail; she tried to get out of the car. A man with a gun motioned for her to stay where she was. Inwardly she was shocked; nothing prepares you for the reality of a kidnap.

Everything seemed to happen in slow motion. She wanted to call out, but her mouth was dry. It wouldn't have made any difference. Two gunmen appeared from the rear of the truck sporting AK-47 rifles and approached Halim and Faruk who were now kneeling on the road and struck them on the backs of their heads. They fell forward into the dust, and lay motionless. She felt guilty for endangering them. She hoped that if all these militants wanted was a foreign journalist, perhaps her captors would let them go without further harm.

The two gunmen got into the back of the car and sat on either side of her. She felt numb. Chloe kept repeating a few well-rehearsed Arabic phrases, "I am your friend, and I mean you no harm, why are you doing this?" It was pointless but the chant gave her some comfort. She was reassured she was doing what she had been trained to do in these circumstances. The newspaper sent anyone traveling overseas on a "Staying Safe" course. It covered simple things like not showing how much money you were carrying, to not looking for alcohol in an Islamic country, to self-defense. The day spent on how to deal with a kidnapping seemed irrelevant at the time she took it. Her instructor had made her practice and practice.

"You need to be able to do things on automatic pilot, your body and mind will shut down with shock when it happens; you have to have faith in your training." She could only hope the captors had read the same counter-terrorist handbook and knew what to do next. If their purpose was to kill her immediately, she was wasting her breath.

They didn't hear her, or if they did, they ignored her. The excitement of a successful mission had left her captors triumphant and joyful. "Allahu Akbar," was the exultant call. Chloe was surprised, they looked like amateurs, and it reminded her of Dick and Jane's celebration in the film, after the first bank robbery, when they couldn't quite believe they had done it. Chloe wasn't sure if this made her feel more or less safe. They were clearly jumpy and right now, they were jubilant. The AK-47's had been obtained from somewhere, this might be their first kidnap operation but they weren't idiots.

It was easy to sit in a training room and have a trainer explain why it was so important to keep calm—your abductors will be excited, fearful, and your life will depend on you keeping the situation calm—and quite another to be in the situation.

Finally, one of the gunmen spoke to her. "We mean you no harm. You are a prisoner of war, we treat our prisoners with honor." His English had an East London accent.

"You speak good English."

"I studied engineering at a university in London. But that's enough. Be quiet." Her captor didn't want to become her friend. She supposed it would be difficult for him to kill her if he liked her. She knew she should cultivate his friendship. It was good to know that at least one of them spoke English.

How did kidnapping a journalist constitute no harm? They progressed in silence. She thought about the journalists who didn't go through a hostage process. Perhaps no harm meant she would be a hostage—but for how long? Statistically you were more likely to be killed than let go, and rescue attempts were rare.

They arrived at a tiny house built of cinder blocks, in one of the poorest areas of western Baghdad. She was directed to the bathroom where the woman of the house looked on in a disapproving manner as Chloe changed into the new clothes she was given. *Is this woman determined not to like me? Are they about to kill me?* It didn't make sense. *Why would I be asked to change clothes?* The intention seemed to be to keep her alive, for now. The woman picked up her clothes, disdainful of the slacks and top, but she clearly liked the new scarf and the coat. Chloe questioned everything, looking for clues as to her future, but not finding any answers.

Her captors had also had a change of clothes, no longer in the black uniforms of a security company, but the ubiquitous check shirts, nondescript pants and well-worn jackets. When they got outside, the modern Toyota, Faruk's pride and joy, had gone. In its place was a dusty Toyota Corona popular in the 1970s. The kidnappers had a plan and were carrying out all the necessary steps to prevent her being found. Chloe was now dressed like a local and unlikely to draw any attention. Patrick could have told the authorities what she had been wearing, not that a black coat and black headscarf were distinctive. She thought about Patrick—he had warned her she was in harm's way. *How did he know? Had he orchestrated this event? Am I getting close to finding the evidence implicating the secret intelligence services in illegal killings?* Her mind was racing, and she was trying to note information about where she was being taken.

They drove.

"Keep your head down."

The kidnapper put his hand on the back of her head, forcing her to look at the floor of the car.

When they arrived at the next house, it was larger and had two floors. They made her go upstairs to the main bedroom; this was to be her prison cell. She was told to sit on the mat in the middle of the floor; the instructions had been in Arabic so she was confused, and it was only through gestures that she grasped what she was supposed to do. She understood some Arabic but it was limited. She sat with her head bowed, partly praying, partly trying to remember all she had been trained to do and wondering what she could say to make a difference.

A few minutes later, the English-speaking kidnapper arrived and the interrogation commenced. What was her name? What was the name of her newspaper? These questions led her to believe they had wanted any journalist, and they hadn't singled her out for any sinister reason. This was nothing to do with her investigation, nothing to do with Walid, it was just business as usual, Iraqi style. The questions continued about her religion, did she drink alcohol? She could honestly reply she now abstained from alcohol. Walid's influence might just save her life.

They had wrongly assumed she was an American and when she pointed out she was French, this appeared to cause some momentary confusion and disappointment, but after a brief discussion they seemed to conclude it wouldn't matter.

"We want the women freed from Abu Ghraib prison. We want you to ask the Americans to do this for your freedom. Women are respected in Islam."

Capturing one woman to secure the freedom of others was an irony not lost on her.

Would it be possible to escape? They had taken her laptop, and her BlackBerry was either in her black coat or had fallen out of her pocket in the commotion at the little house.

She was certain now these were terrorists, and it was not a secret intelligence operation. She thought about Patrick's words, he had said he knew she was expected. The Americans didn't want her to publish, the Israelis probably weren't too keen on her inquiries, and she was uncertain about the British and French. At least when she took on the Mafia it had been a single entity.

Six men arrived carrying a large white sheet, which they unfolded. She thought about the photograph that had brought her to Iraq in the first place. *Is this going to be my burial shroud?* Perhaps they were going to wrap up a rug and make an insurance claim, and Jean Pierre would be proved right.

Chloe was relieved when she realized her cell was about to become a film studio. There was much discussion about where the best place would be to set up the camera, and how to achieve the best lighting. Again, she had the feeling they hadn't done this before and were anxious to get it right.

The English-speaking captor gave Chloe a script and told her exactly how to say what was on the card. He made her rehearse the part several times until they felt the performance created the desired effect. Chloe did everything they asked of her, she cried when they asked her to plead for her life. It had not been hard to cry on cue.

Afterward they brought her some chicken and rice and she ate with the family downstairs. They seemed anxious to make her feel an honored guest, and that they were good.

It could have been easy to like this family in different circumstances. She thought about her trainer talking about Stockholm syndrome, a psychological phenomenon where captives felt empathy and sympathy with their captors. It was a difficult balance, on one hand you were taught to bond with your captors so they were less likely to kill you, on the other hand you were planning to escape and realized any rescue attempt would probably result in fatalities. Her thoughts went back to the way the two gunmen had used the rifle butts of the AK-47 to hit Halim and

Faruk. She wondered if they were alive. Her captors were not her friends.

In the early hours of the morning, the sound of gunfire woke her up. The Americans were obviously mounting some form of operation in the area.

The leader, who had been directing operations at the tiny house yesterday, came into her room. The woman of the household accompanied him.

"Chloe, the American soldiers are close. Do you know why they are here?"

She kept her eyes lowered and shook her head. "No."

"Do you have a cell phone? Or did you use your laptop to bring the Americans here?"

The enormity of his suggestion dawned on her. He thought she was orchestrating her rescue with the Americans and if that was the case, he might as well kill her and have the propaganda of the video. She was chilled and pulled the bedcovers closer to her.

"No. You have my phone and laptop, how can I be using them? You have my clothes. I am not in control of anything I brought with me."

"Do you have a chip planted in your hair?"

"No, let the woman come into the bathroom with me, she can search me."

"If the chip is planted in your skin we won't find it."

"I don't know why the Americans are here." Chloe started to cry, she noticed this man didn't like it when she cried, he gave her tissues when they made the film, it was clear he just wanted to achieve their objectives. She wondered if it was personal. *Does he have a wife, a sister, or friend held in the American prison?*

The woman said something and he withdrew. She approached and threw replacement clothes at Chloe for the new day. This woman was not impressed with her crying and clearly did not like or trust her, the feeling was mutual.

Chloe went into the bathroom washed, dressed, and returned. A little girl of about eight brought up a tray with her breakfast, a green and red pepper with onion omelet with pita bread and fresh coffee. *Is this going to be my last meal?*

It was not long before the leader came back; he had an AK-47 rifle with him this time. If he were going to kill her, at least it would be quick, anything was better than the knife or the sword. The smell of the coffee remained. *Is this my final memory?*

When her colleagues had been abducted and killed in Iraq, Chloe had felt she should honor their deaths by watching the Al Jazeera broadcasts of the beheadings. How wrong she had been. It perpetuated the terror. She realized she could respect those who had died without the mental pictures. She knew what had happened to them, and she didn't need a graphic image engraved in her brain for eternity. He motioned to her to not make a sound and follow him downstairs.

"The Americans are close, don't make a sound or I will kill you." Her English-speaking captor talked low and sounded tense. Now was the moment when she had an ability to influence things. She wondered if her training was correct. Her instinct was to shout out, "Over here!"

"Please don't kill me, I'll make another video, I'm useless to you dead. I don't know why the Americans are here. It's just a coincidence. Please don't kill me."

"We aren't going to kill you, but we need to have you where we can see you, and away from the window."

They pointed to a plastic garden chair and she sat down. Chloe kept her head lowered; she didn't want to give them any excuse to kill her. The jubilation of yesterday was gone, and they were clearly worried the Americans were searching for her.

There was a whispered discussion, they seemed to be discussing where was the best place to be, one man felt she should be in the basement, and there was some discussion about why it was inappropriate. The woman and the little girl left. Both looked scared. Chloe's life was in danger, and it was endangering them too. The leader and the two men cocked their guns and looked apprehensive.

The next moment there was a sound of breaking glass, the room filled with acrid smoke and sharp bangs as if someone had let a firecracker off in the room. She was choking and the tears were streaming down her face. Chloe knew the drill; she needed to drop to the floor. She was in as much danger of being killed by the Americans as the Iraqis at that moment. The air was clearer on the floor, she crouched, curled in a ball making herself as small as possible, watching; the door flew open and in came six soldiers all in full combat gear with respirators. Chloe put her hands over her head. Guns flashed from both sides, and her captors were shot.

The soldiers located Chloe and took her out through the front door to a waiting medical truck.

"Thank you. Thank you. There was a little girl in there! Is she all right?" She sounded as if she was far away, talking in a dream. Was she dead? She decided the stun grenades had affected her hearing.

The soldier went back into the house to check and after what seemed a long time, he returned.

"There's no sign of any women, or a little girl—perhaps they left."

Chloe shrugged and he mimed his answer to her, she thanked the soldier and hoped they were safe.

After a couple of minutes of treatment, which largely consisted of a cooling liquid being dropped into her eyes and an oxygen mask being held over her face, they were on their way to Baghdad airport.

At the airport, Patrick Dubois met her and for one brief moment, she considered if he was behind her abduction, but it didn't make any sense. It was a case of being in the wrong place at the right time. He spoke to her but she was unable to hear him, her ears were still ringing.

He took out a pad and wrote:

You're going to Germany, to Landstuhl base, so you can tell the Americans any information to help them round up all those responsible. Are you okay?

Chloe said, "I'm sort of okay—what happened to Halim and Faruk?"

Patrick gave her a thumbs-up sign.

Her ordeal had lasted two days, she hadn't been treated badly, she had nothing to be traumatized about, but two days can seem an eternity when your life is in the balance.

CHAPTER TWENTY-FOUR

MI5, London

Graeme looked thunderous. He came out of his office, a bull at full charge.

"Briefing room!"

Whatever happened to niceties, like, "Good morning, Louise, did you have a nice weekend? Are you feeling okay?" The phantom pregnancy perks were clearly over. Someone in personnel would have a red face over that mistake.

"Perhaps you better tell me what's been going on," Graeme demanded.

"Art Expert's wife went to Iraq earlier than we had expected, but we arranged to have her kidnapped. We had replaced the driver and translator and arranged to abduct her in the six miles out of the airport to Baghdad in the confusion of a roadside bombing—blanks but lots of noise and smoke, the usual thing. But..."

"Yeah, I bet this is going to be a big but..."

"Patrick was waiting for her at the airport."

"Patrick?"

"Patrick Dubois as in DST Patrick."

"What the hell was he doing there? And why is he always in the wrong place at the right time? What did you do? Did you sell tickets to this event?"

"I don't know but he paid off the translator and driver and spirited Chloe Moreau away. The reports are coming in; information is a bit slow I'm afraid, but it would appear they took the Black Hawk route to Mosul and came back to Baghdad on a Hercules."

"Then what?"

"She checked into the hotel. When she went out for an appoint-ment—"

"What appointment?"

"I'm not sure. Well, they—"

"Who are 'they'?"

"The translator and driver and of course Chloe, well they were stopped at a roadblock, we think, the translator and driver were knocked unconscious—"

"What, the Americans took her at a roadblock?"

"No... She was abducted, but because Patrick had a bug in her coat and they followed her part of the way, they—"

"Who are 'they'?"

Louise looked down wearily at her notes, she didn't know why Graeme couldn't just let her give a report and then ask questions, most of which would be answered in due course anyway, instead of flustering her in this way. He had been home for some sleep and Louise was func-tioning on coffee—large amounts of it.

"Iraqi extremists. We sent a patrol into the area and eventually found her and she is now detained, safe, and out of harm's way."

"Where precisely is she detained?"

"At Landstuhl Regional Medical Center, Germany."

"How does that plan match up with a new Islamic extreme group tak-ing her hostage? Don't you think she will know where she is being held?

So you have now involved us in a diplomatic incident with France—no wonder Patrick is coming in, presumably to protest."

"It was nothing to do with me, it's just what happened."

"You don't think such a drastic change from anything that had been agreed should have been discussed with me first?"

"I didn't change anything. I had a plan ready, but I didn't put it into action because of Patrick. I asked you for a moment to discuss details and tell you about this, and you said to trust my judgment and handle stuff. So I did. But events overtook my plan."

"I am quite sure you must have exhibited some value based decision-making skills when they assessed you for this job. I find it difficult to believe the psychologists could have got your profile so wrong. This is a major problem with the potential for a political storm. So you're going home for the rest of the day."

"But... I did my job. It was a genuine kidnapping attempt and nothing to do with the plan we discussed. I knew you wanted her detained and so she is awaiting a debriefing at the center and if you had been at work yesterday we could all have made progress." Louise was furious, what could she say to make him understand this was nothing to do with her?

"And what's she doing there?"

Louise looked at her watch. "I don't know. Maybe she's sleeping."

"Enough! Look, the only way out of this mess is for me to claim a junior officer exceeded her authority, which won't be wrong, will it? The only acceptable solution is to show we are reconsidering your position here—so you are formally suspended. Go home, relax, and don't talk to anyone. I'll have to send someone from security with you, standard procedure."

Louise picked up her purse, her cell phone, and left. Was Graeme listening? This was nothing to do with her; he couldn't hold her responsible for security issues in Iraq—that was crazy. Why couldn't he listen?

*

Graeme went across to the phone.

"Get me Landstuhl Regional Medical Center, Germany—it's an American medical facility... Duty officer... No, it's urgent." He waited, drumming his fingers on the desk. "Sorry, can you repeat your name again?" Graeme wrote it down. "What's the situation with the detainee?"

"Which one?" An American voice tried to sound helpful.

"How many have you got—no don't answer that. How many pretty French journalists do you have currently in your facility?"

"Ah, the lovely... She is calm, eating, showering, and so far the model patient."

"Calm? Showering? I thought she was sedated."

"No, that isn't necessary; in fact, she's doing okay. We would normally be discharging her, but we've had to wait on CIA clearance and for the French to get here, they are picking her up in the next few days."

"Right, I'll be in touch."

He had no jurisdiction; Chloe might have dual citizenship, but as she was currently living in France and had traveled to Iraq on her French passport, the DST would sort it out. He just wished he could be sure Louise's activities had nothing to do with what happened. He couldn't tell if she was lying.

Graeme saw the alert on his computer screen telling him he had a guest in the arrivals hall, and he waved at a junior employee across the office who went down to reception to collect Patrick. Graeme gathered his thoughts. He would need his boss in on this. He went across to James T's office.

"A word." He quickly briefed James T on the issues in Iraq.

"So what's your strategy?"

"I think we'll see what Patrick has to say first, but if it's going to be a high level incident I think we need to cut Louise loose and contain the issue as fast as possible. I need to see how close we are to getting Art Expert released. I know it's high on Patrick's agenda—maybe we can do a deal."

"I don't think Louise would lie. I'll do some checking and have a note brought through to you."

Graeme left for the interview room.

"Good morning, Patrick."

Patrick leaned across the table and shook hands.

"So what brings you to Thames House?"

"Walid Merbarkia."

"So you have some news."

"Yes, I was in Mosul a couple of days ago, and—surprisingly, considering Merbarkia is enjoying the hospitality of our American cousins in Afghanistan—learned he was seen negotiating some biological weaponry a week ago."

"Is there any confusion over identification?"

"None, it was Chloe's photograph of Merbarkia on holiday taken less than two months ago."

"So you were with Chloe? Right?" Graeme could see a light at the end of the tunnel. He thought telling the Americans Merbarkia might have a brother in Al Qaeda would ensure a lengthy detention while the CIA got information from him.

"I want a bit more than that, Graeme. You see, as Merbarkia is a visual double for this senior Al Qaeda figure, we thought we might use him to flush out a current operation. It's complex, the target seems to be London and maybe the State Opening of Parliament; we're not sure about the date, I expect they are still waiting to see about delivery of materials and availability of operatives."

"Chatter?" Graeme could only hope this was speculation.

"A bit more than chatter. We have a contact with the Chechens via the FSB and it would appear Merbarkia or his double went shopping for some briefcase bombs."

Graeme wondered why the Russians hadn't felt the need to share the information direct with London—or was it the information James T had been talking about months ago? "Hot?"

"Yes, one original refurbished and three new uranium units."

"Shit."

"Mmm… I think it will be a bit more than an annoyance. You could help me with one more item. Merbarkia's wife, Chloe Moreau, seems to have been misplaced. I expect it was a well-meaning incident. When one of our more prominent citizens, and a leading journalist, goes missing, naturally we are concerned. I understood she was going for a debriefing in Germany and would be released yesterday, but…"

"I'll make some inquiries." Graeme hoped he could feign a lack of knowledge and play for time.

"Don't play with me on this. She was wearing one of my lapel pins."

"Really? We are anxious not to be implicated in what was a junior officer's over enthusiastic and unauthorized event."

"What, you don't think Louise is responsible for the kidnapping, do you? I have to say we also had plans to kidnap her, but threw them out. I think we are still cautious after the sinking of the *Rainbow Warrior* in New Zealand. Now that was a plan brushed with stupidity. But it wasn't anything to do with Louise and the Americans have recovered her, she is in Germany, and I want her released immediately. The Americans tell me she is being held at your request. She has dual citizenship and I want her released. The Americans will hear you—being French has little influence at present, they can't even eat French fries, it's Freedom fries, it's all quite ridiculous."

"Um, we have some concerns about her present lines of inquiry." Graeme sought to find a way to work with Patrick on the turn of events in Iraq.

"We have some concerns about her lines of inquiry too, but we have to manage that another way. I'll talk to her editor again, but you have to get her released."

"We are taking steps to arrange that now, but we are using this unfortunate incident to put pressure on the Americans over Merbarkia."

"How?" Patrick grinned. "You mean you're planning to let Chloe think the Americans are responsible for this abduction? I'm afraid that won't work, she knows her captors were genuine Iraqis with a simple agenda, desperate to make changes in the conditions for women detainees."

"Among so many detainees some are bound to be caught up, shall we say, unexpectedly." Graeme raised his eyebrows.

"Let me know how it goes, I won't blow the whistle on what happened. We want to go to Afghanistan and bring Merbarkia back—to try to get as close to him as possible. I am sure you can see the benefit."

"Bagram?" Graeme thought if the CIA had Merbarkia at Bagram no one would be getting close to him.

"No Khandahar."

"We can all be thankful for that."

CHAPTER TWENTY-FIVE

Paris

Ahmed took three Métro trains to ensure no one followed him, before he finally chose a random phone booth to make his call.

"Why are you calling here?"

"One of my couriers has attracted the attention of officials."

"Which one?"

"Merbarkia."

"Has any product been delivered?"

"Yes. Three to London, and the sample is still here." Didn't they know this? Ahmed was surprised at this acknowledgement of incompetence.

"We'll move the Paris sample to London tomorrow. One in place should be enough."

"Same arrangements?"

"No, I'll have someone meet you on the upper level by the taxi stand. Clear?"

"What time?"

"Three. Then you can go, but you need to wait in port for your cargo. Is that clear? You must wait."

Ahmed hung up. He looked around cautiously, and made his way back, slowly looking for any sign of a tail. He saw no one to cause him any concern and laughed when he saw his tail still waiting outside his shop. *I shouldn't let him see me,* so Ahmed used the back entrance.

He phoned the shippers in Iraq, and forwarded the accumulated artifacts to his London warehouse immediately.

*

The surveillance team reported, "Target is back in shop."

"Okay, leave the babysitter in view and come back in."

Martin walked past the surveillance team member watching the front of the shop, smiled at him, and continued on his way to rue de Nélaton.

Patrick looked up from his desk as Martin came in.

"Well?"

"I was glad we had the full team on this one. He took three Métro trains, made one phone call, and returned. I don't think you would take these steps to conceal an affair with a married woman. He's definitely involved."

"Do we know what he said, or who he called?"

"We have the number, Birmingham, England. We're running a check on the address. We are still enhancing the recording of the phone call. But I doubt we'll get much, it was a noisy street. He picked his phone booth with care."

"So what do you think is going on?"

"I would think he is responding to Merbarkia's detainment in Iraq. It could be he was concerned about cash flow—or, of course, it could be one of the artifact packages was going to contain something far more interesting."

"Um... I think I agree with you. I doubt it would be cash flow. My guess would be a delivery. So from now on, we need to open every package for and from the art gallery and forensically check thoroughly for fingerprints, DNA, anything to help. Search every container, package by package. I think we should look out for a new courier. The art gallery can't last long without new stock."

"Do you want me to call Graeme at MI5 to get some information from the Birmingham end of things?"

"No. Let's wait until we have some more definite information. It might be a useful bargaining tool. How long before we get voice enhancement?"

"A couple of hours."

"Right. I want you to make plans to pick up 'Art Gallery'—detailed plans—I think we should assume his shop and apartments have some explosive devices rigged to kill and take us out, which he can trigger remotely or in situ. I want detailed explanations of the how, the where, and the when. Detailed risk assessments—and no one, repeat no one, is to do any fieldwork on this; this is purely desk research at this time. Is that understood? We can't afford for him to take flight. We need to know what types of devices are in the shipments and what the target is. If we time this well, we should get the controller, supply chain, and the cell supplied by this hub, and with any luck the finances raised by this scum."

Martin nodded. He made notes on his pad.

"Oh, and you had better make me an urgent appointment with the senior controller. He will want to be in the loop about these developments. Okay, that's all."

CHAPTER TWENTY-SIX

Landstuhl Medical Center, Germany

It was day five, and Chloe was beginning to wonder what the point of her captivity was. No one spoke to her. A large plastic tub arrived daily containing clean underwear and fresh clothes—the same make and size as she would have chosen, which she thought was very enterprising for a medical debriefing center, until she realized it was her underwear and they had picked up her luggage from the al Hamra hotel, in Baghdad.

Nothing she had done warranted her being locked up. She was an investigative journalist. She was supposed to find deeds committed to defraud and deceive the public. Journalists were supposed to investigate immoderate governments, particularly those that had lost their moral rudder, and keep them in check. *How dare they lock me up and treat me like some doll, going through my possessions and deciding what I should wear for the day.*

It may have been misplaced confidence but she'd had enough and decided to make a fuss. She was more afraid of uncertainty. If they had her luggage they could at least have let her have some books and why not a newspaper? She could be updating her journal, or writing a record of this insane situation.

Chloe began to yell, scream, and dance about. Surely, they—whoever they were—would come in to find out what was wrong.

The door opened, and her mouth dropped open.

"Patrick!"

"Good morning, Chloe. Anything wrong?"

"Anything wrong? Is this your doing? Are you responsible for holding me here?"

"No."

"That's all you have to say?"

"Perhaps you would like to calm down and we can talk about it. Would you like some coffee?"

"Patrick, it may have escaped your notice, but I am a prisoner here and they don't serve coffee to order."

"I'll take that to be a yes."

He turned to the camera and held up two fingers. If they were British, the sign was not polite, if American then he had probably not insulted them.

"Another chair would be good," he said in the direction of the camera. He pointed at her chair and indicated his need of another chair in the exaggerated way people using CCTV for communication seemed to adopt.

The chair arrived first, and they sat down at the table; Patrick turned to the camera and motioned for them to turn the camera off. He waited expectantly and sure enough, the small red light went off.

"All right, Chloe, now we have some privacy. You are clearly mad about what has happened, and I don't blame you. I did try to warn you, although this was not a scenario I had envisaged. Have you been treated all right?"

"You don't think imprisonment is all right, do you?"

"As soon as I knew you had been taken, I engineered your rescue."

"Have you been successful? The fact we are having this discussion inside this cell suggests not."

"It's rather complicated."

"Not really, Patrick..." Chloe paused as a girl in beige slacks and a blue shirt brought in the coffee.

"Thank you, Louise. Chloe here is rather angry at her treatment, so I suggest you beat a hasty retreat. Was there anything else you wanted, Chloe?"

"Yes, I want my luggage—all of it. I don't want to be given clothes to wear each day."

Louise nodded and left.

"Chloe, the situation, your situation, is all wrapped up in Walid's status."

"Have you found him? Is he okay? Is he free?" Chloe couldn't keep the anxiety out of her voice.

"Yes, we have located him. I'm not quite sure how to answer the question about is he okay. He had a heart attack while he was in Iraq and has been undergoing treatment." Patrick watched to see how she received this news, and could not detect any reaction.

"You mean it wasn't extreme rendition at all? He's just been in an Iraqi hospital all this time?" Chloe was finding it hard to follow Patrick. She was very tired.

"Well, no... the good news is the American hospital treated him, saved his life, and the surgery they performed will give him several more years, but life hasn't been kind to him, he's not well."

"Is he free?"

"No, I had hoped to pick you up from here and take you to Afghanistan—"

"Afghanistan? I thought you said he was in Iraq?" Chloe wasn't sure if she was being obtuse or Patrick was obfuscating the issue.

"He was, but now he's in Afghanistan."

"What's he doing there?"

"He's helping the Americans with their inquiries, I believe the saying is."

"Please don't tell me this is spook speak for being tortured."

"No. He's okay. As soon as the Americans are finished with him he'll be back home."

"So you're not taking me to Afghanistan."

"No. I need to know what we are going to do with you."

"You mean you are not here to take me home? No, of course not! That's why we're having this conversation in a cell."

"Chloe, I need you to help me, and I need you to encourage Walid to tell the Americans everything he knows, whether he thinks it is important or not."

"He's helping? Walid? You must be mistaken. They must have the wrong man. They must have the man the market vendor thought was Walid."

"No, that man is Walid's brother."

"Walid would never betray his brother."

"Correct, he won't tell the Americans anything."

"Did it ever occur to them that perhaps he doesn't have any information?"

"I'm sure it did."

"It stinks." Chloe got up and started to pace around the room.

"War has an unpleasant odor."

"Am I being held by the Americans?"

"Why do you ask?"

"Every now and then I hear British voices."

"I don't suppose there's a lot of difference." Chloe thought this was an odd response from Patrick. There was a world of difference between the British and the Americans.

"So what happens to me now?" She realized her chest was tight and she was breathing slowly. It was probably after effects from the stun grenade, or stress from the abduction. Chloe wanted him to say the ordeal was over. *Oh God, please let it be over.*

"That's up to you. I understand you intend to be based in Oxford, so Walid can work at the foundation."

"What, are you reading my mail now? Is that how low the spooks have fallen in France?"

"Chloe, I am going to cut you some slack because I know I would be, to say the least, a little grumpy in your situation."

"Oh thanks!" She sat down again.

"Sarcasm doesn't become you. You should move to England, Walid should be home shortly, that is—"

"How is moving to England going to help?"

"It will, for a start the Brits will be able to apply more pressure on the Americans which—"

"So I'm just to be a pawn..."

"Aren't we all just pawns?"

"You never seem to be a pawn, Patrick." Chloe knew she had let the conversation sink to a petty low level, and found herself unable to rise above her feelings of anger. This was pure bullying; even knowing no harm was going to come to her, she didn't feel safe. She wanted to be out of detention. For all she knew they could have moved her to Afghanistan while she was unconscious. She had no real options but to comply.

"Get settled in Oxford, don't publish anything controversial or sensitive about secret intelligence services and biological weapons scientists and I will work every day to get Walid back quickly. Without my assistance the Americans are likely to keep Walid for months, validating everything they are told against anything he knows."

"That's ridiculous, he knows nothing. What do you mean, don't publish anything controversial? What's controversial? Wearing green this spring, because you think everyone should be wearing pink? What kind of agreement do you want? You need to be specific, otherwise I will be reduced to writing about sports results and the weather." Chloe was shocked Patrick was suggesting some link between what she wrote as a journalist and Walid's detention. He hadn't suggested any breach of national security in her investigation, so she was still free to publish her findings, but Walid wouldn't be getting home anytime soon. She thought about Walid's decision to let his wife die rather than give in to the terrorists' demands, she thought she knew what he would say if he had been present.

She wished she had filed the divorce papers. At least Patrick wouldn't think she could be manipulated in this way. She wanted to say she had no interest in Walid, but she was still married and felt an obligation, old fashioned values drilled into her, and she seemed unable to just say, "So what, I don't care about Walid, and I'll publish whatever my editor likes." She felt this answer would leave her in detention for psychiatric evaluation, and so maybe it wasn't all about Walid, perhaps her reasoning came from self-interest.

"I need you to stop investigating the intelligence services with links to the deaths of bio-med scientists. As for Walid's innocence, you might be right. We are working on options to get him home, you have to believe that."

"And me?"

"I'll need you to sign a confidentiality agreement, we are anxious to keep the method of your release and your time here secret."

"I see. How did you find me?"

"There was a listening device in the black coat, which is how I knew what happened in the bazaar and how the Americans found you."

"But they made me change clothes. They took the black coat away."

"Yes, but although they burned your own clothes, the mother wouldn't let them burn the coat and scarf, and she had them with her. They were new, and she wanted them. A plan foiled by a woman wanting something nice for herself. I don't suppose she's seen anything new for a long time. So we followed the device to find you and mounted an operation for your release. It nearly all went wrong when the woman and child left the house. But in the end, it was a successful operation."

"Thank you. I have one other question."

"Yes?"

"I have a very clear photo of you in black combat gear last month; you'd been following me on my way to the office. I'm sure you remember the day, I was carrying a Target shopping bag."

"Yes, I remember the day, you took a taxi."

"And your reason for following me?"

"I was there to protect you."

"That's fairly easy to say now, isn't it?"

Patrick smiled, and Chloe knew she wouldn't get information from him and she couldn't prove what he had to say.

"Protect me from what?"

"I think you know, as I understand it from Anne Marie, you were mugged later that day."

"You discussed this with her?"

"I wouldn't say discussed, she was furious, because if I had been there to protect you, clearly I hadn't been very successful."

Chloe shook her head, he was like Teflon, nothing stuck to him.

"Why are you so anxious to protect the Israeli and Russian intelligence services? If I publish a piece showing direct links between the scientists and these individuals, will anyone be surprised?"

Patrick shrugged. It was at that moment Chloe realized it wasn't just the Israelis and Russians, it was the French, and possibly the British and maybe the Americans. It was a murky world, but Patrick was rattled if he was trying to suppress the story.

"I'll look after you, find you something really great to publish instead." Patrick smiled, but Chloe wasn't impressed by his promise of a story at some point in the future.

Louise arrived with her carry-on. Chloe went across to check the contents. There were no writing materials. It made the point very well indeed. It might be civilized but it wasn't freedom—that would come at a price. The price was her signature on a confidentiality agreement.

CHAPTER TWENTY-SEVEN

Frankfurt

Traveling through airports always had anxious moments but there were things he could do to minimize the attention of the security forces. He looked around the plane for his target.

There she was, a woman traveling alone with three children, all of whom were tired and fretful. He went across.

"Can I be of assistance?"

She pulled her scarf about her head. Her eyes lowered.

"I'm fine, thank you."

"If I can help you when we land, you must let me know."

She nodded. He felt sure she would need help and sat down, and tried to relax for the rest of the flight.

On arrival, the woman struggled to keep hold of her youngest child, while getting her bag down from the overhead locker. He stopped and got the bag down, helped a child into a coat, and helped her and her three children from the plane. It seemed perfectly natural for them to line up together at immigration. While they waited, he casually asked her questions about her trip, where would she be staying? How long? Did she come often? Finally, he was confident he could pass himself off as a friend of the family.

He let her and the children go to the immigration desk first. He was pleased to see she waited for him to clear immigration, creating the idea he was part of a family group.

He answered the questions based on the information provided by the woman, he told them he was a friend of the family, he would be staying at least tonight with the family but he had friends he would be visiting after that. One of the children broke loose from her grip, came, and took his hand, trying to drag him toward his mother. This act of innocence was not lost on the immigration officer who stamped his passport, a high quality fake, and let him through.

He took the family to friends waiting to meet them and then quietly slipped away before they noticed he was gone. He boarded the first bus to depart from the terminal, not minding where it went, he would leave the bus and take a taxi, but not from the airport.

The taxi dropped him off three blocks from the mosque. He entered the mosque, slipped off his shoes, and knelt in prayer, giving thanks for his safe passage in the work of Allah. The imam watched and waited, and when he had finished, took him through to a side room.

"They will be here at two."

He looked at his watch, thirty minutes to wait. He wanted to avoid conversation and so sat with his eyes lightly closed. Through his lashes, he could observe what was going on around him.

The three young men were punctual. They came and silently sat down on the benches, waiting for his attention. When all three had settled, he opened his eyes.

He spoke of the trials of the Muslim brothers around the world. He asked each questions about the world, their views, what would be the appropriate action to take. Each young man ended his response with, "Death to the infidels."

The third young man troubled him. He motioned to the imam to take the pre-selected young men across to a cell leader who would brief them, leaving the final young man with him. He looked at him, and asked more questions. Clearly, the young man had doubts. His mouth said the right words but his eyes did not. He was a risk to everything, and what was more, if questioned this young man could identify him, even through his disguise. He had survived this long by the intervention of Allah, good instincts, and careful elimination of all unnecessary risks.

"I have a special mission, which I have chosen you to undertake."

The young man was resisting but he was no match for such a man practiced in the art of mental manipulation. Others might call it mesmerism, or hypnotism, but he preferred to think of it as arranging transport to paradise. He told him of the glory his mission would bring, gradually the resistance went and the young man was ready, he would do anything the Algerian asked of him.

"Bring Mahmoud." The imam disappeared at the man's bidding.

Mahmoud arrived and said nothing. The Algerian gave him a glass of water. Mahmoud drank, watching the Algerian over the rim of the glass.

"Our soldier here needs a vest and you need to take him to target B. He knows what to do. You should take him right away and not be too remote."

Mahmoud nodded and took the young man off to perform his mission. He knew if the young man failed to perform his mission, Mahmoud would use a remote control device to explode the vest, and hundreds of people at Frankfurt Haupthbahnhof would learn of this man's jihad and journey to paradise—and many would die.

The Algerian made a mental note, he would now need to get a car to go to Cologne, travel from Frankfurt stations would be out of the question. He left and, after changing his appearance, used a different identity to rent the car to drive to Cologne. There he would take the train to Brussels and Eurostar to London. He stopped at an internet café to book himself a first class round-trip ticket.

He left Frankfurt before the bomb went off, the first class ticket eased his way through security. The rail company did not like their first class passengers inconvenienced by too much security.

CHAPTER TWENTY-EIGHT

MI5, London

James T looked angry. Graeme was briefing the full group on the Frankfurt Central Station bomb attack the previous day.

"Three young men failed to turn up to play soccer for a local league. The *Bundesamt für Verfassungsschutz* (BfV), the German domestic intelligence agency, think that one young man, Aja Al-Sayeed, did not know the other two. For a start, they played on opposing teams and there is no record of them having played against each other before. But, for some reason Aja went with the other two.

"Aja had no history of fundamentalism; he had not recently been to Pakistan. He was married five years ago in Pakistan, he had a wife, and worked at a local insurance company, was highly thought of. He had not visited any mosques that have links with terrorist activity. Perhaps he was being clever and trying to provide information or evidence for the authorities, we don't know. But he ended up at the station with an explosive vest concealed under a padded jacket.

"The other two were under light surveillance by the BfV, they were not expected to be a threat. We all know how that can be deceptive. It is probably the most alarming terrorist attack because it seems they picked Aja at random. There was no chatter about the attack on the networks, all informants have been taken by surprise. The station was not even considered a prime target."

Graeme paused, took a drink of water, and looked at James T. It was hard to believe James could get any angrier about the events.

"This brings me to our involvement; we will give assistance to the Bundesamt wherever possible. We will be actively looking for any links and we need to be alert to the two missing men. Louise…"

Louise used the computer projector to show two photographs of young men of Asian origin supplied by the Germans. She read the descriptions:

"Target One: Farook—we are still establishing his full name, and also what identity he might be traveling under. We have an all border alert. Farook is probably the leader of the pair. He is second generation Asian-German, in a low paid job with the water company and an outspoken anti-American.

"Target Two: Nasir— has been to Pakistan recently and attended a madrassa, which does not imply a problem, but does cause us concern. Again, we have an all border alert for him. He worked at a garage in the body shop as a paint sprayer."

"Thank you, Louise. Now we need to make sure these two individuals are not in the UK. In the circumstances, I think we can assume they would be dangerous. Any comments?"

"Are the Germans sure they are only dealing with one bomb? Could Farook and Nasir have been bombers also? Do we need to consider they may have been among the casualties at the station?" asked James T, concerned about two dangerous terrorists entering the UK, but with resources stretched to breaking point, he didn't need his staff to be chasing ghosts either.

"No, they have established there was one bomb and from the current analysis of the CCTV pictures they haven't seen Farook or Nasir entering the station—but they are still working on it," said Louise.

"Have GCHQ got anything?" Another sharp question from Graeme.

"It depends on how you look at things. The bombing caused so much chatter they are extremely busy. So you could say it's a question of, can they sort out the reaction from any planning initiatives?" There was a knock at the door, Louise went and retrieved a briefing sheet from a colleague.

"Louise?"

"Farook and Nasir took the train from Frankfurt to Amsterdam and changed to a train for the Hook of Holland. We are checking the cameras at our end for facial recognition, but we think Farook and Nasir probably landed in Harwich an hour ago."

James T stood up and looked around the table.

"We need to prevent what looks like a potential major terrorist attack—these men are here for a purpose. This is the number one priority for the next twenty-four hours. I think the Frankfurt bomb, while tragic, should be viewed as the overture. I want every contact checked, every slither of possible information followed up. All rest breaks are canceled until we have these two in custody. Is that clear?"

Make it so, thought Louise, inwardly groaning, she knew she didn't function well without rest. She would see the doctor to get something to help. She could see this was going to be a twenty-four-hour period where she would need all her faculties.

The meeting broke up, and Graeme grabbed Louise's arm on the way out. "My office. Now!"

"Get Patrick on the phone. I don't know where he is but it's urgent. Okay?"

"Okay."

Louise wondered why talking to Patrick would be so urgent in the current circumstances. James T had just made it quite clear Farook and Nasir were the only work priorities.

Louise reached Patrick easily and told Graeme, who asked Louise to stay and put the call on speakerphone.

"What do you make of it all? I suppose we should be grateful it's Frankfurt." Patrick sounded serious and not at all smug.

"It's a bit closer to home. The two known associates arrived at Harwich an hour ago." Graeme brought Patrick up to date.

"So..."

"So, we need to accelerate the release of Walid Merbarkia. If I can get Walid released can you keep tabs on the art gallery owner?"

"Just say the word."

"And Chloe?" Graeme thought Patrick had done a good job in slowing her down, but it wouldn't last. When Patrick had made his arrangement with Chloe, everyone thought the Americans would let Art Expert go quickly, but he was on his way now, and if the medical reports were accurate, he was seriously ill.

"She's still co-operating—but at a price," said Patrick.

"Being?" Graeme sounded cautious.

"I promised her a story." Patrick didn't sound very happy.

"Which I won't like." Graeme knew Patrick would have stitched him up on this deal.

"If there was any other way..." Patrick faded away.

"I'll choose a political scandal and embarrassment any day over explaining we have possibly hundreds of dead innocent civilians to account for."

"That's what I thought you would say." Patrick was relieved; he didn't relish dumping MI5 in the mire. He knew they were good allies, even if relations were often strained.

"Could you pick up Walid from the Americans, take him to Iraq, and provide him with a security detail?"

"Iraq?"

"I would like it very much if you could get him to follow up the art deals in Iraq. I think this may be our only clue. We have no substantive intelligence on where the bombs are coming from or what the targets are. But, we know we're nearly out of time."

"I think I can help you with some information. Ahmed had the shippers deliver his goods from Baghdad direct to a warehouse in London."

"When the hell did that happen? And why the hell didn't you tell me earlier?"

"As you rightly identify, Art Expert, as you call him, is critical to your and my investigations, either the flow of money or goods. We have been waiting on your intervention with the Americans for six weeks. I think you need to look to yourselves for any timing issues here."

"He was too ill to travel. Can you help? Can you pick up Walid?"

Graeme was fuming. Patrick was giving him information so he could say MI5 had been given the information, but not in the best timely fashion. The goods would have been in London for six weeks. The art pieces could be anywhere. He could only hope Ahmed was keeping them in a warehouse for Islamic Art Week at Sotheby's.

Graeme's instinct told him Ahmed Talbi had found a way to deliver the briefcase bombs disguised as works of art.

"I understand you offered Walid Merbarkia a job in Oxford and if you want him that much as your asset, I can only suggest you go and pick him up." Patrick was not going to help them.

Graeme's next call was to get Walid released with immediate effect and transported back to the UK. Louise could pick up Chloe tomorrow; her cover would be a liaison worker with the foundation and she could sort out relocation arrangements. He wanted Chloe and Walid settled in a house in Oxford immediately, somewhere he could talk to Walid and hopefully get more information—he had to hope Louise was on top of all the details, and wouldn't be recognized, she had worked with Patrick in Germany, to secure Chloe's release.

CHAPTER TWENTY-NINE

Paris

J ean Pierre had been surprised and delighted when Chloe had agreed to go to the concert. She seemed so frail since her ordeal and he had no wish to make more problems in her life. After two sessions with the shrink, she had refused all offers of further help. She had declared she had been kidnapped, well treated, and found. This was nothing in comparison with others and she had no wish to make a fuss. They had played a couple of games of squash recently and Chloe was getting better at reading his play. The last match had been close. He had only just won.

Chloe said she had received excellent care at the US military hospital at Landstuhl, Germany, and now it was business as usual. She had been very fortunate. Everyone was acutely aware she was referring to the over one hundred journalists who had lost their lives while reporting in Iraq, and the fact there was still no news on Walid.

Jean Pierre was concerned, Chloe seemed dull, her eyes no longer shone, it was as if her spirit had curled up inside her and couldn't get out. He wanted to know what had happened to her. He couldn't believe it was the result of the kidnapping. She was more resilient than that, he was suspicious that while she was in Germany undergoing debriefing and medical treatment something had happened. He wondered if it was a reaction to a drug or some hypnotherapy or something similar. Perhaps she was on some medication to treat post-traumatic stress disorder. She had asked Anne Marie to go back onto EU stories, which had concerned them both. Particularly now she was nearly at a point when she could publish. A couple more cases, and she would have enough, even for Chloe. Certainly, her behavior was consistent with being sedated, or subdued. He didn't know and didn't feel he should pursue it unless Chloe invited him to. So he was elated when she accepted his invitation to go to a concert.

"I'd love to go. What's the program? You know, it doesn't matter, anything would be lovely."

"I'll get the tickets. Dinner as well?"

"Of course."

She seemed determined to have a good night out. He only hoped he could remain a friend; he hadn't told anyone just how much he wished the relationship could be something more, something permanent. He was completely in love with her and hoped he was hiding it well. It was ridiculous to think he might never have known how he felt about her, until he thought he had lost her.

Chloe had arranged to meet him outside the Église de la Madeleine. He knew this was her making the line of demarcation between a date and two colleagues enjoying a concert together.

She was wearing the same white shirt she had been wearing the day she'd been mugged. He hadn't forgotten those bruises on her wrists. She had seemed so vulnerable. If Walid had not disappeared six weeks ago he felt sure she would have left him by now, but there was nothing like an unexplained disappearance to create feelings of guilt.

Jean Pierre greeted her with a kiss on both cheeks and they went into the church. The neo-classic portico with majestic columns provided an awe-inspiring building to the glory of Napoleon's army. The lighting was dim and they found seats near the front on the center aisle.

As Chloe sat down a waft of her perfume was intoxicating. *Being just a friend might prove hard.*

The musicians took their places and Saint-Saens's *The Carnival of the Animals* seemed suitably innocent. The acoustics in the church enhanced the cello solo for "The Swan" and provided lingering, sweet, and peaceful notes. He watched the cello, held between the soloist's thighs, as her sinewy arms drew the bow rhythmically back and forth across the mellow, curvaceous instrument. He found the image sensuous and became absorbed and emotionally entwined in the music.

He looked over at Chloe and to his surprise tears were streaming down her cheeks. Should he say anything? He watched her closely; no, this was the release she needed.

The piece ended and there was polite clapping, the audience more interested in the interval than approval. He put his arm around her shoulders and she looked up.

"Let's go," they said in unison.

He guided her skillfully through the crowd surging toward the refectory for coffee and wine, and made their way outside where the night air had become cold. He drew her close to him for warmth and support.

"Take me home," she said softly.

"Train or taxi?"

"Can't we walk to your place from here?"

He hadn't expected that.

"Yes, sure."

They walked in silence, his arm around her, comforting and guiding. She continued to cry, seemingly unable to stop. He began to think about how he had left his apartment. Normally when he went on a date, he tidied up, cleaned the bathroom, put fresh sheets on the bed, and made sure there was enough wine chilling in the fridge, rolls for breakfast, orange juice, fresh coffee, but he had made no such preparations.

He let her into the apartment; put the hall light on and a single lamp by the sofa. The soft lighting was normally to aid romance but tonight it was to provide a gentle environment for Chloe.

"Cocoa, coffee, or brandy?"

"Dinner?"

"Of course." He looked in the fridge for inspiration; he wasn't the greatest cook, but he knew better than to get out a frozen meal and microwave it. Normally for female company he would order in from a local restaurant and just serve up, but he had asparagus tips, eggs, cheese, some bread and wine—not impressive but he didn't think Chloe would mind.

He put the asparagus tips to steam in a pan and whipped up the eggs, ready to make the omelets.

"Bathroom?"

He shuddered at the thought—it couldn't be too bad, Madame Guillaume came every Thursday, but he wished he had checked it over. Well, he'd just trust all was okay.

"Through the bedroom and keep going."

He set the table and served the simple meal. He could not believe how arousing it was to watch Chloe eat asparagus tips. He was glad she had stopped crying. He should think of something to say.

"Is the asparagus okay?" How lame was that?

"I love asparagus and it's wonderful. I'm sorry for being such a fool and spoiling the concert."

"Chloe, you are nobody's fool and you didn't spoil the concert. It was a modern piece after the interval—I'm sure we heard the best part. I wasn't sure the acoustics or ambiance of the church was designed for discord, or should I call it modern harmony?"

"I don't know what came over me—self-pity, I suppose."

"Still no news?" What was he doing? The last thing he wanted to do was discuss Walid.

"Not really and the problem is, as you know, things were difficult before he went away. While he was gone, a credit card statement arrived with a bill for dinner on a Bateau-Mouche; Walid used a credit card to pay the bill, but I hadn't given him a card on my credit card account. He must have forged my signature. I can't trust him. But then we did seem to have sorted things out, his life in Algeria had been complicated."

"Chloe, let's get one thing straight: at the very least he could communicate with you. It's just not right to leave you worrying." Jean Pierre was shocked at the credit card information, and wondered why she hadn't started divorce proceedings.

"Yes, I know but..."

"Chloe, there are no buts—you're being too reasonable. You have nothing to feel guilty about. You have done and endured far more than should be expected of anyone."

"I don't remember marrying him," Chloe blurted out.

"What do you mean?"

"I don't remember the day. I have a photo and a license, but no memories, and I can't find the prenuptial agreement."

Jean Pierre understood, she could lose everything, her grandmother's apartment, her savings, her pension. No one wanted to pay that much for a marriage that should never have taken place. He was beginning to think she had either been drugged or hypnotized and made to comply with Walid's wishes. What he couldn't work out was if she had her suspicions or if she was still thinking of more innocent explanations. She didn't offer any further comment.

They ate the omelets in silence.

"I don't have anything for dessert."

"So brandy followed by cocoa it is."

He poured two large measures of brandy, and went back into the kitchen to make the cocoa. He only had enough milk for one cocoa, so he made himself a coffee and decided he should keep his wits about him and not let anything develop to embarrass himself, so he left his brandy in the kitchen. He found Chloe curled up on the sofa relaxing against the cushions.

"Blanket?" She nodded, and he snuggled her up in a soft warm fleecy blanket.

"Can I stay tonight?"

"Of course." His heart missed a beat, but he didn't think this was a proposition.

"I want to sleep with you, held in your arms, and I just want to sleep knowing I'm safe. I'm just so very, very tired. I haven't had a good night's sleep since I got back from Iraq."

Jean Pierre was surprised at this. Chloe didn't usually show any signs of weakness.

"I don't want..."

"It's all right—I do understand."

He collected pillows and the duvet off the bed, they snuggled together on the couch, the softness of her hair falling against his cheek, and finally she fell asleep.

The alarm clock going off in his bedroom woke Jean Pierre. He extracted himself carefully from Chloe, so as not to wake her, and turned it off. He showered, checked on Chloe, who was still asleep, picked up his wallet and phone, and left the apartment.

He walked briskly to the shops, phoning Anne Marie at the same time.

"I want to phone in apologies for myself and Chloe for this morning's meeting."

"You're together?"

"She stayed at my place last night."

"I didn't ask for a show and tell."

"You weren't going to get one. I wanted to make it clear Chloe was a guest, a friend in need and nothing more."

"A friend in need?"

"I told you two sessions with the shrink wouldn't be enough."

"She was adamant."

"I know, anyway I thought as she is opening up and talking to me, I should let the day take its course and let her unload."

"All right, but you need to find out why she dropped the investigation into the scientists when she came back from Iraq. I don't think it's anything to do with the kidnapping or danger, I think she was leaned on. Encourage her to, no, in fact tell her I want you both to go and investigate the next death immediately. The inquiry into Antipov has just been published and there was no mention of those emails she found. It's incredible. So I think you should go to Scotland and investigate the next death on her list, make the arrangements and find out what's going on. I think it will be easier to talk to her if you're both busy. I don't see her just chatting to you all day."

"Right, I'll let you know how I get on."

Jean Pierre completed shopping for juice, fresh croissants, rolls, butter, and milk and made his way back to the apartment. He wasn't sure how Chloe would react to Anne Marie's instructions.

Over breakfast, he broke the news.

"I've just sent our excuses to Anne Marie for this morning's meeting."

"Was she okay about it?"

"Surprisingly okay, she suggested we go investigate the next mysterious death in Scotland."

"How much do you tell her? Are you briefing her?"

"No."

"How does she know about the case in Scotland?"

"I don't know. Didn't you tell her, when you discussed going to Iraq?"

"Possibly. Okay, we'll go to the UK, though not to Scotland but to Yorkshire, England. It's an interesting case and no one will expect us to go there. I sometimes feel I am being played in this investigation, I think I am being watched through Anne Marie. Someone is telling her about what I am doing, what I am finding out, but not the details, it's all very strange."

"Could it be your researcher?"

"Janine? Really?"

"I didn't know Janine had been allocated to you. If she's been doing your, everything has been copied to Anne Marie."

Chloe thought about it for a moment. It would explain why Anne Marie was well briefed in some aspects and totally lacking any information in others.

"Why did you ask Anne Marie to go back to covering EU stories?" Jean Pierre thought the conversation was going well enough to ask the direct question.

"Patrick Dubois asked me to back off, and said he would get Walid home. I don't know if he has Anne Marie's office bugged, or whether Janine tells him everything, but I thought I would let him hear what he wants to hear."

"Seriously? Well, bugger Patrick!"

They both laughed.

"You don't owe anything to Walid except to serve him with divorce papers, so on that basis it would be useful to have him home, but I can't think of any other good reason, and after such a short period of marriage you should just hope you do okay financially in court."

"Maybe. I actually have the divorce papers. But the situation with Walid may be more complicated than I thought."

"Has Patrick been telling you fairy stories?"

"Possibly. It's like being married to two people. Patrick suggested there might actually be two people."

"Yes, and there are gremlins in the system, and trolls under the bridges. Was that the most original theory he could suggest?"

Chloe smiled.

CHAPTER THIRTY

North York Moors

Jean Pierre and Chloe took a flight from Paris to Leeds airport and rented a car to drive to Farthingdale Hall, a journey across the North York Moors. The purple heather was dying back and after the first frost would go brown. Even the bracken had maintained some elements of green; it had been unseasonably warm for the end of October. The wide-open spaces were breathtaking.

The journey gave Chloe time to think. Was she right to go ahead with the investigation? Patrick hadn't claimed any national security issues were at stake. He hadn't made any case for not continuing her investigation. He had asked her nicely, presumably to save any embarrassment to French secret intelligence. If the government didn't keep the intelligence service in check then the press needed to keep a watchful eye. A national intelligence service acting as judge, jury, and executioner needed to be held to account. There was enough evidence for her to engage the public in a dialogue about the issues, it was right to finish this investigation, she already had discovered the "who, when, where, and what." She needed to know "why" this was happening.

"So what did Charles say about the rather lovely Dr Elizabeth Katherine Soames?" Jean Pierre was reading Chloe's file, while Chloe drove steadily along the main road, anxious not to miss the turning to Farthingdale village.

"Nothing."

"How come?"

"Because he discounted this as a normal death."

"But you didn't, why?"

Chloe paused, signaled, and completed the right turn before answering. "Statistically men are twice as likely to choose hanging as their preferred method of committing suicide than women. Women are more likely to poison themselves. I find the circumstances of this woman committing suicide by hanging unrealistic—a characteristic of the other deaths."

"That's it. We're here because of a statistical probability."

"No, a gut feeling, coupled with the fact this scientist didn't have anyone to protest her death. The estate manager said she seemed happy and upbeat and didn't think she would commit suicide. So, someone needs to have a close look. Let me tell you what I know already. Liz, as she was known to her colleagues, graduated from Oxford with a PhD and went to work for the Ministry of Defense. She was briefly engaged to be married to the head of her department when she worked in London. The relationship ended and was followed by a period of six months' sick leave. She requested a transfer away from London and worked briefly at Porton Down. It was rumored she might be 'Rosa' the Russian mole."

"I thought Antipov was agent 'Rosa'? They can't both be 'Rosa.'"

"Exactly. As I was saying, so she transferred again, her friends said this rumor was the work of her ex-fiancé. She was mortified and blamed the death of her grandmother on the humiliation of this rumor. Information continued to leak which, by default, cleared her name, and so after six years' absence she returned to Porton Down and, by all accounts, was a distinguished scientist and part of the team working on the DNA biological weapons defense program.

"On the day in question, she was attending the wedding of a work colleague at Farthingdale Hall. It's a large manor hall, still the residence of the marquis and his fourth wife, it may be his fifth wife by now. The marquis is quite the serial monogamist. To pay for his divorce settlements and the upkeep of the hall, it's run as a conference and wedding venue. It has a large lake with a boathouse.

"Liz left the wedding party and was driven down to the boathouse and no one can say why. She went into the boat dock, grabbed a length of rope, went back upstairs, threw the rope over the beam, and hung herself. She had been on her own for less than half an hour when all this took place. She didn't leave a note, and no one knew of any reason why she would do such a thing. The only explanation was her ex-fiancé was at the wedding. I don't buy that as a reason, so we're here to see the boathouse and talk to the estate manager who opened up for her and see what information is available."

"How did you get so much information?"

"Phone interviews, letters, research print articles, the usual grunt work of an investigative journalist." Chloe doubted Jean Pierre had the patience for such arduous and sometimes unrewarding work; he liked to see quicker results. Chloe's investigations could take months before she had all the information she needed.

Chloe slowed and turned into the entrance to Farthingdale Hall. The black wrought iron gates had a gilt crest recently painted in the center. The car scrunched on the gravel as she drove slowly along, enjoying the views and the sense of grandeur. It would be a wonderful place to get married. She thought about a horse and carriage in June, when the roses would all be in bloom, it would be perfect. Although the gardeners had done their best to make it look festive with clipped box balls in large blue ceramic pots, alternated with mock Georgian streetlamps and flowerbeds filled with winter pansies in random colors, it didn't feel welcoming.

She drove up to the visitors' entrance and they climbed the main stone steps, pulled the metal ring on the stone wall, listened to clang of the bell inside, and waited. A butler opened the door and told them where to find the estate manager's office. They both left feeling the butler's contempt for members of the press.

They got back in the car and continued along the drive, past the stables and the beginnings of a small garden center until they arrived at the estate manager's office. They approached the receptionist, who was wearing a blue wool twinset with pearls. Chloe nearly laughed, the whole place was beginning to be a bit of a cliché. Now she knew the estate manager would be wearing mustard corduroy trousers, a check shirt, and a herringbone tweed jacket, with a rolled up cap in the pocket. The tie would be silk, but well worn, and the accent would have only a slight Yorkshire overtone. She was wrong, Jake Werriman turned up in a tree surgeon's helmet, complete with protective earphones and chainsaw trousers, and an orange and anthracite jacket. He had a short chainsaw in his right hand. The accent was English public school and very rounded and rich.

"Gosh, sorry I'm a bit late, if you hang on here a minute, Kathleen will get you a coffee if you like. I'll get out of this gear and take you down to the boathouse. In fact Kathleen can tell you a lot about what happened that day, she was on duty in the hall."

Kathleen didn't seem to think making coffee for the press and answering questions was part of her job description and gave the minimum answers to their queries, she was impervious to Jean Pierre's charm and that was a rare occurrence.

When Jake reappeared, he was wearing brown corduroy trousers but apart from that Chloe's image of him held true. He stopped briefly to sign a few letters for Kathleen at the side of her desk. She gave him a file, which he put into a soft brown leather briefcase. Then, with profuse apologies for keeping them waiting, they all got into his navy Range Rover, with the family crest on the door, and set off at a gracious pace.

"Do you think you could re-create what happened that day?"

"Sure." Jake turned the Range Rover around and headed back up to the hall, but he made a detour to the back terrace and parked. "I met Dr Soames just over there. She asked me if I could take her to the boat-house. I thought at the time maybe the marquis had given her the note she was carrying, Dr Soames was extremely pretty and just the sort of woman he would choose to seduce at the boathouse. She seemed happy, I didn't think it was the champagne talking, she was sober and chatty. She noticed how well the estate was kept and complimented me and my staff on the smooth running of the event so far. Guests were at a loose end, milling about, the marquee was being rearranged after the formal lunch for the evening event, afternoon tea was due to be served in about an hour and so I guessed she wouldn't be missed for a couple of hours. Something I knew the marquis would also know."

He turned the car around and started the journey to the boathouse. "She was talking about her time at Oxford and I thought she might know the marquis and it might be one of those strange coincidences where he had found an old flame. But afterward the police couldn't de-termine they had ever met, the marquis denied sending a note, as did her ex-fiancé."

"Did Dr Soames's ex-fiancé bring anyone special with him to the wedding?"

"No, they both came as singles, but weren't put at the same table for lunch at the request of both parties. No one saw either of them make contact with the other. The police interviewed all the guests. If it was someone who knew Dr Soames, why didn't they send her a text mes-sage? She had her phone, and we have a good signal for most cell phone networks on the estate, so it was odd to send her a note."

"Did they ever find the note?"

"No." He brought the car to a smooth halt. "Here we are."

The boathouse was a mock Tudor construction, a rose-beige render with mock rustic timber beams in brown wood stain. It was a two-story building with the boats at lake level. A padlock secured the double doors to the boats. Jake led the way up the stairs to the side of the building and to the brown painted door, unlocked it, and they went in. It was a beautiful cottage-chic lounge. The ceiling went up to the rafters. There were two beams across the room, and Chloe swallowed hard, knowing what had taken place. Jake went across to the patio doors, slid them open and walked out onto the deck.

"You can see right up the lake from here and down to the weir."

Chloe and Jean Pierre followed him out. There were signs on the bank telling boat users not to travel further up the lake because of the weir. Jean Pierre asked if it was safe to launch boats from the dock. Jake replied, the signs used to be two hundred yards nearer the weir but the marquis wanted more privacy and didn't want people fishing outside the boathouse, so moved the signs.

There was a clinker-built rowboat on the lake, the angler, sheltered by a large green umbrella, had his line extended to a red and yellow float.

"Do they catch much?"

"Actually the coarse fishing's not bad, some carp and roach. Quite decent sizes too."

Jake's phone rang; he answered, listened, and rolled his eyes. "I'll be right there." He turned. "Look I have to go up to the house. It won't take long, about twenty minutes, give or take. Can I leave you here, and I'll come back and get you in less than half an hour?"

"Sure," said Jean Pierre.

Chloe was glad; it meant they could have a careful look around, without appearing to be nosey.

Jake left, and they both started to look for anything to help them piece together the last half hour in the life of Liz Soames.

"What do you think this room is used for?" asked Chloe.

"I should think the marquis uses it for affairs, casual sex, and occasionally entertaining small parties with a posh picnic."

The sofas looked comfortable but when Chloe sat down it was disappointing, she felt down the front to discover it was a sofa bed. They pulled the bed open; the mattress was already made up with fine Egyptian cotton sheets in a pale aqua, with forest green embroidery scallops on the edges of the top sheet and pillowcases. They put the bed back together and looked up at the beams, both wondering, which one?

The antique Georgian drop leaf table had a high shine, and six dining chairs were placed conveniently around the room. The floorboards were filled and varnished to give a draft-proof, non-rustic effect. A rug in soft pinks and blues was in the middle of the room. It was a feminine room and the sort of room you could take a female companion to and she would relax, there was an extensive selection of drinks on a table, and yet it did not have obvious intentions to seduce.

Jean Pierre's favorite theory was the assassin had come from the lake and so was looking to find moored boats, working out how long it would take to row over, and if the assassin had been waiting below how he would have got into the room.

"What I would like to know is, did Jake open the sliding doors to the patio when they arrived, just as he did for us? If not, your theory is dead in the water, so to speak," said Chloe.

"I don't think so, she could have opened the doors for herself. What's your theory?"

"I don't know, Jake was the last person to see her alive and discovered the body. Why did he come back if he thought the marquis was going to spend the afternoon seducing her? That was rather indiscreet, wasn't it? I think he is probably ex-military, he has a whiff of Sandhurst about him, and it must be hard to have expensive tastes and see all this luxury around you and only have some of the crumbs."

"They don't look like bad crumbs."

"No, but maybe a large cash sum would make him think carefully about doing a small wet job for..." She paused, she didn't know who would have the motive, other than Dr Soames was a weapons scientist specializing in DNA weapons defense, and fitted a pattern of scientists with suspicious deaths.

"I think there's a difference between shooting some rag-top or whatever at the end of a gun sight and stringing up a woman in cold blood. Wouldn't she have struggled?" Jean Pierre looked up at the beam. It would have been quite difficult to get the rope up there in the first place.

Chloe said, "I think we should take a look downstairs, after all Liz Soames was supposed to have managed to get into the boat dock for some rope, and we know the door to the boat dock at the front of the lodge was locked, so there must be a way from here."

They found the stairs to the left of the deck and went down to find the door locked, it took Chloe a couple of minutes to get brave and shimmy her way around the end of the wood siding over the lake water, and around into the dock area. There was a ledge, which made it easy when you knew how. She looked for some rope, but there was nothing hanging up, or in the couple of boats moored there. All the rope was in use or locked away in the cupboard at the end of the boathouse. So much for the theory that "she popped down to get some rope."

They went back upstairs.

"So where do we go from here?" asked Jean Pierre.

"We can ask Jake why he came back—"

Jean Pierre interrupted, "Duck down, quickly, and make your way behind this sofa."

"Very funny," said Chloe, while ducking down and moving away from the window.

Jean Pierre was now flat against the side of the room and reached for the binoculars. "I can see sunlight shining on a lens focused on this room, there's a rifle scope on the opposite bank." He looked through the glasses. "No, not a rifle scope, a long camera lens."

Chloe went over and looked through the binoculars. "What the..."

"How long have we got before he comes back?"

"Ten minutes?"

"Do you think we could run around, check it out, and get back in time?"

"It has to be worth a try and at worst he will think we walked back and we may have to."

They went down the stairs and ran on the tarmac road toward the bridge over the weir. They were both fit, and Chloe more so than usual, she had started running every day since she came back from Iraq, it helped calm her mind and she was planning to enter another charity marathon.

Jean Pierre kept pace with her, but only just and his male pride was hurt by how easy she was finding this run. When they arrived at the camera, Chloe took her own pictures. Jean Pierre was working out how the photos were being stored; there were no storage disks on the camera and it looked as if the camera was motion activated, and sent the recordings direct via the internet to a computer server. The questions were: who owned the camera, had it been in use a year ago when Liz Soames met her end, and was it working now? Why was the camera there? Chloe took out a business card, wrote "Call Me" on it, and placed the card in front of the camera lens. A small red light glowed which suggested the camera was still operating. They ran back to the boathouse, and were still panting when Jake turned up. He looked embarrassed, clearly having decided he had caught them in the middle of sex. They didn't explain.

"Ah, Jake, there were a couple of questions you could help us with. Firstly, we understand why you took Dr Soames to the boathouse, but we don't understand why you went back less than half an hour later."

"When I took her there, I thought I was opening up for a tryst with the marquis. When I found he was still up at the hall, I asked him about the note, and on discovering my mistake, I went to pick up Dr Soames. The marquis wasn't prepared to have the boathouse used as a 'knocking shop' as he put it."

Jake went pale. He was remembering what it had been like to return to the scene. Chloe knew she should have asked him, but she was more interested in the camera they had just found. Chloe was thinking Liz would have arrived, gone down to the boathouse, in heels or barefoot and dressed in a chiffon posh frock, found a length of rope, stood on a chair, thrown the rope over the beam, tied a noose, slipped the rope around her neck, made her peace with her maker, and kicked the chair away. To have achieved all that in the space of just over half an hour required determination and some measure of planning. It didn't seem to add up.

"Jake, could you tell us about the camera on the other side of the lake?"

"Camera?"

"Yes." Jean Pierre took Jake to the edge of the deck, gave him the binoculars, and told him where to look.

"Ah, so that's how she did it."

"So you know about the camera?"

Jake put the binoculars down. "The pre-nup agreement each wife has with the marquis revolves around him being caught having extramarital relations within two years of the marriage. If he's caught his wife gets about two point three million pounds, if he's not caught she gets nothing if she divorces him. For that amount of money, the marquis is used to seeing private investigators, but he thought he was safe here. He didn't know how the pictures had been obtained; he was having the boathouse checked regularly for hidden cameras. I don't suppose he thought it would be possible to get such clear pictures from such a long way away. If you want to know about those pictures you'll need to speak to ex-wife number four, she's in Antigua at present, enjoying her couple of million, I'll find her address in the office. I hope you find out what happened to Dr Soames, she was a pleasant lady and didn't deserve an ending like that, and she certainly didn't seem like she was in the mood to take her own life, you would expect her to seem depressed or sad or something. Look"—he reached into the briefcase—"here are all the pho-tographs and statements from the wedding guests. There are video clips and the police had all these but didn't find anything. I thought they might find out who gave her the note. The police were just happy to call it suicide, a single woman of a certain age at a wedding, she was nearly forty, sees her ex-fiancé, and it's all too much for her."

"Is there anything else you think we should know?" Chloe asked the question and hoped Jean Pierre would keep quiet to let the silence do its work.

"I don't know where the rope came from, it was a blue nylon rope and the marquis prefers white ropes. I can't say for a certainty the rope didn't come from the boat dock, but I don't ever remember seeing it there."

Chloe could only hope the PI had kept the video footage and would give it to her. Jake drove them back to his office, and gave them details of the fourth wife of the marquis.

If there was some video footage this was the best opportunity of see-ing the agents step by step kill a scientist. The evidence would be more powerful than the few photos she had from Emilio's camera, even though they had given some clear pictures of the perpetrators. If the filmed evidence still existed...

CHAPTER THIRTY-ONE

Paris

It was two o'clock in the morning when Chloe's cell phone woke her. She rubbed her eyes blearily, the trip back from Leeds the day before had been long and tedious. She put on the light and checked to find it was an international call. Her first thoughts were it would be one of those asinine telephone-marketing calls from India, so she was off-hand when she answered, but soon sharpened up when she realized she was speaking to the private detective whose camera Jean Pierre had found on the shore of the lake in Yorkshire.

"It wasn't murder, if that's what you were thinking. It was suicide. But it was really strange."

"Do you have pictures?"

"Yes."

"Can we meet?"

"Sure, but you'll need to bring your wallet."

"When would you like to meet?"

"Thursday, in England."

"Where? What time?"

"I'll send you details. It's a burner phone, so you can't reply. If you don't come, I'll be there the next day at the same time."

"I'll need something before we meet."

"I'll send you a sample—nothing very interesting, but just enough to prove I have something."

"All right."

The detective hung up, and shortly after, true to his word, Chloe received two emailed photographs. The first was a picture of the Oxford Natural History Museum with "at two— upstairs gallery," written over the image. The second image was clearly of Dr Elizabeth Katherine Soames, on her last day on Earth at Farthingdale Hall boathouse, in her dusty-pink chiffon wedding outfit. The picture was date stamped, but Chloe didn't need to check the date. Liz Soames stood on the balcony, the doors were open, and she was looking across the lake, directly into the camera—although because it was a sunny day she was unlikely to have picked up the glint of the lens against the bright highlights on the lake. Chloe found herself feeling sad. This woman's life had been cut short when she was in her prime. Her face looked composed, she looked happy and as if she was enjoying the sunshine and the view.

Chloe completed some research on the scientist and again found the inquest was either ill-informed or unaware of key facts. Liz Soames's six-month absence from work was not for depression as stated on her sick notes, which had been emphasized at the inquest. In fact, at the time she was pregnant and being a faithful Catholic had given birth to the baby and had it adopted. Her ex-fiancé had wanted her to terminate the pregnancy and that had been the cause of the rift between them. He thought all religion was superstitious nonsense and had no sympathy for her. He wasn't going to be drawn into a marriage, which he wasn't ready for, and into having a child he never wanted.

It was difficult to reconcile this woman's stand for her baby on religious grounds with the person who had committed the mortal sin of suicide. The description of her being happy that afternoon was also hard to equate with what happened next. Chloe had a large number of photographs and pictures from the wedding to analyze. She wanted to see if she could find out who gave Liz the note that took her to the boathouse that afternoon. Maybe it would give her some answers.

Chloe contemplated phoning Jean Pierre and telling him the good news, that there were pictures, and the bad news, that it wasn't a suspicious death. Chloe's current agreement with Anne Marie was that she would share all new developments with Jean Pierre as they happened. *Ah well,* thought Chloe, *life's full of disappointments,* and she switched off the light and went back to sleep.

At six, the apartment phone rang and kept ringing, annoyed she realized she had turned off the answering machine. Swearing under her breath, she picked up.

"Chloe?"

"Yes."

"It's Patrick."

For a moment, she considered hanging up rather than being dragged into any more of his spook fantasies.

Perhaps he knew she had been to Yorkshire with Jean Pierre and was ringing to reassure her Walid was coming home. So far she hadn't published anything controversial and Walid hadn't arrived home, now she would turn the tables and keep publishing controversial items until he came back. Perhaps he knew what they had discovered at Farthingdale and was going to appeal to her not to publish again. Where was this great story he had promised her?

Although she had discussed a year's sabbatical with Anne Marie, she had decided the job in England wasn't for her. Walid, however, would need his new job as the Sorbonne had sacked him and he would soon be divorced.

She'd had great fun working with Jean Pierre and she didn't need a break. Her investigation in Yorkshire felt like it was going to get a good result. Her gut instinct said there was more to the death than the inquest had suggested, already the presence of the baby in Liz's life, the reason she and her fiancé had split up, and everyone's view she'd been happy at the wedding, left Chloe feeling there was something suspicious.

Chloe's silence on the phone had gone on too long for her to greet Patrick as a long lost friend. "Anything new?"

"Apparently you and Walid are on your way to Oxford, England."

"Walid has a job in England. Should he ever turn up."

"I thought I would wish you a safe journey and say if there is anything I can do, please let me know. You should be smiling by dinner."

"Right. Well, thanks anyway. See you around." Patrick really didn't seem to understand her marriage was over.

"It's going to be okay, Chloe."

"I doubt that very much. No matter what happens next, the trust, the mutual dependency, everything has gone. It'll end in divorce."

"Go to Oxford, get him settled in, it's the least you can do for him, in the circumstances."

Patrick put the phone down first. What was the point of the call? What circumstances?

Chloe got up, showered in the hope it would make her feel bright, alive, and awake; she drank two cups of coffee and was eating a piece of toast when the doorbell rang. *What could the concierge possibly want today?* Chloe had been spending more and more time at her apartment in the center of Paris, and the concierge in Sceaux had become positively nosey since Walid had disappeared; he probably phoned the police every week to give an update.

Chloe opened the door without looking through the security spy hole, after all if "they" wanted to kidnap you, they would.

A young woman in her mid-twenties stood in front of her. She was dressed in a black pants suit with a pale blue cotton shirt beneath. The shoes were classic pumps—beloved of flight crews. Her face was the classic peaches and cream of the British; her mousy brown hair tied back in a low ponytail and her blond highlights were about six months old and needed renewing.

"Chloe Moreau?"

"Yes?"

"I'm Hilary Armstrong. I've come to assist your move to Oxford."

"What?"

"Your husband will land at the Royal Air Force Base, Brize Norton, at three this afternoon, so I thought you might like help to get settled in."

Chloe opened the door wide, to let her in. "So you're a spook." She didn't reply, so Chloe continued, "It's all right, I have friends who are spooks, so why are you here?"

"Your husband should have been with you a few weeks ago, but he wasn't ready to travel."

"Really? What's that supposed to mean? It doesn't usually take him a few weeks to pack."

"He had a heart attack. It was hoped the angioplasty would be sufficient, but he had another heart attack and it took this long to get him fit enough to travel after the bypass surgery."

Chloe absorbed this information. She should tell Hilary to go away, she wasn't interested in a man who hadn't even bothered to tell her he had sons, was paying for them, and visiting them. She wondered if the sons knew he had been ill. Had they been visiting him?

"So why couldn't I have gone to visit him? Why couldn't someone tell me what was going on?"

"I'm sorry, you need to ask the Americans about that. On the bright side, Walid's already left the airport in Afghanistan; an American doctor is traveling with him. Would you like to see some houses in Oxfordshire we could rent on your behalf?"

Chloe thought about it. The flight would take about seven hours. She didn't have long.

"So you expect my husband to work for you?" The anger of the past few months just poured out in venomous questions and this woman had only turned up to help with the relocation. Chloe knew she wasn't being polite or fair, but she was beginning to see all spooks as a large international club, rather than competing forces. They covered up for each other, turned a blind eye if their aims and objectives were aligned.

"We would like to assist with your relocation; we wouldn't like your husband's experience to have lasting effects."

"Two hearts attacks aren't viewed as lasting?" She couldn't contain her sarcasm.

"I understand why you might feel upset. We have all tried the best in difficult circumstances."

"Really—you probably arranged for my detention instead."

She looked embarrassed, and Chloe wondered why. Hilary turned her head to one side, and drew a large breath before saying, "If you would like me to assist you and get you through security onto the RAF base, I can help. If you would like to look at some homes we think you might find suitable, I can help. If I am going to cause anxiety and anger perhaps you would prefer I leave. If you let me know where you are staying I can arrange transport for your husband."

Chloe didn't know why this woman made her so angry. It was pointless to take out her frustration on the only person who was trying, in a very practical way, to help.

"You better come in and sit down. I'm sorry, it's been a trying time. What do you want me to do?" They sat at the kitchen table.

"First of all, I would suggest you pack the personal things you and Walid will need for the next few days. If you are happy with the arrangement, I can bring in a team to pack your other possessions for transport to England on the ferry tonight. They would be with you in the morning."

Chloe just nodded. She left Hilary in the kitchen, making more coffee, and went through to the bedroom. It was easy enough to pack her suitcase, she practically lived out of one. Chloe had gradually been moving her possessions out of the apartment in Sceaux to her apartment in the center of Paris. Now nearly everything left in Sceaux belonged to

Walid, and here was a volunteer to pack it all up. Sometimes for all the wrong reasons good things happened.

She would get him settled and then leave. She wasn't sure what Walid would want. She had put all his things in a box in the bathroom, unable to look at them week after week. She remembered the shock of finding the hair dye to cover gray hair, another lie. The smell of his sandalwood aftershave caught her by surprise. It was as if Walid had walked into the room and was right there.

She wondered why she going to England at all. If Walid was coming home she could just give him the divorce papers and be done with it all. Perhaps it was concern about his treatment over the past few weeks, or maybe it was curiosity, but she wanted to be there when he got back. She looked around at the open shutters in the apartment. It would have been impossible had Walid been here. Did she want to go back to living in a bat cave? Living with permanent fear? In the nightstand drawer were the divorce papers.

She could just go back to Hilary Armstrong, say she wasn't interested, and give her the documents. The problem with Patrick's stories was they had enough truth about them to be plausible. Had there been two men in her marriage? Had she just been a tool? Had Walid used her to avoid problems with a visa renewal?

She finished the packing, downed a cup of coffee quickly, called Anne Marie and told her she was taking a couple of days off, and went to get the concierge. She conducted him through the apartment, they checked and agreed on the utility meter readings and she gathered the essential items from the desk, bills waiting to be paid, her address book, and left everything else for the removal crew. If this was a spook plan to get hold of her research materials, they were going to be disappointed, she would take her personal computer, but there were no files relating to her investigation on it.

Outside the apartment was a black Mercedes with a chauffeur, who put her personal bags in the trunk of the car and opened the door for them. Chloe got into the car. This was a most civilized way to move house.

"Where are we going now?"

"We are going to the Rouen airport and taking a plane direct to Brize Norton, where a car will be waiting for us. We will have time to look at a few houses, make a choice, and get things organized." Something about Hilary seemed familiar.

"Do you have any details on the houses?"

Hilary passed her a folder and she could see the houses were beautiful; they all had an en-suite bedroom downstairs, and were in peaceful and tranquil surroundings in the country, fairly isolated.

"You needn't worry about security, we will be providing security measures and all these houses meet the criteria we need to ensure your safety."

"No one can ensure safety."

"We can minimize the risks though."

One property stood out. Located a mile up a country lane and overlooking fields, the nearest neighbor was a working farm. It was a modern barn conversion, and the internal pictures looked perfect. There was a collection of rooms downstairs to form a master suite, comprising a bathroom, bedroom, dressing room, and sitting room. The windows were small and set back into thick walls, with the exception of the barn entrance, which comprised a double height window overlooking a dining hall with a galleried landing. She thought Walid would feel safe in this house.

"I'd like to look at this one."

"Yes, I think that's my favorite. It's probably on the wrong side of Oxford for you, but I think it would be worth the travel."

"Where is it?"

"Wychmoor Wood."

"Really? I don't recognize it."

"Do you know Wychmoor Wood?"

"Yes, I lived there until I was twelve. My father worked at Porton Down and my mother and I went back to France after…"

"He died?"

"They said it was an accident but I'm afraid my mother and I could never accept that verdict."

"I'm sorry. Is that why you are so concerned about the death of other research scientists?"

"Yes, too much so, I'm struggling to be objective."

"Perhaps I can help you with your research."

"I don't think your bosses would like that."

"We'll see."

Chloe had to admit Hilary certainly knew how to impress. At the airport, they bypassed all security and drove through to a private Learjet waiting by the runway. They boarded, were offered soft drinks, and a flight attendant took her overnight bag. Immediately, the plane took off. Even on private jets, you were usually waiting about for clearance.

After an hour spent in a luxury cream leather chair, sipping orange juice and looking at bright skies and sunshine they landed at RAF Brize Norton. Again, a car was waiting on the tarmac, this time a black BMW 5 series.

Soon they were pulling up a long shingle drive to a recently converted barn. Once farm storage, it was now a beautiful Cotswold stone dwelling. Hilary unlocked the door and they walked in. There's something rather cold about walking into a rented property, as if the owner's soul is missing.

Chloe suspected if Walid was traveling with a doctor he would be spending more time than usual in bed and it was important it would be a peaceful room. She needn't have worried. The room was beautiful. William Morris curtains and bedspread were the only patterns in the room, the flooring was a simple mushroom Wilton carpet and the uneven walls covered in white powdery emulsion with gold framed botanical prints. The architraves were white gloss and sunshine lit the room from the patio doors.

She supposed you would call the style "hotel chic." The layout was great, the bed and chairs were comfortable, and the kitchen was bright and practical, designed by someone who knew how to cook.

"What obligations will I have, if I take this property?"

"None—call it us paying you back." Chloe was surprised. It didn't make sense, why would the British feel under any obligation?

Chloe had to say that she was impressed with the speed with which everything began to arrive. Hilary certainly knew how to get a house warmed up. She worked very hard; she made sure everything was working. She showed her some special security features she was having installed in the house and the garden. Chloe felt sure Walid would feel safe here.

By lunchtime, a fleet of assistants were in the property, ensuring the security features were all installed, in particular the security cameras around the perimeter of the property. Heaven help the local foxes or stray cats.

Hilary and Chloe went off to the pub, just over a bridge, with solid pine tables and wooden chairs. *It's probably so they can install the secret cameras,* thought Chloe, *so they can watch us.* It wasn't a bad lunch.

They went back to the house, the workers had gone, and her only complaint was the squirt of a floral air freshener they had used as they left. Chloe hated plastic chemical smells. She opened the windows to freshen up the place and fifteen minutes later, the perfume smell was gone. Instead, fresh air and some rather rural piggy smells filled the place.

"Okay, I think we should go to the base," said Hilary. "He should be landing at about three."

Her heart jumped. Chloe looked at her watch; she had made herself so busy she had lost sight of the time. *Would Walid be okay?* For one moment, she was back in Siesta Key laughing with Walid at the size of the breakfast special. It would have been a wonderful memory had the inconsiderate man, who claimed to love her, not cleared off the next day without saying goodbye or leaving a proper message. It seemed a long time ago.

"Are you all right?" Hilary appeared genuinely concerned.

"Yes, I'm fine—let's go."

A long chassis limousine was waiting on the curved drive and they glided majestically away. She noticed there was either a scruffy farm worker or a security detail at the gate, and as Hilary nodded at him, she assumed it was security.

Her head was buzzing. Fragments of conversation with the market trader in Iraq, what had he said? "A man like that." Was that Walid? The fear in Ahmed's face, why would an art dealer be so stressed? Why had the Americans kept Walid so long? Surely not just for medical care, two weeks should have been sufficient. None of this made sense. She also realized she hadn't told Jean Pierre about her sudden departure from Paris, and she would have to phone him soon, or there would be a full-scale alert to look for her.

They arrived at Brize Norton's main gate, where a sign declared the alert status was Black Bikini Special. Who decided a security warning had anything to do with skimpy swimwear? Perhaps it was the required costume for terrorists. Chloe could only think of terrorists dressed in a bikini from James Bond movies. Dressing in a bikini may distract the troops but they will still think of you as a potential terrorist. Good to know. In France, the alert status term was Vigipirate, as if Jack Sparrow had left the Caribbean to make mischief on an air force base. They both got out of the car and went into the main guard room to sign in with the RAF security office.

Hilary signed as Louise Chappel, which had surprised Chloe, and she produced an official pass for a good-looking RAF sergeant. She said Chloe shouldn't sign and the sergeant agreed. Spooks, more lies, if she was Louise why was she calling herself Hilary? It was all too confusing. Perhaps Patrick Dubois was his working name.

They made their way to the terminal building. Chloe had seen this building on television but never visited it before. It reminded her of wives seeing loved ones off to battle and coffins arriving with military honors. She tried to put the final picture out of mind. They wouldn't have let him travel if there had been any danger of him dying on the plane.

Louise, or whoever she was, went across to an office with a glass partition window to make a phone call. Whatever did she have to say that was so secret? She left and instead of coming back into the main waiting room went off in a different direction. She came back with an elderly man. He had short white wispy hair that stood on end like a dandelion and formed a halo around his head. He must have been six-foot-two and Chloe guessed he was sixty-five, or maybe a well preserved seventy-year-old.

"I'd like to introduce you to Dr—"

"Iain Carmichael!" Chloe couldn't have been more surprised. He was the doctor who had been on duty at Porton Down when her father had died.

"Madame Moreau. This is a pleasure."

He acted surprised but he must have been expecting her, this wasn't a chance encounter.

"You're here because?"

"Your husband needs some specialist care and they thought I might be able to assist."

"I wasn't aware his heart problems were within your specialty."

"Of course I will refer him to any specialist as needed—don't worry, Chloe, the Americans have provided the very best care. No one wants him to die."

At that point, all further conversation ended as an orderly wheeled Walid into the terminal building. He looked very frail. Perhaps he had needed six weeks' medical treatment. She wondered what else they had been doing to him, apart from surgery.

He stood and kissed her, but found himself out of breath. Getting up from the wheelchair and the long flight had taken its toll.

"Let's go home," she said, "I've taken possession of a property just outside Oxford."

"Where are we?"

"Didn't they tell you?"

He laughed, his eyes twinkling, whatever had happened to him in Afghanistan had given him peace. Perhaps he was just full of drugs and anything would make him happy.

"Tell me anything? No, I think that would be a first!"

"We're in Oxfordshire, England. You have a new job in Oxford."

"And the apartment in Paris?"

"Well, you hated it, I hated it, and so I terminated the lease."

"Okay. So how do we get there?"

"There's a car waiting."

"I think perhaps I should examine my patient to see there are no ill effects," said Dr Carmichael.

"Good idea. Perhaps you could call around to the house tomorrow morning." Chloe gave her best "don't mess with me" look and hoped she and Walid could leave.

"I'm fine, Doc. See you in the morning." Walid seemed used to having doctors fussing over him.

Chloe wasn't sure they were going to be able to get away so easily but Louise, Hilary, or whatever her name was, took the initiative and they were in the car. It was just Chloe and Walid, the chauffeur behind the glass screen, on their way to the new home.

Being alone didn't last long; Louise was waiting at the front door for them.

"Just the last few points."

Chloe groaned and felt ungrateful, Louise had managed everything well, it had all gone smoothly.

"The moving van will be here at ten tomorrow morning, and a right hand drive Renault is being delivered from the local garage. I'll get the driver to just pop the keys through the mail slot so as not to disturb you. Have a good night."

"Good night," said Walid.

"Good night, Louise," said Chloe. Louise looked at her, and Chloe smiled and added, "I'm a reporter, I investigate and I find out the truth about things, and you're not Hilary!"

Louise laughed, shook her head, and made her way up the path.

Chloe showed Walid the bedroom, the fire in the living room, to which someone had added a couple of logs, and the security precautions.

They ate an omelet in the small sitting room, one plate and two forks.

"That was the best food I've had in weeks."

"Not great food in an American military hospital then?"

"Could be better. But, if you like peanut butter..."

Walid smiled at Chloe. It seemed a very long time since they had just been happy together. Chloe remembered how he just left Florida, she couldn't afford to get her emotions engaged, he was charming, but she wasn't convinced it wasn't just part of a plan. She told him she didn't want to disturb his sleep and left him alone in the downstairs bedroom. The bad news about their marriage she would deliver tomorrow.

In the morning, the van drove up with his remaining possessions and two very smart moving men placed items in the spare bedroom, and larger items as directed by Chloe.

As soon as the men left, Dr Carmichael arrived. Chloe left him with Walid and after about an hour, he came to see her.

"My dear, it's not good. I have the file from the Americans and, to my mind, it would appear to be a case of radiation sickness. I need to do some more blood work and the good news is I have a treatment plan. It may not be a long term solution but I think you should agree to treatment."

"Radiation? How? Do you mean he was poisoned? Did the Americans...?" Even as she said, "Americans" it sounded ludicrous. You didn't just get radiation sickness, you couldn't catch it like the flu, so there had to be some explanation.

"The Americans are at a loss to understand where the radiation came from. There are concerns—more about Walid's link with terrorists who might have nuclear weapons than his health, so the investigation has been thorough but they don't have an explanation."

Walid walked in, he was now dressed and didn't look as tired or pale as he had the night before.

"What do you think?"

"Has he told you what's involved?"

She turned to Carmichael.

"We will continue the blood transfusions every week as they seem to be helping, but in addition we will start a course of specific drugs. The effect will be tiredness for a couple of days after the cocktail of drugs is administered, but then you will have five perfectly normal days, feeling your old self and full of energy."

"I'm dying, Chloe, the only question is when, and how much of this up and down can you cope with?"

"Do you want treatment?" It seemed callous to ask Walid the question, but she didn't feel she had the right to make any input into the situation.

"What do you want?"

"It's not my decision."

"Let's try the treatment in a week or so, let's just enjoy now." Walid looked laid back for a man receiving a death sentence.

"I'm sorry, I haven't made myself clear. We need to start treatment tomorrow to have any hope at all of prolonging life, ideally it would have been six weeks ago, but unless they had managed a successful bypass operation, nothing else would have mattered." Dr Carmichael looked first at Chloe then Walid, ensuring they understood his meaning.

Walid and Chloe looked at each other. She didn't know what to say. It would be selfish of her to put him through anything else. If there had been any hope, but there wasn't, it was only a matter of how and when.

CHAPTER THIRTY-TWO

Wychmoor Wood

Louise enjoyed staying at Wychmoor House Hotel. She thought it was probably because she was just so tired she slept well. The sleep was inevitable, but there was a small lingering doubt the quality of the sleep had been derived from the small box she had found on her pillow. The box promised her a good night's sleep. It was a bit of *Alice in Wonderland,* instead of instructions to "Eat me" and "Drink me," the first vial was a nasal spray, and the second was a fine spray for the pillow. It just smelled like lavender water. But, there was no denying the effect.

The rooms created an ambiance fitting a top class country hotel. The blossomy prints framed the tall windows, and the ceiling plasterwork, highlighted in gold, ensured a sense of opulence. The television, hidden in a dark oak armoire, was a high definition thirty-two inch flat screen, with all the premium satellite channels. Louise had been amused to find the en-suite bathroom was twice the size of the bedroom in her London flat. The modern Victorian style radiator heated large white fluffy towels, and Moulton Brown products promised to Energize, Inspire, or Moisturize. Louise wondered if she mixed all three for her shower, would she be conditioned, energetic, and inspired for the day.

It certainly made a change from the usual budget hotels they used on observations or for regional meetings. She didn't think Graeme would leave her in Oxfordshire for long, and certainly not at this hotel, it must be costing a fortune and his department expenses budget wouldn't stand it.

The extractor fan in the bathroom concealed the buzz from her phone, so it was after Louise's shower when she returned Graeme's call.

"Dr Carmichael hasn't turned up at Art Expert's place today. He was staying in the hotel last night. Can you check it out? Oh, and don't get anyone local involved, last problem we had there, everyone was talking to the press. The ambulance men had a point of view—even the editor of the village news made print. So call me for any support. I'm in the car and should be with you in about an hour and a half, give or take rush hour traffic."

Louise finished dressing and quickly downed the remains of the coffee from her breakfast tray. Wychmoor House was a civilized place; it didn't offer a dining room for breakfast. It was all room service with freshly cooked personal selections from an extensive menu.

She arrived at the door to Dr Carmichael's room at the same time as the housekeeper. Louise instinctively knew something was wrong. She would have liked to put this inspiration down to the Moulton Brown shower gel, but Graeme's brief had suggested there might be trouble. She supposed at Carmichael's age, problems did occur. His instruction not to call the local ambulance service was unusual though.

She got out her ID card and approached the housekeeper.

"Could you open Dr Carmichael's room for me?"

The housekeeper looked at her identification. She held the card and looked at the picture and at Louise, assessing the accuracy of the photograph with the owner of the ID.

"I think I better call Mr Speakman-Brown. If there's trouble, he'd want to know." The housekeeper had made a decision, she was not going to help Louise and she was going to leave it all to Mr Speakman-Brown.

"Perhaps you could hurry and in the meantime leave me your keys."

238 | C R HARRIS

The housekeeper paused, but Louise's impatient authoritative gesture seemed to win the point. The housekeeper went back down the stairs, leaving Louise to unlock the door. She knocked, knowing there wouldn't be a reply, and entered the room.

Good quality blackout linings to the curtains ensured the room was dark and she was unable to see anything. As a precaution, she called out Dr Carmichael's name, but she hadn't expected a response. She reached into her handbag and put on a pair of vinyl disposable gloves before switching on the light. She knew she needed to preserve any evidence, in case this was anything other than a natural death. What she saw astounded her. She was used to seeing dead bodies, even bodies of people she was acquainted with, but this seemed like a staged death. There was no point checking for life—Carmichael was alabaster white.

"Graeme, we have a problem."

"Dead?"

"Yes, but unusual circumstances."

"Any publicity?"

"Contained so far, I'm the only one to have been in the room. But the owner of the hotel is about to arrive."

"Tell him it's a crime scene and seal it off. Don't use tape or anything that would upset him, and find out when the hotel guests will have mostly left for the day. I'll send a team over. Why do you think it might be suspicious?"

"I can't quite see Carmichael in the area of autoerotic asphyxia, and well, it looks staged."

"Dear God. Call Special Branch; don't get the locals in. We will treat this as terrorist related—I don't want any information released. Tell the hotel owner Dr Carmichael has died and the police will be there shortly. I'm sure Special Branch will be able to deal with the coroner's office, and the hotel owner's concerns. I'm on my way. I want every piece of evidence taken for forensic examination. If there is so much as a mouse fart in the room, I want the gas bottled and analyzed to see if it was a French mouse—is that clear?"

Graeme rang off, not waiting for her reply.

Louise called Phil Scarlet, she assumed he could either deal with the event or redirect her call.

"I'll be there in five."

She looked around the room trying to take in the detail. She used the camera on her phone to take a couple of pictures to help her with details for her report later.

Dr Iain Alistair Carmichael was naked. His head covered in a black trash bag. His feet tied to the legs of the ladder-back chair from the desk. The belt from the white fluffy bathrobe tied him to the chair and formed a noose around his neck. The end of the tie was in Carmichael's left hand. If this was an accident, presumably, Carmichael had lost consciousness and the plan would have been to let go of the noose and be able to breathe again. What struck Louise as odd was that if this were autoerotic asphyxiation why would Carmichael have shaved a thin strip down his chest to his pubic bone? The pale stripe reminded her of a badger's head.

Louise had no idea as to whether this would have been an effective method of asphyxiating oneself; she couldn't see any appeal in being strangled to enhance the sexual experience. But to take the large white bath towel from the bathroom, place it on the floor, put the desk chair on the edge of the towel as if laid out for some clinical event seemed very odd. There was an empty hypodermic syringe on the floor.

Carmichael may have been well into his sixties but he was still a very sexually attractive and charming man; she couldn't equate this warm man with the image before her.

It was also a very complex set up to complete in the dark.

The discreet knock at the door alerted her to Mr Speakman-Brown's arrival. Louise turned out the light, and opening the door the smallest amount possible to let her slim body pass through, she confronted Mr

Speakman-Brown. A good well-tailored suit, it had to be bespoke to fit this tall, thin elegant man so well. Definitely private school. He looked rather distinguished, perhaps a minor aristocrat, a cousin, or younger son. He had an elegance about him, he gave service with pride not subservient in any way.

"Oh my God, he's dead, isn't he?"

"Yes, I'm afraid he is. It is essential no one will ever know he stayed or died here. You need to think of the reputation of your hotel."

Louise could see this had focused his mind.

"Should I call the police?"

"The police are on their way. They should be here in"—she consulted her watch—"well, about two minutes. So if you would like to go downstairs and greet Mr Scarlet, who will arrive in plain clothes in an unmarked car, we will do all we can to ensure complete secrecy—but I need your assurance of complete silence on the matter. Not even your wife or the housekeeper must ever know."

"Yes. Of course. But won't there be an inquest?"

"I doubt that very much."

"Right, of course...um, well, er, yes...um, I'll go and meet..."

"Mr Scarlet. Meet him and bring him straight up here."

"Right."

Louise wished she had the power of Spock. In *Star Trek* this situation would have been resolved easily, either Bones would have administered some drug to cause amnesia or Spock could have done a mind meld. If the techies could come up with one of those light pens they used in *Men in Black,* now that would be a useful gadget. She brought herself back to the reality of the situation and she knew she would need to get Art Expert to the hospital to see the specialist Carmichael had lined up.

Graeme with his superior persuasive skills might well have better results, but she guessed the only thing to guarantee Mr Speakman-Brown's silence was the thought his precious hotel would become notorious—which wasn't exactly the clientele he was looking for. Still he could always consider holding murder mystery events at the hotel.

Phil Scarlet arrived at Dr Carmichael's room a couple of minutes later. He was slim, trim, hair cut so short it almost amounted to designer stubble. It masked the thin balding parts on his head well. He had a kind face, and he was the sort of man to give you a feeling of confidence, you could trust him.

"Graeme wants this treated as murder, a wet job," said Louise. "His actual words were, 'If there is so much as a mouse fart in the room, I want the gas bottled and analyzed to see if it was a French mouse.'" Phil Scarlet allowed himself the briefest of smiles, she thought he had probably worked with Graeme before and knew the turn of phrase. "I'll see what information Mr Speakman-Brown may have and I need to get my clients to an appointment."

"Okay, see you before you go," he said.

Louise knocked on the door of Mr Speakman-Brown's office.

"Can I get you a coffee or a brandy or something?"

"That's very kind of you, Mr Speakman-Brown, but I won't be long. There are just one or two questions I would like to ask you."

"Right…yes, of course."

"Do you have any surveillance cameras in the hotel?"

"Yes, I'm afraid we have to. We have obvious cameras in the lower parking lot and at the main entrance. But we also have two tiny cameras at the front desk and one at the corner of the stairs."

He opened up the large oak armoire, similar to the one in Louise's room, but instead of the one large screen, she saw four flat screens with excellent quality pictures.

"Do you record any of these pictures?"

"Am I in trouble? Should I have registered this equipment or asked someone's permission or something?"

"No, Mr Speakman-Brown, not at all, these pictures might help us."

"Do you think he was murdered?"

"We are following up all lines of investigation; until the autopsy is complete we have no way of knowing."

"Right, I see. The information is stored on the hard disk of the computer for fourteen days and then we delete it."

"Perhaps I could look at the pictures from the camera on the stairs, say, from seven last night until midnight."

"Of course."

Louise was concerned that, in his current agitated state, the hotel owner would delete the pictures but they appeared on the computer screen on his desk. The pictures flicked on and off as the motion detection equipment turned the camera on and off and a digital clock in the bottom left of the picture let her see the time.

"Is the time on the camera accurate?"

"Yes, the clock synchronizes with the atomic clock at Rugby."

Louise watched herself go up the stairs and concluded the timing seemed to be accurate. She recognized the guests from dinner as they went up and she was concluding she had seen the total complement of guests. She watched Dr Carmichael go up the stairs, and ten minutes later she saw Patrick of the DST go up the stairs. She would never have known he was not a guest. He was dressed in a smart navy suit, dark tie, and would have fitted in to the smart restaurant last night very well indeed. He looked French, understated, and sophisticated.

"This man"—Louise pointed at the screen—"did he stay here last night?"

"No, I don't know who he is. I can check the register." Mr Speakman-Brown was flustered at this inquiry.

"No, that won't be necessary."

She continued to watch and fifteen minutes later Patrick triggered the motion sensor on his way down. Graeme would not be happy. He didn't believe in coincidences.

Just as she was concluding there was only one suspect, another man made his way up the stairs. It was probable he knew there was a camera on the stairs, because he kept his head down, so there was no way to recognize him.

"Could I have a copy of this recording, the reception camera, and the parking lot data from nine last night to eight this morning, please?"

Mr Speakman-Brown put a DVD in the machine and they waited as the information transferred on to the disk. He now seemed calm and confident so she went into the courtyard at the front of the hotel to call Graeme.

"It would appear your initial suspicion may be correct," said Louise.

"Evidence?"

"He's on the hotel surveillance tape. There is one alternative as well."

"Get me a copy."

"Done."

Louise went up to see Phil Scarlet, the police surgeon was present.

"Do we have an approximate time of death?"

"Before midnight. I'll know more when we get back."

The time of death would fit in with either of the two men on the surveillance pictures.

"Murder?"

"Only an autopsy will tell."

"Right. I'll be in touch later."

Louise left the hotel and drove across to the barn. She could only hope Carmichael had briefed the protection team on the events of the day, which would give her some ideas on where to find the specialist. She located the driver.

"He wanted to be driven to the Churchill Hospital, if that helps any."

"I suppose it would be too much to ask if we know the name of the specialist?"

"Sorry."

"Are you ready to leave?" Louise looked at her watch, if there were any traffic holdups, and there usually were in Oxford, they would be late.

"They have a visitor."

"Who?"

"I don't know, some French chap, she seemed to know him and was pleased to see him."

"Right. In future, he doesn't get access either."

"Okay."

Louise composed herself. It wouldn't do for Patrick to work out her suspicions. She rang the bell and used her key to enter through the front door.

"Louise. Is Carmichael with you? He's late," asked Chloe.

"No." She watched Patrick's face. "He's had an accident, he won't be able to go today."

No flicker of emotion. Nothing. Patrick was definitely a pro.

Chloe was about to speak again when Graeme rang the doorbell.

He introduced himself to Chloe and went to meet Walid. Louise saw Patrick off the premises and let Chloe know the real reason Dr Carmichael was absent.

"Walid, I'm Graeme Scott, an officer with MI5."

Walid said nothing.

"We are facing an imminent threat, and I am sorry to inform you that last night Dr Carmichael died."

"Died how?"

"Murder.

"Walid, we have been watching you on your trips to London and can only conclude you have been an innocent art dealer…"

"I have been through all this with the Americans—can't you just share the information and leave me and my wife in peace?"

"Ahmed Talbi, the Paris art gallery owner, has been channeling funds to Al Qaeda networks."

"I don't know anything. I just want to live what little life I have left in peace."

"I don't know if you are aware Ahmed had been exporting crystal, cut glass, in fact any glass objects with sufficient lead used in their composition to disable normal security procedures. These objects went back and forth to Iraq and back to London or Paris."

"No. Yes, I mean I had taken presents to Baghdad last time I went to Iraq."

"The result was just what Ahmed wanted. Security checks in Iraq of materials and art objects coming to France and Britain weren't checked thoroughly, and we now believe that in the last consignment of goods, no less than four radioactive bombs were sent to Ahmed's warehouse in London. By the time we knew of the situation, most of the objects had been shipped to individual galleries, and we are in the process of tracking each item down. We think you might be able to help us speed up that process."

"Three large galleries would take many items; the minor galleries might only take an item every three months."

"Dr Carmichael said he was treating you for radiation poisoning. Do you have any idea when the contamination took place?"

"None. I assume in Iraq and you should question the Americans."

"Yes, I have asked the question but I haven't had a reply yet. The Americans are at a loss to explain your illness, as they don't have any other prisoners who are sick from radiation. Did you look at any burned out tanks while you were in Iraq—they are sometimes contaminated with depleted uranium."

"No. What do you want from me?"

"I would like you to look through some addresses and let me know if any of them look familiar. Are they galleries Ahmed has dealt with before? Or have any of the pieces sold at Sotheby's gone to any of the galleries on this list? That's all."

"I don't know all his clients, only the ones I met. You need to visit Ahmed and get him to tell you."

"We need to find every item from the consignment entering the warehouse in the last six weeks."

"Ask the warehouse."

"We have, but we believe you would know which galleries were most likely to take goods from Ahmed. The goods from Baghdad were not marked as coming from him, but the wholesaler."

"You mean most of the deliveries have already been made?"

"Yes."

"That is unusual. Normally he would wait for me to do deliveries; the clients liked it if I delivered the items and could talk through the provenance and reassure them on the quality of the products."

"If you weren't available, who would he use?"

"I don't know. He would usually wait, even two or three weeks."

"Can you look at some gallery addresses?"

Louise looked at her watch. "We need to leave now to see the specialist. Perhaps we can look at the list in the car."

Looking for the delivery addresses on Graeme's whim that this was how the bombs were getting to London was all very well, but James T, who was interested in finding Farook and Nasir, hadn't, as far as she knew, sanctioned this side of the investigation.

CHAPTER THIRTY-THREE

Bradford, England

Leila had been importing halal baby food for six months before her husband took an active interest in the business. At first, he thought it would not be profitable, just a hobby for his wife, but there was good demand. When his cousin phoned him to take delivery of a package within a shipment for Leila he thought nothing of it. Getting packages to relatives was ongoing for families across continents and he did not hesitate to help.

The chilled halal food arrived on Friday and was placed in a large cold storage room. On Monday, two lads arrived in a white van to take delivery of the small packages placed in each carton of the baby food. The lads were careful handling the boxes and knew exactly which ones to open. Leila's husband felt reassured his cousin would be pleased with the care they were taking. He did not ask what the packages contained or who the young men were.

Farook and Nasir were well trained, they had prepared for this mission for nine months. They said little. The journey so far had been uneventful. They traveled in a plain white Ford Transit van—millions of similar vans were everywhere in England. In the van were maps and more instructions, when and where to change the license plates. They listened to the radio, and chatted about girls from their school days, their school soccer team, what had happened to their friends, and if the French teacher had been having an affair with the history teacher, she was cute, whereas he was a complete geek and they didn't believe the rumors. They knew from the BBC news a bomb had gone off in Frankfurt. They felt aggrieved the lad they met at the madrassa had been selected to carry the bomb into the station. Both men were bitter he had been chosen, but they didn't discuss it much. They had little understanding Frankfurt was just the diversion, a target of convenience to dispose of a potential threat to the security of the terror cell, and their role was far more significant.

To distract themselves from their disappointment they discussed the Eintract, Frankfurt's soccer team, did they trust Willi to keep the team in the Bundesliga or would they be relegated again. It had been a difficult season. The team needed a star goal scorer, and Willi needed more money to get the right squad of players.

The journey was long, and they were bored, they understood the need to stay away from the highways where every car was monitored, but the slow pace of their journey was taking its toll.

Leaving Bradford, they made their way through the night, avoiding the major roads and not exceeding the speed limit, until they arrived at a small village eighty miles outside London. Driving down an unused road to a hay barn, now covered in darkness, they hid the van in the barn and slept in the back on an old and rather damp double mattress. They joked about the van being used as a passion wagon, and how after the event, they would go find themselves a couple of girls for the night.

In the morning, they located the compressor hidden behind some hay bales and loaded it into the back of the van. They placed stickers on the van proclaiming, "Aqua Holdings - Contractors for the Water Industry. Reducing leaks benefits your world."

It was a bright sunny morning but they still had some difficulty locating the grid that concealed access to the water supply for the rural village of Wychmoor Wood. Finally, they found the right manhole on the

CHAPTER THIRTY-FOUR

MI5, London

"Graeme Scott? This is Police Surgeon Geraldine Purse, Phil Scarlet asked me to give you a call regarding Dr Carmichael."

"Thank you for calling and what do you have?"

"It's quite an interesting case. These are preliminary findings and subject to some lab work to confirm the theory, but it would appear Dr Carmichael was murdered."

"Yes, and..."

"I think it went like this. The murderer injected Dr Carmichael with 13.3 mg of ketamine HCl per ml, 1.3 mg of xylazine per ml, 0.25 mg of acepromazine maleate per ml, administered intramuscularly. The common name is Rodent Cocktail, it's used in animal testing laboratories to sedate rodents prior to any procedures. Carmichael was given an injection through his groin, so it has taken us quite a long time to find the site of this injection. He was poisoned—we think probably potassium cyanide."

"How?"

"We are checking the substance now—all I'm going on now is the smell—but I expect the analysis of the stomach contents will show the remains of a cyanide pill. While sedated he would have been made to swallow the pill, the effects are quick. It could have been a form of peptide, a substance naturally occurring and almost impossible to detect in the body, which would cause a fatal heart attack. Dr Carmichael died of a fatal heart attack and not asphyxiation."

"Are you sure?"

"Pretty much so, the lab work, as I said, will confirm this. Having administered the injection your perpetrator bagged and put the noose around the neck of Dr Carmichael. He allowed the limp body to commence the strangulation process while he waited for the heart attack to take place."

"He?"

"Or she. In fact the perpetrator might have left prior to the final moment, knowing death was certain—in which case the total amount of time in the hotel room would have been no longer than five minutes. Dr Carmichael showed no signs of any bruising or abrasion, which would suggest he either knew the perpetrator or didn't believe the person was serious about doing him any harm."

"Amount of skill needed for this method?"

"To be able to give the injection in the right place, I would say low level training. But to know how to obtain the substance in question and knowledge of the dosage to make it effective in a human, that would require a high level of sophistication. The Russians were good at producing peptides for assassinations."

"Are you suggesting Russians?"

"No—something a lot closer to home. I think you should look at the Anti-Vivisection Society or similar. Special Branch are re-opening investigations of three old cases where the verdict of suicide had been given by the coroner, but again the circumstances were odd."

"Anti-Vivisection—where does that idea come from?"

"The parallel with how rats in a laboratory are killed. The deep sleep, some rats are shaved to assist with instrumentation, before experimentation and death."

"Yes, I see the picture—but isn't that a little farfetched?"

"I can't see why any spook would take the time to create such an elaborate scene; he could just administer an injection while Carmichael was asleep and, given his age, leave us all to conclude he had died in his sleep."

"What evidence have you got firmed up?"

"Rodent Cocktail is definite, the site of the injection is confirmed, and the cause of death is myocardial infarction not asphyxiation."

"And presumably the injection takes us away from any thought of a natural death?"

"Right. I'll let you know when we get the lab results and any further information. Any questions?"

"No. Thank you, you have been most helpful. Yes! Just one, why Carmichael?"

"Probably because he worked at Porton Down, in fact he never did any experimentation on animals. He was purely a conventional medical doctor for the benefit of the staff there."

"What a waste of a good man."

"Absolutely."

"Thank you again."

Graeme picked up the phone and called Louise into his office.

"Carmichael was murdered, probably by causing a heart attack, after being sedated by an injection of Rodent Cocktail."

"Rodent Cocktail?"

"Yes, the suggestion is some anti-vivisection group or similar thought, as he worked at Porton Down, he would be involved in animal testing."

Graeme watched Louise's anger. Not good, a professional officer needs to look at these issues with distance.

"So, if we leave this matter to Special Branch, can we stop looking at Patrick as if he is a murderer? I assume the tapes have gone to Phil Scarlet, and we can press on with the small matter of where to find the art gallery packages and if they are live nuclear devices."

CHAPTER THIRTY-FIVE

Paris

Ahmed was concerned the Algerian had left him in place far too long. He should be back in Algeria by now. It was foolish to think if he remained behind to be picked up by the DST it would help anybody.

He looked around the studio; it was time to make some changes. He would need cash. He took three paintings off the walls and placed them in a large art portfolio. He opened a couple of cabinets and took out some exhibits; he worried whether his actions would damage priceless artwork, but it was time to get into self-preservation mode. He needed the appearance of inhabiting the shop, while becoming a ghost.

Ahmed asked the graphics store to do something different from his usual order, in addition to making digital copies for his brochure he asked for a copy of each piece of art, full size on low quality board. He said he would be back for the work in four hours. He went to buy acrylic varnish, burnt sienna powder-paint, and art brushes. He would need to age his new prints to look like the originals before he hung them in his shop.

When he collected his artwork, he couldn't spot the agent who was supposed to be following him. Perhaps he was waiting for him at the gallery; he had followed him to the graphic shop before when he had artworks scanned for the catalogue. When he returned he noticed the agent propped against the lamppost with a newspaper.

Tonight, he would varnish and frame the prints. They would never know he had replaced the originals with copies. He considered how much value he would lose in leaving the frames behind, but he couldn't see any way of spiriting them out of the shop.

He sat at his desk and began to check inventory. This was a regular activity for a Thursday morning. He knew anything he wrote they would be able to see as clearly as he could. He found living under a microscope stressful, and he knew this was part of the cat and mouse game they played. They didn't know whether he was guilty or innocent, in fact if they thought he was guilty of anything he would be in custody by now; no, they were hoping he would lead them to the others. Perhaps the money he sent had been traced. It wouldn't be for much longer.

He would close the store tonight for the last time. He looked around; he had his new identity waiting for him. He would miss Paris.

As he cleared old boxes out from under the counter, he came across an aluminum briefcase. He thought all the cases were in London, so this did surprise him. He couldn't have made a mistake, could he? Perhaps he had kept the original sample hot briefcase, and given the courier a glass vase.

He smiled, now he had enough money to retire on. He dared not open it to check; a sudden increase in the radiation levels would trigger a raid. It might also be there to explode and kill him. The Algerian had a reputation for finishing off any loose ends. Ahmed would assume this was one of the special briefcases and worth a great deal of money. Tomorrow, he would disappear during Friday prayers.

CHAPTER THIRTY-SIX

Oxford

Chloe waited on the orange plastic chair in the waiting room of the Churchill Hospital. She wasn't sure she wanted a pause in the hectic schedule. It was giving her too much time to think.

Did Carmichael fall into the sequence of the biological scientists? He didn't fit the profile, he was a retired occupational health doctor attached to Porton Down—which of course provided an interesting practice. He was sure Walid had been exposed to radiation; the question no one seemed to be able to answer was where he had been exposed. The Americans were adamant nothing had happened while Walid was in their care and they had no other cases among their detainees.

Chloe looked at her watch; it was time to leave for Oxford's Natural History Museum. She felt a fraud playing the devoted wife at the hospital. She was here because she felt sorry for him. It dawned on her that being here, looking after Walid, meant she wasn't finishing her investigation into the biological weapons scientists. It was masterful, she had just fallen in with Louise's plans to be here for Walid, and domestic responsibilities were the best way of slowing down any professional woman. She hadn't been asked about whether she wanted to move in with Walid, it had been assumed she would be the dutiful wife and help look after him. Right, well, she was good at multitasking, she would ensure

Jean Pierre did what she would have been doing and the investigation would continue. She could make phone calls, send emails, there was no reason to stop. Walid would need lots of rest and she could use the time to best advantage, she would make every minute count.

There was something familiar about Louise. Her mind went back to the detention suite in Germany. Patrick knew her. That was it; the house in Oxfordshire was compensation for something nobody had even admitted had happened. The Americans hadn't detained her, she had been held by the British. It was all complete madness. Why would they? Of course, to bargain the release of Walid, and they hadn't been too keen on her line of inquiry. It was odd Louise had offered to get her some information on the death of the scientists. A disillusioned MI5 officer could provide useful information, if she could trust Louise and Louise could trust her.

The bus from Headington dropped her off in Cornmarket, where she went to the bank and collected the five thousand pounds she had ordered in used notes. It probably wouldn't be enough, but it would be enough for a down payment. Then she made her way to South Parks Road, past creamy stone college buildings with their immaculate lawns (with the obligatory "Please do not walk on the grass" sign) and waning herbaceous borders, all set behind wrought iron gates. The museum, built in the neo-gothic style, multi-layers of intricate brickwork, could have been a mainline London railway station, such was its grandeur. Inside colonnades divided the space. She went upstairs and immediately it became clear why he had chosen this space. It was deserted and you could see all around the gallery and had a good view of the comings and goings downstairs. It was nearly two. A young man dressed in jeans and a gray hooded top approached her.

"Chloe Moreau?"

"Yes?" Chloe wondered if this man was going to take her to meet the detective.

"We spoke on the phone." He held out his hand and Chloe shook it, she was still surprised. This man looked too young to be the detective, she had been expecting a retired policeman.

"People are usually surprised, but I don't need police skills, just excellent photographic skills, patience, a client base of rich women, and to be anonymous. Giving you this footage could end my career, so can you make it worthwhile?"

"I suppose it depends what you've got and what you had in mind."

He went across to a glass showcase, got out a ten-inch laptop, and selected a video clip to show her. It showed Dr Soames taking hold of a blue rope. Chloe looked away, she didn't need more images in her mind of people dying. The young man wasn't watching the film either.

"You should watch," he said.

"Mmm. I've seen people hang before."

"Yes, but you haven't seen them hang themselves, only after they're dead. You really do need to watch." He started the video clip again. "You see, she takes a bottle of pills out of her bag and she gets onto the chair and places the rope around her neck. But it's a bit convenient, isn't it? I mean I don't even think the aristocracy would have a servant set up a noose in preparation for a hanging and yet the maid had it all ready for her."

"So do you have the footage of who did this?"

"Oh yes, but watch."

Chloe watched. Liz Soames climbed on the chair, placed the noose around her neck, and took a pill from the bottle she had taken from her handbag. She waited, looking at the lake, took a last look, and swallowed the pill. It was less than ten seconds before her head fell forward and her body twitched, just once, and she seemed dead. The rope held her body up. She was crumpled, but the chair was still in place.

"But it's what happens next that makes this film worth so much." He looked at his watch. "Look!"

Chloe watched as a boat approached the dock and a young woman in a black waitress outfit jumped off the boat, climbed onto the platform, and went into the boathouse. She kicked the chair away from under the body, and prized the bottle of pills out of Dr Soames's hand. She read the label, and placed the bottle in her pocket. She emptied Dr Soames's handbag, picked out a note, put the contents back, and returned to the boat. As she boarded you could see her face. Chloe was shocked. She shook her head. It was Louise Chappel, the friendly MI5 agent, available for hangings, abductions, moving house, and Chloe could only conjecture as to what other functions she could perform.

"How much?" asked Chloe.

"Five grand." Chloe looked at him, she was surprised he asked for so little; he clearly didn't understand the significance of the footage, or maybe he did and he didn't want the responsibility of keeping the secret any more. She knew that if she agreed to his request immediately he would feel cheated, and it was essential to bargain with him, even if she paid him the five grand.

Chloe took a sharp intake of breath, shook her head, and said, "Three."

"Four thousand, five hundred pounds in used notes now, or I walk."

Chloe held out her hand. "Deal."

The young man gave her the computer and Chloe took out the notes, bundled in five hundreds, gave him his money, he counted the bundles, flicked through the notes, and left.

She didn't know his name, she didn't need it, the pictures spoke for themselves. Louise Chappel had some questions to answer: what was she doing at the boathouse? Any good bio-med scientist would have access to some drugs that would bring death faster than hanging, most people wanted a peaceful end, but why did she take her own life?

Chloe left the museum and watched to see if anyone was following her, but didn't see anybody. Perhaps, now she was in England, there was so much CCTV it wasn't necessary to follow her. She thought about her route and decided to return via a Starbucks café where she would be able to email all the materials to Jean Pierre. That should get his heart racing.

She wondered about phoning him, she would like to have heard his reaction, but she would call him tomorrow. She would know what was happening with Walid tomorrow.

This footage should put a smile on Anne Marie's face. Now they were getting the sort of materials she was looking for when she started the inquiry, not just conjecture, but hard evidence, actual names of the individuals within the secret intelligence community.

Back at the hospital, the news was not good. Walid had reacted badly to one of the drug cocktails they had administered, and so they were keeping him overnight for observation. This was not a good start to the treatment regime. Walid wanted to go home. To him this was like detention all over again.

CHAPTER THIRTY-SEVEN

MI5, London

"How the hell?"

"He went to the mosque on Friday which was usual behavior and the tail followed the person they thought was the art gallery owner back to the gallery, only to realize at the last moment it wasn't Ahmed."

"Any leads?"

"Not so far."

"This is a disaster."

No one could accuse Graeme of overreacting. Louise put her head down and continued to look through her emails. It was more important than ever to check emails carefully for any seemingly irrelevant piece of information that might link up to form a clue.

There was one final nuclear briefcase bomb to locate, and the contact who could have led to the capture of the orchestrator of this plot had now disappeared.

Louise noticed a report from West Yorkshire police about an officer called to a reported burglary. When he got to the scene there was no sign of forced entry to the warehouse; the chilled room door was ajar and the padlock, which was on the ground, still had the keys in the lock. The only sign of any untoward activity was six of the packing cases containing the halal baby food imported from Pakistan were open. Inside these cases there was a piece of foam placed on top of the jars of baby food shaped to carry an object perhaps 12 to 14 cm in diameter and about 6 cm in depth. He asked the owner to open a couple of other boxes, which didn't have the foam inserts. When asked to account for the consignment of the baby jars, the delivery was in fact all present and correct, and so without any evidence of a crime the officer was withdrawing from the scene as an angry husband arrived, and confessed he had failed to lock up properly. The man apologized to the officer, but the officer had the feeling the amount of fear and anxiety exhibited by the man exceeded the normal concern about a police officer being on site merely because of the man's negligence. Not locking up properly would not have accounted for the foam on top of the box for something other than the baby food. As the import item came from Pakistan, the routine report was forwarded to the security services.

"Graeme?"

"What?"

"I think I may have found the delivery point for Farook and Nadir."

"Where?"

"Bradford."

"Tell me more."

Louise read out the police report.

"Let's face it, these guys came over clean. They must have gone somewhere when they got off the boat to collect something—and probably pick up transport because we haven't found them on any surveillance footage of public transportation."

Graeme considered the matter.

"Okay, let's phone West Yorkshire police, have them pick up this couple and hold them in separate cells under the prevention of terrorism charges and I'll go ask them some questions. I'll need a car and a driver, Louise. Oh, by the way... good work!"

Louise was disappointed to be left out of the trip to Bradford but she knew she would need to start a search from the address in Bradford to find Farook and Nadir. Now they had a point of departure surely they would be able to find the vehicle, which would be a beginning.

CHAPTER THIRTY-EIGHT

Wychmoor Wood

Mary Butcher was ninety-three years of age. Her family history went back as far as the Doomsday Book. She was a great-grandmother six times over. Four of her great grandchildren lived in the village.

As she looked around the graveyard, she mused, it wasn't kept the way it used to be. People used to tend graves every week. Now she was part of a minority that visited her husband's grave with fresh flowers every week. She was never quite sure what she would find, sometimes one of the grandchildren would leave Grandpa a note, or a picture, which was against regulations. The churchwardens were hot on regulations and cold on maintenance. The churchyard hadn't looked the same since they had insisted all gravestones be laid flat. Something to do with health and safety, they said. You only had to look at the age of the tombstones to realize this was nonsense. *The authorities are good at protecting you from unlikely but predictable accidents and useless at preventing serious events like terrorism,* she thought. Although it was November, the last of the leaves hadn't been collected and the mild weather meant the grass could have done with one final cut before winter.

She picked up the notes and dead flowers, placed them in the Tesco shopping bag she had brought along for the purpose, and put the fresh burnt-orange chrysanthemums in the makeshift vase. It had been the idea of one of the grandchildren. The churchwardens had asked no one leave glass vases at the graveside, as they had become a target for vandals. So, a cut-off plastic Coke bottle buried in the ground became her vase. Frank wouldn't have minded, he would have enjoyed the pragmatic approach, but Mary minded, it seemed disrespectful.

She told Frank all her news; how sad she was that Gertrude had passed away. "It's getting so there's hardly anyone left that I know." She finished her chores and walked slowly home.

Her cottage was too big for her now, but the children wouldn't hear of her selling it, so they moved her bed downstairs and installed a walk-in shower under the stairs. Occasionally one of the grandchildren was dispatched to clean upstairs and check on things.

She took an apron off the peg on the back of the door, hung up her coat, and placed her soft felt hat on top. There would just be time for a cup of tea before Barbara came. Barbara came every night. She wasn't quite sure why she came, but it was useless to tell her not to come.

She held on to the sink. Suddenly she felt tired. Perhaps she had done too much today. As the kettle began to whistle, she realized she was having a nosebleed. The drops fell onto her apron.

Oh dear, she thought. She felt inside her apron pocket for a tissue, but couldn't feel anything, her hand was numb.

The kettle was still whistling when Barbara let herself into the cottage. She went into the kitchen and found Mary on the floor. At first, she thought she had had a fall and the bloody nose was the result. She called emergency services, the dispatcher insisted she conduct CPR until the ambulance arrived, in spite of the fact Mary was cold. It was this action, taken in obedience to the ambulance dispatcher's instruction, which caused Mary to pass the virus to Barbara.

The ambulance crew tried to revive Mary, which resulted in two further victims of the virus, before they called the time of her death. They couldn't take the body away, and told Barbara the numbers of a couple of undertakers who would come. They also told her to phone the police. PC Rowbotham came immediately and called the coroner's office to report the death. He too would catch the virus, as did the funeral director.

Barbara set about ringing Mary's two children living in the village. At ninety-three, it shouldn't have come as a shock, but maybe it was the fact she had been around so long that made accepting her death so hard.

The undertaker took Mary's body to the hospital mortuary so a death certificate could be prepared, but the coroner ordered an autopsy, it was standard procedure. The days of writing "old age" as the cause of death were long gone. Now they needed to have a precise reason. This autopsy discovered Mary's organs had liquefied, the nosebleed was the only symptom in one so old, had she been younger the course of the illness would have been different. This prompt autopsy prevented a large-scale tragedy, and started the implementation of the emergency plan.

CHAPTER THIRTY-NINE

Churchill Hospital

Chloe waited in the corridor. There was always so much waiting around in hospitals. You waited for the doctors, the specialists, the tests, the results of the tests, meals. She didn't know what to say to Walid. He had changed while he had been away, she expected she had too, but he was different. He was at peace. Chloe wasn't sure whether this was his way of preparing for death or whether something else was responsible for the change. A nurse directed her into a private ward where Walid was dozing. Chloe leaned against the edge of the bed and held his hand. It wouldn't be for long, a nurse would move her off the bed as soon as she was spotted. They would point to the chair. Didn't they know you would have to be severely deformed with arms trailing on the ground like some primitive ape to be able to have any physical contact with the person in bed, while sitting in the chair?

Walid drifted in and out of sleep. Chloe couldn't help but wonder if things would have been any better with Carmichael's input into his treatment. She felt the hospital didn't want to be involved in any way with this treatment plan, probably due to a shortage of funds, and she supposed she was grateful to MI5 for whatever input they had into prolonging his life.

"I saw her."

Chloe looked down at Walid. "Sorry, what did you say? I was miles away."

"I saw her. In the water."

"What water?"

"They were holding me underwater to get me to talk. But I died and I saw her. It was wonderful. She had forgiven me."

Chloe was beginning to understand, although he sounded as if he was hallucinating, he was telling her about his experience.

"Your saw your wife?"

"Yes, she had forgiven me, don't you see?"

Chloe did see, she saw all too well. Michael Moreau had been the love of her life so how could she grudge Walid's first wife being so important in his life, even now. Still she needed him to focus on what was about to come, and not on the past.

"So you don't believe in violent protest, but you won't help MI5 to stop the killing of innocent civilians."

"You're asking me to betray my brother, just like I betrayed my wife."

"No, I'm asking you to consider if it is right to kill innocent people to make your case, thousands of people, or individuals, it's all the same, it's useless. And you didn't kill your wife."

"He's my brother."

"Did Ahmed know your brother? How did you start working for him?"

"A letter came into the university from Ahmed, asking for an expert opinion on a piece of art. They thought I could give him an opinion."

"Had he asked the university for an opinion on a piece of art before?"

"No."

"And looking back you don't think maybe he knew you were there?"

"Maybe."

Walid closed his eyes. Clearly, the conversation had taken its toll. She let go of his hand and flopped into the chair.

Edward R. Murrow, the American journalist and broadcaster, said, "No one can terrorize a whole nation, unless we are all his accomplices." Murrow was right—everyone should be involved in anti-terrorism, even Walid.

She went to the coffee shop, it wasn't exactly coffee but it was warm and wet and it gave her time to reflect on her present situation. She hadn't been there long when Louise arrived.

"We've lost our only contact to Walid's brother."

"That was careless."

"We also know there is an attack planned for the State Opening of Parliament—next Tuesday, just five days away now."

"Is that why you're here?"

"Walid gave us some addresses, and we have found three nuclear devices, but our information said there were at least four and maybe five."

"What kind of nuclear devices?"

"Briefcase bombs."

"What—the Russian ones?"

"These were similar."

"And?" What did Louise want?

"And I'm hoping Walid can help us again."

"Suppose I do you a deal?"

"I'm sorry?"

"How about I get you the information, and you get me some information."

"Withholding information about an act of terrorism is an offense."

"So is altering a crime scene, you were at the boathouse when Dr Liz Soames committed suicide. So let's not mess about. You need information and so do I. I have pictures."

Chloe noticed Louise looked uncomfortable. It was a form of blackmail, but she felt she had done enough investigation to conclude there was a systematic murdering of the biological weapons scientists by various secret services and it should be exposed, and now she had some proof of secret service involvement, but still not enough.

"What information?"

"I want to read the files. My father's death, Dr Elizabeth Soames's, something you should know a lot about, you wore such a cute waitress outfit."

"How did you find that out?"

"The Ken Antipov file and any information you have on the missing Iraqi scientists, for a start. Oh, and you could include Carmichael as a bonus."

"You're asking for something I can't give."

"Let's be reasonable, my father died years ago, it can't possibly be secret now, and anyway, it was only an accident. And my publishing your involvement with Soames would be extremely embarrassing."

"Yes, but—"

"Let's start with a simple question. Why did Soames commit suicide?"

"Soames was 'Rosa.' We'd only just found out."

"Why were you there?"

"I was there to see if she made contact with her handler, we wanted them both."

"And?"

"I don't think I can say more."

"I think you have to. You see I have video evidence of everything in the boathouse."

"It wasn't the way it looked. I didn't want her to die. We wanted to talk to her, find out why, who she talked to. It was the last thing we wanted. But every spy has an exit strategy, and when I saw she had been given a note we went as fast as we could to the boathouse but as you saw it was too late. The Russians had provided the pills, which I took, and the note from her bag. If she wanted it to look like suicide, well that suited us."

"If Soames was 'Rosa' why did anyone think it was Antipov?"

Louise hesitated.

"Okay," said Chloe, "you go fishing with Walid on your own. By the way, he's asleep; do you want me to call you when he wakes up?"

"Chloe, I'm sorry. Thousands of people will die if we don't find the bombs."

"Surely Walid isn't the only source of information."

"No, there are several areas we are investigating, but he is our only hope of tracking down his brother."

"And do you think he is going to give you his brother?"

"I don't know."

"Would you?"

"I don't know, I don't have a brother," said Louise in a matter-of-fact way.

"You do what you can and I'll do what I can. I can't say fairer than that. I will also use my contacts in France to see if I can find Ahmed Talbi. He must be somewhere. When did he disappear?"

"He went to Friday prayers and we lost him. Well, not us..."

"Patrick won't be pleased!"

"Um, no, I think telling us they had lost Ahmed Talbi wasn't exactly the high spot of his week."

They both laughed. A bond joined them. It was quite unexpected, but the charm of Patrick had united them. It would appear he had an ageless attraction. In that moment they were an appreciation society, but only from afar, neither of them would want a close encounter. However, they did enjoy knowing he would have been furious at the foul up. His arrogance, his flirtatious manner, all compromised by this failure. Just think of the humiliation of having to tell the English.

"All right, I will do everything I can." Chloe could only hope this was a promise she could keep.

"I'll see what I can do about the file on your father's death." Louise felt sure she could let Chloe see that file, Antipov was dead, and there were no secrets left on that case, none that mattered.

CHAPTER FORTY

Wychmoor Wood

The barn seemed strangely quiet and empty. It was the first time Chloe had been there alone. It had been filled with people unpacking, security equipment fitters, security personnel, and Louise. She felt her privacy invaded when they were here, and lonely now everyone was gone. Even the external security personnel were gone. Clearly, Walid was the only object of their attention. It wasn't as if they cared about Walid at all. They thought of him as naïve; maybe he was, but he was walking his path in the best way he knew how, juggling family loyalty and what he knew to be right.

Chloe looked inside the fridge and opened a bottle of Evian. She marveled and was appalled at the same time by the level of detail Louise had taken with things like filling the fridge. Even down to her preferred brand of water. Perhaps she was getting paranoid and it was just a coincidence.

The response she'd had from Louise when she asked for information had surprised her. It hadn't been a planned strategy. She would get whatever information she could from Walid to give to Louise anyway, so why had she decided to ask her to trade?

Perhaps she had been motivated by watching Walid in the hospital. Seeing Carmichael again had brought back so many memories she thought buried forever. She wondered if she should have asked more questions about the doctor's death. Carmichael didn't fit into the pattern of biological specialists, but it might be interesting to know what sort of accident had befallen him. It could have been heart failure—Carmichael wasn't young any more.

So far, she had established three deaths in America that clearly didn't have satisfactory explanations, and two in England. The Russians seemed to be just falling out of the skies and she would certainly want to check the passenger list before boarding any plane with biological scientists. She was still hoping the air-accident investigation specialist would provide her with evidence. No one could satisfactorily explain why a missile took a plane down. It had to be a suspicious accident.

She could always go back to Iraq and find some more information. With so many scientists missing it would be easy to find some evidence. Mossad were extremely efficient but even they would leave a trail with so many bodies, or missing persons.

She looked at her watch. It was dinnertime. Louise had left plenty of food in the fridge, but she just didn't want to be alone. She decided she would go and try the food at the pub, it would be an opportunity to get more information on Antipov. The pub was about a mile away and she enjoyed the walk on a narrow path between fields, she walked quickly, it was a crisp cold evening.

The Spotted Pig was a traditional whitewashed pub. The window boxes were filled with small evergreens, ornamental pink and plumb colored cabbages, and trailing ivy. Inside the stone flag floor was softened with rugs, the lighting was dim and the brightness of the bar lights gave a welcoming glow. She ordered an apple juice, no ice, and asked for the menu.

The menu was a surprise; it was large and comprehensive, and boasted fresh ingredients. She was expecting some prepackaged, microwaved food, carefully shoveled onto a plate.

She was given a choice of a table in the pub or in the restaurant. The restaurant was perhaps a fancy name for an area to the side of the bar, but it was late and empty so she decided on the round table in the public bar.

The pub owner's wife brought her meal of salmon, poached in white wine, served with the promised fresh vegetables. Chloe thought she might remember her from three months ago, when she had hoped to interview Antipov. She had chatted to this woman, but clearly she hadn't been remembered.

"There we go, ducks."

"Thank you, that looks wonderful."

"We try our best."

"I expect it's quiet around here," Chloe said.

"We do have our exciting times. You remember that scientist Ken Antipov?"

"Yes."

"He lived right there." She pointed at the house on the opposite side of the main road. "You should have seen all the press. It was like a zoo—and they didn't behave much better than animals either."

She paused, and Chloe was just willing her to continue.

"Of course he was murdered. Everyone here knows that. In fact, my husband saw it all happen."

"This salmon is delicious. I thought it was suicide."

"They would say that, wouldn't they. They could hardly say, 'we done him in,' now could they?"

This woman was growing on Chloe by the minute. It looked like she was about to get an eyewitness account.

"Else! Elsieeee!"

"Oh sorry, my ducks, I talk too much and he'll be wanting me to do the glasses."

And with that, her source was gone. Still at least she knew she was eating in the right pub—she might just have to eat here all week.

After her meal she moved across to the bar stool, hopeful the owner might continue his wife's confidences. Unfortunately, he was far more discreet and she knew if he even suspected she was a journalist she would be eating on her own in the restaurant in future and he would be serving her.

"What time do you close?"

"Half-ten. We don't do with all these long hours. Folks around here have got to work."

"Yes, well I better make my way home."

"Where are you living?"

"The barn..."

"Oh right! Just moved in?"

"Yes."

"Quite a bit of fuss wasn't there—all that security."

So much for keeping the security measures confidential, she thought. But that was what happened in villages; a host of dog walkers would pass the scene of strange activity at different times and then congregate on street corners and gossip, unknowingly collating valuable information. Having a dog in an English village was as much to do with belonging to a social grouping as pet ownership.

"My husband had a fairly high profile recently, so the police just thought it would be wise."

"The police can be funny like that, take Ken Antipov, he was a regular here, and one minute the police couldn't do enough for him, they were outside his house all the time, after the BBC said he was a spy. The day before he died they'd all gone. Now, either he needed the security or he didn't, what had changed? The Ministry of Defense hadn't said he wasn't a spy—which of course he wasn't."

"Your wife said there had been a lot of press."

"Yes, and it was funny they all disappeared on the same day as the police went. No one hung around to see if they could get an interview with him. I don't know which came first, the press left because they were bored, or the police because they were told to go. But it was very odd it all happened on the same day."

"I expect they had to go somewhere for a guaranteed story, rather than just hoping for one. They can't wait forever on the basis that they will get a story eventually, and the story seemed dead, the Ministry of Defense didn't make any statement, there was nothing left to say."

"Yeah, story—that sums them up. They're good storytellers, not one of them told the truth for months. Now they are coming back to see if there was a bigger picture. Did you want another?"

He didn't wait for her answer, instead he leaned across the bar, pulled the rope attached to a large brass bell, and called out, "Last orders." He set about cleaning down the bar, putting the towels over the pumps to dry. Saying goodbye to his customers, a pleasant word or comment and usually followed with, "See you tomorrow." Maybe tomorrow night she would get the "bigger picture."

CHAPTER FORTY-ONE

Wychmoor Wood

Walking back slowly, Chloe thought about what they had told her at the pub: "My husband saw it all happen." The pub owner seemed to want to get the story out, and however much he despised journalists, he must know this was the way to expose the truth to the world.

The motion activated security lights on the barn reacted to her arrival and flooded the drive with a harsh glare. The sense of loneliness she had felt earlier had dissipated. She could hear Michael's voice telling her she could do this on her own, and even though he wasn't here to reinforce the message, she realized that losing Walid was not going to be the same as losing Michael, and in fact, she could survive on her own.

Chloe finished writing up her notes from the information gathered in the Spotted Pig, emailed them to Jean Pierre, and managed to calm down enough to contemplate going to sleep. She slept until about five, and went into the small sitting room to watch the news on television. The BBC was covering a terrorist event. They had a specialist talking about viruses and biological weapons. Another commentator was talking about the power of attacking rural Britain. He felt this would strike fear into every Briton. It was different when the attacks were bombs in cities, but when it was the drinking water, the air, the food, everyone was at risk and felt afraid. *Unlikely,* she thought, *it usually made the British more belligerent and determined, some might call it bloody minded.* In deference to the land of her father, she would describe it as resolute.

Chloe changed channel to ITV—the same stories and the host was asking the expert how individuals should protect themselves in their homes and what could the poor people in Wychmoor Wood do to ensure their safety.

"Wychmoor Wood!" She didn't know why shouting at the television was going to help, but she felt like telling him, I'm here, there's nothing going on. They were being advised to drink bottled water, well with a fridge full of still Evian and Badoit sparkling that wouldn't be difficult. Seal up all the windows or create a safe room. *What?* She didn't have any Scotch tape or any other...*Oh, there might be some Christmas tape with the wrapping paper, but heaven only knows where it would be.* It had seemed a luxury, having someone do and undo all your packing, now it had become her worst nightmare. She needed to find all sorts of items and yet she had no idea where any of these things were.

This must be a mistake, she thought, and changed the channel to CNN. They were discussing the Chemical, Biological, Radiological, or Nuclear (CBRN) Resilience Program. How all the emergency services prepared for these events, the steps they would be taking now, the powers they had. She picked up the phone, it was dead, she would have to rely on her BlackBerry.

The man on TV referred to Her Majesty's government's strategy document, how this gave a snapshot picture of the preparedness for such an event and stressed the strategy document didn't reveal all the precautions, because some of these things should remain confidential for security reasons. The national security level had been raised to critical.

She flipped back to BBC news who had decided they should put the whole issue in context by looking at the "rest of the news." *What other news could there possibly be?*

Then they returned to their major news item. They showed a map of Wychmoor Wood highlighting the area under threat, and stating the army from the nearby barracks in Abingdon had secured the perimeter. Saxon Ock Hundred District Council, coordinators of the response effort, had called in the troops.

The security lights came on, someone was coming up the drive. She listened to the crunching footsteps on the gravel, just one person. She waited for the doorbell to ring, but instead she heard the flap of the letterbox clatter shut.

A bright red flyer was on the doormat. How reassuring, put out a notice on red paper. She picked up the flyer, perhaps picking up this piece of paper would put her at risk of, well the news teams hadn't said yet.

The flyer was full of reassurance; if she did everything they asked she would be perfectly safe.

Don't leave your home.

Don't drink the tap water. Bottled water will be supplied in a few hours.

Keep all doors and windows closed.

Keep watching the news on television or listen to Radio Oxford for news updates.

The phone system will be out of service until lunchtime, which will enable the emergency response to be coordinated.

If you normally have a care worker visit in the morning, alternative carers will be provided for today and this is being coordinated by the Department of Health.

Now the purpose of a central national database became apparent. That great white elephant that was costing the British taxpayer millions did have a use.

A mobile Family Assistance Center and Emergency Health Unit will be in place at the village hall by lunchtime.

It is essential everyone stay indoors unless absolutely necessary.

The only thing it didn't tell you was what the emergency was. Did they know? Was it a biological attack? Was it an accident at the Atomic Energy Research Establishment? Unlikely, the wind was blowing in the wrong direction. Now she realized she was being ridiculous. Why would it be just this village? Why not Burford, Witney, and all the villages around Abingdon? No, it was something local and it would have been nice to be told exactly what the problem was. If they knew.

Thank God for Porton Down, she thought. Scientists would be working through the night until they found the cause and hopefully a cure for this problem, whatever it was. She thought about her dad and how when there was an outbreak of plague in Africa he had gone to collect blood samples from the sick and those that seemed immune to the disease, to help to find a cure. She wasn't sure now if it was all innocent aid, or if there was a desire to find a virus they could weaponize, she would never know. What she did know was that they would all be working very hard to contain this emergency and provide a vaccine, if it was a virus.

Chloe watched the news, alternating between channels until they started to repeat themselves and then decided it would be a good time to have breakfast and take stock of supplies. One thing was certain, Walid was in the best place possible right now.

The perimeter was quite close to the barn, and as dawn broke, she thought she would be able to see the soldiers. She had a long lens on her digital camera, and Anne Marie would certainly not be too concerned about getting the composition of the photograph perfect as long as it was exclusive. There was a small round window on the gable end, but she didn't know how to get into the loft to access it.

Dressed in some old jeans, a sweater, and tennis shoes, she set about finding the loft hatch. It was in the second bathroom; the hatch was unbelievably small, and so there would be no easy access loft ladder. The owner of this property did not intend their tenants to get into the loft. She decided she could probably pull herself up from a chair and might break a limb dropping back down, but it was the best she could do. She couldn't move a table into the bathroom and place the chair on top, which would have been her first choice.

Chloe opened the hatch, placed her camera onto the floorboards in the loft before hauling herself into the dark roof space. She could see the dim light through the round window but there was no electric light to guide her passage over the joists. By now, she was beginning to think that she was obsessed with providing news. Anne Marie probably had a hundred beautiful photographs taken from the other side of the cordon and her efforts were insane.

Chloe could see the armed soldiers quite clearly through the telephoto lens. They were dressed in full biological hazard suits and they had placed rolls of barbed wire along the perimeter. Chloe started to take the shots, when she realized without any phones, there would be no broadband and no internet. She had never used her BlackBerry to send large files before but maybe now was the time to find out if it was possible. Chloe realized the roof space was not airtight and there was air movement through the loft. She found herself not breathing, but the damage was done, if this was an airborne virus, which the soldiers' attire did seem to suggest, then she was in a stupid situation, literally dying for a story. If it had been a gas attack the gas would have dissipated by now.

Getting out of the loft wasn't as hard as she had imagined, she had to keep telling herself to breathe. Getting the pictures to Anne Marie turned out to be easy, the television signal was supplied by cable which had an internet connection, and she sent the pictures off to the newspaper and a warning email to Anne Marie's personal email address so she would pick up the files quickly.

What were the signs of the illness? She felt cold and clammy, probably nerves, rather than any mysterious disease. An isolated barn conversion had seemed like a wonderful place to be, and in one way she was pleased, she didn't have any neighbors to catch anything from, but some human comfort in a crisis would have been good too.

Partly because she wanted to have something to do, she started to check out where the movers had put everything. If she could find tape, she could start taping up windows, cracks, and put some plastic over the fireplace.

The news channels didn't seem to have anything new to say until about two in the afternoon. "In 1968 the CIA experimented with injecting chemicals into the water supply." *Water?* So it was a virus in the water supply. The expert talked about the difficulties of getting a virus into the water supply, about the extensive security provided by the water companies. They couldn't explain how the virus had entered the water supply, but there had been a breakdown in security somewhere and the effects would be devastating. She waited for the news story to repeat, and she started to think about her water use. She had showered, washed her hair, cleaned her teeth, but she hadn't drunk the water. She didn't suppose it would make much difference to Walid. It was possible the reaction to the drug might have been unrelated to the drug, and in fact, he was showing evidence of contamination by the virus. She thought about all the people fitting security devices to the barn a few days ago. Louise had been here then. She could clearly remember her drinking a glass of water, and declining Evian, telling her the tap water was purer than the Evian. Chloe remembered saying, "Yes, but the tap water smells of chlorine and tastes awful."

Surely the chlorine... If the water treatment had been effective, people wouldn't be getting sick. Her head was reeling, she had to stop thinking for a moment and relax. Well, she wouldn't be returning to the Spotted Pig anytime soon.

CHAPTER FORTY-TWO

Port d'Alcudía, Mallorca

Ahmed Talbi steered his Sunseeker Predator 75 cruiser into the bay of Alcudía. He throttled back on the twin diesel engines, and watched the light dance on the gentle waves made by the Menorca ferry. He had only been to the Port d'Alcudía once before, and then he had flown into Palma airport and driven to the port.

He was still feeling nervous. Everything had gone smoothly. He didn't know why he felt anxious; perhaps it was the result of the surveillance in Paris day after day. He had changed his identity three times since leaving Paris. The TGV train had transported him to Marseille; next, he had flown to Barcelona, and he had sailed from the port immediately. His planning had paid off; he kept the boat ready: fully fuelled, the water tanks topped up for showers and general use, stocked fridges and freezers, and the store cupboards were full of tinned goods and bottled water.

He was also tired. Although he had used the on-board autopilot for some of the six-hour trip, he hadn't rested properly. He moored stern onto the dockside in the busy Port d'Alcudía on Saturday lunchtime.

Having paid his mooring fee to the harbormaster, he closed up the boat and went below to rest. The gentle undulations of passing boats, and the resultant lap-lapping noise was a lullaby and he was soon asleep. The air-conditioning kept him cool as the sun heated the cockpit.

Rising in the mid-afternoon, he showered and dressed. Meandering along the marina to the boardwalk, he enjoyed the spectacle of the other boats. He liked the fact his was one of the larger and more expensive boats in the marina.

He found his way to a small café, sat down on a director's chair in the sunshine under a maroon umbrella, and ordered a cappuccino and a slice of cake. It was not as good as the French patisserie, but it was sugary and sweet and he felt energized.

He hadn't done anything wrong, he reasoned to himself. He had no reason to be afraid of the authorities. If some of the buyers or sellers donated funds to questionable sources, he wasn't responsible. If the shipments had been interfered with, well it was unfortunate, but hardly his fault. He felt reasonably confident in his defense strategy.

He walked back slowly, stopping off at the small supermarket serving the marina and bought a boat owners' magazine and some fresh fruit. It was four o'clock, he went and made the boat ready for departure. He set the automatic pilot, ready for use later, studied his charts, doing all the necessary checks on oil, water, and taking the boat across to refill with diesel, before mooring again, ready for a quick departure.

He watched all the movements up and down the marina. He was still looking to see if anyone was watching him. It had become a habit. He felt a chill, the sun had gone in and gray clouds covered the sky, he hadn't thought about the weather changing. He didn't have any plans for bad weather. He had just assumed he would be able to execute his escape plan. It was imperative he keep running, the police would not be far behind him. Nearly all his money was tied up in the Sunseeker Predator. He couldn't sell the pictures and artifacts here to generate cash; they needed specialized buyers.

Ahmed had looked at the weather forecast in the window of the marine chandler on his way back to the boat. Gales. Bad weather expected, rising to gale force eight or nine. He hadn't taken the boat out in anything other than fair weather. It was November. What could you expect? His escape plan hadn't taken into account the winter weather in the Mediterranean.

He was trying to remember what the sales clerk had said. It was stable in moderately bad weather but nothing more than gale force six. The hairs on the back of his arms stood on end, he was breathing too fast, he had to leave port today, as the weather would be worse tomorrow. Perhaps he could just leave the marina and moor in a sheltered bay till the storm passed? No, he knew he had to get to Tangiers before the authorities caught up with him, he wasn't going to wait for the Algerian.

CHAPTER FORTY-THREE

Wychmoor Wood

Chloe gave up the unequal struggle with sleep and put the lamps on in the bedroom, it was four in the morning. Sleep was becoming elusive. Normally she could get back to sleep but not today. She turned the television on and listened to the news, nothing new, and the situation in the village was now relegated to fourth place, behind Bush's trip to Europe, Blair's trip to boost the morale of the troops in Iraq, and a sixty-two-year-old mother giving birth because of fertility treatment. The media had been briefed to play down the event in the four villages now affected, in order to reduce the sense of panic in rural Britain.

A van drove up the gravel drive and pulled up with a scrunch, no doubt scattering gravel outside the barn. The heavy door slid back or up to the stops with a metallic thump. Braving the cold, she peered through the curtains to see what was happening.

Chloe decided the first priority was not to have a heart attack; she tried to breathe deeply and slowly. Her heart continued to beat in her chest, but she felt a sharp pain in her sternum, a panic attack was excusable, she was about to be ... what? Arrested? Searched? Surely not abducted again.

Chloe thought carefully, they would have seen the lights, there was no point pretending to be asleep, the only question was whether to get dressed before opening the door. She dressed quickly, and pulled a brush through her hair. The door intercom chimed as Chloe arrived at the door security console and picked up the phone to speak to the party on the other side of the closed door.

"Sorry to keep you waiting."

Through the glass mullion she could see a vision of eight men all dressed in biological warfare suits, green with blue wellies. Had she interpreted the distorted picture correctly? The security lights were flooding the yard. There wasn't much doubt about what she was looking at. Surely, they didn't all want to come in.

"Madame Moreau, I am Phil Scarlet with Special Branch, I have a warrant to search this house. May we come in?"

"Where have you come from? How do I know you are clean?"

"Madame Moreau? We want to search your house."

"Yes, I know, and I am saying how do I know you won't introduce the virus or whatever into my house? What is the purpose of putting a village in quarantine? Where have you come from? You're all wearing suits to protect yourselves from anything in this house or from me. But what is going to protect me from you?"

"Madame Moreau, if we decontaminated between every search it would take much longer to find the perpetrator of this scare."

"Yes, it's only a scare to you, you're all suited up and protected against me and the environment, but who protects me from you and this lunatic?"

"Madame Moreau, we are coming in."

"Yes, that's right, after I have seen you all decontaminate. Otherwise every newspaper will be carrying this story tomorrow."

She watched Phil Scarlet notice the tiny camera above his head—all part of Louise's security features. Chloe doubted she envisaged this situation. She had rigged the CCTV cameras to record onto a disk and Chloe supposed Scarlet would wonder if this conversation was going out live on the internet. She knew he couldn't be sure.

Phil Scarlet seemed to reconsider; he wheeled around facing his men, and made a turning circle with his hand and pointed to the van marked Decontamination Unit.

They were clearly going to search the house. She had no intentions of giving up the computer she had just received from the private detective at the museum, her digital camera, the portable hard drive, her personal computer, or her BlackBerry so she ran upstairs and gently threw them beyond arm's reach from the loft trap into a cushion of fiberglass insulation. She knew her hands would itch from the thought of the fiberglass every time she used these items, but if she survived this, she would treat herself to a new BlackBerry, and a new camera—perhaps Anne Marie would even see her way to replacing these items on expenses.

Chloe arrived back at the front door, and realized eight dripping wet men were going to tramp through the barn. *Better wet than contaminated,* she reasoned.

Chloe opened the door wide and stood aside as bulky green suited men pushed past her into the house. The last two men motioned for her to go into the hall and proceeded to wave a wand all over her—it was like a security check at the airport. The man reading the box attached to the wand evaluated the readings. He asked to swab her mouth with a cotton bud and place it in a glass test tube, and finally to swab her hand with a wipe which he also placed in a marked bag.

She could tell him the results now, Aveda Hand Relief cream, and enough bacteria in her mouth to tell them she had a sore throat she was putting down to nerves and the stress of the last few days.

Phil Scarlet came over. "Madame Moreau?"

"Yes." She couldn't detect any signs of annoyance in this man at her insistence they all decontaminate, but she felt sure he would make some comment about not taking responsibility for the wet carpets when they left.

"How many computers are there in the house?"

She thought for a moment. "Two." *And four, if you count the two in the loft, but I'm not going to count those.*

"I'm sorry, how many?"

Chloe held up her hand showing two fingers and repeated, "Two."

"Could you show me where they are?"

She pointed to the Dell in a leather briefcase. "That is my husband's computer he uses for work at home." She took him into the study and pointed at the desktop machine. "That's my desktop."

Phil Scarlet went across to the security monitor; it was showing the activity at the front door, as the men went in and out of the house the motion sensor set the camera into action, and the activity was recorded onto a DVD. Phil popped the DVD out of the compartment. He waited and checked recent internet and email activity and turned the machine off. He seemed relieved to find the doorstep encounter was not being broadcast live. She realized he knew it could have been.

He made his way back to the dining room, he wanted to sit at the table but the bulky suits made it impossible to sit on the dining room chairs, as they all had arms. Chloe collected the piano stool, placed it in front of him, and sat down opposite him.

"I don't suppose you can tell me why you are here?" asked Chloe.

"Just routine."

"Oh please, routine means you were banging on everyone's door at four o'clock in the morning!"

"You fit a profile—that's all."

"What profile?"

"IT literate and travels."

"I'm glad you've narrowed down the list!"

Phil Scarlet looked bemused; this silly banter had formed a bond between them. He completed checking the computer. They both knew the team should have searched the loft, but there was no way anyone could get into the loft wearing their suits, and presumably, they were under strict instructions not to take their suits off. Gradually the team assembled in the hall. The Dell laptop in its bag was in the hands of one of the police officers, as was a glass jar of furniture polish.

Phil Scarlet started to write a receipt for the items, clearly it was a struggle.

"Shall I write out the receipt and you can sign it?" Chloe just wanted them to leave, glad it was all over. "Why the furniture polish?"

"It just produces a funny reading on the machine; some innocent items produce alarming results. It's nothing to worry about. The early machines couldn't detect the difference between Christmas pudding and Semtex!"

She handed him the completed receipt.

"Thank you, that's an enormous help. We aren't used to these suits, yet. Now, I would like to leave you with a mask."

Chloe thought for a moment. "Do you have masks for everyone in the village?"

"We will have, we are gradually distributing them. We have two and a half thousand and only a population of sixteen hundred to consider."

He instructed her how to put the mask on. The sense of claustrophobia was overwhelming. The smell of the rubber and limited vision reminded her of the dentist as a child, trying to resist the anesthetic, panic as the black mask was put over her mouth and nose, but unconsciousness becoming inevitable as the gas and air did its work. At first, she attributed the breathlessness to panic, but she couldn't breathe. She tried to breathe slow and shallow.

"Just breathe normally," said Phil Scarlet.

She tried gasping for air.

"You're panicking, there's nothing to worry about, just breathe normally."

She just couldn't breathe. The darkness was closing in. She wanted to shout out. She couldn't. She felt herself falling. She hit the floor, and then there was nothing.

She didn't know how long she had been out when she heard voices.

"Chloe! Chloe?"

The voice was familiar but she couldn't place it, she tried to wake up, struggling to surface but getting back to reality was impossible. She listened.

"What happened?"

"Faulty mask—no air to breathe."

"She told me she couldn't breathe, I told her not to panic and breathe slowly. My God, I should have known she wouldn't panic."

"Do you know her, sir?"

"Yes, this is Chloe Moreau, investigative journalist for *La France*, wife of Walid Merbarkia, officially university lecturer but…"

"Oh, I see! The man from MI5 was looking for her a few minutes ago; shall I tell him she's in here?"

"I think you better wait 'til she's awake. Is there a medical attendant anywhere?"

"Don't I need a mask here?" Chloe woke up in a state of panic.

"No, but you will need one."

Chloe wondered how long she had been unconscious. She gathered from their conversation she had been out of action for some time. She was so grateful she hadn't just fainted—that would have been so feeble.

"You better find that MI5 bloke," Phil said. "I'm so sorry I didn't take you seriously when you said you couldn't breathe. I should have made sure you were okay." He smiled apologetically.

She hadn't seen him smile before—he seemed almost human.

"No harm done, and at least I won't have to wear that mask again. You will get me one of those big helmets, won't you?"

"I think that's the least I can do in the circumstances."

Graeme Scott arrived.

"Good news—of a sort."

Chloe wasn't quite sure what to make of Graeme Scott, he'd been aggressive, but now seemed to have his friendly PR face on.

"Could you excuse us?"

Phil Scarlet looked at her, as if seeking her consent to leave. She had no power in the situation to direct anyone, but didn't feel unsafe in Graeme Scott's company, and wanted to know his news. Why did Phil care? Was it just guilt after the mask on the suit not working properly?

Graeme went over and closed the door on the tiny room.

"Where am I?"

"Didn't they tell you? You're in Medivac."

"Just 'Medivac,' but that doesn't tell me anything."

"You're at a special unit created at War Memorial Community Hospital."

"Chipping Norton?"

"Yup."

Chloe digested this information. She must have been unconscious for about half an hour, it seemed a lot less, she thought she had been half conscious for most of the time, it felt as if they had just dragged her out of the barn and across the yard. Still it meant she was ten miles away from trouble and that felt good.

"What happened to you?"

Did Graeme do anything other than ask questions?

"The mask didn't work, and I passed out from lack of air."

"My God, that's not good!"

"You said you had some news, what's happened? Can I speak to Walid?"

"I knew you'd ask that. So…" He smiled and produced his cell phone out of his pocket. "Now it's not allowed for you to use a cell phone in the hospital, it sometimes makes the equipment go haywire. However, I, on the other hand, can make calls of national security with impunity!"

She watched as he dialed the number and hoped they were not interfering with somebody's life-saving equipment.

"Do you want a drink?" He held out a plastic cup.

She drank the water, which tasted bitter, as they waited for the call to go through.

"Walid? I have your wife here who wants to speak to you. Is everything okay? All right then, here she is." Satisfied with Walid's response he handed the phone over.

"Walid?" The phone call passed in a blur of emotions. He was fine, she was relieved and tired. She felt cold and all she wanted to do was sleep.

She must have looked pale or something because Graeme put the oxygen mask back on her face, and kept talking to her. She couldn't hear what he was saying; she was slipping backward into the black abyss again.

"Ow!" She didn't know whether she had spoken aloud or not, it felt like a bee had stung her arm. She was awake now; a nurse in a white gauze face mask was putting an empty syringe into a kidney dish.

"You can go now. Thank you." Graeme motioned for the nurse to leave.

"I'm sorry but the patient needs rest, you need to leave."

"Sorry, but this is too important; I have taken note of your concerns." Graeme had no intention of leaving.

The nurse left. She could see Phil Scarlet waiting outside the door. There was a tense atmosphere and it wasn't related to her health.

"Okay, Chloe, Walid is suspected of either being a terrorist, or linked to those undertaking terrorist acts. The CIA are trying to find links with the Casablanca bombings and the ricin factory in London, the DST may or may not be helping but it would appear DGSE will let Algerian extremists terminate any individuals like Walid whose status is unclear. I need you to help me eliminate him from our inquiries."

"Is that supposed to be a threat?" Algerian extremists had a reputation for terminating individuals and any blood relatives they could find. It would be a win-win situation. Walid was nearly at the end of his life, and everyone would prefer his brother were dead. Algerian terrorists might be a brutal breed, but for a threat to work there would have to be some victims. "Walid is dying without any assistance from Algerian extremists. Walid has a brother though and I think we would all like him dead. What do you want?"

"I want everything you know about Walid, we're running out of time."

Chloe rambled on, answering his questions for some time, everything in a haze. Gradually the headache, the blurred vision, and heart palpitations ended the proceedings.

"I'm sorry, but I just don't feel well."

"I'll call the nurse."

As the door opened, she could see Phil Scarlet, still waiting. He came in.

"How are you?"

"Not too good."

"The nurse should be able to help. She won't be long now."

The tension between Phil and Graeme was extreme. They both left and she found herself drifting in and out of sleep, it could have been seconds, it could have been hours, then her sleep was broken by their low but urgent voices.

"This was wrong—this should never have happened, we're not living in a police state."

"Don't be such a jerk. If scopolamine got us reliable information that will save nearly two thousand lives it's justified. Now if you'll excuse me I have work to do."

My God, scopolamine! They must be mad, why would anyone use such a technique, I'm not withholding information. The nurse could do little. Chloe would learn to live with the hallucinations, the headaches, and the heart palpitations for as long as it took, probably months. She would have answered any questions without the drug. She had nothing to hide. Walid was a lecturer, he made some money on his antiquities deals but it was nothing sinister.

She began to think, it was hard, and her headache was extreme. Was Walid connected? Something was bothering her. Something was missing. What was it?

"Can I get you anything?" Phil looked sympathetic.

"Something to clear my head. I can't think and it's important." Chloe was holding her head in her hand, anything to make the fog go away. It was something Graeme had said, but now she couldn't think.

"I'll take you back."

He helped her up, and they went through the curtain. She realized they had lied about everything; she had been in a mobile unit just ten meters from her front door. She supposed it was insane to think they would take her out of the village or she would have been unconscious for half an hour. It was just a scam to ensure she felt relaxed.

"Yes, he's a lying bastard." Phil spoke with feeling.

"Bloody spooks!" she responded.

They went into the barn and he helped her onto the bed. It was six o'clock on Sunday morning.

"You'll need to sleep off the effects."

"Yes, but I need to remember what I was going to say, it was important."

"Is it about Walid?"

"I don't know, I think so."

"Perhaps you should just give in and sleep. When you wake up, it will come back to you."

"No, it was important. I can't think…"

Phil looked concerned but there was nothing either of them could do.

CHAPTER FORTY-FOUR

MI5, London

Louise made her way to Thames House. It was beginning to feel like some world inhabited by an alien culture, a world where rest and sleep were an option.

It was as disturbing to find three of the briefcase bombs, all of which were viable nuclear devices, as it was to know there were still more out there. These briefcase bombs had not been made by the KGB, but by Chechen terrorists. They had been modified with thin beryllium reflectors either side of the plutonium to increase the effect, and to reduce the weight to eleven kilograms. It would give a ten-ton explosion; it would be effective over four hundred meters and have a hundred-percent fatality within three hundred meters. Although they were only one quarter as powerful, it was enough to create devastation and nuclear fallout.

Louise had been shocked; she thought the Russian briefcase bombs had been a rumor set in action during the Cold War. The KGB replacement, the Federal Security Service (FSB), still located in the Lubyanka, was far more helpful than the KGB would have been. Moscow had changed.

Louise logged into her computer, looked at the large number of emails from admin and data analysis. *Couldn't this be filtered?* she thought. *Surely intelligence officers could be shielded from information overload.*

Louise realized this attack was far more sophisticated than other terrorist attacks on London. The IRA were involved in isolated incidents with
warnings given. Attacking rural England had had more of an impact
than any attack in London had done. The simplicity of the method worried everyone.

The water infrastructure developed leaks—it's what happened to old
pipes. Now, repairmen all over the country were attacked as possible
terrorists, when all they were trying to do was fix a leak. In London
alone there were two hundred and fifty leaks being repaired a day. The
leak crews were asking for police protection. The good news, it would
be harder for Farook and Nasir to repeat their tampering with the water
supply, but by no means impossible. It might be a criminal offense under
section 174(3) of the Water Industry Act 1991 to connect a standpipe to
the water supply, but terrorists didn't care.

Louise took out a piece of paper and decided to draw a link map of
known information. The virus would appear to have arrived in Bradford
disguised as halal baby food from Pakistan. Farook and Nasir (Frankfurt
link?) picked up the canisters? She put a question mark by this piece of
information, but there were no further links to Frankfurt. The Germans
were still investigating the bombing of the Frankfurt station one week
ago; there had been no chatter, no sign an attack was imminent. Their
investigations were pointing at one mosque and it was a balance between community relations and following up leads. The Germans were
sympathetic to the British need for information on an urgent basis. The
trail in Pakistan was cold and although the security services were making some headway, it wasn't exactly a breakthrough.

Monitoring communication channels was continuing, in case Farook
or Nasir made contact with friends, family, or girlfriends at home. There
were a few other possibilities in England, possible couriers of the virus,
but the modus operandi seemed to use sleepers or bring in foreign nationals to avoid discovery.

The briefcase bombs had definite links with Ahmed's artifacts from Iraq, if not with Ahmed directly. The briefcase bombs had come from Chechnya via Iraq and the Russians had lost their source of information. Ahmed had links with Walid and so the circle was complete. Walid was the only information source available.

Graeme was facing disciplinary proceedings because he had used scopolamine on Chloe without prior authorization, which would not have been given before the procedure, but would have been given retrospectively if he had obtained valuable information.

The frustrating thing was relying on others to provide information. It would have been useful to have some contact with Ahmed; Louise knew the French were trying to follow up any leads to find him. She didn't think it had the same priority for them as it did for the British. Could the information she received this morning be useful to the French or Germans? The reality was about getting through the next three days without a major disaster. They had been incredibly lucky so far, the death toll had been so few.

The conclusion to her mind map left some financial links to check regarding the Algerian and Ahmed, and possibly some information might come from Frankfurt or Paris, but otherwise they seemed to have reached the end of useful leads.

Louise started another mind map with Wychmoor Wood at the center. It looked like a bicycle wheel with hardly any of the spokes linked. Carmichael, Antipov, and Chloe's father all had links with Porton Down and had been killed in Wychmoor Wood, or had been living there when they had died.

There was one other thing she would like to check. Had MI6 or someone in MI5, or Scotland Yard, interviewed Patrick Dubois to find out why he had been in the hotel the night Carmichael had died? In the circumstances, any thread might prove useful. It was funny he was in London when Antipov died, was it a coincidence or something more sinister? Walid Merbarkia had also been in London when Antipov died for that matter.

She had just finished her mind maps and lists of other areas to investigate when Graeme sat down at her desk. He looked gray and pale.

"Can I get you a coffee or something?" Louise didn't normally get coffee for male colleagues, it gave them the wrong idea, but out of compassion and concern she wanted to do something.

"Kind offer, but I don't think it will help. What have you got?"

Louise took him through her mind maps. She felt it was probably a juvenile analysis, but it was all she had.

"Good work."

Louise was shocked.

"But, does it help us any?"

"I would say any analysis of what else might be possible would be beneficial. I wanted to say I'm sorry about leaving you to take the rap for the Chloe-hostage Iraq operation. I was wrong."

Louise looked at him. The apology was too late, she had made up her mind she would leave the service as soon as this was all over. She was owed three weeks' vacation, so she would be unlikely to have to serve more than a week's notice. Her father had always wanted her to be an accountant and it was an attractive proposition right now.

"What do you want me to do with this list?"

"I don't know, I think you have put your finger on the problem, we are waiting on the French, the Pakistanis, and the Germans for key data and some feedback from the Russians. I'll phone the Germans, you phone Patrick and ask him what he was doing in the hotel, he might tell you. Any response at all should tell us something, it would be even better if you could get his response on camera so we can analyze the eye movement and body language, Patrick is good, but there are usually some telltale signs of what he's thinking."

Louise's computer pinged, announcing an urgent email. She opened it, not really expecting anything of use. As she began to read, a smile spread over her face. Graeme, who couldn't see the screen, was wondering what caused her to smile when she was clearly tired.

"I think I might just have some news that will be a better pick-you-up than coffee could have been."

"What?" Graeme had no enthusiasm in his voice, only tiredness.

"The Spanish have spotted Ahmed Talbi going through Barcelona airport, and leaving Spain on a small cruiser. Apparently, he has owned the boat for the past three years, and periodically goes out for a week or so and returns—always alone."

"I don't suppose we know what happened to him next?"

"Oh yes! He turned up at Port d'Alcudía Marina, in Mallorca, Saturday lunchtime."

"Where is he now?"

"Ah, well you didn't expect it all to be good news, did you?"

"No!" Graeme thumped Louise's desk in exasperation.

"There is just one thing to make you feel better. He was carrying an aluminum briefcase." Louise watched Graeme; frown to smile to anxiety, in one change of his expressive face.

"Hell. So he might have the last bomb? Let's phone the Americans and see if they have any suitable birds in the area." Graeme was looking less tired. He was reading the briefing note off her computer screen.

"Do we have enough information to ask for a satellite?" Louise was fed up with asking for resources and being turned down.

"I would think so; we are looking at a small window. In the late afternoon, a man matching the description was having a coffee at a quayside café. When the harbormaster went around at five o'clock to collect some dues from a boat two berths away from his, he noticed the boat was gone. It didn't return," said Graeme.

"Wow! Maybe our luck is changing." Louise wasn't totally convinced this was true.

"I'll make the call, can you get a full description of the boat, and send a recent photo of Ahmed Talbi to the Mallorcan police to get a proper

ID from the café. You need to tell Patrick. I'll get a Nimrod scrambled from Kinloss."

"Okay." Louise was amazed at Graeme's energy. She still felt dreadful. She was so tired. Perhaps she was coming down with the flu.

James T, who had been watching the change and energy created by the email, came out to find out what was going on. "Okay, I'll get a boat scrambled from Gibraltar to intercept a small cruiser between Mallorca and Algeria."

"Do we have enough time?" Louise was looking at a map on her computer to work out the geography of the Mediterranean.

"Probably, but it will be close. I'll let the Algerians know, after all we want this man alive, anything else is just a mop up operation—we need information, we need that briefcase. We have a fairly good relationship with the Algerians; they might even scramble one of their new MiGs."

"MiGs?"

"Yes, they've just take delivery of three new MiG 29STMs from the Russians. They might be happy to have an exercise."

"As long as they understand it's a mission to find the boat, not blow the boat out of the water." Graeme looked worried.

James T looked at Graeme and Louise.

"Graeme, I want you to take someone from MI6 with you and get the first flight to Gibraltar. I'll get the navy to return Ahmed to Gibraltar so you will be on hand to conduct any questioning."

"Louise?" Graeme asked.

"Not this time. We need her here. We haven't got anybody to question yet, it may still prove to be a wild goose chase." James T looked at Louise. "I have something else that needs Louise's attention. Just be courteous to Lieutenant Commander Peters. Send my regards." James T smiled.

"Right." Graeme disappeared into his office.

"Louise, sorry I can't spare you to go to Gibraltar, you certainly should be going, you have been invaluable in moving this case forward, but I need you here. Now bring me up to date, what's going on?"

Louise went through her analysis of the situation to date.

"Interesting, but that wasn't what I meant." Distracted, he leaned across her desk and picked up a swab specimen bottle. "You were supposed to send this to the lab three days ago."

"Ah, there it is. I'll do it now."

"Louise, you don't forget, or lose things, so what is going on?" James T asked.

"Suppose I do have the virus, what then?" Louise looked worried.

"Then, I hope the virus is in the first stage because we have an effective vaccine."

"You have a vaccine for this?" Louise was surprised.

"It's a virus the Russians were working on and we had a lot of data about it, so it didn't take long to check the virus and make the vaccine; there have only been sixty cases of the virus, just three in Wychmoor Wood, so it isn't likely you have it."

Louise nodded.

James T picked up the bottle, took out the swab, and gave it to Louise. He waited as she collected some cells off the insides of her cheeks and let her return the swab to the bottle. He put the cover on and wrote her name on the label.

"And if I am sick?"

"Unlikely, but we'll face it, if and when the need arises. Shall we, Louise?"

CHAPTER FORTY-FIVE

Gibraltar

Lieutenant Commander Peters read the signal and checked for any other Royal Navy ships to intercept the small cruiser as it sailed from Port d'Alcudía to some Algerian port. Of course assuming Algeria was his destination could be limiting the prospects of finding the craft, but without further information, and unless the Americans had some satellite pictures, it was as good a guess as any. She considered a press release about an exercise in the prevention of drug trafficking, something about co-operation between Algeria and Britain would do it. She would ask if London could make an announcement, it would certainly make the job easier.

She looked at the commitments for the Gibraltar Patrol Boat Squadron, which was a rather grand title for three inflatables and two sixteen-meter fast patrol boats. The boats were even secondhand, as they had originally seen service in Northern Ireland as HMS *Greyfox* and HMS *Greywolf*. She could release HMS *Scimitar* to take up the chase immediately. HMS *Sabre* would have to complete escort duties, which would take another four hours minimum.

The mission of the Gibraltar Patrol Boat Squadron was primarily to provide security for Gibraltar but it also supported Special Forces. She phoned RAF Kinloss to see when the Nimrod aircraft would arrive to take up aerial reconnaissance.

Having dispatched HMS *Scimitar* to the general region, she hoped she would have some more detailed information to help them find this boat. Right now, it would be like looking for a needle in a haystack.

*

Graeme Scott left RAF Northolt for the flight to Gibraltar. He began to wonder why James T had cautioned him about being courteous. He didn't normally ruffle feathers on a mission. When he arrived at the base, he was shown into the commander's office.

Graeme's jaw fell open. He didn't know why he had expected Peters to be a man, it wasn't unknown to have female commanders in today's navy, but Peters was a delightful blonde and Graeme's first thoughts were if she'd consider dating him.

Behind closed doors, he gave her a full briefing on the current threat to London, about Walid Merbarkia and Ahmed Talbi. It was more than she needed to know, but some educated guesswork about where Ahmed and his small cruiser might be heading would be useful.

Graeme was also aware he wanted to impress her, which was ridiculous. He must be more tired than he realized. She briefed him on HMS *Scimitar*, already en route, and he could join HMS *Sabre* in about half an hour. She reached across to the phone and asked to be connected to the survey team.

"I was wondering where HMS *Herald* was working?... Mmm... Mmm... Well, we have a bit of a shout on and I was wondering if we could count on your support... Yes, national importance... Mmm... Mmm... I know, foul weather. Did you have anything else planned for your Saturday evening's entertainment? Yes, well I thought having the Wessex on board might... Of course. I'll send you details right away." Peters put the phone down.

"That was helpful, we have a survey ship, the HMS *Herald* working in the Med, they're a bit too far away to be handy but they have a Wessex helicopter on board, which might be useful. What we need now is a destination or indication where he went so we can intercept. The Nimrod will be on station in about forty minutes."

CHAPTER FORTY-SIX

Wychmoor Wood

When Chloe woke up, she was in bed at the barn. She felt hungover. A nurse was sitting in the bedroom. Chloe closed her eyes, not quite ready to face reality.

"What time is it?"

"About ten-thirty."

"Ten-thirty when?"

"You were interrogated earlier today. It is now ten-thirty, Sunday morning."

"I've been asleep all that time, or sedated?"

"Asleep."

"What about the mask?"

"They've traced the virus to water contamination, and so now we are out of the quarantine period, unless you have the virus, and you don't; you can go about your business."

The nurse got up to leave the room.

"Where are you going?"

"To get Phil Scarlet, he's been waiting to talk to you. Okay?"

"I suppose so."

Chloe wasn't sure why she was so disoriented. Somewhere nagging at the back of her mind were half remembered things and she just wanted to think clearly not be bombarded by questions again. If it was Sunday only two days remained until the State Opening of Parliament, which would be Tuesday.

Well, there was no point in spending the day in bed; it was time to be up and sorting things out. She'd start with a trip to see Walid, he must have some information that would be useful. Besides, she needed to ask him if there was anybody she should call or talk to, normally family members would be attending him, reading from the Qur'an, and helping Walid to prepare for the afterlife. Was he happy for the funeral to take place in Oxford? Did he have any other requests? Whom should she be notifying in his family, apart from his sons? She hoped he would have some information about Ahmed, who his friends were, did they meet at the mosque, and any other information he might have. Just as she got out of bed, Phil Scarlet arrived.

"Should you be getting up?"

"Yes, there's not much time left, I have a lot to do."

"I would like to ask one question."

"You've been waiting here just for one question?"

"Yes, you said Graeme had made you realize something was important, but you hadn't told him, and you couldn't remember what it was. I was hoping perhaps after a good sleep you might recall…"

"Yes, Walid was sick on our trip to Florida. That means he was exposed to a nuclear device in Paris." Chloe was surprised how easily she recalled this information.

"Okay, I'll talk with the French authorities."

"Yes, I'm going to see Walid and then I'm off to Paris—do you want to come with me or are you going to leave me to Patrick of the DST?"

"Whichever arrangement suits you best."

"Right, I'll think about that in the shower."

Phil left the room and she could hear him on the phone as she went to the bathroom. She put on blue jeans and a jacket, with a T-shirt underneath. She climbed up into the loft space and collected her concealed electronics. She didn't think Phil Scarlet would be interested, he seemed to realize she was working as hard as anybody to find the terrorists. She packed a small bag. She expected to be back from Paris late Monday. If the terrorist plot against London hadn't been uncovered by then, it would be too late.

CHAPTER FORTY-SEVEN

The Mediterranean

Ahmed walked slowly to the boat's stateroom. Just going to the saloon normally lifted his spirits; he loved the clean lines, the elegance of the cream leather sofas contrasted against the warm cherrywood. He pulled on his lifejacket and did it up tight.

He checked the charts; nowhere seemed to provide a private and secure mooring on the island of Majorca. It was a small island to search and if the authorities found him... There were secluded bays providing shelter, but he would be unable to escape, they would be able to cork him up like wine in a bottle, by closing off the exit to the bay.

No, he would have to try to outrun the weather. He cast off and gently made his way out of the marina, he would leave the bay alongside the ferry, which he hoped would disguise his leaving from the shore radar.

His timing was fortuitous. If he had planned his departure more carefully, he could not have met the ferry at a more opportune moment. He felt everything would be all right, "inshallah"—God willing.

As he made his way across the Bay d'Alcudía he felt reasonably confident he would be fine in this weather, it was only the start of the storm. He would be at Algiers to refuel before the worst of the storm broke out and he could make his way slowly down the coast of Algeria toward Tunis.

When he was halfway to Menorca, he left the shelter of the ferry and veered off toward Algeria. He set the automatic steering in the cockpit and went below to make some hot black tea. He stirred three packets of sugar into his tea, to give him energy, and went back on deck. He peered out through the gloom and decided to put on the navigation lights, it would help anybody looking for him, but not showing lights would make him look suspicious. He leaned into the wind and took short steps, steadying himself and moving from handhold to handhold. When he got back to the cockpit, it was hard to see anything in the driving rain. The windshield wipers, now working at maximum speed, weren't clearing the screen. The boat was progressing slowly, far more slowly than he had imagined.

The cruiser was designed to skim the water, but now the boat crashed into the crests of the large waves. At first, the movement was rhythmic, but as the storm increased so did the chaos of the waves. He staggered across the cockpit, bruising his forearm on the console.

He clambered into the captain's chair and tuned in to the forecast on Navtex. The storm was increasing and now expected to reach gale force ten. This was not good news; he tried to increase the speed of the boat but was frightened it would flip. He got out the charts and looked at Menorca as a refuge; it would mean turning back, but he wasn't sure if he would survive a force ten. He slowed the engine right down to see how the boat would react. He let the waves and currents orientate the boat sideways onto the waves to provide the greatest stability.

He'd lifted the blue fenders onto the deck on leaving harbor, but they were rolling and bouncing around. The salt spray hit his face as he went outside. He was only a fair weather sailor and he wasn't enjoying this at all. He clipped himself onto the safety line, and set about picking up the fenders and placed them in the cockpit.

He went back inside, found a towel, and dried his face and neck. The salt made his skin taut; it was going to be a long night. The swell and the diesel fumes were making him feel sick. He went below and looked in a cupboard for the seasickness pills. He had purchased the pills at a pharmacy shortly after he had bought the boat, unsure of what kind of a sailor he would make. So far, he had never needed them, but waves of nausea kept coming. He read the bottle and the warning signs about how the pills could make you drowsy.

"Better drowsy than sick," Ahmed said to himself.

He felt better in the top cabin, and busied himself with the chart plotter. He decided he might as well continue, albeit slower than he had planned, and if he didn't make port before it got rough, well he would just have to sit the storm out. Perhaps he could drag the anchor to improve stability, but decided he wanted to make all speed and would leave any other measures until necessary. He knew nothing about foul weather sailing.

Looking at the instruments was making him feel drowsy, the rhythmic sweep of the radar ensured he didn't run into another ship, also running blind in the storm; the chart plotter and the autopilot were working to navigate his course. He felt better looking out into the storm. There were flashes of sheet lightning in the distance; it was a foul night. He looked at his watch, he wasn't too sure when he had taken the last seasickness pill, but decided another wouldn't come amiss. It must be about four hours.

At the outer perimeter of the sweep of the radar screen, a blip represented a sizable boat coming toward him. It seemed to be untroubled by the weather and making good speed, and Ahmed decided he should change course. It would be one way of finding out if this boat was following him.

CHAPTER FORTY-EIGHT

Oxford

Chloe's visit with Walid was short. The ward nurse told her he had decided not to accept any further treatment in the hope his condition would stabilize and he could make it back to the barn for the last couple of days. The specialist, she said, didn't think any more treatment would help, but Walid would be unlikely to make it back home either. The nurse told her Walid wanted to be buried at his hometown in Algeria.

"Can I get you some tea?" The nurse looked concerned. Chloe contemplated the English belief that a cup of tea sorted out everything. They didn't need a National Health Service, a tearoom worked like some miracle cure-all.

"No, let's sort out everything else."

The hospital said there would be no need for a protracted autopsy. Chloe asked if they could skip the autopsy altogether. Would it be possible to respect his religious beliefs? The nurse ignored this request and continued; Walid did not wish Chloe to go to Algeria with the body, his two sons would place him in the ground alongside his first wife.

At one stage, Chloe would have been upset at the exclusion from his life, but she did not expect anything from him anymore, it was less pain-

ful that way. She did think he was a coward for not telling her his preferred arrangements himself.

Chloe realized the marriage had been over before they had gone to
America, and patching things up was just a patch over a large and moving crack that was bound to open up again. She didn't trust him, and she
certainly wasn't sure what his involvement in Al Qaeda activities were.
If he was so certain violent activity was wrong, why didn't he stop the
current attack, surely he could phone his brother.

Where was his phone? She hadn't seen it in Paris, and it hadn't been
returned with his things from Afghanistan. Perhaps it was still in Paris,
there was a locked storage unit in the garage of the apartment in Sceaux.
Could the movers have emptied it? She should have mentioned it, but
everything was so rushed. She also wanted to ask him about the sickness
and if it were possible he had been exposed to radiation in Paris just before they went to America, it would certainly explain the mystery illness
he had suffered on the plane.

Chloe composed herself and decided a friend from the mosque in
Paris should arrange his funeral. Chloe walked along the corridor from
the nurses' station to the private room where he was being monitored.
She took a deep breath and went in to see him. After the initial pleasant-
ries, she decided to ask him about who he saw the day before they went
to Florida.

"Walid, do you remember how sick you were on the way to America?"

He smiled. "You don't forget an experience like that, do you?"

"No, I suppose not. Perhaps you were exposed to the radiation the
day before we went away. What do you remember about that day?"

"Not much." Chloe was surprised Walid didn't seem interested. She
supposed it didn't matter to him.

"Try to think, it's important."

"Why?"

"They're looking for one more nuclear briefcase bomb, and if you were exposed to radiation in France, then it means they have found all the devices in London."

"Yes, I do remember the day now, I went to see Ahmed in the café, and he had a new briefcase for transporting artifacts. It was ingenious; it controlled the temperature and the humidity. He showed me the first one he had purchased and inside the briefcase was the most beautiful illustrated page of the Qur'an I had ever seen. I opened the box and the gold glistened, even in the dim light under the awning. It was an absolute delight. Ahmed offered the page to me as a gift. I had to tell him I didn't trade in pages of the Qur'an."

"What was his response?"

"He seemed pleased. Maybe he was testing me."

"How did he behave with the briefcase, did he make sure he was shielded by the lid of the case?"

"I don't know." He closed his eyes.

It was difficult to work out if he was trying to remember or if he was just exhausted by the conversation.

"One last question. Have you seen your phone since the move?"

Walid's eyes were open now. Chloe tried to work out whether he was in pain, or... no this was fear.

"No, I think I lost it in Iraq." He turned his face away.

Chloe thought about this response; if he feared her finding the phone then she was on the right track to finding his brother.

"Okay, you look tired. I'll see you later." He smiled, they both lived with the lies between them, she would pursue his brother and he knew it. His death would not be the end of the trail if she could help it.

Phil Scarlet hadn't turned up at the hospital, so she decided to go on without him. She got the Renault out of the parking lot, and made her way down the M40 to Waterloo station.

She treated herself to a first class seat, and started to plan her activities. She phoned Jean Pierre before the train left the station, and asked him to meet her at the Gare du Nord. He sounded surprised to hear from her. There was a silence, she wanted to tell him she found herself thinking about him, but couldn't find the words. He didn't respond when she told him Walid would die within the next few days. She didn't want him to feel she was looking for a replacement husband, so she said nothing.

She felt the key to the problem lay in the mosque. She would find a friend to support Walid in Islamic fashion as he prepared to leave this life, it was the best she could do for him. Hopefully, she could find out what had happened to Ahmed Talbi, maybe find Walid's phone and get a lead on his brother. She was racing ahead; it was ridiculous to think she could make any difference, when several secret intelligence services were involved in looking for a solution. However, she had to try.

Would Ahmed know where the briefcases were? There was only one way to find out and that was to talk to him. Her mind went back to the last time she had been to see him. He was a little man and he was scared of her. He was scared before she told him she was a journalist, his fear was apparently just because she had asked him a question. That bothered her greatly. It was like an admission of guilt. Why would he be scared of her? How much contact had he had with Walid's brother? Was he knowingly funding Al Qaeda? Was he aware of what he was doing, or was he like Walid, just implicated?

CHAPTER FORTY-NINE

Paris

As Chloe left the station, a shaft of light penetrated the gray clouds. The November sunshine seemed reassuringly warm and bright. She looked for Jean Pierre, he said he would meet her outside and he wasn't usually late.

"You look fantastic."

Jean Pierre would flatter any woman and Chloe reminded herself this was who he was and it wasn't personal, she needed to remain focused. She smiled at him; it was an automatic reaction.

They embraced, more of an affectionate hug rather than the traditional French kiss on each cheek. She thought the hug was just too long for a close friend. She hoped it meant more.

"Thank you for picking me up. I hope you've cleared your diary, we have a great deal to do, and only today to do it in."

"Chloe, I love your sense of drama! Any chance of a Pulitzer? Oh no, not in France, my dear!"

"Very funny. Why do you all rag me about the Pulitzer? I didn't seek an award—it just happened."

"Probably because Anne Marie did nothing but go around the office saying she had been made to take you on, and having two Pulitzers didn't mean you were a good reporter."

"Made to take me on? By whom?"

"Does it matter now?"

"Not really, but it explains why Anne Marie always gives me a hard time."

Chloe got in the car and told Jean Pierre what had been happening. She explained the urgency to find out what was going on before the State Opening of Parliament. He became serious immediately.

"Are you all right?"

"I'm not infected, if that's what you mean." He looked across at her, his face registered that she could have been infecting him. It wasn't what he had meant at all, it was a general inquiry about her mental health, and the effects of the scopolamine, which she was choosing to ignore.

"Isn't this something Patrick or someone at DST should be handling?"

"I think, particularly given the fact I need to sort out Walid's funeral, we have a much better chance of getting information. The problem is, if you provide the security services with any information, you may end up being or feeling guilty by association. Information is in short supply at the moment."

"Look, I know you've had a hard time of it in Oxfordshire, but don't you think you're getting a little paranoid?"

"No, in fact I would say I wasn't paranoid enough. I have accepted simple innocent explanations all along, but now I think I am waking up to the fact that someone is trying to kill Walid. I think it is probably his brother. MI5 consider him a serious threat to security."

"Yes, but how does this become your problem? I thought Walid was terminally ill, so it's all about timing isn't it?"

"Look there's other stuff going on too. I can tell you about it on the way but I just have to try to make a difference... It will make a good story." She hoped his journalist's instinct for a "good story" would influence him.

"You reckon we will be able to publish something?"

"Yes, I'm certain of it—now do you want to share a byline or argue?" She put her hand on the car door handle. If he wouldn't help, she'd have to take a taxi.

Chloe watched him thinking, working out the options, analyzing the dangers, and for a minute she wasn't sure what he would do. Then he put the car in gear, and they set off for the mosque. "Set off" was a loose description. Chloe thought she had diced with death a few times of late, which was why she wasn't shrieking at him to slow down, calm down, and get there in one piece. Jean Pierre was a Parisian driver, it was a breed apart, the horn of the car was an extension of his left hand, and the vocabulary colorful. Jean Pierre did not stick with the usual "Zut alors!" and "Merde!" He had bespoke insults for every driver along with pointed gestures. How he found the time or energy, she had no idea; they drove five kilometers in ten minutes, which in Paris was quite something. The Pont d'Austerlitz, named after Napoleon's victory against all the odds, became a new battle scene as Jean Pierre madly overtook cars as they crossed the bridge.

Chloe said nothing about his driving, if she was going to die in his car so be it, there were certainly worse ways to go. She focused on the job at hand. Reading her list of questions to Jean Pierre, he added, between curses, one or two to round out the story. He hated working with anyone on a story, especially as second string. She also knew his skills and charm did overcome all sorts of cultural barriers. He was able to find rapport with most people quickly, and on this story, as a woman, she would not.

"The only thing we can't use here is the potential grieving widow, he is going to be buried alongside his first wife, and I won't be going to Algeria with him to watch."

"Wow! How do you feel about that?"

"Relieved."

"Really?"

"You know things have been up and down ever since we were married, I sometimes feel as if I have been married to two people, a cultured, fun loving, caring individual, and a sullen, withdrawn, violent man."

"And when he's gone?"

"Jean Pierre, the way life has been going for me lately, I will be grateful to just have the luxury of thinking about a future."

Jean Pierre drove alongside the Jardin des Plantes, and they arrived at the Mosquée de Paris. It was grand and beautiful. The problem with asking questions in a large place of worship in the middle of a major city is few people get to know one another. She hoped they would remember Walid, it was a while since he had prayed there, but Ahmed should still be attending regularly.

Chloe put on a dark plain headscarf, so as not to cause offense, and they made their way from the parking lot to the front entrance. She had a good look at Jean Pierre. He aged gracefully, his bone structure helped. The hazel eyes seemed to change color, today they reflected the pale gray cashmere sweater he was wearing under a navy blazer and navy pincord trousers. He looked sharp and tailored in a relaxed way. She was still grateful to him for that night at his apartment, tenderness like that was precious, and she hoped she wasn't throwing it away because of poor timing. If he would wait...

He pulled out his black book and flipped open his phone and made an immediate appointment with an imam at the mosque. Chloe knew it was a good idea to bring him along; he had far more contacts than she had in Paris. Put her in Washington and she would be the same, but the two years she had spent in Paris hadn't been on local stories.

"Okay, this is what we do, you need to look upset, and I will talk for you. Keep your eyes lowered, remember your husband is dying, and you want everything that's best. I don't think we should hit any problems but if I need an imploring look I will say, 'I don't know how we will make progress, time is so short.' Okay?"

"Sounds like a plan."

CHAPTER FIFTY

MI5, London and Isle of Dogs

Louise was about to go out for lunch, she usually ate a sandwich at her desk, but she just wanted a change of air. If she didn't leave now, she knew she would start looking at the files that had just arrived on her desk. They could wait.

She walked along the Embankment and cut up to Starbucks, she knew it would be open, even on a Sunday. She made sure she had a good signal for her phone before collecting a sandwich, an espresso brownie, and a grande mocha-coffee. She was hoping a jolt of caffeine would make her feel livelier. She needed to go to bed and sleep for a week. Only two more days and she could sleep, it would all be over, they would have won or they would need new office accommodation outside of a contaminated London.

She relaxed to the jazz playing in the café. The aroma of freshly made coffee was comforting and familiar. Sitting in the midst of people clutching shopping, talking animatedly with their table mates, oblivious to the problems facing the security services, made her feel optimistic. Freedom to relax and be normal became a privilege. Life had been rough at MI5 recently, but the big picture was worth the fight. Maybe she would stay on and not accept defeat from the onslaught of work.

She had finished half her coffee and half a sandwich when her phone rang. She checked caller ID, it was work. She answered the call.

"Hi, I'm in Starbucks."

"Okay, I'll come and pick you up." James T sounded excited. "We're going hunting!"

"It's all right; I can be back in the office in ten minutes." Louise thought it would probably be nearer fifteen, but that was the best she could do.

"No time. I'll see you in a couple of minutes."

Louise decided she would finish her sandwich and drink as much coffee as she could. She wrapped the brownie in a napkin and put it in her handbag, perhaps she would get to it later.

She arrived at the edge of the pavement the same time as James T in his titanium gray BMW 545i.

"Good news. We have a lead on Farook and Nasir. A successful raid on the Frankfurt mosque gave us some new information. So we're off to the Isle of Dogs."

"Good news at last."

"Yes, Special Branch are meeting us there. You'd better put some body armor on. I have weapons secured in the trunk."

Louise leaned over to the backseat of the car and picked up a body armor jacket. She maneuvered like a contortionist out of her long winter wool coat, and pulled the flak jacket on. She might have been chilly, but the adrenaline rush of being on a raid would leave her oblivious to the cold until it was all over. She folded her coat carefully and placed it on the backseat of the car. James T was humming happily; he didn't get out from behind his desk often. He was like a child on an outing; he loved every minute of it. He drove across London, not speeding but not dawdling.

When he arrived at Canary Wharf, he telephoned to give his position, and made his way to the Asda parking lot, as agreed.

A Special Branch officer met them there. The raid was to take place at a little terraced house close by, no one was sure whether Farook and Nasir were in the house. Biological masks were required for those entering the house. Medical staff would arrive shortly with the antidote for the virus, although no one was sure if the virus would still be viable two weeks later, unless they had received a fresh supply.

James T had the car window open and Louise was getting cold, she reached across the back of the car and draped her coat over her shoulders. James T looked across, realized she was cold, and reluctantly closed the window.

The raid desperately needed to provide two live suspects for questioning. Then maybe, there might be some more information to work on. The way the attack had been set up, it was unlikely Farook and Nasir would be able to give them any information about the nuclear attack, but having them in custody would prevent them from carrying out any further biological attacks.

James T listened to the communications over the radio. He was tense. Louise watched him, feeling as if she was looking down on the situation and not present at all. She hadn't ever had an out-of-body experience before, but she guessed this was what people described. She decided now was as good a time as any to finish her lunch. James T watched as she calmly unwrapped the brownie and proceeded to eat it. He reached across to the back of the car and handed her a bottle of water. He said nothing.

The entry of Special Branch into the house was swift. The old door was no defense against a raid. It suggested they were going to find nothing in the house, the address was a false lead, or this wasn't the original house planned for their stay while waiting to make further attacks.

Farook and Nasir were not there but they had been. They found the property owner and he said the pair had been talking about a warehouse. There were a significant number of CCTV cameras on the Isle of Dogs. Its close proximity to the financial center at Canary Wharf and the incident of the IRA bomb at South Quay meant there was increased security in the area. Once the landlord had given them a description of the car, it didn't take long for surveillance to find Farook and Nasir had crossed the drawbridge at the end of West India dock, and were making their way along the A13 toward Tilbury docks.

"Okay, James, we are looking into possible sites, and we have a helicopter on surveillance in the area. We won't lose them but I think we should make our way toward ExCeL convention center and I will increase the security at London City Airport, in case that's the target."

James T, who couldn't wait to get started, was making his way out of the parking lot.

"Okay, we're on our way—and the description of the car…"

"Pale blue Ford Focus, with a 2004 plate—full details of license plate to follow."

James T looked across at Louise with a big grin, which rapidly left his face as he took in Louise's condition.

"Could your medical team rendezvous with us?"

"Try channel six, his name is Dr Ajay Singh."

"Dr Singh?" said James T, having adjusted the radio.

"Yes, sir."

"I think we have a situation here, can you rendezvous with us, right now?" James T's voice stressed the urgency.

"Okay, we are passing University of East London. I suggest we rendezvous at London City Airport. Should I call in an air ambulance?"

"I think we are probably dealing with flu, but I'd just like an early diagnosis. My agent may have been exposed to the virus." He didn't say which virus, no one spoke of anything else.

James T used the voice dial on his cell phone to call the medical center. He fiddled with the Bluetooth earpiece, turning up the volume to compensate for the noise of the engine.

"Do you have the results for Louise Chappel's recent test?"

"Yes, they're inconclusive. We'd like a blood test."

"She's not looking too well at the moment; can you meet us at London City Airport? We are liaising with Dr Ajay..."

"Singh—sure but I'll wait for his report." The medic sounded calm and confident.

"He's out here on medical support..."

"It will be fine; I'll take a report from him—he can always send Louise to us in an air ambulance if he has any concerns."

As Louise and James T drove past the University of East London, Louise dreamed about skiing on the wonderful sloping roofs of the campus buildings. One of the rooftops had been designed as a skateboard ramp she decided. Did the students ever attempt to get onto the roof? The dramatic architecture always surprised and delighted her and she was glad not to be driving so she could take in the shapes and colors.

They met the medical unit in the car park at London City Airport. Dr Singh examined Louise, took a blood sample, and gave her a precautionary shot against the Wychmoor virus, as it had become known.

"I think it's a simple case of overwork." He looked accusingly at James T. "And a seasonal touch of flu."

"Okay, best to be sure," said James T. "I suggest you go back to the office in a taxi, or go home, whichever you prefer." He looked at Louise.

"What part of 'overwork' did you not understand?" said Dr Singh.

"The part that says if we don't defeat these terrorists in the next forty-eight hours they win." James T looked directly at Dr Singh. His manner dared Dr Singh to overrule his judgment. The doctor packed his bag and mouthed, "Go home," to Louise.

"I'll wait in the car until the raid is over, if that's okay with you two?" said Louise, now embarrassed by the fuss. It was far more likely to be a reaction to the Provigil she had managed to get from the duty doctor to keep her awake and alert and was now wearing off. He had read her the list of side effects and the flu symptoms, while not directly similar, could be attributed to the stimulant. Still it had been effective and she had managed to function without much sleep.

"Sure," said James T before Dr Singh could make any comment.

It wasn't far beyond the city airport that they turned into a small industrial estate. Farook and Nasir had driven the blue Focus into a warehouse at the far end of the estate. Armed Special Branch officers had deployed to cover all the exits. Dressed in black combat gear they piled out of the three vans and took up their positions.

Louise thought they looked like the ants out of a Disney cartoon. They waited and James T gave the order for the raid to proceed.

"What if they release a virus into the atmosphere?" said Louise, rather nervous at all the enthusiasm to go ahead with the raid—if the pair were planning to go somewhere, she would have waited for them to exit the warehouse.

"Best to contain any virus within the warehouse, rather than out in the open," James T said.

Ah, thought Louise, *it was an intentional decision.* She might have known better than to question James T. He was usually right.

The corralling of Farook and Nasir went smoothly, perhaps too smoothly. Both men immediately got out of the blue car, where they had been waiting, and raising their hands, asked to see the German consul.

In the warehouse, they found a white Transit van. Investigation of the van showed all the equipment ready to put the virus into the water supply, but it was impossible to tell when it was last used. The suspects would be taken to the basement of Thames House for interrogation before being handed back to Special Branch.

James T was the only one who seemed suspicious about how easy it had been.

"Get someone in a hazmat suit to collect the virus canisters."

"Yes, sir."

The small team in green hazardous chemical suits, held back in reserve, went to the back of the van.

"Bomb!"

The team quickly dispersed, and James T shouted as he ran to his car, "Get the canisters out of the van, now!"

The hazmat team showed great courage and came out with a metal case, which presumably contained the virus canisters.

James T drove past the team with his trunk open, the hazmat officer did a fosbury flop into the trunk with the metal case and Louise and James T sped away with the man and the virus in the back.

Seconds later, the blast from the warehouse shook the car.

"Nuclear?" Louise voiced the fears of both MI5 agents.

"Let's hope not, shall we?" James T opened his phone. "The phone's still working which would suggest it was traditional."

"Your two suspects are ready now. I would say they are shaken but not stirred," the radio announced.

Louise took in James T's suppressed smile. He would probably have preferred to take the virus and the terrorists out of the way of the blast, but an airborne virus was infinitely the higher risk, she mused. He would want to interrogate these two Germans. One thing was beginning to be clear, in order to avoid detection, the coordinator of the attacks kept each area separate. There was a production unit, which acted separately from the distribution unit, and then there was a deployment unit, in this case Farook and Nasir. The most they could hope for was a contact at the mosque in Frankfurt and confirmation they had picked up the canisters in Bradford.

CHAPTER FIFTY-ONE

Mediterranean

Graeme prided himself on being a good sailor, but he was beginning to feel rather sick in this rough weather. The lieutenant told him to stand out on the aft deck, hold on to one of the guns, and look at the horizon.

Graeme initially thought this idea was probably to ensure he was completely wet through and through, but the fresh air helped enormously. The salt water was icy cold and shot-blasted his face with tiny droplets of hard rain, as if someone was throwing a pack of cocktail sticks into his face. When he felt free of the nausea, and sick of the rain, he went back inside.

He looked at his watch, the Nimrod was tracking what they thought was Ahmed's boat, and HMS *Scimitar* had radar contact and was closing.

"How are we able to catch the Predator?" said Graeme to the lieutenant.

"Bad weather gives us the advantage. We cut through the waves and the Predator tries to skim over them. If it gets any rougher there's a real danger the Predator will flip over, it's not designed for this weather. In calmer weather she could outrun us."

"We need to take Ahmed alive—even if it's a lifesaving mission. We need to get any information he has. Right now it's the only point to continuing this operation."

"I understand. We're doing our best, but if he's looking at his radar he'll know we're in the area, although not, of course, who we are."

The radar operative called over, "Damn, he's changed course."

"Why?"

"Probably to see if we adjust our course to intercept."

"And?"

"We'll hold this course for now, and change when we have to."

"Would you say the—" Graeme lurched across the cockpit. The lieutenant caught him.

"Would I say it was suspicious to change course—not really. You'll just have to trust us on this one, Graeme."

"Okay!" Graeme grinned, the lieutenant had got the measure of him very quickly; it usually took people a couple of weeks to learn he was a control freak.

Graeme would have liked to spend more time looking at the radar, but looking down at the scope made him feel sick; the lieutenant was right, watching the lightning on the horizon was his best option.

"How long before we intercept?"

"Not long."

CHAPTER FIFTY-TWO

MI5, London

Louise made her way to her desk. Whatever Dr Singh had injected into her was working, she felt much better. She unlocked her desk drawer and took out a stack of buff files, with "Classified" printed across in large red letters. Wondering which file to open first, she decided on a chronological order of death, and started with James Robert Culshaw.

Louise wasn't sure what she had expected to see. She felt sure it would not be about a simple accident. Chloe, she concluded, must be a lot like her father. The file concluded Kolenka Antipov murdered James Robert Culshaw.

On the day in question, James Culshaw returned to the test laboratory unexpectedly. Antipov was photographing his results file. The spying activity was obvious and as Culshaw left the lab to inform security, Antipov noticed him. He engaged Culshaw in conversation, before slashing at Culshaw's protective suit with a scalpel. Culshaw hadn't seen the blade and Antipov's actions resulted in an unpleasant death from the nerve agent present in the lab. Antipov staged the event to make it look like an accident. MI5 had quickly concluded the truth of the matter and had turned Ken Antipov into a double agent.

Sometimes the actions of MI5 and the Ministry of Defense at the time were different than they would have been in the current climate. In order to assist Mrs Culshaw in her return to her native France with her twelve-year-old daughter, they had bought the family home from the widow, and given it to Antipov as part of the package deal. It was a sad event. Louise thought Chloe would prefer to know her father had died for his country, and he was a hero. In no way was Culshaw stupid or careless, an absent-minded professor.

Louise picked up the Antipov file, the first part just confirmed the facts she had already gleaned from the Culshaw file, and she turned to the most recent entries. The BBC had announced Antipov was a spy. This was despite the standing Defense Advisory Notice 05 requiring the BBC to seek a dialogue with the Ministry of Defense prior to publishing. An initial and perfunctory inquiry had been made, and the MOD denied the information was accurate. There had been some confusion over the communication. The lack of substantiated facts had not deterred the BBC from publishing their findings, impervious to the effects their reporting would have.

James T had put notes on the file:

> *Meeting set up with journalist Chloe Moreau, reason not known. Suspect Antipov might want to confess re James Culshaw. Breach of security not acceptable. Antipov due to tell MI5 who "Rosa" is.*

> *Patrick Dubois of France's DST seen in London, at Sotheby's sale the day before.*

> *Unexplained DNA of Walid Merbarkia aka Art Expert at the scene. Also present at Sotheby's sale the day before. Losing surveillance seems deliberate with hindsight. Antipov seems to have downloaded either the method to weaponize a virus, or an address to collect a sample of a live virus for weaponization, a waterborne virus the night before his death. Did he pass this information on to Merbarkia? Will analysis show it to be the same virus found at Wychmoor Wood?*

Louise noted James's reference note, was he suggesting the French had something to do with the matter, or terrorists had killed Antipov after extracting technical information? She would have loved to have the opportunity to ask him, but she would have had to answer too many questions as to why she had gained access to the files.

James didn't mention the Russians who could have picked up Antipov and spirited him away to Moscow to face spying charges, or killed him.

Antipov had been dispatched with a quick acting, painless injection. His final breaths had been with a mask over his face, delivering carbon monoxide from an aerosol to ensure his lungs would contain sufficient evidence for the average pathologist to draw the correct conclusion. It was a reasonable deduction that a body left in a shed with the mower running and some evidence of carbon monoxide poisoning had fallen asleep in a tragic accident or committed suicide.

Had the killers not been disturbed in their activities, they would have realized the window of the shed was open, and the mower didn't have enough gas. The pathologist didn't complete the full analysis nor was a full inquest held. MI6 rigorously denied any involvement.

The judicial investigation into the breach of the DA notice found the BBC bore a large measure of responsibility for the tragedy. The BBC had created the situation in which Ken Antipov felt, as an ex Russian citizen, he would not be able to clear his name and had taken his own life. James T had decided the inquest was unnecessary and would merely serve as a further painful event for the family.

Louise noticed a drip of blood on the file cover. *Epistaxis,* she thought. The report into the first symptoms of the waterborne virus used the medical term for a nosebleed. She had had nosebleeds before, but she felt this was probably not a normal nosebleed, although it might be a side effect from the Provigil, maybe, if she was lucky. The problem was she didn't believe in luck. She tore the back cover off the file.

She reached into her desk drawer and pulled out five large gusset sided envelopes, and put the files into the envelopes, taking care not to bleed onto them, she addressed the envelopes to Chloe at the barn. If she hurried, she would make the post office before it was too late.

She put the envelopes into her briefcase. Briefly, Louise considered her action. Chloe should know the truth. If this illness was the virus, at least there wouldn't be any consequences for her to face. Her parents seemed very content with the knowledge they would have a grandchild. She would miss her small nephew or niece growing up. She would miss having her own baby. No one but Trevor would miss her, and if she wrote a last will and testament, she could leave him the flat—a life policy would pay off the mortgage. She got out a piece of paper and realized if she did make a will she would need a witness, she crumpled the paper and dumped it in the bin.

If she didn't die, she could be hanged as a traitor. Maybe the cocktail of drugs and length of duty would mean she could sue the intelligence services under Health and Safety or Human Rights or something and trade off with time in prison. Her nose decided to drip again, she looked for some more tissues, and decided the bloody tissues discarded in the bin were probably a biohazard, so collected them up, shoved them into her handbag and made her decision, the files would go to Chloe.

She took the files out of the envelopes, and ripped off the back file covers. New files had a chip system in place to prevent files leaving the building. She placed her current file in her briefcase and hoped if she gave the security guard one file and pleaded she was unwell, he would be happy to let her through the system without a full check of her briefcase. Perhaps the nosebleed would work in her favor.

CHAPTER FIFTY-THREE

Paris

Chloe walked slowly back toward the car, her eyes streamed tears in an unrelenting torrent. Jean Pierre didn't speak. The overwhelming grief she felt wasn't for Walid, it was for Michael, the hurt was as fresh as the day she made the arrangements for Michael's funeral. She didn't know why it had affected her in this way. Grief was like that. Suddenly, when you felt you were over the hurt, it crept up on you and found a place where the wound was fresh.

She didn't know what Jean Pierre was thinking. Whatever she felt, they had uncovered important and urgent information in their investigation and they needed to move on. Time was running out.

"We should go to the apartment in Sceaux," Chloe said between sobs.

"Is there anything...?"

"It's all right, it's not about Walid. It just brought back painful memories. Don't worry about it, I'm just being silly, I'm tired that's all."

"Michael?"

"Yes, it just reminded me of the day I made arrangements..." The tears flowed again. "Just drive."

"Okay—but I think we should have someone meet us there. I'll ring Patrick."

"Okay."

Jean Pierre got out of the car to make the call. Chloe pulled herself together, picked up her phone, and called Phil Scarlet.

"Hi." She gulped.

"Chloe, are you all right?"

"Yes, just a little tired. I've been to the Mosquée de Paris and Ahmed left or sold his gallery to a friend here. Some of his things are in the shop, including a briefcase similar to the ones in London by the sounds of it. Ahmed went on vacation; he has a boat on the Med, a mooring in Barcelona Olympic Marina—the man thought the boat was a Predator."

"Yes, I think MI5 are checking that out. Anything else?"

"I think Walid left some possessions in the lockup in the basement of the apartment in Sceaux, including his satellite phone, which might give a lead on his brother."

"Chloe, it's really important you don't use the phone yourself. What are you going to do next?"

"Jean Pierre is phoning Patrick Dubois of the DST to meet us at the apartment in Sceaux."

"All right, I'll liaise with MI5 to make sure they know what's happening—good work, Chloe."

She hung up. She was disappointed they already knew about Ahmed, she thought it had been a good lead and new information. But it was ridiculous to think she could find out anything they didn't already know. She should be making sure Walid's last days were comfortable, although probably that opportunity had already gone. He had decided to go back to his roots in Algeria, a place he identified as home. She understood that. Just as she had felt the need to get back to Paris after Michael had died in America. Knowing what she knew now about the Qur'an saying a Muslim should not take protection from a Christian, she was surprised he had married her. Some things with Walid didn't make any sense at all.

Jean Pierre got back in the car.

"Okay, Patrick will meet us at the apartment."

"What did he say?"

"He sounded surprised to hear from me. I suppose he expected to hear from you. He asked if you were okay."

"And..."

"I said you were tired but fine."

"Thank you."

"Are you fine?"

"Yes, I suppose so; it's just been a rather tense couple of weeks."

"Are you sure it's Walid and not his brother back in Oxfordshire?"

There it was. He had voiced her worst fear. That in fact both brothers used her. The reason Walid's mood had swung from happy to aggressive and withdrawn was that there were two people. *No, that's ridiculous. Walid is at the hospital, all the stuff he said about his wife, no it has to be Walid.*

"I'm sure."

"Okay. Patrick said he could be there in about an hour and a half which does give us a little time. Would you like something to eat, a drink, coffee, or something?"

"Not really."

"Would you like a walk through Sceaux Park?"

"That might be nice. Do we have time?"

"Yes, Chloe, we're killing time."

"Before time kills us."

"That's a bit..."

"Only an observation—couldn't we be looking at the briefcase at the art gallery or something?"

"I think that's something for the security services, wasn't it looking at an artifact in one of those briefcase things that exposed Walid to radiation?"

"I don't know, they seem to think so. Walid isn't being helpful about it. Perhaps he thinks it doesn't matter. Do you think they'll find all the bombs in time?"

"Does it matter to you?"

"Yes, of course it does."

"But you're safe here. I mean, you don't intend to go back to London before this is all over, do you?"

"Jean Pierre, I have to." She looked straight at him. She saw the look in his eyes, his feelings for her hadn't changed since the night she'd spent at his apartment.

"Have we time for a coffee in Sceaux?" she said, wanting to change the subject and finding a reason to look away. She put her seatbelt on.

"Perhaps we just go to the apartment and start sorting out what you have in storage; I mean, Walid wouldn't booby-trap the basement. He knew you would go downstairs to find things. It might be more productive, rather than waiting idly by for Patrick."

"Much better idea."

Jean Pierre drove slower than usual as they set off for Sceaux. She was thinking about values and life. *Would you value your brother's life above hundreds of innocent lives?* If Walid knew she was going to be killed by the bomb, she wondered if he would call his brother and stop the attack. It seemed unlikely, but maybe if she made a telephone call to Walid...

Lost in her own thoughts they arrived at Sceaux faster than she had expected. Jean Pierre looked across.

"So what are you thinking?"

"Sorry, all sorts of things—I'm not good company and you've been so kind."

"If you don't mind my saying that sounds a bit patronizing."

"I'm sorry, I didn't mean..."

"It's all right—it's a difficult day."

"Yes, but the problem is, all my days are difficult at present and have been for ages."

"I don't know, these Pulitzer prize winning journalists. The problem is when you've won a couple you just have to go on... and, Chloe, I have to say when it comes to generating news or being the story well..."

"All right—don't get cocky!"

"Mmm, interesting phrase 'cocky'—was that in a ..." His eyes teased in a sexual way. Chloe didn't mean to smile back quite so broadly, but he made her smile. In fact, he made her feel safe, secure in a homey way, which wasn't quite what he wanted. Jean Pierre, a warm duvet, a hot chocolate on a cold night... She couldn't quite see that lighting his eyes with joy.

The concierge was busy at his post, doing something. She had a theory that they always have something on the desk to look busy, but they spent most of their time looking at the comings and goings in the apartments, which perhaps was not a bad thing. All the same, it did mean he was nosey and quite difficult to manage.

"Bernard, I am so sorry. I understand the movers forgot to empty the downstairs storage."

"Ah yes, and you didn't leave any forwarding address. How could the management send you back the deposit....but of course, until the storage is empty the deposit isn't due either."

"I understand, well I'm here now to take care of things. Do you have the key?"

"There's a lot of stuff down there you know, Madame Moreau."

"So I believe. If you give me a key I can get started."

"Where is monsieur?"

"He's sick—I'm afraid he's in the hospital."

"Too bad, send him my best wishes. I thought he looked ill last week, when he dropped by, he said you would take care of the basement." His words lacked conviction. He didn't like Walid. She shuddered, she was hot, but inside she was cold. *It wasn't Walid that came last week; it must have been his brother.* Her mouth was dry. Jean Pierre came across and took her elbow.

"I will." Chloe's voice cracked as she took the key.

"And this is?" Bernard looked across at Jean Pierre.

"A work colleague, and another will be joining us soon, so if you could send him down when he arrives. His name is Patrick Du—"

"Bois." She turned to see Patrick, who embraced her.

"Good afternoon, Patrick," said Chloe.

"Good afternoon, Chloe, well, Bernard, if you'll excuse us we better get on."

So, it seemed Patrick knew Bernard, which was interesting.

Patrick and Chloe walked down the slope while Jean Pierre brought the car down. If she wasn't mistaken Jean Pierre was jealous of Patrick's familiarity. How ridiculous.

Patrick opened the door cautiously and made sure Bernard's view was limited by placing her in direct line between the door lock and the camera.

"Just in case there is any device on the door."

"Spooks! Patrick, did you know Walid's brother was here last week?"

Patrick looked up, for the first time she saw a glimmer of expression not carefully controlled; he hadn't known. She wasn't sure if this made her feel smug, she had at last contributed to the investigation. It had always seemed to her Patrick was in control and knew what was going on.

Jean Pierre joined them and took out a large Swiss Army knife from his jacket pocket. She froze momentarily but realized getting rid of some of the boxes would be a lot easier if they were flat. He was so practical. He either hadn't heard or wasn't going to react to Bernard's revelations about Walid's brother, or maybe he didn't realize it couldn't have been Walid.

She hauled out several cardboard boxes from the lockup for Jean Pierre to cut up and stack on the garage floor. She started looking carefully through the other boxes, seeing what was in them.

"Thrift shop." She passed him a cardboard box full of Walid's clothes. She didn't remember them being brought down here.

"My office," Patrick corrected.

"Really?" Now he had an interest in Walid's old clothes?

"Just to be sure."

"Okay." She shrugged, touched her forehead indicating the insanity of his actions. This left Jean Pierre looking a lot happier, they were bonded together and Patrick was the outsider, he was the spook.

"Patrick. Wait." She pulled at Patrick's sleeve. He was preoccupied looking into empty boxes with the passion of a bargain hunter at a rummage sale.

"There's something wrong." Finally, she got Patrick's attention.

"What?"

"That box, we've never had an air-conditioning unit, let alone four."

"Are you sure?" Patrick looked at her closely.

"Of course I'm sure. And another thing, there used to be a shelf full of books up there and now it's empty. In fact, nothing is where it was when I left it."

"What sort of books?"

"I don't know, they were in Farsi—or so Walid said. I can't say I know the difference between Urdu, Farsi, or Punjabi."

"Could Walid have moved these things?"

"No, I was the last person to come in here." She pointed at a wheeled suitcase. "That was the case I used when I went to America—and Walid was already in Iraq when I got back."

"What are you looking for specifically?" Patrick was now aware this was not just clearing out, there was a more definite purpose.

"Walid had a small trunk which he kept locked. It was a wooden nut-brown carved chest, it looked antique. The handles were brass, as was the lock on the front. In it he kept things that were secret from me, and he always put his phone back in the chest when he finished his call."

"But the Americans took his cell phone off him in Iraq. There was nothing useful on it."

"Yes, but he also had a satellite phone."

"Ah, now that would be more interesting. Would Bernard need to come in here?"

"What, to store some empty air-conditioning boxes and steal some books written in Arabic, I don't think so. Do you want me to ask him? If he comes down here, we'll never get rid of him."

"All right, I think it's time you two left. Leave everything here and I'll bring you the suitcases, and anything else that's yours, later on." Patrick pulled out his phone. "Okay, we're going to need some help."

Immediately a black van came down the slope into the basement.

"Leave! Leave now!" Patrick's voice stressed the urgency of the command. Jean Pierre didn't need any prompting, grabbing Chloe's arm he propelled her into his car, and they left the garage and parked a couple of blocks away.

They sat looking out of the window, it was beginning to rain; the sun had disappeared to leave a gray autumn's day in Paris. The leaves were a brown slush on the pavement and passers-by scurried past with their heads down and umbrellas up.

"Do we wait?" asked Jean Pierre.

"I don't know, I suppose so. We could go to the art gallery and see if there's anything—"

"Don't you think it would be a good idea to let Patrick do his stuff?"

"I wouldn't be here if..." Her voice trailed away, it seemed so ridiculous to think anything she did would make a difference. Yet, she did know she could get information that would not be forthcoming to the police or security services.

"I know, you think they could do more."

"No. I want to rid the world of Walid's brother..."

"Is that your responsibility? Don't you think Walid should be responsible for any views he has about his brother, you only know about his brother because of Walid and he wasn't even the one to tell you. Walid seems to have, in all but name, divorced you, so why don't you feel the same degree of separation?" Jean Pierre looked at her in a way that demanded an answer.

"Look at what that man cost, not only me, but also Walid. He lost his wife because of his brother. According to Patrick, he's more or less estranged from his sons because of his brother. He was pulled into this particular art trade because of him. He is losing his life because of him. I think some of the issues have also affected me. I know you don't share how I feel about this…"

"Chloe, the only mistake you made was marrying the guy for the wrong reasons. He married you so he wouldn't come under the spotlight, which he would have done had he applied for an extension to his visa. He hasn't treated you well and he certainly hasn't ever been honest with you."

Chloe looked across at Jean Pierre, what he said made a lot of sense; the problem was if she agreed with him, she would feel disloyal to Walid, even if he was right.

In the end she didn't have to make any response, her cell phone rang.

"Hello? Okay, when… Right! All right, well I'm in Paris at the moment, I can be back in about four, maybe five hours. I'm sorry, I didn't get that, a nurse? All right, then I'll be there tomorrow night. Oh good! How is he? I see. Thank you. Um, yes, goodbye." She snapped the phone shut.

"They've discharged Walid, or rather he's discharged himself. They gave him another transfusion this morning, and he decided he would go home; he has a couple of days left at most. They've arranged for a private nurse to attend him. They thought I should know."

"And you're just going to drop everything and run home."

"I thought we might have dinner, and then tomorrow, I'll go back to England. Jean Pierre, he's dying. He just wants to die at home. That's all."

"He's made his thoughts about you clear, so why are you running back?"

"Patrick has taken over at the apartment. You tell me I should let the security services do their job… so I would have thought you'd be pleased."

"Pleased? Why should I be pleased? He doesn't deserve you, he never has and—"

Chloe put her finger on his lips.

"It's all right, Jean Pierre, just because I need to go back to arrange the funeral flights, and so on, it won't make any difference, I'm not going to fall in love in two days."

"It isn't that, it's…"

"All right, if you feel that strongly, come back with me. You can stay in the pub in the village. I've been meaning to tell you about the pub. You'll find the owner interesting. It will only be for a couple of days, and as soon as Walid is on his way back to Algeria, you can help me pack up and come back to Paris."

"You're not going to stay on?"

"No, I've told the university I will do a couple of guest, complimentary lectures, but lecturing isn't my thing. Hopefully Anne Marie will let me off the EU stories, particularly after I gave her all those pieces on the Wychmoor Wood virus, and with exclusive pictures, which I see she syndicated to the UK press."

Chloe sent a text to Patrick saying she was going back to Oxford in the morning, his reply was short, a simple "OK."

Jean Pierre parked his car in the garage to his apartment and took her to a restaurant. After a delicious meal, and now feeling very sleepy from the warm food and wine, they walked hand in hand back to his apartment.

Next day they went to the Gare du Nord together and boarded the train for London. Chloe told Jean Pierre about the pub owner and the information he had about Antipov's death. They picked up her car at Waterloo, complaining bitterly about the parking charges, and she drove up the M40, stopping for lunch by the river in Marlow. Then she dropped him off at the pub on her way back to the barn.

As she drove up to the barn, she noticed the security lights didn't work, and there were two men in the hall, it looked as if they were arguing. *What's going on? Perhaps it's just a male nurse, Walid makes a dreadful patient.*

CHAPTER FIFTY-FOUR

The Mediterranean

Ahmed looked at the radar, he was pleased the other boat hadn't changed course, now he would have to make a change in direction. He would be better off in Algiers, he might lose the Predator but at least he would be free. He had friends in Algiers who would hide him. He picked up his cell phone, if he could get a connection they could meet him on the quay.

He looked at the phone, he was surprised how small and fuzzy the figures seemed, he must be more tired than he thought, perhaps it was the pills. He tried to place the call several times but couldn't get a signal. He wasn't sure if his phone worked at sea, or if it was the foul weather.

He got out the chart, was checking the coordinates for the new course, when a wave tipped the boat alarmingly. At first, he thought it would flip over completely, but it crashed back down.

He reduced power, he had it in the back of his mind he was supposed to let the boat drift sideways to the swell.

"Zut!" He simply didn't remember what he was supposed to do in bad weather. He had never intended to sail in bad weather. He looked at the radar screen; suddenly the boat now moving away from his position looked like an attractive rescue vessel.

He switched the radio on, turned the power to high; tuned the radio to VHF channel 16 and started to broadcast his message for help. He depressed the alarm signal generator and counted thirty seconds backward. He thought for a moment, technically it was a Pan-Pan message, he was in distress. *How am I supposed to know if I'll have time to get a Mayday message off later? Another wave like the last one and the boat will capsize and I'll be in the water.* He decided on a Mayday message. His head hurt and he felt tired. He decided he better get out the *Nautical Almanac* and check the exact procedure.

Having transmitted his Mayday message, he concluded with, "Over." He waited, now he would find out about the boat on his radar.

He waited for the response.

"This is HMS *Sabre* acknowledging your Mayday call and changing course now to provide assistance, we should be with you in about twenty minutes. Over."

Ahmed thought for a moment, HMS *Sabre*, the British Navy were a long way from Gibraltar. *Are they looking for me? Surely not, they would have changed course to intercept earlier.* It was a risk he would have to accept.

"Acknowledged, do you want me to let off a flare or anything?"

"A flare would be good in about ten minutes. Over." Ahmed remembered he was supposed to say "over" after every transmission, well they were on their way now, any further conversation seemed useless.

"Over and out." *That should stop further dialogue,* he thought.

"Please keep your radio switched on to let us know of any further developments. Do you plan to abandon ship? Over."

Ahmed thought about this for a moment, and wondered if he would drift into shore from this distance, he thought it would be unlikely but it might be preferable to being taken into custody by the British. He could wait until they were closer to make that decision.

"Hopefully not. Over."

"Perhaps you could let off a flare for us to check your location. Over."

"All right, over." *What do they want a flare for?* They had radar, didn't they? It wasn't a small life raft they were looking for, and he became suspicious. *They said ten minutes, why do they need a flare now?* It was too soon. He was being played, he looked at the radar.

They were close, he opened the locker and took out a flare, he also got out the life raft, and started half-emptying water out of the Evian bottles, it was a precaution so they would float if they went overboard when he launched the life raft. Fresh water would be at a premium.

He knew he should abandon ship; he would launch the raft, and set the autopilot on the Predator for a fast speed so the boat would tip over and the navy would be occupied trying to get the boat right side up to find him. He would take his chances in the life raft, he checked his seasickness pills, he had plenty of pills left, it would be better than trusting the British.

He busied himself with sorting out the life raft and placed some food, a can opener, and the water bottles in a bag designed to float. He thought about the briefcase. If he took it, he could sell the bomb, it must be worth something. If there was a timer on the bomb, then he might be transferring his death sentence to the lifeboat. It had survived this far, and so he put the briefcase onto a length of rope, and tied it to the raft.

He set the autopilot and increased the speed. He grabbed the equipment and leaped over the side. The plan might have gone smoothly had he remembered to detach the lifeline, but he was tethered to the boat. The cable from his safety harness was still attached to the bow rail. He twisted himself round, taking out the knife attached to his belt, and cut the lifeline.

He dropped into the sea. He gasped; it was much colder than he had anticipated. Perhaps he should go with the British, better to spend some time in jail for money laundering than die like this. He struggled to get himself on board, organize the raft, and close the opening. If he streamed the drogue it would be more stable, but he decided against it for now. He let off the requested flare, which he hoped would confuse the Brits, the Predator wasn't too far away when it flipped over, engines screaming.

He wished he had some form of power to be able to get further away from the Sunseeker Predator and British Navy attention. The Predator had been a fine boat, and he knew that he would never have another like it. He grieved for the boat, but also the loss of the paintings and the artifacts, not the loss to the art world, but for the monetary loss. Now he was going to have to figure out how to sell the briefcase bomb.

He watched as HMS *Sabre* came alongside the Predator. They were using equipment to scan the wreck for his body. He hadn't allowed for that, he had felt sure they would assume he was inside the boat and start a rescue mission. As he watched, he realized the life raft had a strong blinking light on the apex. *How can I disengage the light system?* He remembered the salesman's words, this was one of the safest life rafts, it had a search and rescue transponder.

They would have no problem finding him at all. He was sending them a signal, pinpointing his position, and the only thing to do was to look as if he had intended to abandon ship to ease his rescue. He let off another flare, and HMS *Sabre* maneuvered toward his position.

CHAPTER FIFTY-FIVE

Oxfordshire

As she approached the barn, she felt apprehensive. At first, she put this down to fears for Walid. But she had been living with death as a reality for a few days now. As she came closer, she could see two men, they both looked like Walid. Chloe backed slowly away from the barn, and reached inside her pocket for her cell phone.

The security lights blazed into action and Walid's brother came out. She wouldn't have known whether it was Walid or his brother if it hadn't been for the speed of his action and his overwhelming physical strength. Walid was too sick to have this much strength. He pinned her wrists together and threw the cell phone into the grass.

"I don't think so," Qasim growled.

Chloe struggled but it was useless; he dragged her into the barn.

"Look what I've found, Walid, it's your cover story, or should I say your whore?" He spat out the words with contempt. "Did you enjoy dinner on the boat on the Seine, dear? Never seek the protection of the Christian, remember that, Walid? Do you remember learning that from the Qur'an?"

Walid looked down. "What are you going to do with her?"

"Do you care?"

"Just tie her up," said Walid. "What harm can she do now?"

Chloe watched as Qasim thought for a moment, and he went across to the sideboard where she had left some brown parcel tape when she had started to pack, ready for the move back to Paris.

The first piece of tape went over her mouth; she could smell and taste the plastic, she felt like retching. She breathed, slowly and deeply, trying to keep calm. He twisted her around to tie her hands behind her back so quickly that she fell on the stone floor. They all heard the crack of her breaking collarbone. Walid winced. Qasim paid no attention and continued what he was doing. He taped her wrists behind her back and then taped her ankles. He taped Chloe to the cross strut of the hall table, like a pig on a spit roast.

The stone flag floor was cold and she began to shiver. This made the intense pain in her shoulder worse.

She could hear Qasim and Walid talking in the kitchen. Walid was remonstrating with Qasim. Qasim was clearly the dominant of the two brothers and in his current physical state Walid was no match. She glanced through the open doorway. Mostly she kept her eyes closed; she could glean potentially useful information as long as the door was open.

Qasim brought an aluminum briefcase to the barn and placed it just in front of her. She was terrified. *Was it leaking radiation? Will I become sick like Walid?* She found the words of the Lord's Prayer going through her head. She had prayed in the hospital for Michael's life, and God hadn't heard her, so she'd stopped praying. Now, when she thought that Qasim would take her life, with no other source of help, she found herself praying earnestly.

She kept her eyes closed, and hoped her submissive state would lead him to believe she was passive and harmless. She had no idea what the time was, but she guessed it was around one o'clock in the morning.

She could hear some metallic noise, like a nut being screwed onto a bolt. *Perhaps it's a silencer for Qasim's gun?* She could only speculate. She didn't even know if Qasim had a gun. The noise of a phone vibrating on the table stopped him from whatever he was doing; he answered it, the conversation was in German. Chloe's German wasn't fluent but she gathered that a chemical engineer had been caught in Frankfurt and from Qasim's responses he didn't seem unduly concerned.

Chloe didn't think she would sleep, the pain was considerable but there did seem times when she was either asleep or unconscious. She had no idea how time was passing, but she couldn't think of how to escape. In the morning, Qasim would leave, and maybe she would have a chance.

Qasim walked through the hall, paused, and looked at her. Chloe remained still; hopefully he would think she was unconscious. He went through to the bedroom and woke Walid. It was pitch-black outside the barn, it must be early. Qasim came back into the hall and approached the table. He was going through her handbag. What he was looking for? Then Qasim was patting her jeans pockets, she shuddered involuntarily at his touch. He found what he was looking for and reached inside the pocket to take out her car keys. The movement had sent her shoulder into a screaming rage and it took all her powers of concentration focused on breathing through her nose to avoid being sick.

Qasim went back into the bedroom to collect Walid, and she was relieved they took the aluminum briefcase with them. She heard the Clio drive off, she hadn't put any gas in it, and she wondered how far they could get before it needed refueling.

Chloe struggled, but it was impossible, the long oak dining table's central strut was perfect for securing an adversary. Even if she hadn't had a broken collarbone, she didn't see how she could get free, the tape was strong, he hadn't been economical in using it, and he had secured her at her ankles, knees, waist, and shoulders.

The sun was bright when she watched the welcome figure of Jean Pierre walking briskly up the drive toward the barn. Chloe was thinking about ways to attract his attention, would he look through the double height window? Most people were too polite to look into the living area windows as they approached, and kept a fixed gaze on the front door as a measure of politeness. She needn't have worried, Jean Pierre was a reporter and he was interested in everything.

He rang the doorbell and when there was no response, he moved back into view, her loud grunts couldn't be heard through the double glazed units. There was a strong possibility he would just leave.

Jean Pierre had his face pressed hard against the glass to be able to see as much of the inside of the barn as possible. Chloe watched. *Please God, let him see me under the table.* Jean Pierre left Chloe in no doubt he had seen her. He got out his cell phone and made a couple of calls. He went off toward the open barn where she had been parking the Clio.

He returned to the front of the house at the same time as the local police car arrived. The police were aware of the security measures in place, and lost no time in going to the back patio door and smashing the glass.

Jean Pierre took out his Swiss Army knife and cut her free from the table. Chloe screamed as she landed on the floor.

"Hey! Take it easy—you're free now."

"Yes, thank you, but perhaps we could get a sling, some strapping or something. I broke my collarbone last night, it's agony."

"I'll take you to the hospital, they'll fix you up."

"I think I better make some phone calls first. Could you find my cell, it's on the lawn."

"Use mine."

"Thanks, but I need the numbers and they're on my phone."

Jean Pierre returned quickly and she was delighted to see it was still working, in spite of its night out in the damp air and it still had some battery power left. The way her night had shaped up it had been too much to hope for either.

She speed-dialed Louise. "Come on, Louise, pick up." There was no response and her cell phone redirected to voicemail. She left a message, but there seemed little point. Chloe phoned Patrick, he always seemed to pick up his phone, even in the most inaccessible places, but he too was on voicemail.

She decided to try Special Branch, but she couldn't find Phil Scarlet's card. So, she phoned MI5 switchboard, perhaps Graeme was on duty and could help. She couldn't believe it, wasn't anyone working? She explained, at length, to the duty officer who she was and that Walid and Qasim had gone off in her car with what she believed might be a briefcase bomb.

"So to summarize, your husband is in a taxi on his way to London with a nuclear bomb. Is that correct? This message is for...?"

"No, he's not in a taxi—he's in a Renault Clio and the message is urgent for Graeme or Louise Chappel."

"And Graeme's last name would be...?"

"I don't know, I haven't got his card with me. Can't you check an organizational flow chart? Above Louise Chappel's name you should find her boss, Graeme."

"If you could just hold the line one moment..."

"I'm on a cell phone with a low battery..."

Her response was unheard; he had already put her on hold.

"Hello. My name is James T Calder; I work with Graeme and Louise. Can I help you?"

"Hello, this is Chloe Moreau. I'm—"

"It's all right, Chloe, you don't have to explain who you are. What's happened?"

She explained about Qasim, Walid, the car, and the bomb.

"All right, leave it to me, if I think we need your help, I'll send a helicopter."

"I'm off to the emergency room for some treatment for a broken collarbone now."

"How did that happen?"

"It's not important, just stop Qasim—he's quite mad. He will explode the device. Walid can't stop him."

"Okay, Chloe, we'll have to see what we can do this end."

The local police came and asked her numerous questions; as she had suspected, they had found the body of a dead nurse in the upstairs bedroom. She had no answers for them. They took her and Jean Pierre to the hospital, there didn't seem any point in calling an ambulance for a broken collarbone.

CHAPTER FIFTY-SIX

MI5, London

This was James T's worst nightmare, terrorists within an hour of detonation in London.

"Graeme!" James T never shouted, so the effect was dramatic.

"Good morning!" said Graeme.

"Sod good morning, in fact I can't think of anything about it that is good. Chloe called. Walid and Qasim Merbarkia left Oxfordshire in Chloe's car sometime last night or in the early hours this morning. So please tell me we put a GPS tracking device on the car we supplied. "

"Are you sure? Um… I'm afraid there's no GPS—we didn't think it would be necessary, it wasn't one of our cars, we just got the local garage to deliver a run around for a few days until we got Chloe's car over from Paris."

"Graeme!" James T paused, contemplated that the moment for re-criminations would come, but now wasn't the time. "We're not sure how long ago they left; she's been drifting in and out of consciousness. Walid's brother is a rather nasty sort—he shot the nurse. Chloe was lucky to get away with her life and just a broken collarbone. I think we should work on the basis the target is within a three-mile radius upwind of the Houses of Parliament. We know the bombs aren't powerful in terms of an explosion, so the threat is the radiation from a dirty bomb. Please tell me we at least have CCTV operating in the barn."

"No, the Home Secretary was very specific that the warrant for surveillance applied to Walid only, and that the devices were not to be used unless he was in the building. They were switched off when he went into hospital."

James T sighed. "You have a contact at the CIA you can talk to unofficially. I want them to track Walid and let us know where he is."

"How?"

"Of course, officially we don't know or we would put in the strongest complaint, but we believe they are chipping suspects before they leave detention."

"Okay, I'll get on that right away."

"Get another team in here too; we need to plan some traffic control and diversion measures. I need a demolition squad, bomb squad, and a brief sent to the COBRA team."

"Anything else?"

"I'm sure there is. First priority—find the bastards."

James was sweating; he could smell his own fear. He wasn't afraid for his own life, but for the impending disaster unfolding before him on his watch.

Qasim Merbarkia was a ruthless individual. MI5 had been lucky they had contained the virus by a stroke of good luck and an alert pathologist, who noticed strange activity in the blood work of an elderly woman.

There were two objectives, first defuse or contain the blast from the bomb and secondly, make sure Qasim Merbarkia was either killed in the blast or arrested. He'd settle for shooting him on sight, but one thing he felt quite sure of, Qasim did not plan to be in the car, or within range, when the bomb went off.

He picked up the phone and talked the cabinet secretary. The focus of the conversation was whether they should cancel the State Opening of Parliament. It was too soon to say. If they canceled now and there was no incident, they would look weak, and it would appear they had caved in to terrorist threats; cancel too late and the consequences were too great to contemplate.

James T had been happier when he thought the bomb was skimming the waves in the Mediterranean. It had been a great disappointment to find it was a regular bomb with a timing device. He went into the incident room. Any planning would rely on knowing where Walid and the bomb were.

Chloe's car registration had been put into the traffic observation system. Qasim was running this event on an ad hoc basis. Normally he had detailed plans in progress, but James T reckoned this time Qasim had abandoned his original plans and decided to use Walid to deliver the bomb.

Why not, reasoned James T, *he only had a couple of days to live and Qasim would believe Walid would secure his place in paradise with his final action.*

Graeme returned.

"Any joy?"

"Complete denial from the CIA, but apparently he is under observation and they will be back to us within the hour with the information we need."

"Within the hour? It will be too bloody late by then."

"They're on the M11, stuck in a traffic jam," called out Trevor, excited at being called into the incident room. He was a good analyst but this was usually above his level. He punched up the CCTV picture showing the Renault.

"Who?" asked James T in an exasperated voice.

"Walid and Qasim in the Clio," said an excited Trevor.

James T now regretted having asked the Americans for help. He had hoped by going through unofficial channels he would have had more cooperation, but obviously the subject was too sensitive.

"Right, get me a helicopter in the air. Make sure it keeps enough distance to make them think it is just observing traffic; it is essential it has heat-seeking equipment in operation, we need to know we have both men in the car. Do we know if there is any signature from the bomb?"

"No signature was available from the clone bombs, they were too small and, because of the lining in the briefcase, we think it's unlikely we'll be able to tell if the bomb is in the car."

"All right, let's assume the car has the bomb on board. Where is the wind today? Where would be a suitable place for detonation? Do we have a suitable place to contain some of the effects of detonation—a tunnel or similar? Come on, get your systems up—let's work the problem. We need to control, not respond to this."

"Limehouse tunnel?" Trevor sounded uncertain whether he should just call out or wave his hand, so he did both.

"Great suggestion, how will it be effective and what will the containment be? Contact the appropriate CBRN teams and put them on alert, get them in place, three miles from the Limehouse tunnel should be the staging post."

"CBRN?" All these acronyms confused Trevor.

"Chemical, Biological, Radiological, or Nuclear incident teams."

"Oh right, thanks." Trevor beamed.

"Where's Louise?" Graeme asked.

Trevor was wondering the same thing; he hoped being in the incident room would show him to Louise in a new light. He had left her asleep in the flat, she was so tired last night. Surely when emergency followed emergency, the office must just accept sometimes people need to rest.

"She hasn't come in yet," said James T, still smarting from the doctor's admonishing, but the reality was these incidents all ran into each other, and it was impossible to give staff time off when such important issues were at stake.

"What the hell..." Graeme shrugged in an exasperated way. "I'll give her a call... She can't just pick and choose when to turn up." Graeme dialed and waited. "She must be on her way, there's no reply. She doesn't always hear the phone if she's walking in."

James T was going to explain about her health, the doctor, and the need for rest, but decided now was not the time to go through what had been happening while Graeme was in the Med.

"All right, we move everyone off the M11 at the A406—we'll need to make sure the A12 is also blocked. Then we can bring them along the A13 until we get to Canary Wharf, and we can divert the traffic into the Limehouse tunnel. Can someone contact traffic and get priority to flow traffic and get the police to set up the appropriate diversions? We will need the traffic news to be consistent—phone calls from 'the public' to the radio stations describing accidents. Do we have any engineers available yet to give us a prediction on the effect on the surrounding area and to the tunnel? We should have enough data on the nuclear device; I know we have the calculations for conventional explosives. In addition, I want a risk analysis done of contamination of the Thames, the Limehouse basin, Canary Wharf, and a three-mile radius. You had better stop all activity at city airport, and we'll use that as a staging area."

James T was at his best in these situations, his ability to make decisions and multitask was legendary, and he always came out with top marks in any simulations. However, this was no simulation and he wished he had used the strong aerosol deodorant today. His shirt was wet and if he could smell the sweat, then no doubt everyone else could. *They probably had better things to think about though,* he concluded.

The phones were in use all around the room; Trevor kept changing the CCTV pictures on the bank of screens in front of him. He also patched up a traffic flow monitor to show the speed of the traffic on the surrounding roads. Traffic was like water, it flowed in the area of least resistance and it was important the only route available for the Renault was the route chosen for them.

The police confirmed they had units in place. Police motorbikes certainly had merit on these occasions. London traffic was notorious for backing up in the early morning rush.

The next twenty minutes flew past with constant confirmations coming back into the center of all the arrangements in place.

"All right, what effect will this have on the Docklands Light Railway and the Underground? Can we also divert some buses? We might as well limit casualties from this situation as much as possible. Can we get the office towers at Canary Wharf to stage a fire drill—but make sure they muster underground—perhaps in the shopping malls? Can you call HSBC, Citigroup, and Barclays? We must have the contacts for these businesses. Can we look at what arrangements? Can we evacuate the mile around the tunnel?"

"We can do some of those things but we can't start to evacuate the area around the tunnel. We are going to place heavy trucks at the entrances to help contain the blast—we have stopped all traffic going west through the tunnel and the Renault should be there in about five minutes. We will stop all traffic following the Renault into the tunnel. We have a couple of cars available to feed into the traffic flow. The Special Forces are all in place in the tunnel for a prevention operation."

"He's not in the car," Trevor blurted out. He had just received confirmation from the helicopter.

"Who isn't?"

"There's only one man in the car." Trevor was finding different angles with his CCTV camera. He was also rewinding the tape on other cameras.

"Where'd he go?" Graeme was frustrated.

"Damn it, Trevor, we can't lose the Algerian now, look what he's cost us this week alone."

Trevor blushed with embarrassment. He continued to search but there was a blind spot on the traffic control cameras, and that was the moment—well two minutes to be precise—when one of the men got out of the car. The question in everyone's mind was which one was in the car. The helicopter confirmed the car had stopped in the traffic jam and one man got out of the vehicle. In the chaos that is rush hour there was no point asking them to go back and follow the other passenger.

"Call the Americans again, Graeme, and tell them we know where Walid is—could they just confirm, and perhaps they would like to clear their agents from the area, as we are expecting an explosion."

Graeme pulled a face—it was clear he didn't think he would get far with his request. He phoned his contact at the CIA.

"Hi, Graeme, I was just about to get back to you."

"This is a courtesy call…" Graeme explained the current situation and asked if they could confirm if it was Walid in the car.

"As I said before, I hadn't heard of any chipping of detainees. Nevertheless, I can confirm Walid is in the car. Now I think I should make sure all our agents are under appropriate cover. Thanks for the heads-up."

Both men knew they were being economical with the truth. If there were any remains for an autopsy, Graeme would make sure they found the chip. Graeme didn't disapprove of the chip, he just felt the Americans could share the information a little more freely. Graeme turned to James T.

"Good news and bad news, they can confirm it is Walid in the car—but we have let Qasim slip through our fingers. What do you want to do? We can add resources into the area and see if we can find him."

"Work out where he thinks he can go for shelter. He's within the three mile blast area, he must have some plan, and see if we can get some more CCTV pictures. Contact the usual security firms in the area and give them an alert."

"Where the hell is Louise?" Graeme could do with some more experienced personnel he could rely on in the situation room. Trevor was all right, but he wasn't cool under pressure—Louise was an iceberg, so cool. He should have told her how good she was. He phoned again, if she was walking, she should have been here by now. He tried the phone in her flat—still no reply.

"All right, the car is in the tunnel," James T announced, trying to keep his staff focused. Graeme didn't make a good spectator, James T would have preferred to have been in place in the tunnel, but he was needed in the situation room. They watched the CCTV camera pictures from the tunnel on the wall of screens in front of them. There was a flash and the cameras went black.

"I think we can conclude what has happened. Can we get any reports from the ground?" James T was impatient; he hated the hiatus between the action of these Special Forces operations and the feedback to control.

"We're waiting." Trevor tried to sound in control.

"We have some reasonably good news. The team knocked out the CCTV cameras in the tunnel. They have taken Walid down and they can confirm there is no bomb in the car—no bomb. Just one fatality," Graeme announced.

James couldn't see any good news in a losing a nuclear terrorist device. He must find Qasim Merbarkia. He spoke to the Special Branch coordinator and they issued an all ports alert and ensured the photographs circulating were the best available. James T was not looking forward to the inquiry on his handling of this incident.

Could more have been done? Walid had been in protective custody, what had happened to that arrangement? There were still many questions to be answered.

His phone rang. He listened intently. He was nearly purple with anger as he terminated the call.

"The CIA thought we might want to know the detonator in the device is out of date and it won't work. A Russian on a BA flight from Moscow last week had the material and they took the detonator out of his carry-on bag while he was in the toilet and replaced the polonium-210 with an inert substance."

"What?" Graeme was incredulous. "How kind of them to share."

CHAPTER FIFTY-SEVEN

Wychmoor Wood

Chloe winced, it was an involuntary action. Her arm was in a sling and she was under strict instructions to rest.

"Are you all right?"

She looked at Jean Pierre; he'd been supportive without being over-protective. He hadn't even made a pass or flirted in any way. Their relationship worked best when they were being lighthearted with each other. Either she was looking a lot worse than she felt now the pain was subdued with painkillers, or he was respecting her injuries. She felt fragile—but she had a broken collarbone. Perhaps the attraction for Jean Pierre was the chase and now that she was available, he would lose interest.

"I'm fine, stop worrying!"

The phone rang.

"Chloe Moreau."

"Good afternoon, Chloe, James T Calder here, I wanted to officially offer you my condolences."

"James, what's happened? I presume if you are offering condolences that Walid is dead."

"Hasn't anyone phoned you? I am sorry, I thought you were told this morning. Yes, I'm afraid in the process of rendering the device safe,

Walid died." James could have kicked himself, he had assumed Louise would have taken care of this telephone call—she had the best relationship with Chloe. He had assumed she would have made it into work by now, and would have been detailed by Graeme to undertake this task. He would have to follow up with a more detailed inquiry into Louise's whereabouts.

"So does that mean...?" Had MI5 managed to suppress the news—it seemed unlikely. Chloe was confused.

"No, there was no explosion."

"So Walid died...how?"

"The security forces needed to stop him from exploding the device."

"I see." Chloe reflected on this, she wasn't surprised, she felt no anger. She might have felt differently if he had a full life ahead of him, but he didn't, it just made a sudden end.

She continued. "I had the television tuned to the State Opening of Parliament this morning and nothing untoward seemed to happen. How's Louise? I thought she would have been here, in the circumstances."

James T didn't know how to respond to the inquiry, so he made a non-committal reply.

"Needing a break, like the rest of us. The purpose of my call is to find out if we can do anything to help you at the present time."

"Who do I liaise with about the repatriation of Walid's body to Algeria for burial?"

James was about to say Louise, but decided he better get Graeme to deal with it until they knew what had happened to Louise. "I'll get Graeme to call you."

"Thank you, that's kind; the shippers are coming tomorrow, I have decided to pack everything myself—or to put it more accurately, to have Jean Pierre do the packing. Most of the boxes are still packed, and I can't see any point in moving Walid's possessions and sorting them out in

Paris—I might as well dispose of everything here. Louise did an excellent job of moving us last time, so please send her my regards."

"Yes, I think we probably require all Walid's possessions, so I think you can just take your personal things and leave the rest. You have my number; I can only thank you for your support and if there is anything...?"

"Thank you, that makes things easier, I might as well cancel the van, what's left will fit in the trunk of Jean Pierre's rental car. If I think if anything that could help, I'll keep in touch."

She ended the call and turned to Jean Pierre. "You know when Michael died the phone never stopped ringing with condolences and good wishes—that's the first call and I expect it will be the last."

"I don't suppose anyone at the paper knows the situation yet but..."

"I shouldn't think so."

"Chloe, you are much loved and respected by your colleagues at the paper."

"Yes, but it feels like I haven't been there in weeks."

"A lot can happen in a few days and I don't think they'll care about that. When are you going back to work?"

"I don't know, I placed a call to Anne Marie, I'm waiting to hear back from her. The doctor said I should take it easy for a couple of weeks at least."

The doorbell rang while they were in the bedroom. Jean Pierre was helping Chloe to pack her bag. He leaped into action, shot off downstairs, pleased to be freed from the task of folding small silky items.

He came back in carrying several large envelopes and a couple of circulars.

"Whatever is all that lot?" asked Chloe.

"I don't know."

"Could you open the mail for me?"

"Sure."

Jean Pierre handed her a file, which had its back cover ripped off. In the center of the page was the name, James Robert Culshaw. She started reading and her eyes filled with tears. At last, the truth, her father wasn't careless and stupid; he was a hero.

"Jean Pierre, can you see any note with these?"

"No, what are they?"

"I think Louise has sent me the original MI5 archive files. This one is about my dad, and this one is about Antipov..."

"My God, Chloe, won't MI5 have you shot?"

"Technically I believe it would be MI6 or the SAS."

"This isn't a laughing matter, Chloe."

"No, it's closer to hysterical. Bloody hell, they think Walid murdered Antipov after getting a waterborne virus formula out of him. I don't believe it. That liar conned us all into believing he was the innocent and it was all done by his big bad brother."

"What are you going to do?"

"What do you think I'm going to do? I'm going to write my piece about those disappearing scientists, even Anne Marie can't argue with the evidence. Walid is dead, so he can't sue us for defamation of character."

"Don't you think some of this stuff is still classified?"

"I'm sure it is, so I will have to be careful about how the piece—or probably pieces—are written. We also need to make sure that Charles Forbury gets his byline on the whole series. I haven't really thought about what happened to him, but I think it important, he did so much of the groundwork."

"And the fact that one of the murderers was your husband?"

"I think that is especially important. Also, remember my father was one of the scientists who lost his life to defend his country from biological terror. Do we really know who we are living with, and should we give them the benefit of the doubt if they can't explain where they are and what they are doing? I think it's a valid point to make. It's about trust."

"What are you going to do with the files?"

"Oh, write the piece, file it, and ring James T at MI5 and ask him if he would like to pick up his property."

"Chloe, you can be real cool."

"There's a disappointment, I thought you thought I was hot."

"If you weren't injured..."

"Yes?"

"Just don't tempt me."

"I won't, but I'll give in to temptation. Will you? Anyway, I promised you a byline in Paris—so you better help with this lot. Where's my laptop?"

Jean Pierre went off to the study where she had left her laptop.

"Chloe, Chloe—I've found it!"

"Found what? My laptop?" She was feeling tired and so much excitement from Jean Pierre was too much.

"No, the box."

"What?"

"Yes, isn't this what we were looking for in Paris?" He brought out the cedar box with the brass inlay and lock. "And look, the key is in the lock."

She had never seen Walid leave the key in the lock and the box had never been in her closet before.

"You don't think Qasim put it in your closet, do you?" Jean Pierre voiced her worst fears.

"I don't know—there's only one way to find out."

"You must be mad, why don't we just give it to Patrick?"

"Or MI5 or MI6 or DGST or ... you know, Jean Pierre, I'm just going to open it and if you want to wait in the barn, well, I perfectly understand. Me, I'm sick of spooks and I want to know what's in the box. Given the fact Louise sent us these files, a bargaining chip might be useful."

"You're dreaming, you can't negotiate with spooks. They have the weight of the law or the weight of the lawless—depending on your point of view—on their side."

"My box, my decision, I'm opening it. Are you staying or going?"

"You're mad, and if we both die when I get to heaven I don't want my first words to be, 'I told you so.'"

"All right, I'll bear that in mind, I'll say, 'You told me so.' So, we have a plan."

"You think you're going to heaven?"

Chloe grinned back at him. "Do you?"

Jean Pierre shrugged and handed her the box. She opened it. She realized she was holding her breath. She paused for a moment and, turning the box on its side, looked carefully for any signs of wires or other devices as she opened the box. Perhaps there was a skin poison protecting the box and it was too late, she had touched it. For a moment, she nearly left it for Patrick. She found her inner strength, or was it a devil may care attitude, and opened the box.

"We have his satellite phone, so they can track his brother. I would say that's a powerful bargaining tool. Wouldn't you?"

Jean Pierre shrugged. "We'll all disappear. What else is there in the box?"

"Some sort of camouflage net."

Jean Pierre took the unopened packet from her. "What did Walid want with a top of the range, thermally insulated ghillie suit?"

"What's that?"

"A thermal image blocking suit—this one's with the sort of camouflage net you might use if you were hunting deer, while being hunted by a police helicopter."

"Not really his style, he didn't hunt," said Chloe, also wondering what he would want with such an item, not exactly standard gear for an academic.

"Was he involved all along, or did he get coerced by his brother?"

"I am beginning to wonder if he involved Qasim, nothing Patrick told me seems to relate to the truth. Perhaps he was always a terrorist, manipulating, coercing, committing fraud, he probably hypnotized me into marrying him."

"I think the Colombians probably provided him with the solution to that problem, it's a drug called Devil's Breath. Hyosin, as it is sometimes known, or scopolamine, grows on the borrachero trees in Colombia and can be added to a drink. The individual loses their freewill, can be made to do anything, and afterward has no memory of the event. It's a useful rape or robbery drug. You can even just blow the powder into the face of your victim."

Chloe absorbed the information. It certainly made sense. But it was over now and she needed to live in the present and not dwell on the past. "I think we better get on with these pieces while we still have the files, it will be difficult to conceal the files if we have the police around the place. We need to get to a photocopy machine to keep some of the evidence here."

"What about the packing?"

"Are you mad? Oh just shove everything that looks like mine in a suitcase—we can sort it all out in Paris."

The phone rang. They both jumped, the pain shot through her shoulder, up her neck into her head.

"Arghhh."

"Do you want me to answer it?"

"No, it's okay. Hello?"

"Hello, Chloe, and how are you? Should I be offering my condolences? No probably not."

"Good morning, Anne Marie. Were your ears burning, Jean Pierre and I were just talking about you."

"Haven't you anything better to do?"

"Yes, probably—but with a broken collarbone..." Anne Marie would know she was joking, but with the files in her possession, she could afford to.

"All right—I'll buy it, what have you got?"

"I can't say on the phone but it's hot, you'll like it, and it's exclusive."

"I should hope so, if you can't write the piece on the latest terrorist atrocity in London, with all your contacts and information, I don't know who could."

"Right." Chloe longed to tell her what the story was really about, but she suspected MI5 would still have a phone tap in place. "I was wondering if you would be okay about my returning to work at the paper part-time for a few months."

"I'm sure that will be no problem."

It was funny how having some exclusive material made doors open with Anne Marie.

"I'll let you have some copy by four—you might like to hold the front page for the start of the item."

"That good?"

"Oh yes."

"I look forward to reading it." She terminated the call in her usual fashion, she just hung up, and Chloe was left wondering if she would be able to pull off both pieces in time.

"Okay, you do the terrorist plot stuff—chasing around Paris, you know the exclusive stuff we've got—and I'll do the biological weapons scientists."

"Sounds like a plan."

She opened up the laptop and began to type: *Secret Service Linked to Death of Scientists.*

Extract from La France:

Secret Service Linked to Death of Biological Weapons Scientists
By Senior Correspondent Chloe Moreau and Charles Forbury

Death by secret service seems to be the new retirement plan for weapons microbiologists. Loyal public servants should ensure their affairs are in order and not expect to have a long and peaceful old age.

When Don Wiley died in 2001, it was arguably the start of a situation where world-leading microbiologists began dying in mysterious circumstances. A further eleven scientists died in the following six months. The situation has continued and conspiracy theories have escalated. There is evidence these deaths were the start of a campaign to murder hundreds of microbiologists across the globe.

The 1972 Biological Weapons Convention signaled a new era for Soviet Research. Convinced, in spite of the treaty, their Cold War adversaries were creating new biological weapons, the Russians developed comprehensive research and manufacturing facilities. Alexander Kouzminov in his book *Biological Espionage*, exposed Russian infiltration at the Porton Down Chemical Defense Establishment from the late 1970s. In the 1990s, the spymasters at the KGB received quarterly reports from their agent who was codenamed "Rosa."

The knowledge from these labs spread to terrorist groups, in spite of the £20 billion containment package, given to the former Soviet Union by G8 countries in 2002. These weapons, made with relative ease, are difficult to detect prior to deployment.

The activities of the Soviet Union remained secret until Dr David Kelly debriefed Vladimir Pasechnik, a senior bioweaponeer based in the former Leningrad, on his defection in 1989. Pasechnik went on to work for the British. Kelly, a senior scientist at Porton Down, formed part of the international inspection team of the Russian facilities from 1991 to 1994.

Retribution by secret services against spies, dissidents, and aggressors is well documented. In his exposé *Biohazard*, Ken Alibek claims "Laboratory 12" was set up to specialize in substances to kill individuals quickly, quietly, and efficiently. It was also preferable they left no trace, and death should appear to be from natural causes.

A communist defector, Vladimir Kostov lived in France under constant fear of state reprisal from his former homeland in Bulgaria. The weather on 26 August 1978 was pleasant and Kostov and his wife were traveling to the Tuileries Gardens on the Paris Métro. Leaving the platform they took the escalator to the surface, Kostov told the medics that he had felt a sharp pain in his lower back. A tall man, who followed them from the train, had knocked into him with his umbrella. Kostov's back swelled and he developed a fever, but the doctor treating him in the hospital could not identify any cause for the illness.

Three weeks later, Georgi Markov, also a Bulgarian dissident, left his office at the BBC World Service, London, and made his way across Waterloo Bridge. A Bulgarian intelligence officer following Markov stabbed him with the tip of his umbrella. A burst of compressed air from the umbrella's tip drove a platinum-iridium alloy pellet, the size of a ballpoint pen tip, containing 0.2 milligrams of ricin into his right thigh, leaving only a small mark.

Within four days, Markov died in hospital, claiming the Bulgarian Secret Service had poisoned him. The doctors could not identify the cause of illness or death. However, a second postmortem carried out at Porton Down found the small ricin pellet in his leg.

Acting on this information the Paris doctors reinvestigated the wound on Kostov's back, where they removed a similar pellet, and the patient made a full recovery.

Boris Korczak, a CIA agent based in the USA at the time of his attack, was lucky; his kidneys excreted the tiny metal ball and he recovered, after suffering some internal bleeding and a fever.

When Todor Zhikov's regime in Bulgaria collapsed in 1989, officials found a stack of specially modified umbrellas in the interior ministry. KGB technicians had provided Bulgarian agents based in Sofia training in their use. The operational commander widely believed to have been in charge of assassinations using these devices, Vasil Kotsev—a known Bulgarian spy—died in an unexplained car accident. Agent Piccadilly, widely held responsible for the attack is still wanted for questioning in connection with the Markov killing by Scotland Yard.

Now a new pattern of assassinations is emerging, involving the secret service from the west as well as former Soviet bloc countries. Detailed evidence from leaked files shows an ongoing strategy of murder and deception. Having unlocked the Pandora's box of biological weapons, it remains for society to decide if eradicating the knowledge base of those no longer active in this field is the only acceptable solution.

The head of a European defense establishment refused to comment last night, but off the record, he admitted to some concerns about seven of the scientists who died in recent years. "I find it statistically improbable for all seven to have chosen inefficient ways of engineering their own deaths—I cannot accept the verdict of suicide for six of the scientists."

As one widow said, "I knew instantly something was terribly wrong. My husband wouldn't, couldn't have killed himself in that way. They bought our family's silence and talking about it won't bring him back. He was a pragmatist, he would have told me to take the pension."

Tomorrow *La France* exposes the details in an exclusive series of articles.

Dated 24 November 2004

ACKNOWLEDGEMENTS

I have relied on information and accounts from many sources for this novel, but this is a work of fiction. The truth is far more disturbing. The books written by the Russian defectors Ken Alibek and Alexander Kousminov show what the Russian laboratories were achieving. They make a chilling read.

Alexander Kouzminov 2005; *Biological Espionage: Special Operations of the Soviet and Russian Foreign Intelligence Services in the West,* Greenhill Books, London.

Alibek Ken 1999; *Biohazard: The Chilling True Story of the Largest Covert Biological Weapons Program in the World – Told from the Inside.* Random House, New York, NY

Porton Down is currently known as the Defense Science and Technology Laboratory, Porton Down.

Coming soon

A new fast-paced thriller from C R Harris. One that will have you asking could this really happen.

Money for Nothing draws on facts and incidents in the world of espionage and financial greed.

Money for Nothing

Money for Nothing is a conspiracy thriller about a Russian plot to bring down the American financial markets.

Nikolai Pachenko, his wife Galina, and disabled daughter Anastasia, are under threat from the President's Executive Aide, Sergei Ivanovitch. Nikolai must manage a financial meltdown to coincide with the Presidential election in America on 4 November 2008.

When Alistair McAlister, a British fund manager, is ensnared into the scheme, he needs to find a way out, that doesn't involve his own death. It takes his partner Sophie's cunning and scheming to find a way out of the mess. What can they find to bring the Russians to the negotiating table? Can they prevent a financial disaster?

Visit www.crharris.info to find out more.

C R Harris

C R Harris has worked in business and finance in Europe and the USA, making industry-leading programmes on ethical selling in the financial services sector, and contributing to consultancy projects in two of the four major UK banks, as well as key players in the insurance industry.

Her management development clients have also included biological and chemical research organisations, and government departments. Harris would tell you about some of the more interesting events, if they weren't covered by the Official Secrets Act. But these experiences bring authenticity to fiction.

Chris is enjoying the move to a more creative life experience and has an MA in Creative Writing from Bath Spa University in England.

"I like to write stories that make you question your current view of the world and what you believe to be true."

Find Chris on Facebook/crharriswriter
Follow Chris on Twitter @crharris1
Read extracts from the new work and short stories at Exposing the Secrets, Chris's Blog crharrisblog.com